The Island recognized its visitors.

They drifted from beyond the line of the sea with a blink, a fritz of static, burning teardrop-shaped holes in the darkness: a pale boy sprawled out on a yellow raft, copper hair drifting about his face like a crown; a boy and a girl whose arms tangled around each other, heads bent close enough to kiss. All three covered in dust, in death, in the burnt-grass reek of misplaced hope—battered bastard children tugged soundless toward a shore on which they were no longer welcome.

Yet none of them were awake to notice. Had they been, they might have seen the black rocks rising out of the water like avenging angels, the ice-dagger trees swaying a warning. Might have thought twice about returning to the cliffs and coves and hollow trees, or forging back through rock and spring and waterfall. Might have stayed away from the heart of the forest.

But they slept on, their minds flitting petal-thin between fantasy and reality, landing light as butterfly feet in the shadows between nightmares.

And when the ocean spat them onto the sand in salt-chewed offering, only the Island saw, and said nothing.

THESE DEATHLESS SHORES

P. H. LOW

orbitbooks.net

Copyright © 2024 by P. H. Low
Excerpt from *The Scarlet Throne* copyright © 2024 by Amy Leow
Excerpt from *Fathomfolk* copyright © 2024 by Eliza Chan

Cover design by Lisa Marie Pompilio
Cover illustration by Balbusso Twins
Cover copyright © 2024 by Hachette Book Group, Inc.
Map by Tim Paul

Orbit
Hachette Book Group
1290 Avenue of the Americas
New York, NY 10104
orbitbooks.net

First Edition: July 2024

Orbit is an imprint of Hachette Book Group.
The Orbit name and logo are registered trademarks of Little, Brown Book Group Limited.

The publisher is not responsible for websites (or their content) that are not owned by the publisher.

The Hachette Speakers Bureau provides a wide range of authors for speaking events. To find out more, go to hachettespeakersbureau.com or email HachetteSpeakers@hbgusa.com.

Orbit books may be purchased in bulk for business, educational, or promotional use. For information, please contact your local bookseller or the Hachette Book Group Special Markets Department at special.markets@hbgusa.com.

Library of Congress Cataloging-in-Publication Data
Names: Low, P. H., author.
Title: These deathless shores / P. H. Low.
Description: First edition. | New York, NY : Orbit, 2024.
Identifiers: LCCN 2023050058 | ISBN 9780316569200 (trade paperback) | ISBN 9780316569224 (ebook)
Subjects: LCGFT: Fantasy fiction. | Novels.
Classification: LCC PS3612.O8784 T47 2024 | DDC 813/.6—dc23/eng/20231201
LC record available at https://lccn.loc.gov/2023050058

ISBNs: 9780316569200 (trade paperback), 9780316569224 (ebook)

Printed in the United States of America

LSC-C

Printing 2, 2024

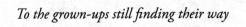

To the grown-ups still finding their way

To Massey Island

these guys bite

had a great time here
what is wrong with you

Marooner's Rock

Mermaid Cove

Cave of Spheres

Northern Cliffs

is this supposed to be a skull?
shut up

Peter's House

heart of the forest somewhere here?
keeps changing

Stone Pillars

Tier's cave (loser)

Why are you so mean to him?
cos it's funny

Pirate Ship

surprisingly well stocked

Western Ocean

To Shinu Island

Map By Tim Paul

PART ONE

When they seem to be growing up, which is against the rules, Peter thins them out...

— J. M. Barrie, *Peter Pan* (1911)

T he Island tracked everything that washed ashore.

An invisible barrier surrounded it, a shimmering wall a hundred kilometers in every direction. Canoes sank in crossing; navigators lost sight of the stars. Later, trawlers and airplanes split themselves against nothing, and the probes they sent into the water returned out of sync or cracked precisely down the middle.

Only the birds arrived unscathed. Only the foxes, floating in on driftwood rafts.

So the Island embraced them with limestone arms and swaying trees—as it did the corpses, the broken gunports. Death is the way of things, after all, and who was it to question the sea?

And then came the child.

A baby, gurgling happily in the wings of birds, a laugh-bright golden creature clutched in his chubby hands. *He* lived. And when he grew into a boy, he flew away and brought others back to play with him: children from faraway lands, sailors reeking of gunpowder and cannon fire, silver-tongued tellers of stories. Cloaked, all of them, in the winged creature's brightness—or else so close to death that they might as well have worn their own wings.

Only then did the Island feel itself filled, a nameless longing satisfied.

So it held still as the humans played among its cliffs and coves and hollow trees. Tousled their hair with cold breezes as they cobbled together homes in forests sprung from five hundred years of patience. Sighed as they hunted and fought and grew up (and yes, they did grow up, all of them except that first boy, whatever else the later stories said—their bones gathering in hidden places, blood seeping thick and dark into ready earth).

And when *they* came—a boy and a girl, to the extent the Island recognized such distinctions, creeping silently after the boy who had stopped growing old; roaming across cliff and cove and hollow tree, through rock and spring and waterfall, and into the heart of the forest—when they touched down on shore, a new beginning, or one as old as the world—the Island knew.

But it kept its silence.

Chapter 1

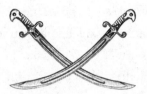

Nine years after leaving the Island, Jordan still hated the city heat.

She shoved her duffel bag back behind her hip, breathed through the soup of air that stuck her shirt to her skin. Sweating spectators jostled and leaned toward the ring below, where two fighters in similar gear jabbed and blocked and danced.

An otherwise equal match, except one of them was going through karsa withdrawal. Even from up here, Jordan could see him shaking.

"Are you really the Silver Fist?"

She looked down. A boy of about ten stared up at her, grubby fingers clenched around a fried dough stick. No parents or siblings that she could see—and he was thin and wary-looking in a way that reminded her of Peter, of the Island, of crawling through forest underbrush with Baron, senses pricked for the rustle of a pirate or a Pale or a hungry feral boar.

An aspiring fighter, then. Or perhaps one already.

She wondered if he'd ever dreamed of the Island. If he'd ever read the Sir Franklin novel or watched the many movie adaptations and thought it, for a moment, real.

"No," she said, serious. "It's just a costume."

The kid cast a long look at her hands. She spread them: the prosth on her right a glove of metal, the click of uncurling fingers masked by the crowd. "Pretty convincing, huh?"

"Sure," said the boy, but he did not shuffle away to his seat. As Jordan turned back to the match, he hovered on her periphery, gnawing his lower lip; stayed until her focus broke like a wave against stone.

"You should get out," she said finally. Smiled with all her teeth. "While you still can. Don't let them use you."

He backed away then, the stick of fried dough in his hand untouched.

The match below was not going well. Third rounds in general tended to be where the most bones broke, fighters both exhausted and amped on their drug of choice, but the karsa addict had fallen to his knees; when his opponent kicked him in the shoulder, he crashed backward and lay twitching on the sand.

As the referee raised his arms, a roar went up through the stadium, half triumph, half protest. This late at night, after the rookie matches and the polite international ones, the spectators hungered for fast punches and faster bets, snapped wrists and broken backs.

This late at night, they wanted a show.

And the addict had failed to provide.

As the medical team—not all of them certified—carried him out, Jordan caught a couple men in suits moving through the stands, wireless headsets hooked around their ears: syndicate muscle, most likely, deployed to ensure a quick disposal of the man's body. The karsa had rendered him useless as a fighter, but they couldn't have him shouting valuable intel in dark alleys, no matter how convincingly it came off as an addict's ravings.

"Pity," the man standing beside Jordan muttered to his friend. A dragon tattoo snaked down his shoulder, wrapped his wrist in flames. "I've been watching Gao Leng since I was in primary school."

"Happens to all of them. They're uneducated, desperate—" The friend's gaze flicked to Jordan. "Hey, isn't that—"

Jordan ducked toward the aisle, their eyes pressing into her shoulder blades.

Two purple cubes of karsa burned in her own pocket. She had deliberately kept her doses as low as she could stand, these past nine years, and not just because Obalang was a stingy arse who would withhold her next canister the moment she missed a rent payment. Karsa tore up your nerves and digestive system; spend too much time in its grip, and withdrawal would leave you vomiting and convulsing until you regretted the day you were born.

But she could not regret the choice she'd made, nine years ago. Not when the alternative, withdrawal from the Island's Dust, would have killed her.

Not when it might still.

As she shoved into the locker room below the ring, a hand clamped down on her shoulder.

From anyone else, it might have been a gesture of encouragement. From Obalang, it was anything but. Jordan rested her right palm casually on top of his tobacco-stained fingers; felt them quivering there, hot and trapped. In a single twitch she could crush his bones so finely he would need a prosth to match hers, and for a moment she reveled in that, even if he held sway over the rest of her pathetic little life.

"You owe me," he said.

Jordan's eyes narrowed. Her landlord-dealer's black eyes were jittering, thin lips parted in suppression of ecstasy. The eejit was sharp on his own drug.

"I said I'd run your errand in the morning."

"What, and count that as payment for a four-ounce can? It's a small deal. Weak stuff. I'll barely get enough to cover the cost of transport." His grip tightened; she shifted back.

"Then why didn't you ask Alya to do it?"

Obalang scowled. His breath smelled of scorpion curry and the rotted sweetness that came with karsa chewing. A hint of the same, she knew, tinged her breath as well. "You're replaceable, girl. I can find a dozen kids on the street quicker and hungrier than you. Don't forget that."

Jordan nodded at the stadium above. Ads for energy drinks and foreign cars blazed across the walls in four different languages, but beneath, the chant had gone up, faint but unmistakable: *Silver Fist. Silver Fist.* "Tell it to them."

Obalang's mouth twisted. It was his word that opened the Underground doors to her every Fifthday night, his karsa that kept her from melting into a drool-mouthed wreck.

Even so, it was not every day that one of his tenants made him big among the ringside betting circles.

"Make sure you win all three tonight," he said as she shrugged off his grip and made for the locker room. "Or I'll give that job to Alya after all."

As the door swung closed, she flipped him a two-fingered salute.

The locker room was, if possible, even hotter. She shoved her bag in her graffiti-encrusted compartment as fast as she could get it off her; fished out a near-empty tube of ointment, which she smeared over her arms and face to keep her skin from breaking. Then she downed the two karsa cubes dry, and the world sharpened, sweet and slow: the bone-rattling thump of eedro music, the shift of a thousand sweat-slicked bodies, the gleam of her opponent's smile as he prepared himself in an identical room on the other side of the ring. Shitty karsa, this—withdrawal would leave her sluggish and achy in thirty minutes, dry-heaving a couple hours after that—but she'd run out of the stronger stuff she'd nicked off errands, and she would ride this high for as long as she could.

And if her right arm prickled a warning beneath the prosth, if the very weight of her bones and blood simmered with the echo of pain—

Through the walls, a chime sounded. Jordan rolled her shoulders, shoved in her mouth guard, and pushed open the door.

The sound almost blasted her back into the room. She'd hovered at the outer edges of this crowd all night, but here at its center, the spectators' fury washed over her like a tide. Her heart was an adrenaline pump, her body electric. As she raised her arms—at once a V for victory and a giant *up yours* to Obalang, who stood, arms crossed, in the front row—the screams swept her up, drowned her, coated her veins in titanium and glowing ore. Two words, pounded into chests and rusted benches.

Silver Fist. Silver Fist.

She fought to pay for the karsa, yes, and for a rat-infested closet Obalang called a room. Fought to keep her other addiction, her Dust addiction, at bay. But as she rolled onto the balls of her feet, felt the slow hard stretch of muscle and joint, she also felt *alive.*

She was a burning star, hungry and inexorable, and she would not be broken.

A pale silhouette sliced the opposite doorway.

Jordan did not blink. She had stayed up nights to study this fighter in the Underground's video archives: his predator's gait, the kicks he snapped like mouthfuls of scorpion pepper. As the ref raised his arms, she mouthed along to the name that blasted from the flat, tinny speakers.

"Gentlemen, I present to you—the White Tiger!"

Jordan's opponent loped across the sand, his white-blond hair shining beneath the lights, and the crowd *howled.*

The White Tiger was the darling of the Underground, tall and lanky and arrogant—*and Rittan,* people whispered loudly behind their hands, as if in explanation. Jordan had fought him twice since she'd first shown up at the back gates of the arena. The first time, he'd knocked her out in seconds. The second, he'd snapped two of her ribs and whispered, as the medics carted her away, that he went easy on little girls.

But Jordan had come back. She'd wrapped her broken bones, iced her bruises. Learned to throw a punch with the full weight of gravity dragging her down, to stay light on her feet even when no Dust from the Island kept them in the air.

All in all, she'd gotten decent at fighting on sand.

And tonight, she would win back her pride—and her next week's worth of karsa.

As they bowed to each other, the Tiger's eyes locked on hers. His irises were giveaway Rittan, the cold pitiless blue of movie stars and senators' sons, and at the sight of them, an old heat seared across Jordan's chest.

"Pity you think you've already lost," he said, the words crisped by his accent. "It might have been a good match."

"Pity you're an arrogant kweilo," Jordan countered. "It'll be fun to beat you."

They stepped apart, and the scoreboard clock flicked into a countdown, digits burning red against the faded wall paint.

Ten seconds.

At the edge of the arena, Obalang flicked a cigarette. *Three for three.*

He did this sometimes, when someone big had bet on her and he was behind on rent or drugs or whatever increase in tribute money the Hanak were demanding from him that week. These days it was usually two for three, minimum, or that she hold out for a certain length of time—which gave her lower audience ratings, but fewer broken bones.

In the past few months, however, she'd been losing him fewer bets. Had even thrown a few matches on purpose.

Six.

The Rittan's white tank top was a paper ghost. The memory of his video matches sketched across the backs of her eyelids: the dancer-like lift of his back foot before a kick, a phantom gap between raised hands. She just had to catch him in real time.

If only it were that easy.

Three.

Fists raised, a meter and a half apart, they crouched as one.

Two.

She needed this, she told herself. A hundred times more than he did.

One.

Another chime rattled the air.

They circled each other. Jordan's ears pounded blood and bass; she didn't dare blink. The Tiger did not bounce as some of the newcomers did, established no rhythm that would betray his first strike. His fists were points of light, the metal studs on his knuckles jeweled like snake eyes. The crowd above them stirred and murmured as sweat clung to their backs.

This late in the night, they wanted blows. They wanted blood. They wanted—

Strapped down to the hospital bed, screaming as Dust withdrawal burned through her veins—

Focus, dammit.

In Jordan's periphery, Obalang scratched his nose.

She lunged. The crowd roared as she and the Tiger became a flurry of limbs, and she fell into muscle memory, blocking again and again as his kicks and alloy-capped fists barreled toward her. A roundhouse wrenched her left arm in its socket and she slammed it with her other forearm, teeth rattling as he shoved her to the ground. Then his heel smacked her shoulder—a starburst of pain, too close to her head—and she was rolling away, back on her feet, her eyes acrid with sweat. Her chest heaved. No shame in breathing hard, here. As they circled each other again, her vision embrittled into sand, light, shadow.

This time, he attacked first.

He fought with the grace of someone trained in classical martial arts—quick and elegant, kicks snapped perfect from the knee. Countering even the punches from her right hand with blows that would have fractured her ribs again if she'd sidestepped a millisecond more slowly. When she showed up five years ago, she had fought with the unrefined flailing she'd picked up on the Island: a child who'd always had the option to fly away, snuggle back into bed at the end of the day. But she'd figured out gravity. Figured out her arm. Now she lashed out with all she had, struck kidney, elbow, crotch—

Another chime, the clock over their heads blazing zeros, and amid the surge of shouting and uncreative slurs involving her anatomy, the ref shoved between them, arms outstretched. Jordan spun away and wiped her face—though that was a stupid move, since sand gritted her knuckles. The White Tiger limped, still tender, toward his locker room. A one-minute break, and no question that she'd ended on top.

Two more to go. A splash of water from the drinking fountain, a stimulant patch slapped on the back of her neck, and she strode back out to the center of the arena.

Even crouching with his legs slightly too far apart, the Tiger looked murderous.

"Just remember," she called as time ticked down, "I took it easy on you."

He bulldozed into her with a thud and she crashed breathless to the sand, kicking and struggling as his knees pinned her midsection. A silent fury in those glacier eyes, a studded fist swinging down toward her head, and small suns exploded behind her eyes *shit shit shit*—

She threw out an elbow, bucked her hips. Dove for him as he tipped off-balance. Her vision was fuzzing in and out—one moment narrowed to the bead of sweat at his temple, the next dazzled by the shine of the surrounding fence. Then she was punching torso, neck, head, her pulse a crack-snap of bone, red echo of tearing teeth—

"Time," someone bellowed, "*time*," and multiple refs' arms vised around her, carrying her off the ground; the Tiger's chest heaved as he glared and staggered to his feet. They had bowed to each other only minutes ago, yes, but there was no thought of sportsmanship inside the match itself—only this animal hate, the blue lightning of her body, the tang of ozone on her tongue. As Jordan was set back on the sand, she raised her arms again, and the crowd bore her up, heady as the name she had chosen for herself.

Round three.

The White Tiger was desperate now: humiliated by a girl, even if she was slightly more augmented than he was. It would make him reckless, but also dangerous. If he managed to get the upper hand, she had no doubt he'd break *all* her ribs tonight.

The clock blinked down its intervals.

One last time.

They circled again, briefly—both of them hot and loose now, the ring blurring with the sweat in Jordan's eyes—and then he rushed her once more: head shot after head shot, lightning jabs and arcing kicks. Pushing her out of center, aiming for the knockout. She blocked, both arms shuddering with impact, huffed as his fist caught her full in the chest. Pivoted away, panting, toward the wire fence, the pounding sea of faces.

And paused.

Something was wrong.

Her ears felt stuffed with cotton. The taste of iron clogged her tongue. She was standing at the bottom of a giant fishbowl, the crowd a sick sea of gaping mouths and dead eyes, and a slow convulsion twisted her gut—separate from the pulse of her shoulder, the bruises blooming on her arms. A high tight tremor in her knees, her spine.

She thought of Gao Leng, twitching in the sand, and a cold void slid open inside her like a door.

Jordan edged farther away, both hands raised and clenched to stop the shaking. Obalang might have fucked her over—might have discovered she'd been skimming from clients, degraded the karsa he gave her on purpose, and then bet against her so he would profit anyway. But if he hadn't—if this was the usual dose and it was her body that was habituating, demanding more—

When she was thirteen, she had sought him out at the convenience store near her parents' house: a shifty, greasy-looking bastard with only the shopkeeper's gossipy suspicions to recommend him. She had bought herself a few years, thinking to stave off the Dust withdrawal shredding her system hour by hour, and paid for it in people she'd left behind.

But she had always known it would return. Pain, after all, was the only thing that stayed.

Three paces away, the Tiger cocked his head. Understanding loosened the set of his shoulders—and wary triumph.

Jordan met those hard blue eyes. Jerked her head: *Well, come on, then.*

And when he plunged forward, his leg a flawless scythe toward her temple, she let her fists drop just enough that her head snapped to the side, and she tumbled into the dark.

"What the fuck?" Obalang snarled as Jordan emerged from a back entrance of the Underground, still bruised and raw despite the anti-inflammatory patches she'd slapped over her shoulder and temple. One of the other fighters had tossed her an extra cube of karsa for the withdrawal, but she now owed them a cut of A-grade from tomorrow's deal, and lurking beneath her skin was the promise that this would happen again—and again and again, until her body gave up altogether. Obalang shoved her against the wall, and the world jarred. "You threw that match."

"I didn't," she said, shouldering around him, but he stepped in front of her, the tip of his cigarette flaring orange.

"I don't need to show you the godsdamned replay. You dropped your fucking hands."

Jordan sighed. She had taken her time in the locker room precisely to avoid this. The reek of old sweat and rotting food filled the passageway, turning her stomach; across the street, people stumbled laughing out of bars, chattering in Burimay and Hanwa and Yundori, and she briefly envied them—the way they could lose themselves in the city without bracing for a knife or a fist or the cold kiss of gun to temple.

"These things happen," she said evenly. "I'd fight better if I had a cut of the A-grade—"

"No," Obalang snapped, as she'd known he would. "And you're still running that errand tonight. Two a.m., or I'll sell that silver fist of yours to the Hanak bosses. It'll almost pay off the debt you just racked up, along with your next three weeks' worth of karsa."

Jordan shifted her gear bag on her hip. She'd always expected to part ways with Obalang eventually—though whether by hot-wiring a motorcycle and hightailing it out of the city, or being shot and dumped in an alley like this one, was yet to be seen. Now, as borrowed drug sang in her veins, she imagined their relationship as a timer, counting down.

Three weeks' worth. Even if she skimmed off deals, called in every favor owed her, she would break by next Fifthday. And the fighter she went up against then might not be as merciful as the White Tiger.

She would rather die a quick death than a slow one. Would rather go up in flames while she was ahead than shrivel in a slow decay of consequences.

At the edge of her hearing, a little boy's giggle, as if from inside a black-mouthed cave.

And now?

And now?

And now?

"Everything pays a price to survive," Obalang said. Darkness eddied over his face, thumbprints of shadow dappled by the light of a nearby restaurant. He ground his cigarette out on the wall. "I've paid, all this time. And I'll keep paying."

"As will I," Jordan said, and walked past him into the brightness of the city. She would pick up his godsdamned karsa—but not on his behalf, or the syndicate's. By this time tomorrow, she'd be long gone. "I'll be there. Two o'clock sharp."

Chapter 2

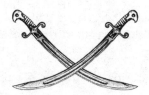

Baron always knew when the thunder was coming.

As he stared at his computer screen, the pages of his calculus textbook blurring into a senseless tangle of symbols, a warning thrummed in his ribs, the arches of his feet. Not impossible, or even difficult, to predict—he had, after all, been running on three hours of sleep and a cocktail of legal stimulants for a lightless smear of days—but the dread that fisted behind his forehead was no less potent for having been portended.

He shoved away from the desk, pushed back the keyboard on which he had been tapping uselessly, and it rammed into him with monsoon force.

His lungs seized. His breath came in gasps.

Thirty percent of his final grade in one of the two classes he wasn't failing, and he didn't understand half the practice questions.

He had shown up to every lecture, even when he'd lain awake the night before listening to the frantic judder of his heart; hunched over problem sets through the dark narrow hours of early morning. Yet the concepts slipped through his fingers like water, his Bs dipping to Cs and then Ds as the sometimes-doable puzzles of double and triple integrals gave way to a nonsense blear of theorems and proofs.

And now?

Vectors yawned at him, mocking, and Baron's eyes blurred with sudden heat.

You just have to work harder, he heard his father say, the way he did every time Baron dared express the remotest difficulty with classes. *Just because you missed a few years doesn't mean you can't catch up.*

A few years. Baron was twenty-two, but being held back multiple times for subpar test scores meant he was only a sophomore. Less than halfway through.

He took off his glasses. Focused on cleaning them with the corner of his shirt, though his grip had gone so lax that he was just as likely to drop them on the floor. *Breathe.* The lab was in an engineering school building—even at one in the morning, students milled through the halls with steaming cups of coffee. Outside of his private study room, he couldn't let them see him like this: scattered and shaking, his mouth gaped on the edge of a sob.

Get your shit together, he thought, and the voice in his head sounded remarkably like Jordan's.

But he couldn't, he couldn't. His throat had closed; a lead weight crushed his sternum. He was everywhere and nowhere, collapsing and flying apart.

Breathe.

Adrenaline shot through his palms. He didn't think he was going to die, but gods, he wanted to. Every nerve in his body vibrated toward it as if by gravity.

Breathe.

He looked, as he always did, toward the single narrow window, high on the wall. The world softened without his glasses, unreal—the sky a vague bruised velvet, downtown San Jukong a mere calculation of lights. But it helped him get his bearings back, if not his lungs.

Reminded him that he was safe in the broadest sense of the word; that the world was vast, that he could be more than just suffocating.

"Hey."

Baron whipped around so fast his neck spasmed.

Jordan—he shoved his glasses back on, although who else would fail to knock?—leaned against the doorframe, short hair dripping onto her rumpled shirt collar. Her duffel bag was slung over her shoulder. "Been here all night?"

Baron swallowed. His pulse rampaged in his ears, trapping him in a suit of marble, and he wanted to laugh, wanted to cry, wanted to *open his fucking mouth*, but his jaw was glued shut, his throat a skein of wire.

Finally he managed, "How'd you get in?"

She raised a brow. "The door?"

"Oh."

She spoke to the ceiling. "The light was on in the window. And I didn't think you'd—"

"Gone the fuck to sleep, yeah," Baron said, and then he was breaking in earnest, his gasps headed toward wheezes. A strangled sound escaped him, like a leaked balloon.

"Hey." He blinked and she was in front of him, her bag digging into his knee, and his heart lurched and the world was spinning and she was not the kind of person one fell into—she was the last person in the world one might fall into—but this was enough, it had to be enough, because otherwise he had nothing. "You do the five-five thing?"

Five-second inhale, five-second exhale, according to the doctor she'd forced him to see. His chest hurt. "I—I can't."

"Three body parts you can feel?"

He clenched his fingers. Curled his toes. Knuckled the ache at his temples, from week upon week of thin grey sleep. "Yeah."

"Things you hear?"

"You."

Her eyes like dark pools, searching. "That's one."

He clamped down against the urge to fold into fetal position, or scream. "I don't understand this vector stuff at all."

"The little arrows and shit?"

"I—yeah." Baron lay his head on the desk. Counted to five on his next inhale, five out. *Breathe.* He could do this. Manage these few seconds sitting somewhat upright, listening to the blood roar in his ears. Treading water, moment by moment, and hoping he washed back up on solid ground. "I only got a D on the last midterm because one question was so similar to the example I found online. I copied the steps, I don't actually know what's going on—"

"I thought you were seeing a tutor."

"They're all booked for finals week. Though I'm failing most of my other classes anyway, so it doesn't matter." Baron closed his eyes. Willed the storm to subside, the adrenaline to drain out the back of his skull until he regained some semblance of control. As Jordan rummaged through his desk drawers—*she doesn't even go here*, he thought, and a brief, weary consternation washed over him at the thought of one of his classmates peering through the glass door at this particular moment—he forced his jaw to unlock. Listened to her steps across the linoleum, the squeak of hinges.

Behind his eyelids, integrals burned gas-fire blue.

The squeaking paused. "You got any food?"

There. A concrete task. Baron forced his legs to uncurl from the chair, pointed at a drawer she hadn't searched. "Yeah."

"Nice." Jordan plucked two cold pork buns from the white bakery box and stuffed both in her mouth at once. Muffled: "Thanks."

As she settled cross-legged on the floor with her prize, Baron sat back into his chair, the knot behind his forehead loosening slightly.

"Are you still taking—?" he ventured.

"Yes." Jordan grinned with her mouth full. "You want?"

"I'm fine."

"It could—help."

They did not often speak of his—problem, not unless he was dealing with it directly. But he appreciated the attempt. "No, it's just—"

"Illegal?"

"Yes, and—"

"Addictive?"

"Yes, and—"

"Not looked upon favorably by the gods?"

Baron rubbed his eyes. "I didn't mean it like that."

"Everyone pays a price to survive," Jordan said, taking another bite. "As someone told me recently."

Baron stared, nonplussed. It was a rare moment that she seemed to let her guard down—when she was not the grown-up version of the Lost Boy he'd known on the Island, swaggering and swearing with the best of them. Not the girl who, every morning for five years, had made her own skin bubble and boil as she shaped Dust into a glamoured right hand that would allow her to appear as Baron's Twin, unrelated though the two of them were.

He wanted to ask where she'd been tonight, how she'd gotten the bruises that mottled her forearms. But he suspected he didn't want to know.

"How's the arm?" he said instead.

She raised her left hand, with the attendant pork buns. "Same as usual."

"The other one."

"Response time's a little slow."

"Have you tried turning it off and on again?"

"Yes, and no, I'm not giving it back to you for maintenance so you can keep it for another *four days*." She curled the mechanical fingers halfway. "Besides, I've gotten syndicate secrets soldered to the inner panels. If you're caught with it, they'll sink you straight into the sea."

Baron cast his eyes ceiling-ward. He'd been engineering prosths for her since middle school, tweaking the experimental models his father brought home from the hospital where he worked, but now this one needed repairs and there was no way in Taram she'd give it up for the week or so he needed to make them. "If you'd just give me half an hour—"

"Nope."

"Your loss."

Jordan pointedly licked char siu juice off her fingers. Baron swiveled back toward the computer, his father's voice rattling again at the edge of his hearing.

It had been easy for him to leave the Island. Peter kept no one against their will; the day after Jordan left, Baron had simply asked to go home, then waved goodbye to the remaining Lost Boys as he soared back across the ocean. But he had missed out on far too much: By the time he alighted back on the sill of his bedroom window, thirteen years old and five years missing, his peers were spending the entirety of their waking hours at cram school, squinting at biochemistry equations and dense histories of Burimay sultans until their eyes refused to focus beyond the distance of a screen. In high school, he'd gained a reputation for tinkering, rewiring the prehistoric computers and ID readers he found in old storage rooms; had even won a prestigious engineering contest, the prototype for which had led to an update for Jordan's prosth.

Yet he'd still failed his entrance exams twice. In every way that mattered, he might have been better off simply dropping out.

Though even that was only half the problem, he thought as he scrolled aimlessly through the pages of incomprehensible symbols. He could recover from failure itself. His family was not wealthy, but he had a safety net he could bounce off again and again until it broke or his parents got fed up with his leeching. No, it was the idea of the enterprise as a whole—being trapped in fluorescent cubicles for the rest of his life, the endless flood of deadlines and demands. Year after year of struggling to breathe.

Why? he thought, and the word fell through him like a motorcycle sailing off a bridge. *Why? Why? Why?*

"Baron," Jordan said suddenly. "I have a proposition for you."

Baron's hands hovered over the keyboard. "You may propose."

She snorted. Then: "I'm leaving tonight."

He spun around in his chair. Jordan's head was tipped back against the wall, her lashes curved dark over those twitching pupils.

"Where?" he asked.

"I think you know."

A new rill of adrenaline coursed through his palms. His ears rang. "I thought the karsa was helping."

"It barely works anymore." Her eyes fixed on him, at once dead and fever-burning, and Baron was suddenly afraid. "And when it stops—" She swallowed, and the cords of her throat tightened. "I need to go back to the Island."

"No."

Her eyes narrowed. "Come again?"

He made a strangled sound. A different kind of storm was barreling through him now: grief and fury and hysterical laughter, a hundred memories unfurling with the brightness of a dream. "Isn't there a doctor who could—I could ask someone at the university—"

She yanked down her collar, exposing the mottle of scars he knew ran across her chest and upper arms. "Is there a single other person who'd believe me if I told them where these came from?"

Baron's mouth clamped shut.

When they had both just returned from the Island—when Jordan's stitches were still healing, and an IV fed a steady stream of painkillers into the crook of her elbow—she'd raged to go back. She would plunge a sword through Peter's heart; cut him to pieces for the Dust he had torn away from her, for leaving her with nothing but gravity and something beneath her skin that, when it flared up, left her shaking and vomiting blood. After her parents found karsa stashed beneath her pillow and kicked her out, she'd met Baron on street corners, in parking lots. Made plans to save up and take a ferry out to the edge of the sea.

Then he'd gone back to school, and she'd never spoken of it again.

"It's right there." Jordan leaned over his shoulder to poke at his computer, and a map of the world unfolded in a private window. Clumsy red lines crisscrossed continent and ocean, streaking from Burima and

Ritt and Yundo and Gann until they vanished in a patch of darkness off the coast of Hanwa. "And don't give me that look, you graphic design snob. You can read it, can't you? Here." She tapped a smear of sea, zooming in. "The centroid of the triangle made of Shinu, Kep, and the Massey islands. Nineteen planes lost in the past twenty years. The constellations visible from that area match up with what we saw on the Island, as does the climate, and the stories."

Baron's mouth opened, closed. "The stories," he said at last.

"Says the boy who beheaded Captain Hook's first mate with a single stroke."

"I'm not—"

"—that person anymore?"

There was a dangerous glint in her eyes. Baron nudged the computer mouse and watched the dark triangle recede.

He'd always dismissed their Island conversations as just talk, or an excuse for her to bum a couple of his red bean pastries—the idea that they would actually seek the place out again was laughable. The Island wasn't *theirs* anymore—in fact, the more he tried to remember it, the more it felt like their childhood storybooks come to life, or one of those disappointing Rittan adventure movies where magic swallowed the main characters, claiming fate or prophecy, then spat them out again when they got too old to keep the audience's interest.

The Island had marked them, to be sure: in the topography of scars beneath Jordan's shirt, the way Baron recoiled from even the flash of a kitchen knife. But it was the Outside world that was supposed to beat them down now. The slow march of days, and cubicles like lit coffins.

They had grown up, after all.

Though if he said that out loud, Jordan would probably choke him with his own engineering project.

"I'm not," he said simply.

To his surprise, she regarded him without judgment. "You don't need it anymore."

Baron pushed his glasses up his nose. His Dust withdrawal had not been nearly as strong as hers; by his second week Outside, he'd hardly noticed. Only dry eyes when the wind blew a certain way, quickly remedied with prescription droplets. "I suppose not."

"Is there really so much to look forward to here?"

"Maybe it isn't about looking forward." He curled his fingers around the edge of the desk. A piece of gum had lodged beneath, and he grimaced and stuck his contaminated hand beneath the wall-mounted hand sanitizer unit before continuing. "Maybe you just walk on because you know you have to. Maybe you keep your head down and work because the people you care about will need your income someday, and you don't know why they cling so tightly to life, you don't even know if they know themselves, but you want to give it to them."

"And that's worth sixty years shut up in an office building somewhere?"

Sixty years. The echoes of his *whys* drizzled off the cliff like rain.

"I don't know," he said weakly.

"Baron." Jordan stood, and there was an urgency in her voice that in anyone else he might have called longing. "Come with me."

"I don't know if—"

"You can return to *this* anytime." She motioned at the cramped lab, the campus grounds unrolled outside the window. "Don't you ever miss not being bound by gravity?"

Of course he did. Every morning he woke with the ache. "There's more to life than flight."

"What, like capitalism?"

"Like—trying to see what's out in the world, instead of hunkering down inside a memory and desperately trying not to grow up."

Her eyes flashed. She thrust out her forearms: bruises purpled, turning ugly. "In case you haven't noticed, I probably won't."

"That's not what I meant."

"I'm sure it wasn't." Her voice was low and hard. "*You* don't have to remember anymore."

Baron shifted in his seat. For nearly nine years, ever since they had returned from the Island at age thirteen, he and Jordan had circled each other at a careful distance. She slept, somewhere. Ate more than the pastries she nicked from him, judging by the way she still nearly matched him in height. Earned enough to afford a consistent supply of karsa.

The unasked questions thickened on his tongue.

"Stay with me," he said.

An inscrutable expression crossed Jordan's face. "What, and mooch off your paycheck in exchange for cleaning your apartment and bearing your children?"

Baron's cheeks flamed. "What? No. I'm just saying—"

She grinned, jitter-eyed. In the set of her mouth something bittersweet and final.

"I hope you have a good life, then," she said, swiping away the map on his screen. Her arm brushed his, warm and then gone. "Or whatever you want to call it."

As she hoisted her bag onto her shoulder and shoved open the door, the vise squeezed again around Baron's lungs. Jordan regularly slipped out of his life for days at a time; as she refused to get a phone— syndicate hackers would latch on to anything, she said—he had no way to contact her.

But she'd never claimed to be leaving for good.

"Wait," he said.

Her hand caught the edge of the door.

The word hung in the air, condensing like smoke. He still had three problem sets left to finish, he thought wildly. Not to mention an engineering project whose code he needed to troubleshoot and two papers he hadn't even started. He couldn't simply go chasing after some half-remembered blot of land in some apocryphal region of sea.

Not to mention his parents would hunt him down and murder him first.

And yet. His chest was still tight, the underside of his skin scraped raw with the echo of fear. What was he hoping to become, anyway?

One of the suits who boarded the magrail year after year to spend his best hours hunched over emails? The faithful son who plunged through the storm for his parents, until he either broke down in public or stopped feeling anything at all?

When would it *end*?

"I'll come," he blurted before he could second-guess himself, and Jordan smiled.

Chapter 3

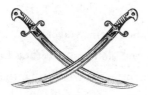

San Jukong was never truly quiet—cars and motorcycles thrummed over grey-ribbon highways, downtown First Circle a low constant roar—but San Jukong University campus was where it came closest. The place supposedly exemplified modern Rittan architecture, a cavalcade of concrete and glass buildings interspersed with trees and sloping lawns, maintained more for show than spatial economy. Yet in Burima, everything was cheap—manufacturers were bribed, building inspectors were bribed, construction workers were underpaid—so the dormitories and lecture halls they passed had a faded, dead look, as if they had stood for decades instead of just a few years.

Jordan drew up at the outer gate, its curlicued iron bars hammered into some hollow semblance of a past-century Rittan estate. Sweat slicked her back—Burimay humidity, even at night, was thick enough to swim through—and a pang went through her for the Island's cool breezes, the dusting of snow across dark pines in winter.

"This is what your tuition pays for?"

"This," Baron said stiffly, "and career prospects."

"Of course."

Baron hoisted his bag higher and walked on ahead of her.

Even as a thirteen-year-old, she knew, he'd dreamed of attending school here: ogled the groups of button-down-clad students debating bioethics on the courtyard steps, the math and science club members plastering the walkways with chalk and paper flyers. Paused, always, before the marble facade of the Kan Auditorium, where the Franklin Medal was draped around the neck of the top engineering student each year.

Instead, here he was, not even two years in, running away.

He would back out, no doubt, once they hit the train station or boarded the plane—when he realized, fully, that she meant what she had proposed. No one ever stayed; she had no right to expect him to.

But this last walk across the grounds together—across the unfolding campus green, the library's concrete bulk—it was enough. Had to be.

His eyes were still glassier than usual. Jordan had seen it before: fighters' heads between their knees in the locker room, ragged breaths easing as they slapped tranquilizer patches on their forearms. But it was not a thing that was said out loud.

"Are we going by plane?" he asked. When she nodded—thinking, as she did so, that neither of them would ever refer to it as *flying*—he said, "Then won't we need, ah, tickets? And some form of ID?"

Jordan smirked. "Your concern is touching. But we have a private ride this time."

His mouth twisted. Beneath the distant gleam of streetlights, he was pale as the moon. "A coworker?"

Here was another thing they never spoke of: what she did during the day. "Sure."

"And what about your—karsa?"

"If we reach the Island on time, I don't need to worry about running out. We'll have Dust soon enough."

"Dust." He said it like a curse.

"Yes."

A flash of memory: the bright winged creature flitting around Peter's head, its tiny clawed hands rubbing together like a beetle's; Peter's mortar and pestle mixing its golden wing powder with a pirate's ground-up bones. His high-pitched giggle as he dipped his fingers in and drifted off the ground.

"You want to steal Tink," Baron said.

"Yes."

"And a few funerary urns."

"If needed." At the look on his face, she added, "Having second thoughts?"

"Naturally." He shrugged his backpack higher on his shoulders. It had taken him an eternity to pack, even with her drumming her fingers loudly on his dorm room wall: a box of nutrition bars, his toothbrush and toothpaste, three changes of clothes, two full pump bottles of hand sanitizer, and a small wad of cash, stuffed into a climbing backpack she would bet her life had never actually been used for climbing. "And third ones."

"You don't have to do this."

He stopped, turned to her. "You know," he started, and then seemed to think better of it.

"Spit."

Baron shook his head. "We were the Twins," he said, fixing his eyes on a swaying stand of palm trees. "We were Peter's, before anything else. Before we even got to be *kids*, almost. And I was thinking—"

"Oh no."

"I was *thinking*," he continued, pulling a face, "that everything that's happened since, all this"—he motioned at the sprinklers, the smog-hazed streetlights, the campus buildings still and dark as mausoleums—"maybe the Island *is* the reason I don't know how to live in this world, you know? Not just because we missed so much school. But because we always knew there was a different kind of place out there. Different physics, different rules."

Jordan thought of long nights tilting her prosth against the single shitty outlet in her rented room, of sucking grains of karsa off her thumb in the roach-infested dark.

Well. As long as he had his reasons.

"All right," she said. "So we'll state for the record that this wasn't just my bad idea."

"It was, but—"

She punched him in the shoulder and he winced, protesting—and then they were tussling at the edge of the green, sweaty and half laughing, and Jordan felt a strange sense of familiarity, as if she was returning to a place she had lived long ago.

Peter had come for her entirely by accident.

She was sleeping over at Baron's apartment that night, her five-year-old sister wailing as Jordan carried her nightclothes and toothbrush just next door. Baron's parents were polite, if a little perplexed—they had expected a tumble of boys, when their son spoke of an eighth birthday celebration. But it was pleasant anyway, just the two of them, slurping peanut noodles and orange slices at the dining room table before retreating to Baron's bedroom to finish their homework.

They were settled beneath his blankets, drifting toward sleep, when he said, "What's that?"

Jordan opened her eyes.

A boy crouched in the open window.

The apartment was on the tenth floor.

"What do you want?" she asked.

The boy drew himself up. Even at his full height, his head barely brushed the frame. "My name is Peter," he said, jumping down from the sill to hang suspended in midair. Jordan's eyes widened. "And I'm looking for my shadow."

"It's not here," Baron said, with the instant knowing that came with having one's sock drawer organized by color and thickness of material.

Peter frowned. A light flitted around him, the size of Jordan's fist and flickering like a light bulb. As he raised a finger, it twined around his wrist: a tiny face, gossamer wings, faint ridges of exoskeleton tracing its abdomen and shoulders. "But I can smell it."

Jordan yanked off the covers, tucking her right arm behind her back. Her classmates teased her incessantly about it—in fact, along with Baron's thick glasses, it was part of the reason they had banded together at school—but if she started wearing a prosth, they would have taken it as a sign of defeat. In any case, her arm was long enough that, if she angled her shoulders right, most people didn't notice right away.

The patch of dark beneath Baron's desk had caught her attention earlier that evening, deeper than the surrounding shadow and strangely jagged. She snatched it up now and held it to her chest, heart thundering.

It was cashmere-soft, the coolness sliding against her skin like star-brushed night. Soft, and strange, and altogether *real*.

"I'll trade you this," she said, "if you take us with you."

Peter looked dubious. "Both of you? But I was looking for a Tudo."

Baron's eyes met hers in the dark. Their third-grade teacher had just read the Sir Franklin novel aloud to them in class; they had watched the movie together in Jordan's apartment as her younger sister bounced and twirled and pretended to be a fairy.

In both versions, there was Peter and Tink and the wicked pirates, and an island that shifted and groaned in the small hours of night. In both versions, Peter was attended by a small posse of Lost Boys: bespectacled Tudo, and the Twins who finished each other's sentences; vicious Kuli, and worldly Slightly, and towheaded Jack, the Ama's boy.

And in both versions, the girls always had to do the chores.

A plan unfolded in Jordan's mind.

In most of the stories she'd watched and read, the magic only reached out once—the grimoire, the amulet, the key to a forbidden door. Some invitation, easily overlooked by the rest of the world, to a realm where you could defeat a shadowy dark lord or drive off an invading army with a small brave band of magical companions; where you could become *more* than the homework dumped on you every night or the cruel words your classmates and parents tossed out because they knew you'd be punished for hitting back.

Adventure had presented itself to Jordan Makta, if she was strong enough to take it.

And she thought: Perhaps it was the only chance she would ever get.

"We'll be the Twins," she said, dangling Peter's shadow in his face. "Promise that we're coming with you first."

"Fine," he snapped, and snatched the darkness out of her hand. To the winged light now flitting around Baron's lamp, he said, "C'mere, Tink."

A sound like bells, and then those translucent wings dusted the errant shadow with gold. Peter drew a small leather pouch out of his skeleton-leaf pocket, dumped its grey contents—the powdered bone, Jordan would later learn—onto the golden dust and stirred both into the shadow with his index finger. In seconds he was jumping around the room, shadow bounding after him, and crowing about his brilliance in finding it.

As Baron cautiously slid off his glasses, receiving the Dust Peter blew into his cupped hands, Jordan's plan shattered outward, lightning cracked across a midnight sky.

If she went along as she was, she was bound to get caught—if not by Peter, then by the Lost Boys. Other children were like bloodhounds, she had learned from school: They would see her arm, and single her out, and notice when she had to use the bathroom in private.

But Dust was not just for flying. Dust held things together, bent the rules of the world like light through a prism. And her lie about the Twins might get them onto the Island, but if she could mold herself and Baron into exactly the same image, if she could convince Peter that they were truly interchangeable—

They would have more than a few hours, flying like this. They would have years.

"From now on," she whispered in Baron's ear, "pretend I'm a boy."

He gave her a sideways look—gauging her already-cropped hair, the jut of her chin—and nodded.

And so, when Peter sprinkled Dust on her forehead—when Jordan felt an intoxicating sense of well-being swell inside her, a tug at the base of her navel—she caught an extra pinch and rubbed it on the end of her right arm.

It burned. Bent her over breathless, her skin seared raw by the thing she was asking it to do. But she screwed her eyes shut and *imagined*, and when she opened them again, something like a hand shimmered from her right forearm, limp and wet-looking as clay.

A shadow. A glamour.

"Does this mean we'll never have to grow up?" she asked, pitching her voice lower. Baron spoke with a slightly different cadence, but there would be time enough to work that out. He caught her gaze again, finally comprehending.

"No." Peter launched himself backward out the window and they followed, Jordan's head spinning with vertigo as the street stretched thirty meters below them. "I'm the only one who stays."

"So what happens to the other, ah, Lost Boys?" Baron asked.

Peter's teeth glinted in the city lights. "They grow up," he said, "usually." And as they flew out into the night, Jordan did not look back at the apartment complex, at her parents in their study or her sister sleeping fitfully in their shared bedroom; did not bother to think, for even a moment, about what Peter might mean. She was eight years old, and all the stories were real, and if she could choose any future for herself it would be this.

Chapter 4

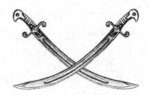

Tier cradled his fifth—sixth?—seventh?—shot glass and thought, eloquently, *Fuck*.

The 8&8 Bar was a favorite of his whenever he stayed over in San Jukong: straight off the airport shuttle line, but far enough away that his fellow pilots wouldn't stumble into him on their own quests for oblivion. San Jukong was an international city, and a red-haired Rittan did not attract nearly as much attention here as he might have in Zachen or Rezé. And so, after his last flight for the week, he'd all but sprinted to the low building—near-solid shadow, save for the neon lining the bar—ordered a few volcanics, and burned the tremor at the edge of his mouth straight to Taram.

He should have known, by now, that he would go down with it.

Tier did not drink in-flight, but something about being on land cracked him open. The steel thrust of skyscrapers and highways, perhaps, or the lingering gazes of the Rittan expats he passed on the streets—any one of them potentially his father's associates, eager to report on the wayward youngest son in this distant tropical backwater.

Or perhaps it was simply the crush of other bodies, pressed in against the hot night: all the sweating and talking and *touching*, loud voices and sticky shoulders shoving his back when he least expected. After the clean isolation of his cockpit, it made him want to claw his own eyes out.

Nevertheless, as Jordan Makta clamped her metal hand over the empty chair across from him, Tier wondered if he shouldn't have drunk *quite* so much.

"Ey, kweilo."

"Don't call me that," he slurred, tipping back his seat. A silent breath of relief—the words slid out glass-smooth when lubricated by alcohol.

"No?" Jordan leaned against the table, her thumb tracing the initials etched into the wood. A few patrons had looked up, idly curious. "Would you rather I called you Mr. Ardm—"

A crash, breaking glass. Tier was on his feet—had slammed her shoulders back against the wall, his breath coming fast and hard. "Not here."

Jordan grinned, all teeth, her near-black eyes glittering malevolent in the bar's faint glow. "Let go, or you'll be crying every time you piss for the rest of your life."

"What do you want?" he snarled.

"To not have to repeat myself." A faint pressure at his hip, metallic and unforgiving, and he jerked back, heat blotching his face. "I could do the other end, too, if you'd like—"

"Fuck off." Tier retreated farther, startled as his leg brushed the tipped-over chair. But he had stood up too fast; the floor was tilting, the ceiling a fluttered wingbeat, and when he reached for his drink, he inclined a hair too far forward and crashed headfirst into the back wall. Pain flared through his skull. "Ngh."

"Tier," Jordan snapped. A small victory for him, that she'd used his forename instead of his surname, but it no longer felt like one. "I have a job for you."

With no small amount of effort, Tier righted the chair and sat, his head still throbbing. "Obalang sent you?" he asked, attempting to recover some shred of dignity.

"No."

"Then who?"

Jordan seated herself opposite him, placed her elbows on the table. "I sent myself."

Tier snorted. The two of them had worked together before: him flying private planes, karsa tucked in secret compartments and the false bottoms of transport crates; she a runner parceling out portions, poking at the borders of Hanak territory. Every time, that quirk at the corner of her mouth, as if she would find him laughable no matter what he did. Every time, the best part of the op had been watching her step off the plane. "Why in the ten hells would I ever want to work with you again?"

"What about forty million mir?"

"Bullshit."

Jordan leaned forward. "I could've asked Ikhai, instead of dragging myself down here to deal with your drunken arse."

"So?" he shot back, nearly losing his balance again as he waved down a waiter for another drink. "Go. They'll laugh you off the jet bridge. Runners run drugs, not ops."

She said, enunciating slowly, "There's a reason I haven't yet."

Several pulses of overhead eedro, and then the memories filtered in: the slow churn of clouds against his windshield, her shadow sliding over his control panel as he veered slightly off his official route; the careful, probing questions about the triangle formed by Shinu, Kep, and Massey; the star chart stuffed beneath one of his display screens, marked with speculated latitude and longitude and a sketch of an island. *The* Island, with a scrawled note claiming she had once been there, lived there. He had never acknowledged the missive, but on his next flight out, he had navigated to the coordinates she'd marked, heart thundering in his chest—and found nothing.

A glow-in-the-dark shot had appeared at the center of the table. Tier knocked it down, felt the room around him smear further into oil slick and shadow.

"You still think it exists."

Jordan raised a brow. "I *know* there are five centuries' worth of buried shipwrecks in the surrounding area. And that you need more than latitude and longitude to find it. There's something—else."

As close to an apology as she would ever give him. He made a face. "If it's being young and innocent and heartless, I doubt you're any better off than I am."

"If I said it here, you'd have no reason to take me." Jordan lifted her chin. "I'll tell you once we land. Forty mil worth of treasure."

Tier pressed his fingertips together (though they kept slipping, mismatched, and eventually he conceded to clasping his hands). *Forty million mir.* As a child, he'd made a habit of disappearing into other worlds—first through animated princess movies that got him beaten by his older brothers, then via more *suitable* comics and webtoons whose heroes punched out both villains and witticisms with flawless panache. They gave him a way to leave his body for a while, when he could not stand the feel of his own skin. By the time he discovered the Island forums, based on the famous children's book—an amalgamation of headlines, court records, historical documentation of shipwrecks and plane crashes that hinted at an anomaly off the Gulf of Enju—it was only the next step on a road he had long been traveling.

Then he'd left home, and his father had split his inheritance among his brothers, and that preoccupation had grown into something more.

Those ships: hundreds of years drowned, loaded with bullion and precious relics. Cargo planes vanished with crates of diamonds, carrying syndicate and government comms that could be sold for a fortune. If Tier could unbury them—if he could, at last, prove he was worth something—he could return to Ritt and reclaim the birthright of which he had been stripped.

And if Sir Ardmuth's people always hovered at the edge of his awareness—if their covertly taken photos ended up plastered across

Rittan tabloids, and his father denounced him yet again as an eejit and a lost cause—well, fuck them. He was already gone.

Another shot, luminous blue, but when he reached for it, Jordan swatted his hand away. "Is that a no?"

"N-no," he blurted, and his cheeks heated again—he'd never figured out how to answer a double negative. "I mean yes. I mean, I'll meet you at the Cindan Airstrip tomorrow at two—"

"Now."

"I said *tomorrow* at—"

"Or I'll knock you out and ask Ikhai."

"No other syndicate pilot will believe you."

"Try me," she said, and her eyes were flat and cold as a shark's. He did not want to find out, when she left him unconscious in the back alley, whether she'd leave his credit cards on him. Or his balls.

"All right." Tier stood, the floor still sliding beneath his feet, and willed his eyes to uncross before he sat back in the cockpit. "All right. Fine. But I need at least an hour to run preflight checks."

Chapter 5

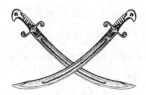

Baron couldn't look at Tier for too long.

It wasn't that he *wanted* his face to heat at the sight of the drunk Rittan. Not that he wasn't aware of all the ways this man's people had cracked open trade sanctions by force and burned to the ground entire nations who refused to comply. And even with adrenaline still jagging through his chest, it was impossible to miss the blatant disgust radiating from Jordan as they took the train out of the First Circle. *Our pilot,* she'd introduced him, and allowed Tier to attempt a greeting in chewy, mangled Hanwa before Baron responded in Rittan.

And yet. There was something about the curl of red-brown hair falling in Tier's eyes, the crisp lines of that pilot uniform, that made Baron dizzy.

You eejit, he thought as Tier checked the controls; as Jordan's hand hovered over the small plastic-wrapped package tucked inside her bag. They'd stopped at an apartment complex on the shabbier side of the First Circle before boarding a second train—and then there was the plane itself, all sleek white metal and pale diffuse lights. *This is not the time for—*

"Baron," Jordan said, sliding into the copilot's seat as if she flew for a living, and Baron's head snapped up, violet flaring through his vision.

"Yes?"

She smirked, knowing. "You should talk to him," she said in Kebai, the southern Hanwa dialect they had both grown up speaking. "He has an utterly charming personality."

Baron flushed. "It's not like that."

Her grin broadened. "If you need any pointers—"

"I can manage on my own, thank you." Baron's stomach twisted. He had never met any of Jordan's previous flings, and did not want to. Enough that he had to imagine her mouth on some stranger's, their pleasured groans in the dark.

She winked. "Then I eagerly await your demonstration."

"What are you talking about?" Tier slurred, irritable.

"The price of cabbages." Jordan propped her feet against the side of the windshield. "Settle down and get us off the ground, Rittan."

Tier glared at her blearily but did not seem to have the energy, or perhaps the courage, to push her further. Baron wondered how she'd persuaded him to join them; why the pilot flinched every time she moved close. Decided, again, that he didn't want to know.

"He looks like that anime character you like," Jordan said thoughtfully as the engines thundered to life. "What was their name again?"

"Saints," Baron groaned, burying his face in his hands.

"He even has the same eye color—"

"I'm *begging* you—"

"Speak a language we all know," Tier snapped. The plane lurched forward and Baron staggered, his elbows banging hollow against the back wall. "And find a seat."

"We were wondering if you needed anything," Baron said hastily in Rittan. He could feel Jordan's eyes on him, but didn't dare reciprocate. Embarrassing that she could read him so easily, but at least this was an issue he could quickly let go of. "Water, tea, coffee—not that it will counter the impaired judgment due to alcohol, but—"

Jordan made a sound of amusement, and Baron's cheeks went hot again. To his surprise, however, Tier did not scoff.

"Kind of you," he said, low, and Baron fixed his gaze beyond the windshield. Save for the runway lights, the darkness was thick, absolute, the type that had folded over the Island after the sun slipped beneath the horizon. "But I can get things myself, after we switch to autopilot. The passenger seats are open. Feel free to spread out. And"—his eyes briefly met Baron's, as vivid blue-green as the sea—"get some rest, if you can."

"The shadows under your eyes have shadows," Jordan added cheerfully, and Baron nodded before stumbling out of the cockpit as fast as his weary legs would take him.

He woke groggy and disoriented—his mouth tasting of sleep, a dull throb behind his right eye. His bones gone slow and heavy, as they did after every time he lost control.

"You awake?"

Baron grunted, his eyelids weighted and sliding. "Ngwhat?"

"We're about forty-five minutes out."

He forced one eye open: Jordan beside him, a darker shape in the dimness. The lights had been switched off in the cabin, save for the glow of the exit and restroom signs. "Nuh?"

"From the Island." Her hand brushed across his forehead, feather light. Pushing the hair out of his eyes. "Remember?"

He did. A murmur of pine branches, the touch of salt breeze against his face. Crimson gargles of blood, as knees folded to the forest floor.

Reckless, to return. A death wish for all of them. But once Jordan was involved, Baron would have thrown himself to the Island wolves and called it a joy.

He struggled the rest of the way awake. A heavy blanket had been draped over him—Tier's, he suspected—and he nearly fell out of his seat attempting to untangle himself. Jordan grabbed one corner and pulled, and then he was cold, and dizzy, and he still couldn't quite feel his legs.

"I'm so tired," he said, and it felt like a confession.

"I can tell." A twitch at the edge of Jordan's mouth like displeasure. She blamed the Island, he knew: for the way he caved into himself at the slightest provocation, the adrenaline that lanced his lungs at just the sound of children's laughter. These long periods of exhaustion after the storm took him, in which he stumbled around as if drunker than Tier.

Speaking of whom. "Is our pilot—?"

"I kept him alive for you," Jordan said, teasing. "If you really want me to—"

"No, I do not."

"I was going to say 'stop being such an arse.' "

" 'Course you were." He unbuckled his seat belt and heaved to his feet; before he could collapse into the seat immediately adjacent, her hand was at his elbow, bracing him upright, half dragging him toward the cockpit.

"How long've I *slept*?" he slurred as she slid open the door.

She raised a brow. "Through the night, like a normal person."

"Why didn' you—*wake* me—"

"You really have to ask?"

Dawn had broken, a faint pink line of sunrise that limned the edge of the world. Tier was slumped in the pilot's seat, head tipped down to his chest. Beneath the lightening sky, he looked almost Erendite: Dark blue veins showed through his near-translucent skin. His hands, resting on the control panel—though the autopilot did most of the work— were scattered with freckles.

"Slacking?" Jordan said loudly, and he shot up so fast that Baron might have laughed aloud, had he not been preoccupied with focusing his eyes. "It's a miracle we even got off the runway."

"What do you want," Tier said flatly. He smelled of cologne, with an undercurrent of vomit; Baron angled his face slightly upward, trying not to make a show of breathing out of his mouth, and wished it was enough to free the moths fluttering in his stomach.

"You asked how we would find the Island." Jordan thrust out her prosth, the upper third of her right forearm exposed beneath her rolled-up sleeve. Among the bruises curved a faint crescent-shaped scar, barely visible in the cockpit dimness. "I have Dust stored in a sac inside my skin."

Baron swayed back against the wall. "You *what*?"

"Not much." Jordan's right hand dropped back to her side. "But that's what got us there nine years ago. If we each take at least a token amount, we have a decent chance of breaking through the barrier."

"How do you know?" Tier asked, turning reluctantly around in his seat. "In all the stories, doesn't Peter have to bring you?"

Baron stared. Tier had not questioned the existence of Dust or its efficacy—had spoken as if Peter and the Island were as true as this plane—and Baron wondered what someone as obviously grown-up as the pilot might want with such a place. The Island was *for kids*, as the old ad jingle went, that taunting cry of automatic exclusion via inexorable time. Surely Tier wasn't hoping to be initiated into the Lost Boys at his age.

"Peter might not matter," Jordan said.

"Why not?"

She swallowed, her left thumb ghosting over the crook of her right elbow. Turned to Baron. "Remember what he said, the first time we came?"

He nodded. Their first flight across the ocean had been wheeling stars and moonlit grins, the metal and smog of San Jukong fading at their backs, Jordan laughing beside him as dolphins arced out of tinfoil waves. And then, hours in—a hum in his bones, like the brushing of two like-polarity magnets, as they laid their hands against the invisible curtain that veiled the Island from grown-up eyes.

And Peter had crowed, *The only adults that get in are dead ones.*

"I don't think Peter means anything he says," Baron said doubtfully.

"I know." Jordan dragged a hand through her hair. "It doesn't explain how the pirates washed up alive. Or the Pales, for that matter. But why else did all those planes and ships disappear? Where do they *go*? In the original story, the Island is tucked on the other side of sleep. If most of the passengers were sleeping, or got caught in a storm—there were a couple of those, too—"

"Sleep and death are different things."

"Maybe. But maybe it's the unconsciousness that counts. Or something else. If Dust can't get us through the barrier, we might be able to fall asleep and float through like flotsam—"

"That's a lot of assumptions," Tier said.

"I know. Which is why, in the worst case—" Jordan pointed up at the remaining stars. A cluster of three made up the Fox's Tail, its tip glinting faintly red. "Second on the right, remember?"

"Er." Tier's eyes flicked up, uncertain. "And we just—keep going?"

"Or turn around if there's still nothing."

The pilot scowled. "So you've just wasted thousands of mir worth of my jet fuel for a guess."

"For a chance at forty million," Jordan said crisply. "Don't you want to at least look?"

Tier had opened his mouth to reply when a blipping white dot shifted on the radar screen, and he went still.

"What's wrong?" Jordan asked, leaning closer, but the pilot only pressed his lips together, freckles stark against the blanch of his face.

"N-nothing."

"You're a terrible liar." To Baron: "Someone's following us, aren't they."

Baron leaned forward, squinted against the tight pulse of a returning headache. Sure enough, the dot had crept closer, the green radar circle a dull glowing target.

Then another flicker in his periphery, from some kind of camera screen: a sweep of dark wings, machinery bristling from the plane's underside.

"It looks," he said, still hazy, "like it's—armed?"

Blink and Jordan was gripping Tier by the collar, her eyes cold with fury. "Who the fuck is after you?"

"Don't," Baron said uselessly.

"Get your hands off me," Tier drawled—his accent strangely stretched, almost Meirian—but his face had blotched red, spit frothing at the corner of his mouth. "I—I'll report you to the syndicate."

Jordan's grip tightened. "All I have is one packet of karsa. I'm not high up enough on the ladder for someone to come after me with a Saintsdamned war plane."

"I'm just a pilot—"

"Ten hells you are," Jordan snapped, and he flinched. "You own this fucking jet."

"How do you kn—"

"*Don't lie to me,*" she said, and then the pilot's face spasmed and he was choking, sputtering, his hands flapping frantically against her arms.

"Jordan," Baron said, but her face was like stone, and she didn't let go.

Tier had turned a disturbing shade of purple.

"My—my father's people," he gasped. "They've—they watch me. Ever since I left Ritt—"

Baron's heart clenched. "*Jordan.* He can't breathe."

"And what do they want now?" Her voice was low, toneless. "Why are they after you?"

"The Island," Tier said, his mouth contorting again, and Baron saw, beneath Jordan's arms, the pilot's fingers twitching in small helpless motions. "They—want to d—develop it."

"But what do they think they'll achieve by following *you* th—"

A massive explosion rocked the plane. Baron tottered against the back wall as sirens began to wail; emergency lights bathed the cockpit red.

"Fuck," Tier coughed. Jordan had released him, and he slumped back in his seat, rubbing his throat. "Get in the cabin and eject. They won't care if I die, they want the location—"

A second impact, and the plane swooned. Tier went pale.

"They might have skimmed a wing," he said, and then he was hunched over the controls, frantically pressing buttons, his profile flattened by the emergency lights into bloodred silhouette.

"Come on." Jordan motioned Baron back toward the cabin and he followed, eyes fixed on nothing. In his high school physics course, he had calculated how quickly a person would be rendered incoherent if a plane depressurized at an altitude of *x* meters, how forcefully they would hit the ocean if they fell from such a height. For years, he'd skirted around the idea of death: cyanide and multistory parking lots, midnight highways and ties knotted from ceilings; had only ever lacked the courage to act. That he should be blown apart in the first airplane he had ever boarded, alongside the only person he'd ever considered a friend, was to be pitied, perhaps—a severance at the start of a journey, a drowning-out of possibility.

Yet he would be free, as well, from the sixty-plus years of spreadsheets and strip lighting that chained him to the shore he'd left behind. Would finally be allowed to stop fighting.

Somehow, he could not bring himself to be afraid.

"Dust," Jordan said, and then there was a small plastic baggie stuffed into his hand, its bottom lined with a grainy brown sludge. Baron's heart skipped.

"Jordan—"

"I'll open the emergency door." The flash of a knife, vanishing into her pocket. She tipped her head pointedly away from her bleeding right arm; beneath the flicker of the lights, she was oddly wan, almost sick-looking. "Take a couple of those flotation devices under the seats. When the door opens, spread the Dust out on your skin before it blows away."

"Er." Baron peered beneath the lower cushion, his head pounding in time with the sirens. "Are we *jumping*?"

Jordan's answer was lost to a colossal *boom*. The walls convulsed this time; Baron staggered sideways, and she caught him by the arm, her elbow sharp against his ribs. "Come on."

He fumbled one bright yellow life jacket from beneath the seat, then another, inflated them with his breath coming short and fast. "What about Tier?"

"After he got a fucking fighter plane on our tail?"

Then her hands were on his, the baggie tipped sideways, and Dust zinged euphoric through his skull. He'd forgotten the headiness of it: the first wind of spring, honey in the comb, sky arched blue into infinity. Actual magic, distilled in his veins like wine.

"All right?" Jordan asked, looping the life jackets over both their heads, and Baron grinned, though his hands were slick with her blood. "Let me know if—"

"'mfine," he slurred, dreamy-slow.

She smirked, no doubt as high as he was, and yanked the exit lever. Wind roared through the gap; waves surged beneath, fast approaching.

The plane tilted—though whether it was by Tier's hand was up for debate—and several more alarms joined the cacophony.

"Let's go." Jordan held out her hand, similarly grimed with Dust and blood—which, he now saw, was leaking from a sort of flexible pocket embedded in her forearm. A passive implant, undetectable to all metal scanners, built to break only when punctured.

Too small to fit more than an afternoon's worth for a single person.

"How do you know it'll be enough?" he asked, fighting the dizzying sense of well-being: It wasn't real, none of this was real.

"I don't." Jordan nodded at the door. "But unless you have a parachute inside that giant backpack of yours—"

Baron stepped forward, joints swinging loose with each step. His knees had gone weak; he could not stop himself from looking down at the grey curtain of rain, the infinite drop.

He was so tired of falling.

He only had to do it one more time.

"And stay upright, keep your feet together," Jordan was saying, as if from a great distance. "We're still a few kilometers up."

Baron nodded, then dragged in a gasp: He was already losing oxygen. Thunder rose in his ears; clouds churned at his feet.

This was not the Baron his parents knew. Not the Baron *he* knew. That person would have kept his time on the Island firmly partitioned in his subconscious. That person would only have broken open in the privacy of his own dorm room; would have let adulthood shatter and rebuild and shatter him again, until all that remained was a hollowed husk.

He took Jordan's hand, a somewhat incongruous smile twitching across his face as more Dust shot through him like sunlight.

Then a groan shook the plane, and the engine thrum crescendoed into a shriek, and they jumped.

Chapter 6

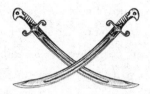

A red light flashed on one of Tier's control panels—the emergency
doors flung open—and then Tier knew he was alone.

Two seconds after the alarms had begun to sound, a barrage of
shots ricocheted off his wings and fuselage, a concussion of punched
metal and shattered glass. He'd radioed in on every frequency he could,
shouting that he was a civilian, that he was carrying passengers, and
received only silence in reply. Now a dozen sirens howled through the
cabin; one of the pressure gauges had burst, and something rattled dangerously. He was running on fumes. If he didn't eject himself from the
aircraft with the one-person life raft folded beneath his seat, the plane
would plunge him under, and he would either drown or be trapped in a
waning bubble of air, asphyxiating slowly from his own exhales.

And yet. His calculations placed the Island two minutes off the
horizon line; the virtual pin he'd dropped on the coordinates blipped
steadily closer on his nav screen. He only needed to fly near enough to
let the currents carry him in alive. Though, as he knew nothing about
said currents' direction, that still meant as close as possible—

The plane rocked again, bucking him face-first into the dashboard, and his head rang. The whole cabin was tilted on its side now, descending rapidly, the waves below a stippled expanse of copper and iron. Beneath his wavering hands, the displays flashed odd colors, the altimeter whirling, and—he looked closer.

The radar screen was empty.

"Fuck," he shouted, and the word hung in the air, flawless and unfettered. The Island had emerged on the horizon—or at least *an* island, pine-wreathed peak crowning the water line where his maps showed only ocean. He reached for the raft, fumbling for a plastic tab beneath his seat—it *was* some sort of tab, wasn't it, and not one of the rarely used buttons on the side panels?—but the emergency protocols were a nauseous jumble, and he was groping for a single edge in the dark.

The plane's nose yawed downward, the engines sputtering their last resistance to gravity, and Tier bit down a scream.

You know this.

The cockpit rattling apart. Alarms a continuous blare. He squeezed his eyes shut.

You fucking eejit. You know this.

Years ago, in another life, his family had stayed in a small village off the coast of Narwith for the summer, one of the few vacations in which he'd ever been allowed to tag along: small white cottages drenched in sunlight, seagulls awhirl through forever-blue sky, his mother's laughter bubbling up like a surprise. Tier had flown his first plane there, a small red-and-blue Noctera parked on a dock by the water; ducked his head as his father, settling into the passenger's seat, turned on him the full force of his attention. *Remember this*, a low murmur, large strong hands wrapping Tier's around the red emergency handle in the cockpit ceiling, *and this*, the latch at the window, *and this*, reaching along the bottom of the seat for a lever and pulling until Tier heard the click, the sucking whoosh of air. *Just in case.* The last time Tier could remember the two of them touching without pain.

His hands ghosted the motions now, tentative. The memory of

sunlight rose on his skin, light and potent as liquor, the warm solidity of his father's fingers curled around the bones of his wrist. A man he'd admired, once, because he hadn't known anything else. A man for whom he still could not help feeling, in the end, something like love.

This was his history. This was his legacy.

This was the only thing Tier had left.

Remember.

He pulled the lever and fell out of the shrinking sky.

PART TWO

I'm sure you've heard the stories... They're all true enough.
—Leigh Bardugo, *Six of Crows*

T he Island recognized its visitors.

They drifted from beyond the line of the sea with a blink, a fritz of static, burning teardrop-shaped holes in the darkness: a pale boy sprawled out on a yellow raft, copper hair drifting about his face like a crown; a boy and a girl whose arms tangled around each other, heads bent close enough to kiss. All three covered in dust, in death, in the burnt-grass reek of misplaced hope—battered bastard children tugged soundless toward a shore on which they were no longer welcome.

Yet none of them were awake to notice. Had they been, they might have seen the black rocks rising out of the water like avenging angels, the ice-dagger trees swaying a warning. Might have thought twice about returning to the cliffs and coves and hollow trees, or forging back through rock and spring and waterfall. Might have stayed away from the heart of the forest.

But they slept on, their minds flitting petal-thin between fantasy and reality, landing light as butterfly feet in the shadows between nightmares.

And when the ocean spat them onto the sand in salt-chewed offering, only the Island saw, and said nothing.

Chapter 7

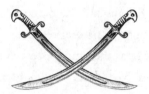

Jordan blinked awake, sand gritting her eyes.

For a moment she was back in the Underground arena, reeling from a head kick, the crowd jeering as she fought her own weighted limbs. Victory still floating above, if only she could pick herself back up and seize it.

Except for the sun slashing down like teeth, the pebbles and seashell shards pressed into her cheek. Except for the roar of ocean waves, and the brine-tinted breeze, and the taste in her mouth of raspberries and rain.

Then she registered the slope of the skyline, and her breath caught.

Those peaks. Those trees. That cliff. Familiar as her own knuckles, their jagged edges an embrace. She had slain pirates and Pales here, played and fought and flown and *lived*, and she was standing again on its shores and breathing its air and all of it was real, all of it.

She swallowed a laugh, or maybe a lump in her throat. Because despite everything, the first thought that came crashing through her was *home*.

"Baron," she said. "Baron, get up."

His lashes fluttered, showing the whites of his eyes. They were lying out in the open, a couple meters from the sea-foam line of the water—and, judging by the angle of the sun and the mountains at the Island's center, they'd washed up on Peter's side. Despite the shift of its forests and caves and ravines, the Island's borders always remained vaguely crab-shaped—Peter and his Boys' circle of hollow trees on the northeast pincer; the pirates' ship grounded on the southern bay; Pales camped to the west, a motley assortment of Rittans and Meiri and Glennans known Outside for leaching weaker nations of natural resources but pared down, here, to what Jordan thought of as their most essential form—cannibals. One sandy arm of the pirates' bay edged Jordan's periphery, but here, a Boy might stumble across them at any moment, and then the imitation bird calls would go out, patterns she still remembered for washed-up corpses and hostile invaders, and they would close in.

None of them would remember her face.

"Oh." Baron had shot upright, one hand patting the sand as if he'd expected a bedside table. "Jordan—is that you? Have you seen—I can't find my glasses, and—oh, *Saints*—" And then his breaths were coming short and sharp, his face tipped toward the sky.

"Baron," Jordan said cautiously—at times like these, he did not always hear her. "We're still alive. Breathe."

He sucked in an inhale, an ominous scrape running beneath. "Sorry. Sorry, I just—"

"Five in, five out."

He closed his eyes. Tucked his head between his knees, fingers digging into the ground, and Jordan could almost feel the race of his heart, the whipcrack of adrenaline through his veins. It had gotten worse, recently; almost every other day, she would walk into his dorm or study room and find him gripping the edge of his desk, white-knuckled and fighting for air.

Shitty of her, to be a contributing factor. Yet he had come with her anyway—had agreed, knowing what it would cost him.

She tried not to think about what that meant. What he might do for her, if only she asked.

When Baron had recovered enough to speak again, he raised his head reluctantly, mouth twisted with chagrin.

"They were expensive," he said, as if in explanation, and she let him have it. "Er. Where are we?"

Light-strobe bursts of memory: whirling sirens, wind boxing her ears, the impossible rise of her body into rosy dawn. Then the explosion above her head, consuming white. A vast blank seared in her memory.

She and Baron could have drowned in that absence. Could have been dragged with the plane—and, perhaps, its arsehole pilot—to the bottom of the sea.

But now—

Now—

"I was just going to tell you," Jordan said, and a grin spread across her face, so wide it could have cracked her open. "We're on the Island."

His mouth opened, and then closed. She saw the question of whether she was joking bloom and die on the tip of his tongue.

But she would never joke about this.

"It—worked?" he said finally, sifting sand through his fingers. "I'd always thought it would be—harder, somehow. To get back through."

Jordan had only ever crossed the barrier *into* the Island the once, when Peter first brought them here—light rippling through the air like a gauzy curtain, a sub-bass hum coursing beneath her skin. The line between Inside and Outside, Before and After. *Grown-ups can't feel it*, Peter had informed them, and she'd felt a little rush of delight, as if she had finally arrived at a kingdom that might belong to her.

"Dust," she said simply, and Baron's gaze flicked to her prosth— or the still-weeping cut a few centimeters above it, though she dared not look there. She had asked the quicksurgeon for threaded stitches instead of liquid ones, the scar marking its place not a declaration but a necessity.

"Are you—quite sure?"

"Smell the air," she said, throwing her arms out. Around her, the cool sharp scent of pine and weathered stone, the caws of Everbirds borne along the wind. "Listen to the forest. There's nowhere else on earth—"

The first salvo of pain shot down her spine, searing the world red.

No, Jordan thought, as the rest of her words withered in her throat. Her pack lay a couple meters away, crusted with kelp, and she scrambled over, fumbled with the zip, though her prosth had gone slow and unresponsive. Inside: a small plastic baggie that used to hold karsa, now salt-soaked and lined with only a faint smear of purple.

The godsdamned thing hadn't been sealed properly.

"Fuck. *Fuck.*"

"Jordan?" Baron's eyes were wide—pools she could have fallen into, if falling had ever been a choice she could make. "What's wrong?"

She turned, every muscle in her body strung tight and aching. A tremor was building inside her chest like a nitrogen tank primed to blow. "I'm fine."

"You're going into withdrawal, aren't you."

" 'Course not."

There must have been some sharpness absent from his gaze, though she couldn't much tell the difference. "How can I help?" he asked, with a gentleness she did not deserve, and this was why she had left him for days at a time Outside, this was why she had always been afraid of coming too close: because she was always going to burn herself down, and he could only ever watch.

"Well, don't *look,*" she snapped, and then her spine spasmed and there was no reasoning with the pain, no moving through it—her shoulders locked and Baron's hand was at the small of her back and she coughed, retched, her vomit shot through with threads of dark red.

Oh.

Heat pulsed through her insides, raced across her skin. Proof, she thought with a weird fucked-up relief she didn't have the energy to process, that she hadn't made this up.

"Jordan," she heard Baron say, but she was not here—she was an acid convulsion, a lightning pulse. The final stage of karsa withdrawal, at the shittiest possible time.

At the edge of her hearing, a little boy's laughter.

And now?

And now?

Jordan curled into herself, breathing hard. Her jaw ached from being clenched; green spots blitzed the corners of her vision.

She imagined running a sword through Peter's soft pale stomach, punching in his perfect milk teeth.

He had turned her own body against her. Even if Chay, the Boys' Ama at the time, had been the one to point out Jordan's transgression, it was his command that had riled up the Boys into charging after her, his thirst for blood that sent the wolf tearing into her skin.

And for that, he would pay.

"Jordan," Baron said, more urgently. "We should go. If we're really on the wrong side of the—the Island—"

"Right." Her voice like ashes. She squeezed her eyes shut, heaved upright in a dizzying burst of motion. "I'm fine."

He said, quietly, "I'm sorry."

Jordan exhaled and wished she could leave her body.

Walking was excruciating. She pointed Baron to a cave in the distance, toward the pirates' side of the Island—it had been dry there even at high tide, the one time she could recall playing in it. A wide low mouth opened into a high platform, a rocky ceiling punctured with light. But with every step, lightning sang through her legs; her breath rattled, as if vomit clung to the insides of her lungs.

Baron draped her arm over his shoulders, his free hand gentle around her wrist. She realized that, when he bent like this, they were precisely the same height.

Another throb in her chest, deeper, and she garbled a sob.

"I'm sorry," Baron said again. "I shouldn't have—we could have had a life, in Burima."

As if it had been his decision. Jordan pressed her fist against her diaphragm. A cramp had tightened between her ribs; her tongue was a corpse in her mouth.

"Should've listened," she said thickly, "when your ba told you to stay away from me."

"That's not what I meant."

"'Course not." Swallowing was difficult, as was opening her swelling eyes. "You wanted to feel like—like you'd done at least a few things right. After the Island."

"That's not true." A pause. Then, as if from a great distance, she heard him say, "What in Taram is your problem?"

Her problem, she thought, hazy. Turning the words over in her head like smooth stones. They had both lost touch with reality, somewhere in the last nine years; clung to their secret history as if it made the mundane hurts of growing up any more profound. And the gods or probability or fate had dragged them to the edge of the world to be taught, once and for all, that time only moved one way. That the small empires they'd raised had since fallen, or only ever stood in their own imagining.

That, in the end, they were just two fools who had believed a lie.

"What do you think is my problem?" she mumbled.

"When most people find out they're dying, they usually try to make the most of the time they have left." Baron sounded more bemused than hurt, but she sensed the strain beneath each syllable. "Not, well—"

"No," she said. "*Usually*, they don't put up with being lectured—"

"You think I'm *lecturing*—"

"Did you want a fucking goodbye?" she snapped, and then the pain arched through her again and she spent minutes or hours leaning too heavily against him, her breath a razor in her throat.

"Just take your time," Baron said wearily, and she hated him for it. For being there when she lashed out, and staying anyway; for all the strange lands they might have explored together, if they'd only started sooner. But she could barely move, and so she let her eyes slide closed, tunneled all her focus into placing one foot after another in the sand.

When she'd fled this place, nine years ago, it had been natural. Expected. If falling was a consequence of gravity, exile was the logic of the Island. What she wanted now, though, was against the rules. Returning defied physics; she was fighting the world itself.

And if the Island called for her death instead of her life—if it chose to kill her upon return—she would be powerless to stop it.

Another wave of bile rushed up her throat, and she choked, vomit spattering her shoes. *Godsdammit.* Five years of Underground matches had trained her to throw punches, not let herself be *wracked* like this, her knees on the edge of buckling. She'd done better as a thirteen-year-old—well, less kid than corpse—passed out on the sand of San Jukong Beach with her wounds already beginning to fester.

Dying slowly. Since then, it was all she'd been doing.

"A few more steps," Baron said quietly. "We're almost there."

Jordan raised her head. The cave was still at least fifty meters away, and she wondered how much of it he could even see—a shadow, a promise?

"Yeah," she said. Her tongue tasted of rotted meat. "Yeah, we are."

Ten meters away, her legs gave out at last, and Baron grunted as her weight dragged him toward the ground.

"How far is it, actually?" he asked as she knelt, breathing hard. His face was strange to her without his glasses, his eyes wide and dark as Island night. Even with the shadows beneath them, he looked unexpectedly young, and she thought: She had pulled him into this. If he did not find Dust, if he could not fly far enough to escape this place, his death would be on her head. "At least tell me if we're going in the wrong direction."

Jordan's spine was a rictus of pain, her left arm and shoulder sore from trying to hold on to him.

"Almost there," she said, and her voice was small and far away. "I swear."

As Baron bent, gesturing for her to drape her arm back over his shoulder, a memory washed over her of softer sunlight, mossy stones dappled with the shadows of waving pines. It was one of those days Peter had gone off on his mysterious trips, and the Boys had drained the wine bottle of Dust to the bottom—*Mer-lott*, Tudo had pronounced the faded label, *rhymes with mer-maids*; Kuli's retort, *That's not how rhymes work, stupid*—and she and Baron had slipped away to dive for fish: flicker on the water like molten glass, murmur of wind on the back of her neck. Baron's gasp as a trout thrashed between her hands, a wild alienness in the flat coins of its eyes.

She hadn't understood, then, that she'd been happy. The weight of secrecy had pressed down on her, cool and damp as cave-shadow; her glamoured arm had burned day and night. Only now, as the pain swallowed her whole, did she wish she had known.

She was eight years old, the Island unspooling before her in a grand puzzle of moss and stone, Peter's ragged troop of Lost Boys whooping and clapping as she and Baron touched down amid the ring of seven hollow elms. Her legs and shoulders slotted perfectly into the throat of wood and she belonged, she belonged, she belonged.

She was nine years old, lounging with Baron against the stump of the Never Tree, their every gesture and facial expression tuned to such precision that even Wen, their Ama at the time, could not tell them apart.

"Just look at them," one of the Boys said, "staring at you like freaking clones," and she grinned Baron's grin, tipped her head back to laugh at the same angle that he did, and in the Lost Boys' eyes she saw the beginnings of fear.

She was ten years old, sword steady in her hand, back-to-back with Baron as pirates surged below. Peter wailed alone on Marooner's Rock after the captain had slashed him open: "Hook wounded me, I can't fly or swim." But she and Baron darted between the pirate ship's sails— quicksilver fast lest they got cut and thudded helplessly onto the deck, Dust-flight rendered null by the drawing of their blood—and the two of them were invincible, one creature, sharp blades keening as they cut grown-ups into forever.

And when Baron sliced open the captain's first mate, in a mess of blood and steaming innards—when the captain jumped into the jaws of a crocodile lurking beneath the currents (and every captain did, eventually, drown or leap off a cliff or swallow poison rather than succumb to the humiliation of death by Peter's hand)—a wild joy wheeled through her: that she was young and lethal and *right*; that she would always be on the side of the story that won.

She was thirteen, and bleeding.

Fresh from battle, her sword still slick with gore, the Boys gathered on the corpse-studded beach as Peter crowed his own praises. A hot gush between her legs; the Boys gone silent; the spreading blot of dark against her light brown furs.

And here was her Twin: blood crusted on his fingers, a nasty gash along his left shin. The planes of his face somehow unfamiliar, though she glamoured her own every morning in imitation—as if the bones underneath had shifted overnight, hollowed into new valleys of dubious purpose.

"Jordan?" he asked, his voice wavering, and she was not sure if he remembered what this kind of blood meant, not sure if he had ever known, but in the set of his mouth she saw the end of the world. "Ama's coming."

Jordan turned.

Their mother was picking her way across the gore-stained sand.

Chay, their new Ama as of a year ago, whom Peter forbade from coming on missions because killing was not for womanly eyes. Chay, who wept over Everbird chicks that fell from their nests and buried them beside the creek with dried roses to mark their graves.

Chay, whose pet wolf loped with sharp-limbed grace at her side.

A blink and she stood before Jordan, comprehension spreading across her face like a stain.

"Peter," she drawled, stretching his name into an incantation, and Jordan wanted to die. "Do you know what happens to girls when they grow up?"

"No." Peter sauntered over, scratching the wolf behind the ears. "What happens, Ama?"

Chay smirked, and the wolf growled, its long teeth shining in the light.

Jordan was thirteen, and fleeing.

Through the forest, wet still squelching between her legs, knives biting the edges of her skin as they whistled past her into the brush. A hedge reared up on her left, and she plunged in—hitch of raw breath, thorns flaying her open—and then she was through, she was through, scrabbling down a muddy slope toward a knot of white birch trees wrapped in glowing strands of sun.

The birches had been her and Baron's meeting place. Their secret.

She realized only then that she'd come to say goodbye.

He was waiting at the base of the largest trunk, his eyes the burnt umber of autumn leaves. She had to float a few centimeters off the ground to meet them level, and only then did she feel the first twinge of sadness: What would happen when they were both bound by gravity and she had to look up?

"I'll find you again," he said, and one last gift had passed between them, the leaf-packet of Dust that Jordan would later bury in her right arm, before the wolf leapt through the trees and tore the skin off her chest.

Chapter 8

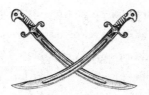

Tier was fairly certain he had died and been thrown into the tenth court of Taram.

His head pounded. His tongue tasted rancid, and sunlight knifed through the softs of his eyelids, spilling bloody heat. Gods knew he'd been hungover before, but there were hangovers, and then there was obliteration.

Though, he supposed, it was no more than he deserved.

Pins pricked his arse, crept beneath his shoulder blades. He was lying on warm sand, his face raw from sunburn. His intestines felt shriveled as shed snakeskins, and he couldn't remember if he'd vomited—a maggoty aftertaste stained his breath, something dead and not long removed. Far off, the rumble of stone, or perhaps a massive engine; whispers writhed under a skein of rotted air.

Where was he?

The question congealed inside him like old blood. After his fifth drink or his sixth or his eighth, the tip and the swallow had become automatic, urgent even, the void in his rib cage giving way to numb and thoughtless heat as the bodies around him laughed and sweated and sang.

Some people drank to feel more comfortable in their own skin. Last night, he had left his altogether.

Tier groaned and cracked his eyes open.

A beach, as he'd expected. Past the wavering line of sand, thickets of pine trees merged into a forest that rose into a mountain; on his other side, ocean waves piled all the way to the horizon, an unceasing oscillation of blue and gunmetal grey. The sun hovered at its apex like a burst egg. He lay near a bright yellow raft—*from the plane*, he thought dimly, though he could not quite remember why. Only the ember of a cigarette tip, the soft blue of a glow-in-the-dark shot, warmth tingling through his hands and chest and the stubborn knot of his mouth.

And then the glint of a metal arm, and a film-strip slice of Jordan's face, and sirens howling red red red—

The plane.

Tier struggled to lift his head. His boots had been kicked off halfway, and his socks were stiff with salt.

The *plane.*

Shit.

His father's people, from the Burimay branch of Ardmuth Industries. It would have been so easy for them to overhear his exchange with Jordan at the bar; easier still to track him from there, to the jet he always flew. Forty million mir was small change for them, but there was the cultural mystery, solved, there was the perfect excuse to make him disappear.

And now he was stranded and half-cooked with sunburn, and his plane was twisted slag on the ocean floor.

Naïve, he heard his father chide, with the same condescension he'd used when Tier had been half a meter shorter and crying for some toy dangled high above his head. *If you let yourself look weak, someone will always use it against you.*

Tier lay back on the sand and breathed, let the hollowness bloom inside his bones. Behind his eyelids, the waves gave way to polished mahogany, the musk of his sweat ceding to the tang of waxed citrus.

I took an opportunity, he thought. *I'm making my own path.*

This is a treasure hunt, his father's voice said briskly. *Pure speculation, and less than half the inheritance you threw away.*

"No." A stiffening of his lips, his throat. He hadn't gone to the 8&8 Bar just to get wasted—alcohol loosened his mind's hold on his tongue, enabled some shabby imitation of normalcy. But last night's round had long worn off. "You n-n-never would have given it to me."

Of course I would have, if you'd shown me even once that you were a worthwhile investment.

"Fuck you."

Ah. Silk-smooth, a touch of aspersion. *Reverting to profanity again, I see.*

Tier ground his teeth, wet his parched mouth. His own mind baiting him, he knew, but he could not fight it, not when that voice reached through his skin and prodded all the dark places beneath.

"That was on purpose," he shot back—except his first *p* fractured into a dozen pieces, and by the time he reached the end of the word, his face was hot, his chest heaving.

From a distance, he heard the click of a belt buckle, like a gun safety switching off.

Say that again.

Again.

Correctly.

No.

I deserve this, Tier thought, heat arching his throat. *I deserve it all.*

He staggered to his feet, almost blacked out again as pain jackknifed through his skull. His skin felt flayed, as if every time he moved, he would crack open and drip blood onto the sand. He needed shade. Clean water, too. A creek gurgled at the edge of his hearing, and he shuffled toward the forest, clamped down a wave of nausea as the ground shifted and rolled beneath his feet. Perhaps this was the Island, but perhaps it wasn't—maps of the place varied wildly from story to story, forum post to forum post, and he was not high enough in the air to note any landmarks besides the central mountain. Either way, wiser to find cover than stay out here in the open, being roasted alive.

He was halfway across the beach when he saw the footprints.

Two pairs: adult-sized, shoe treads. A churn of them about ten meters from where he had woken, fading as beach turned to mud turned to pine-needle-padded forest floor.

Fading, but not gone.

At the tree line, Tier knelt cautiously. He'd been taught to track, allegedly, forced to join Boy Scouts in primary school, but his troop mates were more likely to shove him into a cold river than follow a deer with him through the woods, and his tongue had locked up when he tried to explain to the troop leader what was wrong. Even now, the thought set his temples throbbing, a stone in his throat that made it difficult to swallow.

Your own fault, whispered his father. *You never really tried.*

"Stop," Tier spat, and walked faster.

The footprints led him to a rust-colored cave, its opening low enough that he had to duck. A glimmer of light beyond, a soft ragged gasp, and he tensed—suppose this *was* the Island, and whoever was inside saw him as competition for the treasure? Suppose they were armed? But they might have food, too, and supplies, and if Tier was wandering this place alone without even a knife, they were bound to find him eventually.

He pressed his tongue against the roof of his mouth, willed his spine straight and his shoulders back.

Brief darkness, like cloud-shadow, and then the cave opened around him like an exhale. A voice rang out in Hanwa—a high tenor, wary. "Who's there?"

Tier stopped. The cavern was approximately circular, its floor worn flat by erosion or footsteps. Parts of the ceiling had crumbled, and thin streams of afternoon sunlight slanted across the floor, cast the jagged walls in harsh relief.

Jordan was curled beneath the nearest outcropping of wall, her face sheened with sweat. Beside her sat the quiet college student she had inexplicably dragged along, hands fisted in his lap. He'd spoken fluent Rittan on the train, but seemed skittish as a rabbit; had barely looked at Tier since they'd been introduced.

"It's just me," Tier enunciated—slow, flawless. The King's Rittan. "I washed up here, too."

"Tier?" Baron twisted the wrong way around. There were still dark smudges beneath his eyes, and in the shifting light he looked haggard, he looked old. Switching to Rittan, he said, "How did you find us? Where—"

Tier rubbed the knot in his jaw, tried to soften his tongue against his teeth. "I'm by the entrance."

"Oh." Baron turned approximately in Tier's direction, raised one hand ruefully to his face. "I—I lost my glasses in the crash."

"And her?" Tier motioned at Jordan—though, sober, he didn't want to risk stumbling over her name. "What's wrong?"

"Karsa withdrawal." Baron's eyes narrowed, his focus still slightly off from Tier's face. "She lost her supply as well."

"Oh." Tier's cheeks heated at the implied accusation. But of course he could not expect forgiveness, not when the explosion had destroyed everything they'd needed to survive in a place like this. Of course even Baron would hate him, for plunging his friend into that kind of pain. "I'm sorry."

"Are you?"

"I—what do you mean?"

Baron's mouth thinned into a line. "You don't seem to particularly like each other."

"Well, no," Tier said honestly. "But I don't have a way back out of here, either."

A deep sigh, and then Baron leaned back against the rock wall, thumbs pushing slow circles into his temples. "Okay," he muttered to himself, "okay, okay," and Tier had shifted onto his heels, on the verge of slinking back out into the forest, when Baron added, "The people who were chasing you."

"Yes?" Tier said cautiously.

"You didn't think they would?"

"I—" he started, and then stopped. What could he say—that he'd made a habit of being too drunk to care? That he'd been reaching toward escape for so long that it no longer mattered who he took down with him? "I didn't think—"

"No one does," Baron said, and then flushed. "I mean—"

"No, I'm sorry." Tier stepped closer, surprised to find that he meant what he said, and Baron's cheeks pinked further. "I was d—drunk. I shouldn't have offered. And you got caught up in this—"

"I chose to come," Baron said, raising his chin. "No one forced me."

"Oh."

They both turned to Jordan, still unconscious—her hand fisted at her side, a vein standing out in her clenched jaw.

"She needs Dust." The lump in Baron's throat bobbed as he swallowed. "And since I can't see enough to—to get around, I was wondering if you could—"

Tier pushed down a flinch. He had felt no pang of recognition, when he'd returned to consciousness on the hot sand, no sense of arriving at his final destination after so many years of wandering. Yet what were the odds of him washing up alive here, after his plane had gone down in a ball of flame? What were the odds Baron would be looking at him with such utter seriousness, as if Tier held the key to everything he'd ever wanted?

"You think we m-m—" Tier began, and bit down on his tongue. A fault line fracturing through the press of his lips, the slight touch of his teeth. Shit, he needed a drink. "You think we—are on the Island."

Baron nodded.

Tier thought back to the wild flicker of his control panels, the radar just before the crash a blank circle of green. "But if—if Peter is here, and the Lost Boys—"

"You owe us," Baron said, low and fierce. "The Boys drop Dust everywhere they fly. Just get to their side of the Island—on the northeast—gather up at least a palmful, and leave as few footprints and broken branches as possible."

"My clothes," Tier said. "They don't exactly blend—"

Jordan's back arched against the ground, a groan peeling out of her throat, and Baron smoothed her hair back from her forehead, his hands shaking.

"Please," he said, and something vicious and ugly reared through Tier's chest: that no one would care if he walked straight out of this cave into the ocean; that no one had cared for a very long time.

He didn't know if being asked to risk his life—for Jordan Makta, of all people—made that better, or worse.

"Fine," he spat, and stormed out before he could change his mind.

Chapter 9

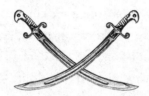

Baron's denial wore away slowly.

It outlasted Jordan's cursing, as they'd collapsed together into the cave: of Peter, the Island, Chay, her parents, the wolf, Baron, the day she'd been born. It did not break after Tier's footsteps faded into the susurrus of trees, the bright high cries of birds. But as the hours passed—as the sun gilded the cave, and then slipped out of sight—something inside Baron began to crumble.

Jordan's forehead was feverish; her breaths, when he hovered a hand above her nostrils, came short and spasmodic. He had no idea how quickly Dust withdrawal progressed, but she had used again after nearly a decade without. Could that accelerate the process? Was it possible to overdose?

Or had her body adapted, by now, to need karsa more than it needed Dust?

He was so alone.

"Jordan," he said hoarsely. "Can you hear me?"

A keening from the back of her throat, remote, terrifying. He twined his hand in hers, shifted his crumpled jacket so her head nestled in its folds. In high school he'd volunteered at a local hospital, but never actually handled patients; only ever heard the screams and cries beyond the curtain.

Heat radiated off her skin, small suns blooming every place they touched. Her lips moved, less than a murmur.

"Sorry, what?"

"Press down," she choked, arching out of his grip. "Down."

"On what?"

Her fingers curled weakly around his. At her throat, the mottle of old scars—wounds she'd hastily sealed with Dust, those nine years ago, to fly away from the Island, but which had bloomed with pus and infection in the days after—frothed damp like the integument of some massive worm. Baron recoiled.

"I'm sorry," he said. "I don't understand."

She moaned and swore, and as another twitch jerked her sideways, he fumbled with his jacket to keep her head from sliding onto stone.

It was his turn to be strong, he told himself, tipping his eyes toward the cavern ceiling. Jordan had propelled them out of San Jukong, gotten them halfway across the ocean with a warplane on their tail; the least he could do, now, was keep from breaking. But as the last of the light burned away, as his vision flattened to black and silver, he was a child again, borne helpless toward a wide and unrelenting sea.

Then she began to plead.

"Baron." It might have been a command, but her voice was a thing raw and split open, and there was no sound he wanted to hear less in his life, except that it meant she was still fighting.

"I'm here," he mumbled.

"Not that hard, you arse. Just press down."

"On *what*," he said, louder. The sky had withered to smoke. He couldn't remember which direction the sun had gone.

Her hand seized his, an iron grip, jerked it toward her neck. "Push. Hold. Stop breathing. Easy."

He was shaking, his fingers a smear of grey on grey. He imagined the ridges of her trachea moving against his palms, the shattering stillness when it stopped. "Gods, Jordan."

"No gods to save us now."

"I know," he whispered, and then his face screwed up and he was sobbing into his sleeve, so hard he thought he would vomit. Pathetic, when he was barely suffering in comparison. "I know. I know. I know."

"Baron. Look at me."

Breathe. Swallow. Gasp.

"Closer."

He leaned in: nose to nose, breath to breath. Beneath a silver shard of moonlight, her eyes were half-lidded, lashes like feathers.

"Please," she said softly, and the last dim dregs of his hope—that Tier would return, that she would recover enough to help him find food and clean water; that they would, at some point, *leave*—tumbled headlong into the void.

He thought: She had asked many things of him, but never like this.

He thought: On the dark nights he'd imagined giving her all he had, his *all* had never included letting her go.

He knew: After all this time, he was still selfish. Down to his beating bones.

"No," he said, more firmly than he'd expected. "I can't. I won't."

Jordan's hand twitched. "Fuck you."

He realized she was trying to make a fist.

Chapter 10

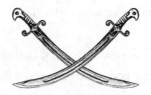

Tier could have sworn the forest was *moving*.

He'd been walking for hours—white-slash sun softening to gold and then dusk as he padded between trees, his face so blistered that even frowning brought on a blaze of pain. The jitter beneath his tongue and teeth had faded into the quiet, until the only things in his head were birdsong and the heartbeat surge of ocean waves.

But as he turned—northeast, as Baron had directed—a boulder leered at him, carved as if with a knife into the shape of a face.

And it was a face he had already seen.

Tier sat abruptly on a log. His head was a dull whirl, his throat dry; his eyelids unstuck loudly every time he blinked. He remembered, in a daze, that finding clean water should have been first priority.

When he attempted to stand again, his knees gave way beneath him, and he lay unmoving with his face in the dirt.

Somewhere in the back of his mind, he'd always suspected he would die alone. And what more peaceful way than this? Curled in the belly of a forest, wind shushing the trees, a creek in the distance burbling cold and clear. He could forget the debt he owed Baron and Jordan; forget the raw desperation with which Baron had looked at his friend; forget the way his own heart had been stripped bare at the sight. When he was thirteen, locked in his family's house in Ritt as his father and brothers flew to Akhara for a meeting on oil futures, he had spent a weekend reading about dehydration—the way it shriveled one's skin, made blood go sluggish, induced a dizziness like the whiskey he snuck from his oldest brother's shoe closet. The way death could pull over you like a warm blanket, and it wouldn't hurt at all.

But he wasn't ready.

Ships full of gold still awaited him at the bottom of the sea. As did the Ardmuth International Airport, where he would step off a new jet, smirking as he unloaded crates of bullion and precious gems in front of shouting photographers. And his father, hurrying from his limousine onto the runway, mouth agape with rage and a feeling he would soon recognize as pride.

If Dust was real—if the Island truly possessed a golden powder that allowed you to fly—

Tier reached up—for the log, for anything—but the forest slipped away like a memory.

He woke to cold water splashed in his mouth.

His dreams had been labored, uneasy—the long, echoing flagstone halls of his family's estate; the heavy wooden door of his bedroom, locked from the outside; the nest of centipedes his third brother had once left on his study chair, so Tier had run from his bedroom shaking and sputtering and been unable to string together a coherent sentence for three days after.

As dark branches crystallized around him, knifed through by moonlight, he thought: If this was death, he wanted a do-over.

Another slop of water and he choked, spluttered.

"Easy," said a girl's voice, and then there was a hand on his chin, tilting it up. "Easy."

He swallowed, his teeth clacking against the rim of the cup. Somehow, he'd been propped back up to sitting; a young Hanwa woman held a ceramic mug to his mouth, her face limned in moonlit silver.

"Hold still," she said as he raised a hand to her wrist. "Or all that water's going on your jacket."

Her Rittan was perfect. She sounded like a news anchor. Tier dropped his hand, mouth flooding with guilty relief.

"Who are you?"

"My name is Chay." She set down the mug, now empty, and unscrewed a small plastic canister. Before he could speak again, she had swiped a greyish ointment across his forehead, and the red throb of his face diminished slightly. "That's for the sunburn. Our neat little Island trick."

Tier widened his eyes: a difficult task, as the lids were nearly swollen shut. First Baron, and now her—with her flawless Imperial Rittan, her solemn pronunciation of the Island with a capital *I*.

Her threadbare white dress, sewn in precisely the same style Sir Franklin had sketched in his novel.

"The Island," he croaked.

"Yes."

As Chay daubed ointment across the bridge of his nose, Tier tilted up the slits of his eyes further. She was bird-thin, her dark hair gathered in a wispy braid that hung down to her waist.

Her knees, which poked out from beneath her hem, were covered in bruises.

Unease threaded through him. As a Scout, he had learned the basics of hunting and fishing, but it seemed food here would be difficult to find.

"How long have you been here?" he asked, twisting back into an Erendite accent before he could trip on the *b*.

A tiny crease formed on Chay's brow. "A while. I should be—I should be nineteen now."

"Really."

The crease deepened. "Yes," she said with greater confidence. "Nineteen exactly."

"And do you live with anyone? Do you have a f—a family?"

"Of course." This answer she seemed sure of. "It's me and Peter and the Boys, in our house underground. I doubt you'd fit into any of our trees"—she looked Tier up and down, and he flushed—"but if you visit at night, you'll probably be able to avoid them."

Her thumb was still trailing his cheekbone, and an unfamiliar heat coiled in his gut, arched the soles of his feet. No one had ever tended to him like this; he could not remember the last time anyone had touched him at all, outside of a bar fight. As she dabbed at the hollow behind his ear, he curled into himself, placed his elbows on his knees to hide the rising sign.

Gods, the things he would do for a whiskey right now.

Chay was watching him curiously, as if he were a sculpture on display in a gallery. "Are you all right?"

"I'm—f-fine." The tremor at the edge of his lower lip again. *Pause. Breathe. Slowly.* "I just—backache."

Chay lifted her hand, each finger crowned with a dollop of ointment. "Would you prefer I stop?"

"No," Tier said, too quickly. A fresh sweat broke out on his forehead, his jaw locking like stone. Through his teeth, he added, "N-not if you don't want to."

Her fingers traced the back of his neck, the grey salve painting an instant swath of relief across his peeling skin. Tier pressed his forehead into his hands with a muffled moan.

"What is this stuff?"

"It's mostly paste from a plant that grows on the cliffs," Chay said. "Though I added a little Dust to speed things along."

"Dust," he echoed.

"Yes. Head back up, please."

As she anointed his eyelids, he thought of Jordan's outstretched hand, dawn pouring through the cockpit; her promise that Dust would slip them through the barrier around the Island. When the emergency door had hurled open in the main cabin, he thought she'd taken that promise with her—yet he had washed up on the Island anyway.

"There you go," Chay said cheerfully, pushing to her feet. Standing, she couldn't have been more than a meter and a half tall. "Take a look?"

She drew a bent-handled serving spoon from her pocket. *A mirror,* Tier thought, edged with rust.

He bent toward a bright shaft of moonlight. Peered obligingly—and froze.

The sunburn was gone. His skin was pale as winter, the blisters on his nose and cheekbones vanished beneath his freckles as if they had never been. His cheeks, when he raised a slow hand to them, were soft as an infant's.

Chay beamed as he handed her back the spoon. "It's my own recipe. I use it on Peter and the Boys, too."

Peter. Tier shook his head, then stopped as his brain sloshed unpleasantly inside his skull. If the Peter that Chay was living with was anything like the one Sir Franklin had written about—if the Island's cardinal rule was *no grown-ups allowed*—

"Why are you helping me?" he asked, touching his face again—and he almost didn't mind, for once, that he hadn't shaved in two days.

Chay shrugged, looked away. "You didn't look like a pirate."

"Then what d—what did I look like?"

A small smile lifted the corner of her mouth, and Tier's stomach swooped, as if he were falling from another plane.

"I thought," she said quietly, "that once the sunburn went down, you might be a prince."

Chapter 11

Chay smiled as she placed the pan of pork ribs inside the firepit. She had spent the day in a whirl of busyness—washing dishes, darning socks, making sandwiches for lunch as Peter's and the Boys' swords clanged over her head. But the whole of the Island seemed to have been lit with some pure fire: Sunlight dashed across the clearing where she wrung out the wash; the creek gushed sweet music over jewel-toned pebbles; a mermaid's tail flashed iridescent from a distant shore. Even the seven hollow trees, with their woody throats that opened into the little room underground, danced in the wind, as if they knew the song her body was singing.

Tier.

She had not meant to help him, when she'd found him lying facedown in the mud. Peter, of course, would have killed him on sight. But on their evening outing, the Boys had shot off toward the lagoon, shouting that they didn't want their mother *pestering* them all the time, and she did not want to think about the supper she had packed for them, the fluffy bread and pork fat they would mash between their pearly white molars; did not want to think about the grey static behind her temples, or the saliva gathering in her mouth, or the way she might devour the basket's entire contents if she dared lift its lid.

So when she caught the moon-flash of an upturned face through the trees, she hurried toward it, and busied her hands, and stretched her hunger one more hour.

And then the surprise—the piercing blue-green of his eyes, and his long, slender fingers wrapped around her wrist. And then the strange weakness along the insides of her knees, and the shadow of a thing she'd only just been learning when she arrived on the Island at nine years old, and its weight now draped over her shoulders like prophecy.

"Amaaaaa," Kuli drawled, hovering over her shoulder. "Is it dinnertime yet?"

"Just a few minutes." Steam licked Chay's face as she nudged the lasagna along the sturdy metal cooking rack. "Go play with Jack and Tudo."

"But I don't *want* to play with Tudo."

"Then go play with the Twins."

"Fine." Kuli stalked off, drawing two daggers from his belt as he sprinted upside down across the ceiling.

Chay sighed and fed another log to the flames.

Given the tree roots tangling the walls, the merry bonfire Peter demanded be kept going at all hours should have roasted them alive years ago. But it was surrounded by a tidy circle of Dust and belief; even the drafts that blew down the hollow trees, flaring the colorful scraps of cloth she had pinned across each opening, could not break it out of its boundaries.

"What's that wonderful smell?" a voice boomed from above, and the Lost Boys broke from their games, rushing to the base of its owner's hollow tree.

"Peter, I beat Jack at marbles today—"

"Peter, can you make Ama tell the story about the girl with the apple and the mirror—"

"Peter, can we have a *little* more Dust?"

The recipient of this supplication tumbled out the mouth of his tree, the golden blot that was Tink chiming above his head, and Chay's breath snagged. It happened every time—at the perfection of his little pointed face, his eyes like oceans, her heart filled with something vast and warm and unassailable. Washing over the tightness of her hunger, the guilt that poured out of her like blood.

Every night that he returned, her center of gravity recalibrated: Here was the sun, here was her anchor. She let it move.

"Hullo, children," Peter said, brushing off his shoulders as if his skeleton-leaf shirt was a woolen suit.

"Hullo, Father," the Boys chorused, catching on.

"And Ama." Peter held his arms out toward Chay, magnanimous, and she hugged him dutifully, felt the echo of Tier's cheekbones beneath her thumbs as Tink yanked the tail of her braid. "How is the best mother in the entire world?"

"Ready with dinner," she said, smiling, and somehow it was easier when she looked into his eyes, when the golden thrill of his Dust brushed the edge of her senses. "I fixed all your socks and cleaned the sheets, so you Boys better keep them—"

"Okay, no need to nag," Peter said, waving her away. "Where's the food?"

Chay busied herself as the Boys settled around the Never Tree stump that was their table. It was not difficult; there were spills to clean up, and smears of tomato sauce to wipe off faces, and Ael—her pet wolf, who had roused himself from the foot of the Boys' giant bed to sniff at Peter—to keep from tripping over. The Boys did not ask why she wasn't eating: She had assured them that mothers ate after their children did, though she couldn't remember if this was true of actual mothers or only waitresses at restaurants. She supposed it didn't matter. Even if it was just a story, it suited her purposes.

The backs of her eyes pounded, as if she had been beaten upside the head with a mallet.

She had first chosen hunger as a matter of necessity. When she was nine, Peter had alighted on her windowsill and she'd followed him into the sky, chasing a sister who had vanished from her life four years before. Not long after, blood blossomed between Jordan's legs, and Chay had realized emptiness was the only way she could stay. But ten years in, she'd come to *like* the lightness of her steps, the gap between her thighs. The way her white dress, threadbare though it might be, still barely strained at the bust or the waist.

When she gnawed on a carrot after she had put the Boys to bed, she was immortal. Light-headed, she was strong. And if she saved her body, if she lasted forever—if she earned her way into this story, over and over—Peter would have no reason to cast her out the way he had Jordan.

Even if it was her fault the other girl had been exiled in the first place.

Ael snapped at a piece of pasta Jack was dangling over his head, and guilt stitched itself between Chay's ribs.

"Tell us a story, Ama." Peter flitted above the table, Tink sparkling an aura around his shoulders. "The one about the maid and the glass slipper—"

"Flipper," corrected Slightly, who took great pride in his memory of Outside.

"What about the one about the poison mirror?" Kuli chimed in.

"Or the boy and the radioactive spider—"

Chay steadied herself against the Never Tree stump. Seven plates of pork ribs yawned before her, crusts of fat and a smoky sauce she had mixed herself, and her traitorous mouth watered.

She thought of that last bright morning, the dark burn of Jordan's eyes. Thought of Tier lying prone in the mud, and his sharp-edged jaw, and the almost incongruous pink softness of his lips.

Thought of all the things she had already left unsaid, and how adding another should not weigh on her so much more.

"Pleeeaaase?" Kuli begged, dancing on the table, and the rest of the Boys took up a chant: "Sto-*ry*, sto-*ry*, sto-*ry*—"

Somewhere outside, an animal cried like an infant, wrenching and unearthly. Chay cleared the Boys' plates, dumping the scraps into the fire with a sizzle that knotted her stomach. She had saved three tomatoes to eat after the Boys went to bed—she and Ael alone by the fire, unsweet juice stinging her mouth, small pale seeds sliding between her molars like secrets.

She raised her right hand, a fist.

"You have to be quiet if you want to listen," she said, and they fell silent—watching, hungry. The only time of day she could ever get them to do so.

Chay shifted on the block of wood that was her seat. The cushion she had sewn to cover it was wearing thin, and she'd been mortified when Peter had pointed out a matching hole in the seat of her dress. The Boys had laughed for days.

Ael padded past her, his shoulders solid and strong beneath her trailing fingers, and she pushed away the memories of teeth and blood and shredded-open skin. Inhaled slow, closed her eyes.

It was quiet. Gloriously quiet, like the beginning of the world.

"Once upon a time..."

Chapter 12

Jordan woke shivering uncontrollably.

Darkness all around, broken only by a breath of moonlight above her head, ocean waves stirring beyond the narrow mouth of the cave. Nearby, water dripped, magnified as it echoed off the cool stone walls.

She did not remember entering. Did not remember the bright afternoon being muffled by cave-shadow, or the pine branches that sheltered the hole-riddled ceiling glowing gold as the sun set. Only the sick quiver between her ribs, the infuriating give of her knees.

She tried to push onto her side, and met resistance.

An arm was draped over her shoulder, fingers curved elegant in midair. She shrugged it off and rolled back onto stone, her head whirling.

Baron lay beside her, the white moon of his face utterly at peace.

Jordan attempted to swallow, though her throat was so dry it crackled. *Baron.* She vaguely remembered screaming at him, in the interminable hours of withdrawal: cursing everything that had brought him to her; begging him to end her life. Subjecting him to the ugliest fact of her body, the rot she'd sworn never to let him see.

White spots skimmed across her vision, a mockery of stars. The pain had dulled into a slow monotonous thing, or else her gag reflex had exhausted itself. Either way, she was hazy with dehydration.

And he was still here.

Or perhaps they had both died and gone to Taram.

Behind her, someone cleared their throat.

She shoved to her feet. Too fast—a muscle spasmed in her back, and she curled into herself for precious seconds, teeth gritted against tears. When she straightened again, a lantern had flared in the cavern dark, illuminating Tier's face, pale and drawn.

"You." She lunged toward him, though her prosth had gone dead—damaged, perhaps, in the explosion—and she swung slightly off-balance before steadying herself against the wall. "The fuck are *you* doing here?"

His eyes flicked up, cobalt blue in the firelight, and she felt a grim shot of vindication. He *did* look like that one rip-off of an irritating character in Baron's favorite anime series.

"A *thank you* would be more appropriate," he said stiffly.

"You got us in a godsdamned plane crash."

"I also got—" Tier bit his lip—was he *nervous?*—and said, "I got Dust for you."

"You what?"

"Your—Baron asked me to." He fumbled with something in his pocket; pulled out a plastic canister so familiar that, for a moment, Jordan's vision blanked.

"That's—" she breathed. The container seemed to pulse beneath the lantern light: an artifact that belonged in a museum, time put on loop. "Fuck."

"I ran into the Boys' mother," Tier explained, answering the question she hadn't asked, and her curiosity, if that was what it had been, soured. She didn't want to think about who had replaced Chay—or where the Ama might have gone, after her body had betrayed her in turn. "She—put it on my sunburn, and I—made friends with her and asked for the rest."

"You made friends," Jordan repeated, and Tier scowled.

"And brought back Dust ointment for your withdrawal."

So she owed him a debt, or else he was trying to pay off his. "I didn't ask you to," she said automatically.

He snapped, "You weren't in any condition to ask."

Lantern flicker, far-off croak of bullfrogs. Something crawled beneath Jordan's skin, as rotten and uneasy as the taste of her own mouth. Bad enough that she had leaned on Baron, that he'd sat by her side like a nursemaid as she groaned and thrashed on the floor of the cave. Bad enough that she'd pushed him toward panic—and she'd felt it, a couple times, like the zing of ozone in the air before a storm. But Tier was syndicate, and Rittan. He would hold any sign of weakness over her head, probe for cracks until he could thrust his fingers in and grab what he wanted.

"Fuck you," she said.

To her surprise, Tier only leaned his head back against the wall. "How'd you know I owned that plane?"

Jordan grinned—this one was easy. "That time I scraped my knife against the outer paneling. You nearly frothed at the mouth."

"Ah." Something shuttered behind his face. He'd shoved her around then, too, like the big man he was always pretending to be, and she'd flicked the blade toward his throat. "Would you really have killed me?"

"What do you think, kweilo?"

"I told you not to call me—"

A rustle in the distance, and they fell silent, wary. As Tier shoved his lantern behind a rock, wincing at the faint clank of metal, Jordan tugged at Baron's arm and he blinked awake, eyes dark and wide as the sky.

"Jordan?" he whispered, and she put a finger to his lips, goose bumps pricking the back of her neck.

"Someone's coming."

She lurched into a fighting stance at the mouth of the cave—a reasonable defense position, if she could cut them off before they surrounded her. But she still felt like she'd been run over by a motorcycle; her right hand was a useless lump. And her opponents might have swords and hatchets and pickaxes, a wolf with bared teeth and black claws—

"Don't move." A gravelly baritone, closer than she'd expected.

Jordan did not lower her fists. The forest mocked her from above, a vast faceless rustle of lichen and bark. Not the Lost Boys, then. But Pales and pirates roamed the Island, too, and she was not particularly reassured.

Her throat burned. "Show yourselves."

A heartbeat of quiet, pricked by cricket song. Then lanterns flared to life, one by one, and the pirates stepped into the cave.

There were about a dozen of them, Hanwa and Yundori and Burimay—taken together, too dark to be Pales—all scraggly beards and haunted eyes. Swords and crossbows hung from their belts or were slung across their backs, and she thought: Strange for the weapons to not drag on the ground, as they did for the Boys. That they could fit, be grown into.

And—hands with missing fingers resting on those belts. A wooden post in place of a leg. An eye replaced with a round dark stone.

Jordan steadied herself against the wall, reeling from something she could not name. "We need Dust," she said. "And water."

The pirates looked as one to a dark-haired, clean-shaven man in an extravagant maroon jacket. He was neither the tallest nor the strongest-looking, but there was a military steel to his posture, a tilt to his chin as if he was accustomed to being listened to.

"The three of you washed up from Outside?"

He spoke in Rittan, with the clear inflectionless accent of someone who had lived around the world. Baron had shuffled to her side, a question on his face, and she thought: She could not shrink back again, leave him to pick up her pieces.

"We used to be Lost Boys," she said. "We"—*I*, she thought—"escaped Outside, but the"—*my*—"Dust withdrawal was too strong, so we came back."

"Jordan," Baron said, a warning.

"I see," the captain remarked, in a tone that set Jordan on edge. "Some of us have experienced Dust withdrawal as well. But it has always been relatively mild—"

"Listen." Jordan gripped her right hand in her left, and the prosth came off with a faint sucking sound. A few of the pirates' eyes widened infinitesimally. "I glamoured myself a whole fucking hand every day I spent in this place. Don't tell me withdrawal is *relatively mild.*"

"Jordan," Baron said again.

"I can work for you. Fight for you." She popped the prosth back on, capping the odor that had billowed out with its doffing. "I just need a bit of Dust."

Something closed off behind the captain's face—hesitation, she thought, or perhaps she had played this wrong, and the pirates had never touched Dust at all. Then he bit out, "What happened to your arm?"

"Oh, just a crocodile," Jordan said airily. She had in fact been born with the limb difference, but fuck him for asking. "As it goes."

A weighted pause. Then the man turned abruptly back to his crew. "The two boys can come with us," he said, voice raised in verdict. "The girl is more trouble than she's worth."

"The fuck—" Jordan started forward, bristling as a couple other pirates drew their swords, but a thickset bearded man with a wooden peg leg held out a placating hand.

"We could use another fighter," he murmured to the captain, quiet enough that only a couple other pirates—and she—could hear. "Gods know we've got few enough as is."

Jordan tensed as the two of them exchanged fierce whispers; as the captain's gaze swept over her again, her ragged Outside clothes and bruised arms and dead prosth.

"She's a walking mutiny waiting to happen," he hissed. "Trust me, Jack Two. I have a sense for these things."

"But say she does just want Dust. Say we keep a close eye on her."

The bearded pirate—Jack Two—glanced back in her direction. Raising his voice: "And you have reason to help us, do you not?"

Jordan nodded, reluctant. She hated the idea of relying on these strangers; had lived long enough in the armpit of the First Circle to know what such armed and desperate men could do. And she did not particularly care to join the pirates' full-scale attacks on Peter and the Lost Boys when she only needed to steal Tink.

But they had a common enemy, and weapons. Not to mention she was hazing out again—a sick curdling at the base of her stomach, the space between her temples gone knotted and grey.

Soon, she would hardly be able to breathe for the pain.

"I do," she said.

Another look passed between Jack Two and the captain, thick with a history she did not understand. Then the captain dismissed the other pirate with a flick of his hand and sighed.

"You might remember Peter and the Boys hunting us down, before, when we tried to leave," he said, not quite looking her in the eye. "So we do need to defeat them first. And we have a bit of a Dust shortage, so you'll have to split a pouch with your—companions, for now. But if you fight for us, if you fight well, we'll give you an equal share of whatever we scavenge."

"Deal," Jordan said.

"Are you sure—" Baron started in Kebai, leaning close, and she gripped his shoulder, holding herself upright.

"They have Dust," she whispered in the same dialect. "And they haven't killed us yet."

His lips thinned into a line. "All right," he said. "But I don't like it."

"*I'm* not here to fight."

Tier's voice, slanted oddly again toward an accent not his own. Jordan turned. The Rittan had uncovered his own lantern, the amber flame casting his face in harsh angles. His canister of ointment was nowhere to be seen—stowed in the crisp black lining of that pilot's jacket, perhaps—and she had a sudden vision of tackling him head-on, clawing at his pockets until he gave up enough Dust to put her back together.

They may have been facing these pirates together, but she hated that she owed him. Every atom of her body rebelled against it.

"He wants your treasure," she said flatly.

Tier's mouth twisted in displeasure, but he did not deny the charge. "I hear there are shipwrecks around this island," he said. "I'd like to fix one up and—bring some of what I find Outside. If that's all right with you."

The captain switched his attention to Tier, and Jordan sensed a lightening in the way he held himself: an eagerness, an instant trust.

"We could do with some money, once we leave," he said—ignoring Jack Two, whose expression had gone carefully neutral. "I'm sure the nearest countries would pay decently for some three-hundred-year-old bullion."

"But only once we've defeated the Boys," added a round-faced Yundori man with glasses. "Or they'll just set our sails on fire again."

"We can pursue multiple ventures at once." The captain pinched the bridge of his nose in a way that suggested this argument had been hashed out many times before. To Tier, he said, "So you'll give us a twenty percent cut in exchange."

"In exchange," Tier repeated, as if confused by the concept. "I—er—"

"Trying to take without paying again, Rittan?" Jordan mocked, and he cut her a ferocious glare.

"You're one to talk."

"Go fuck yourself."

"*Jordan.*"

Baron stood beside her, his gaze fixed on a spot a couple handsbreadths from the pirate captain's face. Quietly, in Kebai, he said, "He did find you Dust."

"Because you asked him to."

"Yes." Baron swallowed. Despite the lantern dimness, the faint pink that had risen high on his cheeks was unmistakable. "But he risked his life anyway. And fighting"—he lowered his voice—"it's not as if I—"

"I know," she said. One morning on the Island, when they were ten or so, he had flown into battle with her and started shaking so hard he'd dropped his sword; could not face a sharp blade afterward without flinching. She had fought for two, after that—kept him facing skyward as she jabbed at pirates and dodged Pale axes—and none of the other Boys had noticed the difference.

She'd never asked what happened. *If* anything had happened, or if the years of bloodshed had just crashed over him all at once, an obliterating wave.

"So." The captain cleared his throat. "A cut of the treasure"—a nod at Tier—"and two fresh bodies for the war machine. That sound about right?"

From Baron: a near-imperceptible catch of breath, his hands curled into his chest. But when he spoke, his voice was steady. "Sure."

The captain grinned with all his teeth. "Then we have ourselves a deal."

Chapter 13

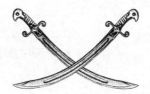

The walk was a blur of shadow and sky. Pine needles pricked Jordan's cheeks; roots reached up to stumble her; the undergrowth rustled, glinting with yellow eyes. Baron, at her side, walked with his feet stretched out before the rest of his body, feeling his careful way over rocks and patches of mud.

She twined her hand in his. His palm was damp, his pulse hummingbird-fast.

"You okay?" she murmured in Kebai, low enough that even Tier, directly behind them, would not hear.

Baron nodded jerkily. Tier had offered him the canister as well, but he had blanched at applying what he'd classified as a *paste* to his eyes. "Are we close?"

"Should be." She thought she'd known this side of the Island: the curve of coast down from the Boys' headlands to the northeast; the stone pillars, jutting a hundred meters out of the water, that kept the pirates from sailing up from the south. But the woods had shifted and tangled in her absence, slopes and ravines rendered foreign by thickened roots and heightened trees.

She said, inclining her head toward Tier, "You think I should forgive him."

Baron's face twitched, and she could have laughed—he had always been so easy to read. "I don't—*feel* that way about him, if that's what you're asking."

"It wasn't, but now that you've brought it up—"

For a full ten seconds his mouth worked in silence, twin creases forming between his brows. Then he said, in a furious rush, "Sometimes when strangers are nice to me, I get—nervous around them. But it isn't *real*. It's not—" A swift glance at her and then away, his hand gone slick with sweat.

"It's not what, Baron?" she asked, and a slow smirk spread across her face. "Are you saying I should be nicer to you?"

"What are *you* saying?" he shot back, his voice tinged with desperation, and promptly tripped over a divot in the mud.

An hour or so later, the moon high above their heads, a ship emerged along the line of the beach, one Jordan knew as if in dreaming. It was smaller than she remembered—salt-eaten planks, thick scrolls of rope-bound sails, two masts ragged against the matte black sky. But the rest of the Dust had leached out of her system; there was a dangerous give to her right knee when she put her weight on it, and her body had become a thing outside herself, a shadow smeared to charcoal.

"It's past the Boys' bedtime," said the bespectacled Yundori man, who had introduced himself as Mateo, the ship's cook. "They probably won't attack until morning."

"And what then?" Tier swayed a little as they climbed the gangplank up to the deck. He looked as exhausted as Jordan felt; she pushed away the reminder that he'd walked half the Island to find her Dust. "Do they just—descend upon you like locusts?"

"We meet them in the woods, most of the time," the captain answered. Jordan had heard some of the men call him Aku, though she didn't give two shits—he'd turned his back on her as if she did not exist. "And we're plenty armed. I can show you, even if you're not planning on—" And the two of them slipped down into the hold, talking almost amiably.

Jordan rolled her left shoulder. She had pulled a muscle as she'd convulsed on the floor of the cave—yet another ache on top of the bruises from the Underground, and the residual shakiness withdrawal had left in her bones, and a slight ringing in her ears from the exploded plane. But none of that would be enough to stop her, tomorrow. It couldn't be.

"So," she said, when Aku's and Tier's voices had faded. "Dust."

Mateo waved toward the gaggle of pirates that remained on deck. "Hoi, Dau."

A young man sauntered over, shoulders hunched. He stood half a head shorter than the rest; the colorless trench coat draped over his shoulders looked like it had tumbled through several oceans before ending up on his narrow back.

"They need the works?" he said, and Jordan startled at the high timbre of his voice—but of course. She could never have been the only one.

"Are you also—" she blurted, and the pirate raised a brow.

"It's *they* to you."

"Ah," Jordan said, "all right," and Dau offered her half a grin like forgiveness.

"They're our quartermaster," Mateo started, as Dau drew a small leather pouch from their pocket, "maybe a Lost Boy before your time—" But a long shadow blinked across Jordan's vision, her whole body crumpling toward the deck, and then she was being lowered to the planks, Baron's arm around her shoulders. His voice—*may I touch you?*—was a muffled echo, and she nodded without knowing why.

He rolled up her sleeves, cool fingers gently kneading in Dust. She inhaled scattered gold and chalky bone, felt the smoke behind her eyes marginally recede.

"Better?"

She had asked him the same question many times—Dust sprinkled in his corneas, on a hill in the dark. Mud for sight.

"I'm fine," she said. "You use yours?"

He raised the pouch Dau must have given him, his lashes scattered with gilt. "Enough to see that you're two breaths away from passing out again."

She breathed twice in rapid succession, and he rolled his eyes.

Mateo—who, in the face of the captain's indifference, seemed to have taken it upon himself to be their welcoming committee—had perched himself on a crate across from her and Baron, watching them curiously.

"We're mostly grown-up Lost Boys, here," he said. "The ones who didn't want to go back to schools and offices when we grew up, and survived Peter trying to kill us for it."

Jordan frowned. "I didn't know anyone else *had*. Survived, I mean."

"Most don't." He bowed his head, as if in brief prayer. "But did you ever wonder why you rarely saw pirates washing ashore?"

Jordan tilted her head back against the wooden rail. The gut twist of withdrawal was fading again as Dust crept in, her nausea tapering off, but she felt unmoored, cast out into a lonely sea. If only she'd known, nine years ago. Who could she have been, if she'd stayed? What kinds of deaths could she have kept from dying?

"Ah," she said. Watched the splash of some deeper-sea creature against the smudge of the horizon. "But you're not the Lost Men, huh. Or—the Lost Men and Dau."

"Do you like being called a lady?"

She shuddered. "Shoot me first."

"There, see."

"Why's the captain got a stick up his arse?"

Mateo snickered, even as Baron, halfway through spreading more Dust across Jordan's forearm, stiffened with apprehension. "Well, you know how the story goes. And he has both his hands."

"Ha," Jordan said: So he saw her as a challenger, even if she'd been a girl at the same time she had been a Lost Boy. Yet among the things that seemed to be etched on the bones and blood of the Island—like the number of Boys on Peter's crew, or the way Amas never used Dust except to arrive or depart—was the quick and gruesome death of every man who had dared seize command; she wanted no part in that fate. "And he thinks he'll have to, what, get chomped by a crocodile to stay in charge?"

Mateo shrugged. "Everyone interprets the stories differently."

"But he trusted Jack Two enough to take his advice."

"They were Lost Boys together," he said, as if it was that simple. And maybe, for the two of them, it was.

A thunk—Dau had pushed open the hatch, hauling a heavy burlap sack.

"These were March's and Nicola's," they said grimly, allowing it to fall open, and Jordan gaped at the flak jackets and bulletproof vests that spilled out alongside the swords and shields. Mateo had stilled; Dau inclined their head slightly. "They should fit you two well enough."

"Thank you," Jordan managed. Beside her, Baron's mouth had dropped open, and she elbowed him in the ribs until he sputtered an echoing appreciation.

"Figures," he muttered to her in Kebai, and she almost grinned.

At some point during those nine long years in San Jukong, fighting and running and charging her prosth at three a.m. as cockroaches skittered across her apartment floor, Jordan had resigned herself to meeting Peter, if she ever did, with him on the high ground. It was, after all, what grown-ups had done since the beginning of time. But what if the rest of the Island had been as much a farce as her and Baron's glamours? As Dau handed them shields and flasks of water, a broadsword for her and a rapier for Baron—she already admired the quartermaster's judgment of character—something unfurled inside her, though it took a long time to name: hope.

"Right, then." Dau pointed at Jordan as she hefted the sword, its leather grip steeped in someone else's sweat. "Get a feel for those. Then find yourselves a cabin—"

"Or two," interjected Mateo.

"Or two," Dau amended grudgingly. "Though if we get any new

joiners, you're sticking to one. And keep drinking water. Tomorrow, we fight."

The interior of the ship was surprisingly clean—the floors recently swept, porthole windows scrubbed. A handful of walls had been knocked down to clear room for hammocks made of old sails, which gave the impression of billowing curtains, or large white birds.

An echo, Jordan thought, of Peter's house underground.

"What about these?" Baron had stopped before a pair of adjacent empty rooms, marginally wider than the closet Jordan had once rented from Obalang. She peered inside: narrow cots, dim portholes, bare walls.

And the ocean beneath, hushing like a heartbeat.

Home.

The rare times she remembered her dreams in San Jukong, they were always of running—up the next skyscraper, through train tunnels and alleyways, into wood-paneled halls dogged by Peter's laughter. But walls stood between her and danger now. Walls and people, plural, who had promised to keep watch for her, and she for them, at least for tonight. Their word would have meant fuck all to her in San Jukong—enough of her so-called friends had defected to other syndicates, enough colleagues gone on errands and never come back. But here, wrung out by Dust and karsa withdrawal, her clothes stinking of vomit, she was too exhausted not to believe.

Jordan staggered into the first cabin, collapsed on the cot, and was unconscious in seconds.

PART THREE

In every story, there is a Technicolor screen: black / white /
    red / green
In every story, there is a chance to restore the color
If we recover the flotsam, can we rewrite the script?
                    —Sally Wen Mao, "The Toll of the Sea"

Chapter 14

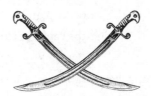

B aron."
Flicker of light, curve of shadow. The dregs of thick, uneasy dreams, a syrupy gold that sank his limbs into the mattress.

Something poked his shoulder, and he groaned.

"You awake?"

The space between his temples was stuffed with cotton, the blankets—no, furs—piled on his chest pleasantly heavy. He reached for his glasses before he remembered, and then his eyes slid closed again, and he drifted.

"Baron."

Jordan. He wished, dimly, that he could explain his exhaustion. Wished sleep were not already closing back over him, warm and slow and inevitable.

"I think—" he slurred, and found his mouth as gummed up as his brain. "Adrenal glands—out of juice."

A hand at his chest, undoing the first button of his shirt, and he swatted it away clumsily.

"Shit." Jordan's voice, far away. "They really are."

"Mmh."

Her weight sank into the side of the cot. A blur swung from her hand, drawing close—the leather pouch Dau had given him yesterday.

"Dust?" she asked.

He unstuck his mouth again. Managed: "Sure."

It hurt even more than he remembered. A boiling through the delicate gel of his eyes, and then his vision sharpened to a painful amount of detail—every whorl in the wooden planks of the walls, every diamond facet of ocean wave beyond the cabin porthole. The elegant curve of Jordan's lashes—

He wiped his streaming eyes. "Saints. Was it this bad before?"

"Pretty sure your vision got worse."

She was watching him carefully; he could not read her expression.

"First battle's today," she remarked, and the air was weighted with all the things they had not said. "You don't have to come if you don't want to."

Flash of steel and blood spurt, the wet sound of entrails spilled to ground. Baron blinked, hard. "I said I would."

"You just fell from an exploding plane. Aku will give you a pass."

He wondered how she knew—or if she and the rest of the world had always been breaking what he'd perceived to be the rules, and he was the only one foolish enough to believe them ironclad. "But if you go into withdrawal again—"

"I won't."

"All right, you won't. But I can still hold a sword." Baron attempted to swing his leg over the edge of the cot, but overshot and landed flat on his back. All the breath huffed out of his lungs.

"Case in point," Jordan said, standing above him.

He lifted his head, dazed. "Ow."

"If you say 'fuck,' I'll stop giving you shit for the rest of the day."

"You'd—give me more."

"Touché." She held out a hand and he hauled himself up, paused again as the walls spun. "Well, if you're sure. Let's get geared up."

"Do the pirates drink coffee?"

"I think so. Come on."

His fatigue sharpened into a headache as they made their way through the bowels of the ship, past men groaning out of bed or sprinkling Dust on wounds in various stages of healing. Jordan greeted them as if they were already old friends—"That's Ellis," she murmured in his ear, "and Rien, and Koro, and Nilam, and Sander"—but Baron was even more out of his body than usual, his limbs gone leaden and uncooperative, and in the five seconds that Jordan let go of his hand, he banged his knee twice on a meter-high shipping crate and promptly forgot every name and face.

But she did not question his resolve again, and after he'd obtained a steaming tin cup of black sludge from the galley, she pushed open the trapdoor, both of them squinting against the cold brightness of the sky.

A map of the Island had been sketched in charcoal on the deck, more pirates gathered around the captain and Jack Two as they mused over the Boys' most frequent points of attack.

"They love cutting down our bridges," Dau explained, stepping back so Jordan could look closer. As Aku shifted his group of men pointedly away, the quartermaster pointed at the slim rectangles drawn beneath the curve of the Boys' territory: the rocky columns that jutted off the coast, between which the pirates' precarious rope-and-wood suspensions were the quickest route to Peter's little house underground. "They don't know we pick up their leftover Dust, but pirates aren't supposed to build things, so they've sensed something's fishy."

"And which forest paths are they using?" Jordan asked, leaning in. "Is the big ravine still there?" Then the two of them were pacing around the drawing, Dau pointing out choke points and the Boys' favorite sites for open battle, and Jordan's eyes lit up as she discovered the Island anew.

Baron leaned cautiously against the rail, curling his arms through the gap to keep from tipping back into the ocean. On the other side of the deck—Port? Starboard? He'd never been able to keep them straight—a few pirates were donning body armor, oiling wickedly sharp blades. Tier peeked out of the hatch, his hair as rumpled as his suit, and slunk off toward the forest with an axe and a bundle of smaller tools before anyone could attempt to make small talk.

Mateo, his sword only half sheathed, caught Baron's eye. "You want to practice?"

Baron's windpipe vised shut.

"Have already," he said in Rittan, so flustered by the lie that he forgot to add the subject that would have made the sentence grammatically correct. "But thank you."

The pirate winked, and Baron's face warmed. The other man's glasses were round rimless affairs whose arms curved all the way around his ears; they looked old and strange enough that they might have been fished out of the sea. "Well, let me know if you ever want more."

"Er," said Baron, and lowered himself to sitting.

There had been a night on the Island, when he was ten. He'd woken in the dark needing to pee, fumbled up the edges of his hollow tree and toward the trench the Boys used as a latrine. But then the gasp beneath the blustering wind, the scrape of bark against his palms as he ducked behind a thicket of pines. Then the slashed throat, the wretched dying gargle, the hot gush of scarlet beneath the halo of Tink's light.

He had never told Jordan about that night. Not because he thought she would laugh—she wouldn't, if she sensed his sincerity—but because the words for what had happened simply would not come out of his mouth. Boys had quietly disappeared from their ranks before then, when their voices cracked or hair started growing in unsightly places; Baron himself had beheaded plenty of pirates, sliced open Pales like the boars the Boys spit-roasted on the beach.

How could he explain what this one death had done to him, or why he'd spent the next few years dreaming of corpses?

How could he tell her that, of all the deaths the Lost Boys had doled out, this was the first he had felt, in his bones, could have been his?

"Baron."

Jordan stood over him, broadsword at her hip, and lightning fritzed through his palms.

"Yeah?"

"It's time." A glow lit her face in the early-morning light, as if a fire had been kindled from within. And he thought: If this was the day he died, at least he would have seen her like this. "Last chance to back out."

He would not kill, today. Would not leap in front of a Boy's sword, either, not when Jordan would see and hate him for it; not while the captain—Aku—still held the promise of Dust and treasure over her and Tier's heads. But for nearly nine years now, he'd dreamed of dying for a cause. Of pouring himself out for another until he was beaten and broken and flayed.

Of his body having *meant* something, besides the shame of never having figured out how to live.

And if it happened on accident—the slip of a blade, an arrow thudding home—well, no one would blame him, then.

Baron tilted up his chin, looked his Twin in the eye.

"No," he said, and his voice did not waver, his hands did not shake. "I told you, I'm coming with."

It was only an hour later—as he lay in the mud, shoulder to shoulder with Jordan—that he began to regret his decision.

The forest was a slow green undulation, gilded in morning light. Pirates crouched behind bushes, their mud-smeared faces and body armor hidden behind thick sheaves of dead grass: Mateo on Baron's right, Dau and Jack Two up ahead with Captain Aku.

On his left, Jordan was a brewing storm, all adrenaline and simmered heat.

"Relax," she murmured in Kebai, bumping his elbow. "The Boys can't risk getting cut or they'll fall out of the sky. They won't touch you."

"I know."

Baron shifted, wincing as the hilt of the sword dug into his rib cage. He would rather have his throat slashed by a Lost Boy than spend endless decades shut in a fluorescent cubicle. Would receive greater accolades in Taram for dying in battle now than from a heart attack at seventy, sprawled on the floor of an empty apartment, no one still alive who loved him enough to mourn.

Yet hesitation pushed up against his teeth. Neither he nor Jordan had touched a sword in nine years, and he remained uncertain of the physiological effects of Jordan's Dust withdrawal. He himself was still sluggish from the residual sleep debt, the lack of decent caffeine.

He didn't mind giving up his life, but he was a little afraid, just now, that it would hurt.

And, too—the ghost trace of Jordan's hand around his, in the gathered dark. The echo of her voice: *Are you saying I should be nicer to you?*

He didn't know, he thought as the Lost Boys' laughter floated through the sun-struck air; as Aku raised a hand, signaling the pirates to fan out between trees. He didn't know anything at all.

Then the children fell upon them, howling war cries, and the early-morning stillness combusted into steel-edged motion, and Baron scrambled upright and drew his blade just in time to block a ringing strike from above.

The fight was more vicious than any he could remember. The Boys had the advantage of flight—Aku had long ago ruled that the pirates would use Dust for healing only, as the Boys didn't know they had it—and so blows rained on Baron like gravity, his forearms juddering to the bone as he braced the shield above his head. His shoulders began to ache within seconds; his sword flailed through empty air.

A burble of laughter trailed behind his left ear, baby teeth pearled in sunlight.

The Boy who had set upon him, sensing weakness, drove down even harder, and an incongruous heat unfurled behind Baron's eyes.

He couldn't do this. Couldn't fight, couldn't remember.

Couldn't stand the possibility that he might now be the villain.

His heel sank into something soft, and he stumbled back from the seashell curve of an ear, a chest splattered with blood. A pirate whose name he hadn't yet bothered to learn.

Saints above—

"Hey, meat puppet!"

Baron's head snapped up. Another Lost Boy—a Slightly, judging from his dagger-tipped staff—sneered down at him from a pine branch. "You're holding your sword wrong."

Baron tried and failed to stop his hands from shaking. He should have run while he'd had the chance. What a joke to think he could still hold his own here; could still *believe*, when all he had to fight with were the ruins of his former lives, a script that would never be finished because no one cared enough about the ending.

The forest closed over his head like the lungs of some vast, living organism: the jutting branches its alveoli, microscopic air pockets filling the spaces in between. In distancing himself from the pirate's corpse, he had backed out of the semi-cleared space where the others were still fighting. Here, the waking sun seared gold across the Boy's shadowed upper lip, the matted hair that covered his shins.

Baron felt a twinge of pity despite himself. This Boy would soon become the very thing he had trained for years to slaughter.

"There are many ways to hold a sword," Baron forced out, despising the wobble in his voice.

The Boy raised his staff. "Too bad yours is getting you killed," he might have said, and then they raised their respective weapons— Baron's reflection sliding off the metal, his face thrown back at him in blurry fragments.

He had done this before, he told himself. Many times.

He couldn't breathe.

Then—

He was not sure what happened next. Later, he would wonder if time had slowed the same way for the Boy, the way birds hung for a wing-beat in midair before they were blown back in the wake of a passing train. All he heard was the thud, the indrawn breath, and then the Boy was ground-bound and sprinting away, his staff a faint swinging line against the lichen-crusted pines.

Baron sank to his knees. His teeth were chattering, though a small, detached part of him noted it was not particularly cold.

"You're holding your sword wrong," Jordan said behind him, and he smothered a bout of hysterical laughter. "How much of this *do* you remember?"

"A—a bit." Sort of. Triumphant whoops and her arm thrown around his shoulders, a bright fantasy of laughter and belonging. But the two of them had never belonged to the Island as they were. Never without their glamour, their masks, their walls.

They had never truly been children, he thought. He could see that now, under the adventures and conquests. They had been toys, played with by Peter and then cast aside; had paved the road of his forgetting with blood.

"Are you absolutely sure about this?" Jordan dragged him to his feet, her sword reflecting torch-bright where it was tucked beneath her other arm. Even as fractured as his vision was becoming, she seemed lit from within—fire and marble, obsidian and melted glass. The only sharpness in a world of dull things.

Baron swallowed, flexed his fingers. His own body was barbed wire and razor blades, the howl of a typhoon pounding onto shore.

"Stop trying to get rid of me," he said faintly, and his voice was not his own.

"Then don't let them get inside your guard," she bit out, "use your reach—oh, fucking hells—"

A pair of Boys had broken away from the main knot of fighters, screaming toward them with blades outstretched.

"Gods help us," Baron said faintly, and then the real fighting began.

Chapter 15

Jordan had missed this.

The rush of bodies, blades and teeth ignited by the rising sun, Lost Boys shouting as they lashed out and tumbled away. Her locked-up prosth meant she had a club instead of a shield, but she was lighter on her feet this way, and then there was her new reach—here the strike she'd never have gotten before, an eye, other people's blood and she didn't even blink—and a laugh bubbled in her throat, the same wild wheeling as beneath the Underground spotlights, because this was it, this was *her*: sand in her mouth, sweat streaming down her eyelids, sword-clang reverberating up her arm. This, now, the weapon she had made herself into, and if she was going to die here, she would do it this way—on her feet, blade in hand, veins seething copper and neon and dark fire.

"Ready?" she said to Baron at her back, and it was not quite like old times but it was close enough.

Silver slash—knee, gut, the sole of a foot. A roar in her ears like a breaking dam. The Lost Boys' bodies came in fragments, glimpses of pale ankle and soft belly, a grunt as Baron's shield pushed someone

away. She opened a nick in a heel and another Boy took his place—
Tudo, from his spectacles, hurling a hatchet toward Baron's head—

As the axe clanged off her sword, she caught the flash of a face in her periphery, a dart of white.

"You." A girl's voice, knifing the morning air. "You weren't supposed to come back."

Jordan's blood went cold. Across the clearing, the Lost Boys, many of them bleeding now and thus ground-bound, were sheathing their weapons, turning toward the voice's approximate source. As were—her stomach sank—the pirates.

There was only one person on the Island in front of whom the Boys and pirates would not kill. Wholly improper for a lady to see heads coming off, the uncouth spurts of blood.

Jordan turned.

Chay stood behind her, a moon-white dress—of the same cut she'd worn the day Jordan left the Island—billowing in the wind.

She was much shorter than expected, if Jordan could have expected anything at all—her wrists slim as saplings, her shoulders bony and breakable beneath the sunlight seeping through the trees. Were they standing side by side, Jordan doubted the other girl would even come up to her chest.

And yet. The set of that mouth. Those eyes, the same color and shape as her own.

A buzz filled Jordan's ears, a physical sensation of grey spiking out of her hands and shoulder blades. She thought of broken wings.

"Chay," Jordan said hoarsely. "You're still here."

Her younger sister smiled. "I had no reason to leave."

Peter looped behind Chay, mischievous blue eyes and dimpled smile, and Jordan tensed: It was his giggle that haunted her dreams, the phantom glint of his gold-inlaid sword that caused her to whip around in the middle of busy San Jukong intersections. But his expression was blank, the dagger between his fingers spinning with no special vengeance. He did not remember her face.

"Who's this?" he asked, and his voice was a perfect peal of infant laughter.

Chay's gaze was steady. "No one."

My sister.

Jordan noted, with some detachment, that a tremor had started in her left hand. If she had known—if she'd had even an inkling that Chay was still here, her bones not yet sliced out of cooling flesh to bolster Peter's Dust supply—Jordan might have shot straight toward the little house underground and strangled her and her wolf (grey and stiff-legged, now, limping behind Chay with a tepid growl trapped between its teeth) herself.

But she could not run a sword through *this.*

Chay's eyes like mirrors, staring back, alive. The slight upturn of nose, like Jordan's, like their mother's. Jordan hadn't been able to see it at the time—she had been thirteen years old, her sister ten, both their faces still unformed dough—but nine years later, the resemblance was startling.

And the starkness of Chay's collarbones, the bony arc of rib cage beneath that dress. The jarring difference in height.

Chay had stayed a child, to play the part of Mother. But what price had she paid to do so?

"Maybe you should get back to cooking," Peter said, patting her gently on the shoulder, and her head bobbed as she slipped back into the woods, her skirts shrinking to a pale ghost sliver.

An indrawn breath, as if the trees themselves were waiting. And then the slow slide of steel: the Lost Boys and pirates, unsheathing their weapons again in unison.

Jordan rolled onto the balls of her feet, shifted her grip on her sword. A high whine threaded her hearing, flattened her world to the line of Peter's blade. She herself was not blameless—had been aware, at thirteen, of all the times she'd chosen the Boys over her sister, sneered at the Ama's girlhood; the ways she had slammed shut the gates of the story she'd built because she was terrified of being left outside its bounds.

But she had spent the rest of her life being punished for it. Dust withdrawal and their parents and karsa and Obalang were more than a fair trade.

Nine godsdamned years.

Above her, the pine branches shivered—gilded thorns, fractal glass.

"And now," Peter said, leveling his blade at Jordan, "it's your turn to die."

She was three years old, tumbling across the porch as some aunt or cousin scolded her to be careful, the lizard she'd snatched from the outer wall of the apartment squirming between her cupped hand and right forearm. Her parents would be home any minute, and Ma would yell at her for tearing a hole in her pants again, but if her father was in a good mood, he might let her take the elevator down to the park, to let the lizard go.

The front door opened and her parents stepped in, a pink bundle wrapped in her mother's arms.

"Look," Jordan exclaimed, thrusting the creature toward them, "look what I found," but Ma only snapped at her to hush and then nodded at the bundle.

"She's sleeping."

Jordan scowled. "Who?"

"Your little sister," Ba said, his voice a tenderness she could not remember ever being offered to her, and Ma stooped low so Jordan could see. "Isn't she darling?" And something slipped from Jordan's fingers that she'd never known was hers to lose.

She was five years old, thrashing on the floor as her mother tried to force her into a pink dress and itchy tights.

"What is *wrong* with you?" Ma demanded, as Jordan wrenched away from her grasping hands. On the sofa, Chay sat in her own frilly pink number, quietly sucking her thumb. "Just put them on. Why can't you be a good girl like your sister?"

"Fuck her," Jordan shouted, a word she'd heard an angry man screaming in the park, "I don't even want to be a girl," and then pain exploded across her face and her mother was leaning above her, breathing hard, open palm raised like she'd do it again.

She was seven years old, seething with frustration as she struggled to open a soda bottle her Second Uncle had given her. The next room over, Ma and Ba paraded her sister's ballet skills before the extended family, all twinkling eyes and encouraging coos as Chay trotted in her tutu.

As the grown-ups applauded—as Second Uncle gave her a soda, too—Chay looked through the door at Jordan, her eyes shining innocence.

"Nnf nnf," she grunted, clutching her own bottle with the inside of her right wrist. "Nnf"—and then Jordan was on top of her, punching and kicking with a viciousness she usually saved for the kids at school, and above her sister's screams and their parents wrenching them apart and the shouts of *how could you* and *what were you thinking* and *she's only four*, Jordan found herself sobbing so hard she thought she would vomit.

She was eight, soaring out Baron's apartment window into the boundless night. Later she would tell herself she did not look back, did not even think about those she was leaving behind, but the truth lodged in her throat was this: As gleeful as she was to ditch the bullies at school, neither did she regret abandoning her family.

She was twelve, her knees and elbows chapped and splintered from wriggling down a hollow tree that no longer quite fit. Wen had flown home that morning, claiming she missed the smell of newsprint and pencil shavings and her parents' morning coffee, and a new Ama stood in the kitchen of the underground house, arms wrapped shyly around the same white cotton dress that Wen had worn.

"My name is Chay," she said, beaming, "I'm here to help with spring cleaning," and then her gaze landed on the Twins, her brow creasing like the beginnings of a question, and dread shivered across Jordan's skin.

She was twelve, swathed in black-glass night, the knife in her hand steady against the soft of her baby sister's throat. She was twelve, and weakness meant death, and the edge of the blade spoke when words were not enough.

"Don't tell them about me and Baron," she whispered harshly, and watched the attempts at memory flicker and die against Chay's long lashes—this was not the *jiejie* she had built up in her mind, in the many years of Jordan's absence. "I'll know. And I'll come for you faster than they could ever come for me."

She was twelve, only half guilty at the envy radiating from her sister's gaze, the way the younger girl hovered at the edges of the Boys' adventures as if hoping to be invited in. Jordan was twelve, and despite time and the Island blurring her parents' faces and the name of her street, she remembered that feeling: the whispers in the schoolyard, the prick of mechanical pencil tips against her arm and the nape of her neck; the two-meter radius her classmates had kept from her after she beat up the main perpetrator, as if *she* were the rabid dog.

But she had carved out a home for herself, on the Island. Marked a boundary in Dust and blood. And she would kill, would *be* killed, before she allowed it to be taken from her.

She was thirteen, and bleeding.

She was thirteen, and Chay glided toward her with that incredulous sneer, all traces of softness burned out of her by a year of being walked past like a wall.

"You didn't even know, did you?" she mocked, and Jordan pressed her knees together, desperately trying to ignore the red gush of warmth.

"Shut up."

"No one told you?"

And then Chay explained, in great detail, what happened when a girl became a woman—how their wombs grew padded with the softness they needed to bear children, then flushed it out once every moon.

When Jordan refused to show the Boys her wound, Chay laughed.

"Just look where it's dark," she'd said, and Jordan had only gaped—legs frozen, sword slack in her hand—as the wolf and the Boys closed in.

She choked.

She never choked. Not punching bullies in grade school, not facing down pirates or sharp-toothed mermaids twice her size. Not even, technically, at her first Underground match—gravity had dragged at her heels and fists, then, left her wide open for a head kick, but at least she'd kept moving, at least she'd tried. Now, as Peter's sword sliced a gash across her left arm, the world went ponderous and strange—the light limning the trees a soft sheath of unreality; the blood ribboned across her skin, so red it looked false.

"What?" Peter taunted, his voice mockingly familiar. "Tired already?"

She watched her knees buckle as if they were someone else's. Hands seized her shoulder as other blades clanged above her head, and then she was being dragged backward, her left arm a conflagration, darkness smudging the edges of her vision.

No.

Peter was getting away. *Tink* was getting away. And Jordan had not spent nine years wallowing in the cesspool that was San Jukong, had not crossed half an ocean and flung away even the thin safety net that running karsa for the syndicate had given her, just to pass out the moment they swerved back within reach.

Someone seized her arms, her ankles, and she kicked: a satisfying crunch, a muffled curse. Her sword wobbled bright through the empty air—she had tried to stuff it into her right hand, wrap the clenched prosth fingers around the unforgiving hilt—but it fell in the mud. A touch on her wrist and she screamed.

"*No.*"

Around her, the twang of a bowstring, high-pitched cries, the sharp copper seep of spilled blood. The wounded Boys were pulling back, Peter a golden glow at their head, and she stumbled after them one last time, jagged with pain. She would destroy Peter. Without Dust, he was nothing. Without Dust, he would grow old and die like the rest of them, and she would sit back and laugh as the shame of it tore him apart—

More hands at her waist, her neck, and she threw back an elbow. Felt the startled huff of air.

"It's me."

Her teeth bared in a snarl.

"It's just me."

She lashed out with her bloodied fist, her vision thumping black.

"Jordan."

"Fuck off."

"Hey. Hey. Look at me. I'm right here."

Baron. Her eyes blurred.

The trees were an emerald curtain now, pulling closed between them and the Boys, and in the sudden quiet she was weeping, great heaving gasps locked between her teeth, more tears leaking from her eyes—traitorous bastards—than she had shed in the last nine years. She'd gone soft, she thought with disgust. She should not have needed someone to cling to. But her slashed-open arm was a bolt of pain, and she had no one else left.

She curled into Baron, who didn't speak, didn't try, only held her and breathed and understood.

Slowly, notch by notch, she brought herself back. Shut the hurt in some far-off corner of her body and pushed to her feet—avoiding Baron's hand at her elbow, and the sight of her wound (peeled open like rotted fruit, perhaps; vertigo bloomed through her at just the thought). As the pirates' stares pressed in on all sides, the echo of Baron's collarbone warmed her forehead: a bridge, a scar.

"I have to go after them," she said hoarsely. "Now that they know we're here."

He was still kneeling in the dirt, a smear of blood—hers?—drying on his forehead. "Jordan."

"What?"

"It's all right. We're still alive." His face was sunlight and open sky, and Jordan wondered just how wrong the stories of the pirates had been—how many of them, too, were villains only pretending. Behind him, a flock of Everbirds flowed out of the trees, a river of ink. "We'll have other chances."

"This is the Island," she said flatly. "All our chances ran out years ago."

A tiny curve at the corner of his mouth. "Then we'll make more ourselves."

She laughed, a wet, choked sound, and when he took her right elbow, she did not pull away. "You know who you sound like?"

"Let's not go there," he said primly, and she scoffed.

The captain and a handful of his men stood a few meters away, arms folded, faces sliced bright and bloody beneath triangles of sunlight. Jordan glared, hating that they had seen her weak more than they had seen her strong. That she now owed them *more* than she had last night, when she'd collapsed onto their ship and gorged on their Dust.

More trouble than she's worth, Aku had said, as if she were a stallion in need of breaking, and she was already proving him right.

"We have more Dust back at the ship," Dau said softly, eyeing Jordan's forearm.

Black spots swarmed her vision. "At what cost?"

"You fought with us," Jack Two said. A nick on his cheek wept dark red. "You fought *for* us. Our Dust is yours now."

Jordan cocked a brow at Aku, who dipped his head sardonically.

"Welcome to the crew."

Blink and a door slammed shut in her face, the shouts of *demon child* and *no daughter of mine* echoing off concrete walls. Blink and that greasy rat Obalang was staring too long at the prosth Baron had rigged for her, his eyes a naked calculation of whether she was more valuable whole or broken down for parts.

Blink and she was surrounded by strangers studying her with, if not warmth, at least intent. It was not quite belonging—her and Baron's places here still hinged on her sword fighting ability, and she doubted any of the pirates, even Dau or Jack Two or Mateo, would shed a tear if karsa withdrawal killed her in the next few hours. But it was more of an alliance than she'd ever been offered, since her days as a Lost Boy.

Jordan stepped forward, swayed as the pain nearly blinded her.

"Hey. Easy, easy."

A hand under her elbow, her armpit, a quick knotting of cloth into a tourniquet. It was a testament to how shattered she was that she couldn't find the energy to object.

"Ah," said Baron, "you've gotten blood all over my shirt."

"There was already blood all over your shirt, you arse."

"Good, good. Keep talking."

Baron egged her onward, and a disembodied cloud of other voices. But her legs were shaking, and blood had crusted hot and sticky across her front, and in the end, her eyes closed and she slid out of her body.

Chapter 16

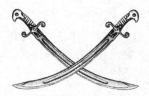

The fear had come not all at once, but slowly: a thief without a shadow, stealing into a room without light.

Nine years ago, she'd washed up on a beach outside San Jukong—arms and chest throbbing blood beneath a thin layer of Dust-conjured skin, pain a river in which she could drown. But she hadn't been afraid, then. Nor on the nights that followed, as medics slit open her pus-filled wounds and stitched them back together; nor when her parents burst into her just-reclaimed bedroom, their shouts of *ruined the family* and *don't come back* piercing her in places even the wolf's claws could not reach.

No, the fear had come after, in the dark red pit in the throat of a white toilet.

She was using the surprisingly clean communal bathroom in Oba-lang's building by then, and knew she hadn't been injured. It didn't matter. As she stared at the monster her own body had produced—as the smell of iron clotted the back of her tongue—she felt the hot uncontrollable gush spreading through her Island furs, the shear of wolf's teeth across her skin; heard again the scream that slashed a line between her Before and her After.

Flash of dark like a wingbeat, and she was sprawled face-first and gagging on Obalang's tile floor.

And for the first time since she'd left the Island, she thought, *This is fear.*

There was no shame in calling it that. Fear could be useful—prick your intuition when reason did not, steel you to fight harder when someone less afraid would have lain down and surrendered. But the thing that had cracked open inside her was a different beast.

This was the kind of fear that paralyzed. The kind that made one weak.

Jordan could not be weak, not anymore.

So she went to a quicksurgeon.

"I want drugs," she said, handing him the rumpled stack of mir she'd saved from her first Underground win—her meals for the next week—and the man's eyes did not widen at the cash, or the cap of steel over her right arm. "The kind that will take away my period."

He gave her two pills, which she swallowed dry while seated on his office toilet. As they burned through her—this was the sloppy way, far cheaper than monthly pills or implants stuck *up there*—the smell of blood filled the room, cloying and red.

She pressed her forehead to the cold wall. Exhaled, slow, out of her mouth. And that last time—that is, if one were to tell this like a story, with an ending noosed tight around her throat—that last time, she did not black out.

When Jordan returned to consciousness in the bowels of the pirate ship, dread had settled in her like a weight.

She had done much, over the years, to avoid the sight of her own blood: coated her skin with sealing ointment before Underground matches; slapped on bandages blind under her shirt; showered, after bad karsa runs, with her eyes closed and her wounds screaming. She'd even bought herself a pocketknife as a means of rehabituation, but passed out immediately after nicking her ankle and never tried again.

Perhaps she shouldn't have been surprised that, nine years later, her skin had barely broken, and she'd queased out like the damsels in the old Rittan stories.

Worse—she winced, remembering—Baron had seen.

Something wrapped tight around the throb of her left arm, and she trailed her right elbow along its edges, feeling for bumps and patches of tenderness: a cloth bandage, or perhaps the tourniquet from earlier. She breathed out through her mouth. It wasn't bleeding on *her* as far as she could tell; that should have been enough. But the moist heat against her skin, the slow seep, the *smell*—

Jordan cracked her eyes open. She was lying on her cot; the porthole beyond had brightened to a near-fluorescent afternoon white, the lanterns through her half-cracked door dim in comparison.

Baron sat beside her, unrolling a length of old sailcloth.

"Oh, good," he said when she made a sound. "I thought you might have hit your head."

Her throat closed. "Not ruling that out."

"You don't remember?"

"No," she lied.

She scanned the room. A roll of gauze was tucked in her own pack, mostly dry by now from its soak in the ocean, but she didn't quite trust herself to move—it was as if her joints had come loose, swung open like door hinges inside her limbs. Besides, with Baron hovering at her shoulder, she would have to look down to apply the bandage, and if she passed out again, it would be a dead giveaway.

The alternative, however, was getting infected from a cut that was probably surface-level, and that was a stupid way to die.

She would have to risk it.

"Wait." Baron looked up as she shifted her good arm. "I was going to cut open a portion of your sleeve to clean the wound."

"Or you could take my clothes off entirely," she countered, and grinned at the look on his face. "It's fine. I'll do it myself."

Baron waved the roll of makeshift bandages. "You're turning down free medical care?"

She paused. "Fair."

"It won't take long." He snapped on nitrile gloves of doubtful provenance, drew out a small pair of scissors. "I'll—er—cut the hole now."

"Do enjoy yourself."

Baron rolled his eyes but let her lever herself upright, her eyes fixed on the ceiling, to give him a better view. The wetness was spreading: not quite *there*, but still uneasy, a serrated edge scraping under her teeth. Quiet snips as the tourniquet fell away, a tug of fabric as Baron lifted it off her skin.

Then the blade touched her arm, and darkness slid over her, an eyelid closing.

"What was that?" Baron snapped, rubbing his head. She had cuffed him—her right hand floated sharp in the center of her vision as the rest of the world went soft and slippery.

"Shit," she said. "Sorry." She was breathing too fast. Blood burned under her eyelids; the heat of her left arm had crescendoed to a dull roar.

It wasn't that she feared touch. She would almost have welcomed another roundhouse kick from the White Tiger, a spray of arrows from the Lost Boys—those would have at least proven something, whether or not she was alive at their conclusion.

But the scissors were a soft sinking in, like teeth.

In the dark—a little boy's giggle, a flash of small hands.

"Jordan. Hey." Baron's voice was thin but firm against the nausea pressing its thumbs to her throat. She gripped the edge of the cot, clenched her toes.

She would not be weak. Would not be broken. Would not allow herself to be saved, not when she'd stolen the story to begin with.

"Go on," she said tightly, and Baron continued to cut.

Holding still was excruciating. She counted the planks across the ceiling, then the rusted bolts holding the porthole in place—anything to distract her from the steady sharpness above her skin, the pulsing flow beneath. Her morning dose of Dust was wearing off; the world was curdling into a grey smear, the salt-steel smell of the ocean a nauseating blandness that clung to the insides of her nostrils.

"Lucky for you," Baron said, setting down the scissors at last, "I won't have to attempt tweezers. It doesn't look like anything went in."

"Okay," Jordan said.

"But I'm, ah, going to have to press the sides together so I can apply the Dust that Dau gave m—"

"Do it then."

"All right. Sorry." He wiped down the area with another piece of cloth—she hissed through her teeth at the sting—and pressed on a bandage with slow deliberation. Cool relief pooled through her: some of Tier's ointment, perhaps, added to the gauze.

"And here I'd just been using cotton swabs and vodka," she said, at which he sighed.

"You'll live."

"Thanks, doc."

An itch crawled beneath her skin as Dust knitted her cells back together. Jordan braced herself, and looked down.

Sealed, the wound was ridiculously small. Embarrassingly so.

She'd expected to see her forearm split into meaty lips, oozing flesh and yellow discharge, but there was only a neat rectangle of cloth, held in place with a metal clasp. The hole Baron had cut in her shirt barely as wide as her palm, and not a single spot of blood.

"Shit," she said, nudging it with her frozen prosth. "It really was nothing, wasn't it?"

Baron fiddled with the extracted flap of shirt fabric. Now that she posed less threat of crushing his skull in, he looked a great deal more relaxed. "I mean, you should still keep it as dry as possible," he said, "and limit yourself to speaking only at mealtimes—"

"Oh, go stuff your diagnoses up your—"

He drew himself up indignantly. "Who's the fake doctor here?"

"I am, clearly, as I have diagnoses for your diagnoses." She stuck out her tongue. "Or if you are, why don't you grab me another pouch of—"

"You're the one refusing to follow directions."

"My morning dose is wearing off." Jordan raised a brow. "And good fake doctors *always* keep their patients adequately sedated."

"Dust isn't a sedative."

"Pacified, whatever."

"Words *mean* things in medicine," Baron said sternly.

"Sure, doc."

Baron disposed of the waste in the washroom, scrubbed his hands, and then sat back down at the foot of her cot. For a while, they simply watched the ocean shimmer through the window, the thin clouds drifting through bright blue sky.

There was very little chance she would succeed, Jordan thought, in capturing Tink on her own. Her mind was still a minefield—today had made that abundantly clear—and she would not paint herself an even greater fool before the pirates by charging forward alone and in denial. Yet the pirates wanted the Boys stripped of Dust, too. Wanted to go where Peter could not follow. If she could stay alive on their Dust supply—if she could find a way to fight for them without coming into direct contact with Chay again—perhaps she could convince Aku that a quick theft was better than this open war they had been waging for generations. Perhaps a bunch of grown-up Lost Boys was exactly what she needed to take Peter down.

A knock on the door, and Mateo poked his head in, his eyes lighting up as they found Baron.

"There you are," he said, jarringly cheerful. "I'm afraid I didn't quite get to thank you for this." He motioned at the fresh line of stitches trailing down the left side of his face, vivid black against light brown. The quirk at the corner of his mouth shifted into a grimace. "Or apologize for swearing quite so much. You didn't deserve it."

To Jordan's immense surprise, Baron's face pinked, and he muttered something about a lack of anesthetics.

"When did you learn how to suture?" Jordan demanded, and he ducked his head.

"I just—watched?" he said, and in spite of the composure he'd maintained as he cleaned and re-dressed her arm, there was a hitch to his breath now, his hands flexing awkwardly in his lap. "Dau was stitching up Jack Two, and I wasn't injured myself, so—"

"Well, he's quite good for a first-timer," said Mateo, winking. "Smart of you to keep him around." Then he slipped out the door, and left Baron sputtering and blushing and apparently incapable of looking Jordan in the eye.

Chapter 17

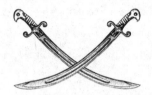

Tier was not a fan of dinner parties.

He'd been dragged to plenty, growing up. Fidgeted for hours in stiff suits and pinching shoes; smiled for the inevitable cameras; said as few words as possible when his parents' well-meaning C-suite and socialite friends tried to loop him into their conversations. The pirates' bonfire on the beach should have been nothing alike—grease smeared their cheeks as they ate roast boar with their hands, and the dress code was an odd assortment of suits and tank tops and coveralls, whatever salt-soaked tatters had washed up on the beach. Yet the same sourness tinged the back of Tier's throat, the same expectation that he *enunciate* and *project*. It made his head pound.

At least there was whiskey. He snagged a tin cup of the stuff from an outstretched hand, chugged until his eyes stung.

Chay's fingertips ghosted cold along the nape of his neck.

She had touched him so easily. As if it were natural. As if it had cost her nothing. And he could feel himself hungering for more—her hands molding him into the shape of a person, making him real. Her eyes, without an image of who he used to be, finally seeing him into perfection.

No, he thought, scratching at a cut on his jaw—he'd shaved at last, albeit with a blade that snagged with every other stroke. No girl—woman?—he'd just met could heal him, with Dust or affection or anything else, and he would not demand it of her. Only when he had gathered all his treasure—when he had patched up a ship and prepared it to leave this place, his future glittering with gold and fame—would he offer her a place beside him, if she wished. A quiet overture, a new beginning. He could not simply spill the mess of himself and expect her to pick up the pieces.

Though it felt like he'd already spent half his life breaking open.

"Oi, redhead."

Tier raised his head, smiled thinly. No one ever seemed to remember his name. "Yes?"

"You eating?" It was the captain, broad grin and outstretched arms. Three other pirates sat around him in the sand. "The meat's excellent tonight. Very tender."

"I will soon." The alc hadn't kicked in yet—wouldn't really, for another two or three drinks—and Tier refilled his cup from the barrel, acutely aware that he had twisted his words into something of a Glennan brogue. "Mind if I join you?"

"Not at all." Aku introduced his companions: a Rittan named Seida, cold grey eyes and curled upper lip; two Hanwa men, wiry and sharp-boned and close enough in appearance to be twins. Each endowed Tier with a solemn nod.

"Where are you from, by the way?" asked Seida, with a played-up kind of nonchalance. "I can't seem to place your accent."

"I'm—ah—" Tier gripped his cup, frustration stiffening his tongue. If he professed to be from Ritt, Seida would question his earlier pretense in front of the captain. But pride would not allow him to claim another country of origin, and he'd have to put on the same humiliating accent every time he interacted with these particular men. He cleared his throat, felt his face turn giveaway red.

"I've—traveled a great deal," he managed, and then took a large enough swig of whiskey that he started choking and coughing too much to properly explain.

He'd spent all day in the coves Aku had pointed him toward the evening before. A veritable museum of ruins—crates of rubies and pearls, shards of porcelain, Espish coins centuries old—and he'd passed a blissful blur of hours excavating what he could from the shallower mud, piling it beside the skeleton of a ship he thought he could patch up with a couple fallen pines and some tar. Strangely, he found himself enjoying the work—it was slow and quiet, a pure physicality to plunging into the water and struggling back up again with his haul. He did not have to worry about stumbling through takeoff and landing announcements, or botching the negotiations for a job. Not that he often *did*, at least enough for anyone else to notice, but the shame from the few times it had occurred was a constant vise around his throat, smothering him.

Then, near sunset, the burly pirate with the peg leg, Jack Two, had appeared at the cave mouth to check his progress, direct him back to the beach for supper—where a full dozen strangers were gathered around the spitted boar, watchful and leering. Tier had felt eight years old again, frozen in his seat at an important company function. Knowing that if he tripped on a sentence, he'd be locked in the cellar after; beat his own fists bloody pounding the door in the thick dark.

Aku and his companions were staring at him now, expectant. He realized one of the maybe-twins had asked a question.

"Excuse me," he said, and pushed back to his feet with a vague mumble about needing air.

Past the bonfire glow, past the soft grey strip of shore, the Western Ocean rippled black against the impending night, frothing here and there as sea creatures broke surface. The first stars had emerged, white pinpricks against the orange-streaked sky—more distant than from his usual airborne vantage, yet still so near and bright he could have reached out and gathered them in his hand. He unhinged his jaw, trilled his tongue across the roof of his mouth. Focused on the clench of his fists in his jacket pockets, the slow sinking of his boots into the sand.

Again.

Again.

No need to be frustrated.

Why are you so angry?

Beneath the ship's hull, Jordan and Baron sat with another gaggle of pirates, Jordan laughing and tossing back whiskey as Baron picked at his mushrooms with a battered-looking fork. Tier's nostrils flared. The two of them had fought as part of the crew today; earned the pirates' respect and camaraderie, as his father would have said, *like real men.*

Tier didn't give a single runny shit. But that did not make the jealousy that sang through him any easier to bear.

"—would have lived at least a few years there," Jack Two said, waving a pork rib in the air. He seemed more relaxed around Dau, leaning easily against their shoulder as they bolted down their own portion. "Remember how he always used to tell us about his mother shutting his bedroom window on him?"

"You believe that?" Jordan asked—not mocking, just curious.

The pirate shrugged. "He does speak Rittan. And his ideas of what mothers and fathers do align at least somewhat with the Outside."

"Eh," Dau said, their mouth full. "*I* still think Peter learned everything he knows from the Boys."

Jack Two arched a brow. "So he just, what, flittered over here as a baby?"

"Or he's not even human. Who's to say?"

Tier drained the last of his tankard. The beach had gone pleasantly hazy, his tongue and lips and jaw almost loose enough that he could speak without thinking, and he meandered back to the whiskey barrel, almost grinned as warm liquid splashed his knuckles on its way to his cup. He counted his sips this time, one for every three waves that crashed onto a fixed point on shore. A perverse pleasure filled him as his vision blurred.

"—taking all of it."

Jordan, at his elbow, with that infuriating smirk she wore every time she spoke to him. He stepped back—swaying a little, to his surprise, as sand slipped beneath his feet. The night had gone unsteady without him quite noticing. Above him, the ship's twin masts spiraled toward his head, a *thwap-thwap-thwap* he did not hear so much as feel.

"What do you want?" he snarled, and was pleased when the words slid out in the Imperial accent he'd grown up hearing. "We're even now. Stay out of my way and I'll stay out of yours."

"*Even?*" Jordan's voice was low, dangerous. "That plane crash nixed my karsa supply and broke my prosth."

"Ask me if I give a shit."

"Baron and I might not be able to return to San Jukong because your father's fucking panopticon spotted us with you—"

"How'd you learn a word like 'panopticon'?" Tier shot back. "Your college boyfriend teach you?"

A heartbeat of silence: Jordan's eyes gleaming in the firelight, the slow-motion crash of ocean waves. Then an impact in his gut like he'd been shot, and he was spewing vomit onto the whiskey barrel and his own clothing, gagging loudly as he fell to his knees.

The pirates' horrified murmurs washed over him, a full assemblage of stares fixed on his back. Jordan stood over him, her face a mask, right fist pulled back as if still in preparation.

"*Now* we're even," she said, and walked away.

Tier wrapped his arms around his stomach and moaned. He felt like a cracked egg, all shattered shell and leaking yolk. This was his brothers all over again: the centipedes crawling out beneath his chair cushion, the white-stained underwear piled on his pillow, the constipated expressions and goggled eyes as they mocked his stutter.

Even here, at the edge of the world, he could not escape his unbelonging.

"Fuck you," he choked, spat—although through the wet blur of his vision, all the pirates looked the same. "Fuck. You." And then he staggered to his feet and fled back to the ship like a scolded child.

Chapter 18

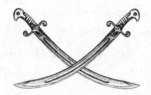

Baron shivered as he pulled the blanket tight beneath his chin.
Deep night had fallen around the ship—wind moaned against
the windows, the sea beyond drowned in moonlight. Aside from a
couple pirates standing guard in the rickety crow's nest, the crew had
settled into their hammocks and cabins, tossing and snoring in time to
the creak of the wooden walls. The air down here all smoke and rust,
the sour tang of old fear.

Behind him, Jordan shifted, her bandages lumpy against his spine.
In theory, Dust should have patched her up completely; he had given
her the rest of her day's ration, the precious golden grains vanishing
into the flayed mouth of her flesh like sugar on a tongue. But after she
punched Tier—*Deserved it*, she'd muttered as Baron sprang to his feet,
Rittan arse—she had leaned too heavily against the ship's hull, eyes
glassy, and the old terror surged in Baron's chest.

A terror that still clung to him as he lay awake beside her, listening
for a hitch in her breath, a dangerous slowing. How much blood was in
one body. How little she could stand to lose.

Behind his eyelids—the gleam of sharp teeth, the mauled mess of her arms and torso.

And the memory of Chay, ten-year-old Chay, her triumphant sneer fading as her sister's blood spattered her dress.

He had doubted she was still alive. His parents frequented the same temple as the Maktas, even if they were no longer neighbors, and had heard nothing about the return of their second daughter—*Such a tragedy to lose two children*, their friends would murmur, *even if they were both girls*. But Peter allowed any child to leave the Island of their own free will. Chay had known the signs; Baron had expected her to depart before she was exiled the way her sister had been.

"Jordan," he whispered, unsure if she was still awake.

A few slow breaths before she responded. "Yeah?"

"Did you know? That she was still here?"

Her spine pressed into his. She did not have to ask who he meant. "No."

"How did she stay, without—"

"If you don't eat enough, your period doesn't come," she said harshly, and Baron flinched. "Most girls knew that, at our school."

From beneath the flimsy door, the groan of a hammock; torchlight cast a faint miasma against the dark. Baron had heard the whispers, in middle and high school—the outcasts pantsed when they began to bleed, their faces rubbed in the waste or shoved into toilet bowls. The ones who starved and dehydrated themselves so they would never be caught in the bathroom alone.

Chay hadn't been old enough for that. Shouldn't have been. But she'd known all the same.

"You didn't," he said, and a sudden weight pressed on his chest, made the air in his lungs scratchy and thin. It felt almost like grief. "You didn't kill her."

Jordan made a sound. "She was unarmed. And—you saw her."

"Yeah," he said quietly. "Yeah, I did."

"Gods." Jordan shifted on the cot, the press of her bandages easing against his back. Gradually, her breaths slowed again. Outside the window, the waves murmured heartbeat-hypnotic, and Baron could almost hear words in the slip of the tides, tales of storms and high winds and leaves translucent beneath sunlight.

He tried to remember Chay, before they had all arrived on the Island. Those years had blurred to color and echo, but he could guess at chubby baby cheeks, blunt-cut bangs, a small soft hand wrapped around his pinkie. The rising wail, every time he and Jordan abandoned her for a game of street ball or made-up adventure: *Wait for me. Don't go.*

"I'm going to kill him," Jordan said eventually.

The night warped and shifted around her, impenetrable, listening. Goose bumps rose on the back of Baron's neck.

"*Can* you?"

She rolled onto her back with a grunt, her face tilted toward him. Her lips were parted slightly, lashes oil-black against her sun-browned skin, and even though Baron had spent the day attempting to stitch up badly injured men without anesthesia, his breath caught in his throat.

It was dangerous, he knew, to live for someone else—they would inevitably let you down, or break under the strain. No one else could be his reason, or his way out. But under the full weight of her attention, he felt as if he was falling again: his legs, dangling awkwardly off the edge of the bunk, suddenly leaden, his tongue strange and languid between his teeth.

"Yes," she said simply. "It might be more difficult than I expected. But there's a difference between us and him. We learn. We adapt." A bitter twist to her mouth. "*He* forgets."

"And stays perfect forever," Baron murmured—a line from the Sir Franklin novel, which he had read obsessively upon returning Outside as if searching for his reflection.

"That Rittan was full of bullshit," Jordan said, tracing Baron's calf with her big toe. A strangled sound came out of his throat, and he kicked her away.

"Well, so are you."

"You shouldn't kick an injured person while they're down."

His stomach dropped—still falling. "Said person must not be very injured if they're kicking back."

"That's not how it works." Her left arm folded over his, and realization clicked into place: the way she'd pointed her face away from the implant in her forearm, almost blacked his eye when he'd tried to bandage her wound. She did not like the sight of her own blood. Was perhaps—he hardly dared think it—afraid.

And yet. The heat of her hand, resting on his shoulder. The dark stars of her eyes.

"What are you—" He swallowed, dizzy. His sternum a shallow bowl. "What are you doing?"

Her breath brushed his ear as she leaned close. "Do you want me to stop?"

"I—well—no?"

Her hand traced his shoulder, his waist, the slight pouch of his stomach. His breath quickened, warmth flickering through the soles of his feet, and when she rucked up the hem of his shirt, he gasped and went stiff.

"Maybe don't *think* so much," she whispered. As he attempted to relax, every cell in his body radiating heat, her lips softened on his, and he did not move away.

She was not the first person he'd kissed. There had been another, the year before uni, with a bubbling laugh and long black hair and a penchant for romantic comedies. When it ended a week later—she had, of course, dumped him—he realized he'd been trying to prove something to himself: That he wasn't afraid of losing Jordan. That he already thought her a lost cause. But now—

Now.

Around them, night unfolded. The half-light of the lone lantern unraveled his skin, left him drowning in the smell of salt and smoke and wood soaked in sunlight. And he didn't know why she had chosen him, after all this time—if she had finally seen the truth blazing in his eyes or begun to want him on her own; if that morning's blood spatter and blazing sunlight had been her first taste of death that felt true. But her lips were startling in their softness, like flower petals—for all her humanity, he often imagined her to be made of stone—and a tremor passed through him, fault-line deep, new lands birthed from the earth's molten core.

The last time, he thought, was nothing like this. *That* had been the trial run. This was the breakthrough.

Then her hand trailed down farther, the only time he could remember her doing something gently, and he swallowed a groan.

"*Jordan,*" he whispered, blushing furiously.

An odd expression crossed her face. On anyone else he might have called it longing, but on her it simply looked out of place, like a stranger dressed for the beach at a black-tie party. "Tell me to stop."

His head spun. Every lapping wave flung him skyward. "I—no. It's all right."

"All right?" she repeated, raising a brow. "Just all right?"

"That's not what I—that's not—I don't—" he sputtered, and then she was touching him, again and again, her mouth on his hot and sweet and urgent, and when his body arched into hers, unthinking and full of need, her smile curved against his like moonlight on still waters.

And yet.

All his life, Baron had been afraid.

His first five years on the Island, he'd lain awake staring at the lumpy shadow of Jordan's false hand, terrified her Dust glamour would melt away as she slept. Upon returning Outside, a new weight had pressed down on his sternum at the reams of homework and after-school exam prep, too-bright screens blurred to gibberish before his eyes. His parents were there, too, however much Jordan ribbed him for being beholden to them—fists clenched on the sidelines, berating their only child as he failed to do the single thing for which he had been conceived.

He'd despised his own fear, his own guilt. And he so wanted to say this was the moment things changed, the pivot point on which his story turned. But as Jordan tugged at his pants—as he put tentative hands on her waist, felt the pucker of scar tissue and hard muscle—he could not stop the adrenaline from needling his palms, the light wheeze that scratched the back of his throat.

"Sorry," he said, and turned his face away. *Breathe.* "Sorry. Sorry."

"Shit," she said quietly. She was luminous—lips slightly parted, guard down, as if he could be more than his storm, more than his fear of letting go. "Did I do something?"

"No. No." Baron choked a laugh—even *this* he could not get right. "It's just—the bed—" Heat bloomed in his cheeks. He would have buried his face in his hands, except that there was no room between them for his elbows, and he was still awkwardly touching her back and he didn't know how she'd take it if he stopped or rolled away and he'd never *lain* with a person before and—"There are no bedsheets. We couldn't wash the cot, we'd have to just lie in the—in the—*oh gods*—"

The barest twitch at the corner of her mouth, but she did not laugh.

"It's okay," she said, and she spread her palm flat above his pounding heart and he gasped and gasped, mortified by the wetness coating his lashes, the way he could not hold a good thing in his hands without crushing it beneath his fear. "We don't have to if you don't want to."

His heart hurt. "I'm sorry."

"Don't be." She winked. "At least we're not in one of those sailcloth hammocks."

"You—" He turned, bleary. "Sailcloth—there are—?"

"Yes." A wicked grin. "Last night. I heard some *quite* evocative moaning."

He dragged in another inhale. Counted to five. "Ah."

"Would you like a demonstr—"

"*No.* Thank you."

They lay there, quiet but for the lap of the waves and the sharp cut of his breath, until the tightness in his chest eased, until the thunder of his pulse subsided to a murmur. This should have been the easiest thing in the world, he thought, his mouth twisting. To lie beside someone who wanted you. To have nothing else asked of you but to stay in your own body, to love your own life.

He was still so tired.

Baron cleared his throat. Said, with a weak laugh, "I bet none of your other partners were this level of batshit."

"You're not batshit," Jordan said immediately. A shuffle of blankets, and she pushed herself up on her right elbow. "And those were just hookups."

"As opposed to?"

"I didn't want to ruin what we had." Her eyes were ocean-dark, her inert prosth a bridge between them, and he thought: that she would allow him to hear her voice like this, half confession, half prayer. "And I wasn't sure you felt"—she gestured vaguely at their still-tangled legs—"well."

"Oh," Baron said faintly. Some kind of truth there, at least in part. He hadn't started off wanting her, not the way his uni classmates had talked about *doing* girls as if they were adventure park rides, or the way construction workers whistled at the well-endowed Meiri exchange students who sauntered across campus, hips swinging. It was not even the same way he'd felt, for a few humiliating moments, when he saw Tier at dinner—he could still look Jordan in the eye, still hold a conversation without his face morphing into a furnace. But he and Jordan had been in the same room on the night Peter came for him, lumped together by virtue of their Hanwa features. Had rubbed each other the wrong way for so long they'd sanded themselves into something approximating fit.

And then—

"Why now?" he asked, touching his kiss-swollen lips. "What gave it away?"

She reached up, brushed his hair out of his eyes. Said, instead of answering: "Why did you fight this morning?"

"Why did I—fight," he repeated, because his verbal reasoning had scrambled again at her touch. "Well, we've made it this far, haven't we?"

"But you didn't have to come to the actual battle."

Flash of sunlight on sharpened steel, cherub-cheeked smiles and pealing laughter. The tremor in his hands, as the Lost Boy mocked his sword grip. "I wasn't afraid to."

"Weren't you?" Lantern light flickered across the planes of Jordan's face, cast her eyes in deep hollows. An intentness there like realization. "You're terrified of swords," she said, slow. "But you're not afraid to die."

Baron swallowed, fixed his gaze on the ceiling. "Yes, that."

Silence, too long, and he was half afraid she would punch him in the face, half afraid she would confess that his final flight would shatter her like glass. Jordan had traveled the lands of death far more than he, their first time on the Island and afterward—but if he knew anything of her at all, it was the determined thrum of nerve and blood, the continual *yes* of her heart to her body.

They had dared return to this place because she wanted to live.

"Baron," she said, and he flinched as if struck.

"It's not a big deal," he mumbled. "I just—I knew it was a possibility, given what we're trying to do, and—"

"Baron. Look at me."

He turned, eyes prickling again. His body a bruise, and he wanted to sleep and never wake, he wanted to fall through the floor and sink into the ocean depths. "What?"

"You're not sacrificing yourself for me like some knight in a Rittan fairy tale."

He blinked. "I didn't say I was dying for *you*."

"Well, *that's* great to hear," she snapped, and the silence that crystallized between them was colder and more brittle than the last.

She could not leave him, here. Could not snatch a red bean pastry and duck out of his dorm until he pieced himself back together. There was only the catch in his windpipe, the blaze of her eyes; only the blanket tangled between their bodies, clammy with sweat.

Only the war they had fought, once, and all the ways it had fought back.

As the ship creaked—as pirates snored in the hold, and night thickened beyond the porthole—Baron wondered at both of their missing pieces. Wondered if someone else might have called them loneliness.

"Baron," Jordan murmured.

"Hm?"

Her thumb trailed the line of his jaw, the dip of his throat. If he closed his eyes, he could almost imagine it felt like forgiveness.

"You'll be all right," she said, and her voice was a blade and a fire and a hope he had never dared. "We'll be all right, I swear it. If you stay."

Chapter 19

The laundry seemed to multiply every time Chay did it.

She hunched in the middle of the creek, shuddering as cold water flowed across her calves and ankles. The Boys' furs were piled on the bank—stinking of wet musk, flies gorging themselves on the crusts of dark blood. A full day had passed since their battle with the pirates: plenty of time between meal preparations to scrub at least a few. But Chay's head had begun to pound by lunchtime, and she had stumbled through the rest of the day halfway outside her body.

Slash of dark eyes, burning hatred. Sword sheen too close to her face.

Her sister had grown taller since they'd last met. Her hair was no longer shaved so close to her head (only razors ever seemed to wash up on the Island's shores, and blunt ones at that); a mountain range of scars twisted across her upper arms, at which Chay could not look for too long. But Jordan moved with the same unbearable swagger she had put on as a Lost Boy. Or even worse, thanks to the steel club of her right hand; the blade she hefted so easily, now, in her left.

As if she had been practicing all this time.

Chay scrubbed Slightly's shirt with a stone, and the water clouded with rust. She had believed a different story about the Boys, back then. Had not understood that, when they spoke of killing pirates and Pales, they were not always pretending.

She had not expected so much blood.

Her eyes blurred.

She could not remember what she'd been thinking. Could barely even recall how much time had passed—and she would have forgotten entirely, if not for the cuts she made at the mouth of her hollow tree upon every year's first snow. There was a vague recollection of crying, at age five, as Jordan pried off her clinging arms; of Baron's empty bed in the middle of the night, covers thrown wide; of the smudge of grey-gold Dust on the floor, and the grown-ups' laughter when Chay insisted her feet had risen off the ground after touching it. Then she'd crossed an ocean to find her sister and found a Lost Boy instead, and a hard lump of resentment had swelled in her throat every time Jordan grinned at Baron instead of her. But that last morning—as Chay wandered toward the clamor on the beach, gaped at the blood dark between her sister's legs—was curiously blank, a room of mirrors forever reflecting. Had she screamed first at the wound, at what it meant, and so caused Peter to ask her what was wrong? Or had she smirked, recognition lancing through her—that, like a bright new dagger in her hands, she now held the means to hurt Jordan in turn?

Chay heaved Slightly's furs onto a flat rock, where they streamed cold water. The Boys themselves were playing by the cliffs—*No girls allowed,* Kuli had bawled as they departed—but the cold had settled deep in her bones, sharpened against the quiet, and she almost wanted them back just to distract her.

The smell of roasting fish, burnished with sea salt, and her throat tightened.

"Chay?"

She turned, dizzied, gulping. Tier was picking his way over the rocks—balancing, with one hand, a whole trout roasted and spitted atop a plank of wood. He had shaved, too, the line of his jaw pale and smooth and foreign.

Chay breathed through her mouth. The smell was overwhelming.

"Tier," she said, scanning the forest. "You shouldn't come out into the open like this. The Boys—"

He held out a hand.

"Walk with me?" he asked, solemn, and she banged her knees in her haste to leave the water.

It was a hazy morning, shifting into afternoon. Sunlight lazed across the high branches of the pines, traced fallen trunks and moss-thick stones in honeyed gold. Chay clasped her elbows, shivering as the water dried on her legs. All manner of mushrooms burgeoned beneath these pine needles, puffy white or brown and ruffled like girls' dresses; she could say she was foraging for Saturday dinner.

Not that it was necessarily Saturday Outside, but she and Peter often decreed it to be so anyway.

"You're cold," Tier said, stopping. There was a new glow to his face, the way the Boys looked when they discovered a new hideout or a buried cache of swords, and she reached up and touched it again, as she might have one of the Boys'.

His cheek was smooth, warm. It pinked beneath her palm.

"A bit," she said. Wind blew through the space between her torso and her arm.

"Do you want my jacket?"

Her hand drifted down, fingered the material. She did not remember much about Outside fabrics, but this was smooth, immaculately stitched. Well-made, even if the sleeves were a little torn.

"I couldn't."

"Just," he said, and then stiffened for some reason, bit the inside of his cheek. "Just for the walk."

"Is something the matter?"

He looked at her, flushed. Proffered the fish. "I, er, made you lunch."

"Oh." Her voice had gone strange, disjointed. No matter how much her head ached, she had always been able to muster the brusqueness to corral the Boys, but Tier was disorienting somehow, like turning a corner to find a meadow instead of the usual looming trees. "You still want the jacket, then?"

"Oh—ah. Yes. No. Wait." He looked lost, for a moment, before setting the fish tray on a couple of rocks and draping the garment around her shoulders. It smelled of smoke and salt and a trace of *him*, foreign and familiar all at once.

"Thank you."

Beneath the jacket, he wore only a white T-shirt, salt-stiff and tight around his shoulders. Chay looked, and then looked away. This was what she imagined the Boys becoming, when they left the Island: their wiry arms hardening to muscle, a faint line of definition at their stomachs in place of baby fat or hungry hollow. The thought stirred a warmth in her, even as it made her afraid.

Tier motioned at the fish, half a bow, and she felt a matching pink rise high on her cheeks. "Ladies first."

She ate.

She should not have, did not want to, but Tier was carefully slicing the flaky white meat with a bent fork and knife, those lambent blue-green eyes flicking to hers, and so she raised the fatty chunks to her lips, and rolled them between her molars, and mashed bits into the grass when he wasn't looking. *Stay strong.*

Once Tier had collected his treasure, he would leave. If she broke now, if the time bomb inside her swelled and ripened and burst, she was the only one who would bear the consequences.

"I've been diving in the coves," Tier said, when the sound of their chewing had grown strangely taut. "It's peaceful enough, when the mermaids aren't there. The water's warm, and there's a boat I'm patching up behind the cove with the st—the, ah, stalactites, and—will you tell the Boys?" A sidelong glance at her, a flash of bright sea.

"They don't care." Chay kneaded fish oil into the dirt. It was true: The Boys stuffed coins and jewels into hidden places the way Everbirds stockpiled food, then promptly forgot where they had hidden them. "Take what you like."

"You don't want it either? The jewels, the gold?"

Chay shrugged. "The things I value, no one can take away from me."

A pause. Tier placed his bent silverware on either side of the wooden plank—proper Rittan manners, even in this place—and set his hands on his knees.

"Chay," he said. The flush in his cheeks had gone blotchy, spread to his ears. "They're not—hurting you, are they?"

In the pine branches above their heads, a flock of Everbirds hopped and cawed, gossiping in a language she could not understand. There were so many ways to hurt and be hurt, she thought. She would wither to dust before she could count them all.

"Of course not." Her voice came sharper than she had intended. "I'm their Ama."

"You are," he agreed. "But if there's ever anything, anything at all, and you want someone else to—talk to, or—"

"Tier," she said. A hardness had closed over her chest, was creeping up her throat. She did not want to be *helped*. Especially not by someone born in a body like his, someone who would never be caged in a cycle of swelling and bleeding, swelling and bleeding. Who would never fear losing control for a quarter of his life, or understand why she'd carved herself hollow to escape hers.

Her fingers were still greasy. She would have to scrub them with mint to rid them of the smell.

"You've been kind to me." She pushed to her feet, not looking at him. His jacket still swamped her, folds and folds of cloth, and she handed it back, shivering violently as a breeze cut through her dress. "But I have to go."

"Chay, wait," Tier said.

Her legs moving slow, as if in a dream. Her eyes blurring for no reason she could discern. Only that she had been given warmth, and was giving it up. Only that she hated being cold.

"Chay," he repeated, louder, and she hesitated.

He was still sitting before the bones of the roasted fish—one elbow propped on his knee, an auburn curl blown across his forehead. The kind of boy who sprang out of a story, she thought. The kind born to gallivant across rugby fields and drive fast cars, who had never looked down at his own body and longed to slice it apart with a butcher knife.

For a moment, she allowed herself to despise him for it.

"Are you sure you don't want this?" he asked, holding the jacket out toward her. "I'm not cold."

"You're not?" Her voice a broken reed.

"No. Really."

"But—"

He stood and piled it into her arms, and Chay clutched the fabric and began to cry.

He stayed with her for as long as she would let him.

There was still laundry to wash, she tried to explain, though her voice came out a garble. Still lunch to serve, as the Boys inevitably remembered her when they got hungry. Even working nonstop, she labored beneath an endless mountain of tasks, ever growing. But she pressed into his chest anyway, and he held her to him, his arms steady and strong.

"What's wrong?" he asked, as the sobs wracked her over and over. "What is it, Chay? You can tell me." But she could not confess the ugly things she had done to keep herself special, chosen; could not speak of the price she'd paid, to stay the only heroine in a story not merciful to girls.

"I'm sorry," she whispered, and felt her own face wrinkled and ugly as a baby rat's. Her hands clasped around each other still ice-cold—the jacket had remained bundled in her arms while she cried. "I—you were trying to be *nice*, and—"

Tier made a low sound in his throat. "No need to apologize."

She raised her head. Sunlight slanted across his face, illuminated the scattering of freckles across his cheekbones, the rosy bow of his lips. Clean-shaven, there was something vulnerable about him, and she could imagine him as a child splashing through some clear Rittan creek; as a gawky teen kneeling at his bedroom window like an altar, dreaming of the Island in the falling dark.

"Will I see you again," she said, watery, "before you leave with all your treasure?"

"Yes," he said. "Yes, I will. I mean, you will. I mean—"

A laugh shot out of her, high and unexpected. "Okay," she said, curling her hand around the crook of his elbow. "I'll hold you to that."

His mouth worked, soundless. "Please," he said at last. Then he bowed deeply, in the way of Rittan knights to their queens, and slipped back into the trees.

Chapter 20

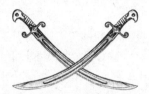

The pines clicked their branches, restless, as Tier picked his way back to his makeshift camp. He could hear the Boys, now—snatches of breeze carried laughter and fervent debates over who had climbed the cliff fastest, dealt the most damage to which pirates. Across the beach, a flock of Everbirds thundered skyward, a rush of glossy wingbeats. Salt wind buffeted his bare arms.

He wished he had asked Chay for more of that ointment.

Chay.

In another life, he might not have thought her beautiful, with her puffed-up face, her swollen nose, the hard knot of her misery. But when she had pressed into his rib cage, her tears soaking into his shirt, a confused chorus had risen beneath his skin, at once exultant and thick with grief.

That an arm might loop through his, gentle as breath. That touch was not just another word for pain.

And yet—perhaps he had presumed too much, in thinking her sadness familiar. They had only spoken twice, and only once when he was fully conscious. Pathetic of him, to fixate on the first person who had ever shown him interest for reasons beyond work or his parents' money. He had read too many comics, watched too many epic movies. Drowned himself in the wrong kinds of stories. Even if they'd saved him, as a kid—even if they'd let him believe in something beyond his brothers' torments, the latest humiliations at school—they had ruined him, too. Deluded him into thinking he could be the kind of person who made the long, heroic speeches, who might command battalions or boardrooms with a fluency easy as breathing.

Weak, chorused his father and brothers, and Tier pushed them away.

The forest thickened, a rumble of boulders and muddy undergrowth that seemed almost to be closing in on him. It had been easier, today, to walk a straight line toward Chay, as if the Island had observed him that first time and decided he meant no harm. And now his return, as well—the pirate ship a sliver of wood in the distance, the salt smell of sea unfolding amid the sharp pine-green.

"Interesting route you're taking," said a familiar voice, and Tier went cold.

Jordan leaned against a tree behind him, sword swinging from her right hip.

"You," he spat, though he kept his distance this time. The bruise across his abdomen was still raw as fresh-ground meat, and after his hour or so with Chay, the fault line along his jaw had cracked open again, his capacity for *articulating* pushed to its limit. "Don't you have b—better things to do than follow me?"

"That depends on where you're going," she drawled, and Tier's brain fizzed out, a grey blip of static.

She knew.

She *knew*.

He imagined her stifled laughter from the brush, as he draped his jacket over Chay's shoulders. The sardonic moue of her mouth as Chay sobbed into his chest. He didn't know which was more humiliating— that he'd been watched, or that it had been *her*.

And then Jordan added, "My sister."

He was not aware of what he was doing until he'd done it. A wild lunge, fists flailing, and then she shifted her stance and his boots slipped on damp moss and he slammed into a tree. The world fractured: stone, sky, bloodied tongue.

Jordan's drawn sword was a quicksilver edge in the afternoon light.

"Always the same," she said evenly as his shoulder throbbed, along with half his face, and he hated her as much as he had ever hated himself. "You kweilo. Snatching up whatever you want and then plugging your ears when someone tries to tell you what you took. Well, Chay is my sister. And you've heard that Boys die on this Island, yeah? She tells Peter when to kill them."

Tier braced himself upright. Some kind of insect had smeared greenish-brown on his white undershirt, and a roar filled in his ears, splintered sound into nonsense.

"No," he said. And then, because swearing was safe, "You fucking liar."

Jordan spread her hands—the prosth balled into a fist, ready to strike. "Why would I lie to you?"

"Why would you not?"

"Ask her, then." A gleam of black eyes, like some deep-sea monster that had crawled out of the mire beneath the coves. "Ask her what happened to the old Kuli, and the old Slightly, and the old Jack, and the old Twins. The Boys still age on the Island, as you well know, and—"

"Fuck off."

A breath, and Jordan's sword was a finger width from his face.

"You asked me why I was here," she said, and he did not answer; was preoccupied with the quivering blade, his eyes crossing as it neared his nose. "I was her and Peter's first collaboration, and I am *this* close to passing their lovely lessons on to you. Don't get in my way, and I won't get in yours."

Above the forest canopy, a gull sliced across noon-blue sky. Tier wet his cracked lips.

"All right," he said peevishly, motioning at the sword. "Enough with the d-d-d—"

His stomach dropped. Heat sheared through his chest.

Damn. Damn.

Jordan had stepped back, something closed off behind her face, and humiliation washed through him, hot and sick.

Saints *fuck.*

They'd made a habit of goading each other during syndicate ops, prodding each other's weak spots, but she'd never had this—the crack in his armor that ran all the way to his heart.

"Dram—" he started, switching to a lilting Erendite accent, but a sound came out of his throat like he was trying to swallow his own tongue, and instead he scooped up a handful of stones and hurled them at the nearest tree.

Why are you still trying? came the whisper in his ear, and through the sharp smell of split cedar, he caught the faint scent of citrus and wood polish. His father's office. *You lost a long time ago.*

"Shut up," he snarled, hurling another rock. When he was twelve, the last time his parents had really made an effort, he had run out of the house in the middle of a tutoring session; been discovered by his brothers in the rose garden, stammering defiantly that he couldn't stand the old woman anymore, that he would simply have to speak this way for the rest of his life. She had been the nation's most venerated speech pathologist, and from then on, his family had treated him not just as a failure but a spectacle. "Shut up, shut up, shut up—"

"Are you done?" Jordan said, and Tier whipped back around, rage still churning beneath his ribs.

"Fuck you to Taram," he barked, his face on fire. But before he could stalk back toward his caves—damn the ship, damn the pirates and the laughter that always hovered at the corners of their mouths—Jordan had sheathed her blade and disappeared; left him standing in a circle of dirt, shaking and on the verge of tears and wishing, nonsensically, that he could go home.

Chapter 21

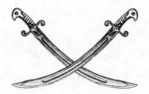

J ordan hoisted herself over the deck rail, adrenaline singing through her veins.

She had not ventured out just to rib Tier—in fact, she'd only spotted him on the way back from scoping out the Boys' house and correctly guessed his intentions. But dealing with a volatile Rittan was the least of her issues. The pirates were stuck in permanent stalemate; brute force attacks from the ground would not suffice against the Boys' flight, especially when no one had guns, and Aku was highly resistant to drawing on their hoard of Dust in battle until they gathered enough to strike decisively.

"We need to end this with one fight, if we use Dust at all," the captain was saying to Jack Two as Jordan snagged a tin cup of abhorrent-tasting coffee from the central pot. The sketch of the Island at their feet had been scribbled over with a new layer of detail: land routes and bridges, meandering trails and squares that denoted scavenging outposts. Aku paused infinitesimally as her shadow slid over it, but gave no other indication that he had noticed her. "Flying uses the most Dust out of everything. Everyone would get half an hour or so at most—"

The sky had gone overcast, the clouds flat and cool and colorless. Baron shuffled to her side, his hand twitching awkwardly in the gap between them, and she caught it, squeezed. She hadn't taken him to be one for physical affection, but she'd woken that morning to find his face mashed against her upper arm, pinkie hooked around hers, and something immense and complicated had shifted beneath her rib cage like a bruise.

Jordan had never been with anyone she considered a friend. Her previous intimate encounters had taken place in anonymous eedro-booming bars or the low-lit Underground arena passage the fighters had dubbed Arena Two, both parties knowing they would walk away at the end of the night. She'd only allowed herself to be split open because it was not real, only cried out names in the throes of ecstasy because they meant nothing to her.

And in terms of friends, she'd only ever had the one.

But here at the edge of things, where memory and Dust withdrawal might unravel her with impunity, she would take whatever Baron offered—knowing, of course, that it would not last.

The captain cleared his throat and Baron snapped to attention, spots of color rising high on his cheeks.

"Sorry," he whispered, as if for both himself and Jordan, and then yelped and almost fell over as she circled her thumb along the inside of his wrist.

Aku sighed, as if he'd been begging for their attention in the first place. "Do I need to repeat that?"

"You want to fight the Boys on Pale territory," Jordan summarized, "to show the Pales how strong we are."

"Exactly," Jack Two said, and promptly received a look from Aku that said *don't encourage them.*

"But why not steal the source of their advantage?" Jordan rested her chin in the crook of Baron's shoulder; he let out a scandalized sort of hiccup but did not shrug her off. "If we got our hands on Tink, and they couldn't produce any more Dust—"

"Not to state the obvious," Aku said dryly, "but Tink is always with Peter."

"And Peter is always with the Boys," chorused several other pirates, as if it was a chant they passed back and forth every time the subject came up.

"Exactly. You wanted one strike," Jordan said, and behind her eyelids, she saw the electric shimmer of San Jukong at night, the hot blast of a firing gun. "Make this it. Burn the house down, flush them out, take the fairy before Peter can disappear into the forest."

"That wolf will smell the kerosene halfway across the Island."

"Spike it with Dust." Jordan sipped her caffeine sludge, grimaced. "And the smoke will keep the Boys from finding each other. So we'll catch Peter by himself."

The captain's gaze flicked to her prosth, his lips pressed into a line. But Jack Two stood expectantly at his shoulder, and Dau and a handful of men were nodding along, and at last Aku pivoted toward the deck, arms thrown wide as if in welcome.

"We're lighting the Boys' base on fire," he shouted, as if it had been his own idea, and the pirates thumped their fists against their chests and roared.

An hour later, Jordan found herself trooping with Baron through an underground passageway toward Peter's house, the better to avoid any Boy or Pale scouts skulking through the woods. Anticipation flickered beneath her skin. A canister of Dust-laced kerosene swung from her wrist, smelling only of water; in front of and behind her, lanterns bobbed in the dark like stars. And she was not on the team charged with capturing Tink—Aku, being captain, had the first crack, along with a thick-muscled swordsman named Nilam—but this was *her* plan. No one had missed the way she'd stood shoulder to shoulder with the captain and Jack Two as they discussed angles of approach, or helped Dau hand out lamps and fuel and chips of flint.

Not that she was gunning for a leadership position. But the pirates would owe her, if they triumphed. Would look on her with more favor when she revealed what she had actually come for.

"So," Baron whispered—in Kebai, as the two pirates directly behind them, Imni and Omni, hailed from northern Hanwa and thus were unlikely to understand. "Are you going to steal her from them, after?"

Tink. No way of saying her name, which they'd never bothered to translate, without the others catching on. Jordan shrugged, caught the lamp sliding off her prosth before it hit the ground. Behind them, the two other men—she could not bring herself to think of them as *the Twins*—muttered in an unfamiliar dialect, lanterns stretching their shadows along the damp stone walls. "After the pirates are safe."

Baron's brows drew together. "But then—wouldn't they come after us, too?"

She felt a rush of affection: that he would not automatically side with them, just for being the larger organization; that the two of them might, for however long this lasted, still be an *us*.

"You heard Aku," she said. "None of the pirates have withdrawal, not really. And if neither side has Dust, maybe they'll figure out how to live together without killing each other."

"Maybe," Baron said, unconvinced.

"The Boys will grow up eventually." A giant stalactite loomed out of the shadows, and she ducked around it. "In a few years, they'll all be on the same side."

"And if some of them want to stay on the Island, but keep flying?"

"I'm sure we could work something out."

"With swords?"

"I mean—" At his expression, she amended hastily, "We could come back. A weekly or monthly restock, though it would be a pain in the arse during storm season—"

"And be the arbiter of who gets Dust and who doesn't?"

"Would you rather it be Peter?"

"So chatty," one of the pirates behind them said pointedly in Rittan, and the two of them lapsed into silence.

The hollow trees, as they emerged squinting into the light, felt oddly airless, high towers flattened by afternoon glare. Laughter floated from the waist-high red mushroom chimney in its center—and faint scolding, so familiar that Jordan blinked twice to make sure she wasn't dreaming. Beside her, Baron's lips were half-parted, and he was swaying slightly, as if he had been struck.

Just the Boys, eating lunch.

The Boys, and Chay.

Adrenaline crackled through Jordan's shins.

She could not choke this time. She would light her fire and get out of the way, give the captain and his strike team as clear a shot as possible through the smoke. But Peter's sword still sheared across her memory, the dizzying well of blood. An ache beneath her sternum as if she'd been punched.

No.

A dark swoop to her vision, and she leaned against the nearest trunk, cursing silently. If she passed out now, the pirates would have to drag her back to the ship, which would open them up as easy targets. And she could not live like this—blindsided by history, defeated by ghosts.

A splash of petrol, pungent and thin.

Jordan looked up. Silent hand signals had gone out among the pirates; Imni, Omni, and the others were pouring their kerosene buckets in tandem around the bases of the trees. Downwind from the openings, to buy them a few more seconds without that godsdamned wolf.

She inhaled, allowed the vertigo billowing through her body to settle into a general wooziness. It was not karsa—not the sharpening of the world into razor edges, the wheeling high, titanium for skin. But it was better than nothing.

She realized, as Baron knelt to strike the spark, that they were burning her sister's tree.

Chapter 22

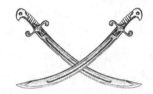

Dread pooled in Chay's gut as she cleared the Boys' plates.

Lunch had been wild boar and garlic bread crisped over the firepit, the ingredients she couldn't scavenge from the Island's hillsides gathered instead from the improbably dry packages—flour, spices, yeast—that periodically washed up on shore. (*The Island's gifts to its Ama*, Peter called them. She never reminded him that those gifts were passed on almost entirely to the Boys.) As always, her mouth had watered despicably at the sizzle of fat, the oil glopped into the pan. But every mouthful that nourished the Boys, that slipped away the hourglass grains of their childhood, was one that did not end up inside her.

Is this strength? asked a voice that was not hers. *Is this courage?*

Chay dumped the Boys' scraps in front of Ael and shivered. Crying had wrung her out, left her hollow, as if she'd been flayed open and stitched back together and the seams did not quite fit. She couldn't remember the last time she'd wept in earnest, and she did not like the raw scratch of her throat, the puffiness of her nose.

Yet Tier's jacket lay heavy on her shoulders. Not exactly warm, but a shield between her and the drafts that blew down the hollow trees.

It had been so long, she thought, since someone had been *kind*.

Which was enough for heat to prick her eyes again. Chay turned toward the wall, swallowed hard. She had made a place for herself, on the Island—molded her body and mind into a story she could finally belong to, when Jordan had looked at her and seen only a liability.

And so: She could get through this. Had no choice but to get through this.

The Island was the only place she would ever belong.

"Amaaaaaaa," Peter sang behind her, and she knew without looking that he was skimming across the ceiling, that mischievous glint in his robin's-egg eyes. "It's story time. Can you tell us a new one?"

"Yeah," Kuli said. "The old crap is so boring."

"I did like the one about the spider and—"

"Shut up, Tudo."

"Yeah, Tudo. Nobody asked you."

"Amaaaaa, Kuli's being meeean—"

"Boys." Chay clapped her hands, her back still turned. A pause—one more breath, to smooth the edges of her facade.

They had not asked where she had found the jacket. They had not noticed at all.

When she turned back around, her smile was flawless.

"All right, darlings," she said, and the Boys crowded forward, elbowing each other in the ribs as they settled at her feet. "I've got a new one for you. Once upon a time there was a boy from a faraway land..."

She spun a tale of high adventure—a prince born to great wealth but made poor by his father's gambling, forced to journey across the desert to restore his family's name. There were dragons and floating cities, androids and streets of slick rainbows. Her throat was still cracked and dry from that morning; conjuring duels between armored tigers did little to soothe it, or sharpen the dull grey fog between her temples.

But she was not as cold as she had been. The fire crackled at her back, seeping into the dark of Tier's jacket, and her shoulders loosened, the clench of her spine. As if she had stepped out of a smog-thick city into clear-skied countryside, and realized what she'd been breathing before was not air.

What if, she wondered, the boy met a girl? What if she asked for an adventure, too, and he took her with him?

A low growl broke through the cadence of her voice, and she tensed. Ael had risen from his place by the fire, hackles raised. *Danger.*

The Boys' heads had all shot up at once.

"Pirates," Peter bellowed, and the spell that was story time popped like a soap bubble: Chay rendered invisible again, a doll tossed on a shelf as the Boys acted out the narratives that mattered. "To arms, to arms! Doors in thirty seconds, hup-ho!"

As the Boys scrambled for swords and knives and axes, refilled the leather pouches around their necks with the old wine bottle they kept full of Dust, Chay turned and turned on her heels, her pulse quickening. She had watched Tier vanish over the slope of a hill, assumed he'd made it to whatever camp he must have set up near the mermaid coves. But if he'd returned to "help" her, if he had decided Peter and the Boys were just children playing with knives, oh, she should have warned him, she should have told him these were not just boys.

And if it was Jordan up there, with her sword and her fury—

Chay breathed in again, and smelled petrol.

"Fire," she shouted, and she could feel it now, the breeze flickering through the pinned-up curtains too warm and thick with ash. "Get out, Boys, all of you, *now*," and then they were shouting, jumping, a flash of bare feet disappearing up wooden throats that might burn them alive. Her own hands gripped the mouth of her tree, brittle and unlikely; heat blew back her braid, the fabric of her dress, and Ael bayed at her heels, yellow eyes blazing.

She breathed, breathed again. Free, at last, from the cold.

There was not enough air.

Go.

That voice again, not hers, and she heaved herself up her hollow tree.

*   *   *

The smoke was a living thing, a breathing thing. As Chay emerged aboveground, coughing, the elms were already pillars of flame, crowns blazing gold against the roil of dark. *No no no*, a feral scream, Kuli or Jack or Peter, she couldn't tell who, and then a *howl*, singeing the hairs on the back of her neck.

"Run, Ama!" Peter tugged her arm, the perfect gentleman when she was in danger. But he did not offer her Dust, and she did not have the breath to ask for it. "Run!"

She stumbled backward, fell. Her palms stung with pine needles; pain rang through her tailbone, but the heat was a giant mouth devouring and so she hitched up her dress and lurched back upright, every breath a gasp, legs churning as if underwater. Shadows loomed out of the undergrowth, gleaming eyes and sword edges singing white, but she slipped between them, a ghost, a memory of herself, until heat no longer clawed at her back, until the blaze was beyond the next hill, until the air eddied cool around her legs and she was safe, safe, safe.

Chay braced herself against a tree, spitting ash. Her lungs heaved; her knees and shins were raw with cuts, the forest floor a switchblade opened only in flame.

"Peter," she coughed, because she did not dare speak *his* name, even here. The right sleeve of the jacket had been scored by a branch, and mud caked the front, but otherwise it was fine, *she* was fine. "Peter. Jack. Tudo—" Another step forward, and her legs did not give out so much as slide from beneath her hips. The ground convulsed, sickening. "Kuli—"

She was still trying to find her balance when the clearing exploded.

Chapter 23

Baron crouched behind a stand of boulders, shirt collar pulled up over his nose and mouth, and tried desperately not to retch.

He had managed, this time, to observe the proceedings with something like detachment—his hands striking the flint chips together; Aku and Nilam spiraling through the canopy with Peter trapped between them; even the explosion, which Baron had predicted by virtue of the Boys always leaving their wine bottle of Dust behind and warned the pirates of accordingly. As steel clashed over his head, muffled by the close-hanging smoke, Baron retreated to the thick of the forest, breathing shallow through his mask of shirt fabric, and scoured the trees for signs of the others.

Minimal engagement, Jordan had promised—the pirates would light the fire, Aku and Nilam would grab Tink, and they would all slip away before the Boys realized what they had lost.

Then the body had thudded down beside Baron like a bird shot from the sky.

Numbness crept over him as he crawled toward it. His vision in flashes: a clenched hand, an acne-scarred cheek, the gash Peter had drawn across his throat laughing like an open mouth. *Aku*. The man's maroon coat was rucked across the mud like some extravagant, broken plumage; blood oozed a puddle around his head, and the smell of urine tanged the smoky air.

"I'm sorry," Baron choked. He knew Jordan had not been fond of the captain, knew Aku would have let her be slaughtered by the Boys rather than allow her to take a shred of his authority. But the dead were the dead, and they deserved what meager respect he could offer. "I'm so sorry."

"Baron?"

He looked up. A shadow was moving between the trees, vague in the rippling heat. But he would know that stride from its barest gesture, a single flickered frame.

"Over here," he called, and then she was staggering toward him, another man's arm draped over her shoulder, the ash smear of her face almost indistinguishable from the surrounding trees.

Closer: Nilam, his head lolled sideways, arms limp and dragging. The wound above his heart a million light-years wide.

Baron rocked back on his heels, and it felt like free fall.

"So he got his final duel with Peter." Jordan's eyes, rimmed pink, flicked down toward Aku. Nilam—Nilam's corpse—slipped out of her grasp, and Baron grimaced as its thick limbs splayed like a marionette's.

"Yeah," he said. Bile tainted the back of his mouth. "But all *we* did was start a fire."

They both looked toward it—seven towers of orange, a devouring city. Earlier, the pirate scouts had double-checked that the ground was still damp, in hopes of containing the conflagration, but the trees were old and tall and would burn for a long time.

"The Boys will be pushed aboveground, at least," Jordan said. A new cut gaped across her shoulder, and Baron could not tell if the blood staining Nilam's shoulder belonged to the dead man or to her. "We won't have to squeeze down any of the hollow trees to get to them. This is almost over."

"Jordan," Baron choked out.

"Yes?"

He rubbed his eyes. An all-consuming sense of unreality had fallen over him at the sight of Aku's corpse—at the man who had been shouting orders just an hour ago, now spilled out for the earth to drink. And Nilam, blood congealed down his torso, his eyes frozen as if in surprise. Baron slid them closed; shuddered at the warmth that dusted his fingertips.

"They're dead," he said, his throat thick. "All that fighting, and they're just—gone."

"If we don't get moving," Jordan said, though not harshly, "we will be, too."

He wrapped her shoulder with a strip of Aku's undershirt, felt her full-body flinch as his fingers accidentally brushed the wound ("Sorry." "Don't."). As he pulled Aku's arm across his back, the sword clamor faded; he wondered if the Boys and pirates had moved elsewhere, or retreated to tend to their injuries.

They began to walk—back toward the ship, the corpses' heels dragging mud. A muscle pulled along Baron's spine; his head spun from inhaling smoke. Charcoal sweat slicked Jordan's face, and he wondered about infection: if particles of ash could contaminate the blood, if her arm was swelling, if she was running a fever—he pushed down a wild laugh. Impossible to determine that when they were trudging past a *forest fire*, and the only thermometers within reach were cracked and waterlogged antiques buried in silt beneath the mermaid coves. And the Island made no promises—no one would draw him a warm bath, after this; no one would wash his gore- and mud-crusted clothes while he slept, or heat up breakfast when he woke again. And he was so tired of *feeling* all of it, because feeling meant hurting, meant being afraid, but maybe this was what it meant to grow up in the end, to see the tide rise and know you were powerless to stop it—

"Hey," Jordan said hoarsely.

He could taste his lungs, all burnt flesh and char. "Yeah?"

"You're doing it again."

He shuddered a breath, choked against the pain that knifed his sternum. Squeezed his eyes shut. It must be tremendously boring, he thought, for whatever minor god up in the heavens was recording his life—every storm a catastrophe, every slight malfunction ballooned into a system-wide alarm.

Aku's arm slipped, and Baron fumbled for the man's waist, pressing into rib cage and lean muscle.

He could not do this. He absolutely, fundamentally could not do this.

" 'It,' " he choked out. Adrenaline pricked the soles of his feet. "Yeah. Yeah, I know."

"What if you, ah, set a beat? Breathe in time with your footsteps."

Baron looked down at his shoes—battered and fraying, the leather barely recognizable beneath the mud and ash. *In. Out.* Embarrassingly loud. But better than looking at either of the corpses, or at her. *In. Out.* His shoulders ached; his legs trembled. *Out.* Jordan edged a step ahead and then paused, contemplating a patch of incongruously blue sky *in* and here was his throat sealing shut, lightning through his ribs *in* what if they never captured Tink *in* what if Jordan ran the pirates out of their Dust supply *in* they had chosen this and now *in* there was no way out *in* but hadn't he wanted *in* hadn't he chosen—

in

in

in

"Baron, take a break," Jordan snapped, "take a fucking break," and Baron lay Aku back on the ground and tucked his head between his knees and breathed and breathed and breathed, his face radiating shame.

Chapter 24

Jordan propped her bandaged arm against the ship's railing and watched the waves roll dark beneath her feet.

Past midnight now, the sky a vault of jewels, the wind edged in cold. The fire had died down—Peter's hollow trees indistinguishable from the rest of the forest, this far out at sea, but she could see no flicker of amber, no small, misplaced suns.

It was the first time she'd ridden the ship off land, despite it being a functioning vessel. A precaution, perhaps—several patches crowned the hull, and its two masts were scarred in the aftermath of swords; she had a vague childhood memory of bashing them with a torch. Aku and Nilam lay wrapped in spare hammocks, arms crossed over unmoving chests. They would be buried in the depths—an homage to how they'd reached the Island, and to keep the Boys from plundering their bones.

Pain throbbed through her forearm, marrow-deep and terrifying, and she turned back toward the sea.

There had not been enough Dust, this time, to patch her up entirely. On her return to the ship, Dau's hand had braced her elbow, then her shoulder, and she'd felt a slow squeeze of flesh at which she'd nearly blacked out, a golden itch of congealing tendon and muscle and vein. But the ache lingered. The gaping mouth of the wound—which she only imagined, as Baron wrapped her arm again—had not fully sealed, and a hot wetness pressed against her skin, the air tinged with iron if she breathed in too deep.

She thought of that karsa-addicted fighter, Gao Leng, shaking and irrevocable, and nausea bloomed in her stomach.

We won't have to squeeze down any of the hollow trees. They had flushed the Boys out permanently, or at least given them one less place to run. If they were hiding in some dank temporary cave, she might simply stroll in, snatch Tink from Peter's sleep-stilled shoulder—

"Jordan?"

She turned. Dau had risen from where they'd knelt beside Aku's body, murmuring something like a last blessing. Most of the crew had already done the same—heads bowed before the dead pirates as if praying to saints, last secrets whispered in their late captain's ear. None of them had shown the remotest surprise when Jordan and Baron had emerged from the forest with the bodies; from that, and the number of weapons in the ship's armory attributed to unfamiliar names, she had concluded that pirate deaths were not uncommon.

But just because you were nursing old wounds didn't mean new ones hurt any less.

Dau nodded across the deck. "You're welcome to say a few words, if you'd like."

"—the reason they're dead," someone muttered, but when Jordan whipped around to scan the ash-greyed faces, she could not tell who had spoken.

The crew parted for her anyway as she made her way across the deck. In their captain's absence, they seemed not quite sure of where to stand—though Dau, Jack Two, and Mateo had begun to drift toward her, which bubbled a feeling like laughter through her rib cage.

Cold spasmed down her back, and she ground her teeth against the shudder. *Fever.* A clock ticking down too soon.

The pirates watched her, and in their hooded eyes she saw grief and rage and resignation.

"Aku," she said. Her boots creaked the planks. "Nilam."

The men's hammocks had been stitched closed, save for around their faces, and the thick canvas hid the red yawn of the captain's throat, Nilam's pulped wound of a heart. Ironic, that their blood had not bothered her as she and Baron hauled them through the trees. Perhaps she should have been ashamed—her brain's shutdowns contingent on some twisted narcissism, the betrayal of her own skin daring to break. But the only thing that kindled inside her now was a slow-burning fury.

Aku may not have liked her, but he and Nilam had fought tooth and nail just to survive. And in the end, the alternative had been so quick. So easy.

"You deserved better," she told them. The other pirates had paid their respects in relative privacy, but the chill was spreading through her body, and her arm and shoulder radiated heat; if she knelt, she was afraid she would not rise again. So she shifted her weight against the pitch and yaw of the deck, and let her words carry.

She hadn't known them long, she said. But she knew the Island, knew what it took to carve out even a semblance of a life here. Respected them for staying. Wished she could have met them earlier.

"It was an honor to serve," she said, and stepped back.

A shift of shadow, behind her—Mateo, eyes shining before he turned away.

The ceremony did not last much longer. Tier spoke next, slurring and reeking of whiskey, then Baron, his expression shifting and wild, gaze frittering away from hers. At last Dau and Jack Two heaved the bodies overboard—a twinned splash, like a punch in the chest, and the hammock-shrouds vanished beneath the waves.

Jordan braced her back against the ropes, fighting to stay upright.

It was becoming more difficult. The seed of a spasm clenched her spine; nausea roiled through her every time she turned. Above her head, the ship's masts seemed surreal and weightless, etched in chalk against an endless slate of black sky.

She still harbored a half-baked plan to slip away tonight, after the burials—to steal Tink before the Boys realized how vulnerable they'd become outside the hollow trees. But as the crew filed belowdecks and she, attempting to follow, slid sideways into the doorframe, she realized she was going to lose a hell of a lot more time than she'd anticipated.

"You're in withdrawal again." Baron appeared at her side, a doubled crease between his brows.

"Astutely observed, doc." Pain jagged her left side with every step; hammocks and racks of weaponry loomed out of the torch-dusk as she swayed toward the washroom. She managed to kick open the door before everything in her convulsed, and something yellowish and stringy splattered the floor. She coughed, spat. "Godsdammit."

"I'll clean up," Baron said immediately, and she despised this—the rising stink, the crew's studiously turned backs. The fucking pity in Baron's eyes, when he'd been gasping at the caress of her fingers the night before. But her stomach was an open wound, the inside of her head cotton-thick. She blinked and he was on his knees, scrubbing the planks with a washcloth.

"I can do it," she insisted, though her voice came out strange and dim.

"I'm almost done."

Another twist of heat, and she shoved past him and retched into the basin. *Fuck. Fuck.* Her teeth were clattering like motorcycle engines. She had only needed one more night.

"I'm sure Dau can spare some more Dust," Baron said, maneuvering the washroom door closed between them and the pirates' curious eyes. "You could borrow against tomorrow's share, or we could split—"

"I can last the night," Jordan muttered. "If I borrow, it'll just—keep borrowing—"

Her toothbrush appeared at her elbow, and his toothpaste, the bright logo incongruous against the weathered planks. When she had brushed and spat, she pried open the washroom door, the ship's bowels a slippery flash of dark.

"We can go to my cabin." Baron, at her elbow. "Purely for, ah, purposes of medical supervision—"

"Don't make me laugh or I'll puke on you."

A nudge at her stomach—a chewed-up plastic bucket, likely meant for bailing. "Please aim. I'm tired."

"Okay," she said, as another tremor spasmed through her. "Okay." And his shoes stepped into the echoes hers left, and his knuckles grazed her newly wrapped bandages, and it was almost enough to hold her up.

Chapter 25

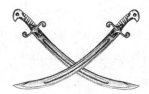

Baron did not watch Jordan sleep.

He felt his way along the dark hold, one hand along the wall to make up for his Dustless vision, the smell of her vomit rising lightly from his shirt. She had kicked him out after a few minutes of mutual tossing and turning—*You're hovering*, she'd snapped, *take a lap, I'll be fine*—but he sensed that another wave of pain had seized her, that she did not want him seeing her ill any more than he had to. Yet even as he shuffled forward, fingertips trailing off the weathered edge of her cabin's doorframe, fear thrummed beneath his skin—from the heat that had radiated from her forehead when he'd pressed his lips to it; the chatter of her teeth, as she'd pulled the thick furs tight around her shoulders.

Jordan may have mocked him for his seclusion within the university bubble, but he'd spent his fair share of time downtown. Seen the greasy-haired teenagers begging and shaking outside hawkers' stalls, the old men curled beside gutters who even the medics couldn't be bothered to cart away. There were stages to addiction, he'd read on the internet after Jordan was kicked out of her parents' apartment. Casual experimentation. Problem usage.

Dependence.

Baron's hand met the edge of another doorframe, and he leaned his head against it, exhaled slow.

Jordan was definitely addicted to Dust; had probably become addicted to karsa, too. Either way, the Island could not give her what she needed.

"You all right?"

He straightened, squinting. A shadow blocked his way, tall and swaying slightly, though he could not make out its features in the vague flicker of the hold's lanterns. Heat rushed to his face. "Sorry, I can't—who—?"

"It's Tier," his interlocutor said quickly, and Baron's flush deepened as he recognized the timbre of the pilot's voice, the slight waft of alcohol. "Are you—er—looking for your cabin? I think it's behind you."

"Ah," Baron started, "I'm just"—and then spent a full five seconds groping for a verb—"taking a walk."

A supremely awkward pause, the darkness between them yawning and stretching, and Baron *felt* the moment they realized, in unison, that he wouldn't be able to tell when he had returned to his own door.

At last, Tier shuffled backward, a small sound his throat like a cough. "She's in withdrawal again, isn't she."

"Er." Baron was briefly disoriented—Tier, attending to Jordan's health?—before he realized her retching would have been difficult for anyone on the ship to block out. "Yes. Unless it's infection, or, well. Something else."

"Ah." Another silence, albeit more thawed-out than the last. Then, unexpectedly: "You still love her, though, don't you? Even if she— No matter what she does?"

Baron blinked. He hadn't pegged the pilot as someone particularly interested in *feelings*, especially not with as new an acquaintance as Baron. And, too, he dared not think of what he felt for Jordan as love—not yet. Even if she'd kissed him, even if she'd meant it, pinning such a word between them would imply that, in all the time he had known her, he had never dreamed of drowning, or of being impaled on a Lost Boy's sword. Never lay down on his dormitory cot and wished he would never wake again.

Though he wasn't quite inclined to disclose that to Tier, of all people.

"Jordan has done a lot of things," he said evasively, and then stumbled backward until he stood at her door again, his face hot, something trembling deep in his rib cage.

The wood paneling gave way at his touch.

Jordan had fallen asleep at last, he saw as he worked the latch, inched backward toward the bed. Her shirt was rucked up halfway, her bandaged arm laid out crosswise to facilitate circulation; as he arranged himself neatly at the edge of the cot, tugging the fur blankets over his chest, he could feel her encroaching on the handbreadth between them—shoulder to shoulder, spine to spine.

And fear filled him again, for a death that was not his.

For the past nine years, from the night she'd first told him about using karsa, he'd imagined her end, the final flare of a dying star; had resigned himself to loving her from a distance, while he could—and in the clawing, desperate corners of his mind, vowed to go first, or shortly after. But then last night: her mouth softening on his as if it had been sculpted to fit there. Her hand trailing his rib cage, despite the overactive stutter of his heart underneath—

Warmth worked its way up Baron's neck. He closed his eyes, pushed down the thunder that doubled his pulse. *The worst possible time—*

"You awake?"

The speed at which his eyes sprang back open was highly embarrassing. "Yes," he said, and flushed harder as his voice cracked.

She mumbled something he couldn't decipher.

"What?"

The cot groaned—she had rolled toward him, her breath a cloud of mint. "Want to distract me?"

"Distract?"

She drew her thumb along his jaw and he stilled, heat coiling beneath his navel. "Provide various complimentary medical services. Pain relief, and so on."

"Oh my gods."

"Is that a yes?"

"Aren't you—*going through withdrawal*? I mean—" He had lost his words again. He was reeling. "Are you sure—"

"Yes," she whispered, "and we'll get the bedsheets washed tomorrow, swear on my life—" And then they were curving toward each other in the dark, fumbling against the worn wooden planks as the ocean murmured and the Island stirred in its un-sleep and the pirates beyond snored or passed the time in their own ways. He dared not touch her bandages, but her lips found the dip of his temple, the curve of his ear, and though he could barely wrap his mind around the next month, the next year—could not envision himself returning to Burima, or rebuilding anything like a life—her hand guided his downward, a softness he had not allowed himself to even think about, and in that moment he would have poured himself out for her, he would have given her anything.

Chapter 26

Jordan blinked awake in the middle of the night, her arm pounding in time with her heart.

She was not sure what had woken her. The sky through the porthole was a plush, star-studded black; the preceding hours had not involved sleep as much as slurred fragments of memory, a reaching beneath her skin for a warm languor that might dull the pain. Beside her, Baron had gone so still he could have been catatonic; in the seam of light from the covered lantern, his lips were slightly parted, dark hair mussed across his sweaty forehead. A more than decent distraction, she thought, eyeing the mark that had bloomed on his throat. About an hour in, she had finally caved and dosed herself with another quarter-pouch of Dust— but perhaps this could lower the threshold she needed to keep going.

A shift beyond the door, and she stilled.

It was not so much sound as feeling, intent. She slowed her breath on instinct, braced herself against the lingering tremor of withdrawal. Took inventory, as she had in her old apartment: broadsword leaning on the far wall, daggers tucked in her waistband and at her back.

Perhaps Jack Two stood outside her door, making his rounds; perhaps Dau was handing out the day's Dust rations earlier than usual. But Jordan had not survived nine years of First Circle San Jukong by assuming benevolence beyond her walls.

A metallic clink, so soft it could have been a sigh.

Then the door banged open: a rush of bodies and steel, faces wrapped in black cloth, and she threw one knife *thump* as the lantern blew out. A muffled scream *Baron* and her heart dropped and she threw again, a guesswork in the dark, another thud, a grunt of pain—

Light flared through the cabin—Dau, lit from below, murder in their eyes.

"Stop," they roared, drawing their sword. "What in Taram are you doing?"

The men—two of them—were crumpled on the ground, Jordan's daggers embedded sloppily in one's chest, the other's eye. Before Dau could help them up, Jordan staggered from the cot and slashed both their throats.

And then she turned.

Baron had sat up in bed—shirtsleeves shredded, his arms and face a mess of blood. But his shoulders were shaking, his mouth a rounded O as he gulped for air.

He was still alive.

An unfamiliar heat rushed to Jordan's eyes. "Baron?"

His hands curled at his throat, wide eyes staring at nothing. "Saints," he wheezed, his breath coming too fast. "I can't—no—*aah*—"

"Baron. Hey." Her arms around him, squeezing hard, and he tilted his head toward the ceiling, hyperventilating so hard she thought he might retch. "I killed them. They're gone."

"They're—" Cough, gasp, and his whole body shuddered. "Who?"

On the floor, a muffled thump. Dau had yanked the cloth masks from both attackers' faces—Imni and Omni, empty black eyes mirrored even in death.

"They tried to kill us," Jordan said—her voice separate from the rest of her body, loud and clear enough for the whole ship to hear. Then, lower, to Dau: "Baron needs Dust. He can use mine."

"Saints." Dau plucked the knives from the dead twins' slackened grips. The lines of their face were drawn deeper when they looked up, as if they had aged five years in as many minutes. "There have been fights before, on this ship. Those who wanted too badly to be captain, or gained a taste for killing and couldn't stop, even among their own crew. But most of us here—we were Lost Boys. We grew up seeing Peter—we *know* what it's like—" And their face filled with such a desolate grief that Jordan averted her eyes.

She sprinkled Baron's wounds with Dust from the corpses' pouches; fixed her eyes on Dau's lantern as Baron, with shaking hands, did the same for the reopened cut on her shoulder. Then, with the assistance of Dau—and Jack Two, who had woken to the quartermaster's shouts—they hung hammocks in the main hold, as if any of them had a chance of sleeping the rest of the night. Baron dropped his bundle several times, his eyes glazed; an electric current ran beneath Jordan's skin, edging the room in nearly karsa-sharp detail, and she found herself pacing the ship end to end, checking with every lap that Imni and Omni still lay dead on the floor.

By then, most of the other pirates had roused, squinting suspiciously from their hammocks.

"Self-defense," Jordan said, motioning at Baron to show his slashed-open forearms, and the two of them filled in Dau's more orderly retelling of the affair.

Then silence, an uneasy shift in the air, and Jordan studied the rest of the pirates one by one. A few of them nodded acknowledgment, but a handful held her gaze a moment too long: Jack One, and Rien, and the grey-eyed Rittan who'd often sat with Imni, Omni, and Aku during meals—Seida, she remembered after a moment—before they looked away.

Of course, Jordan thought bitterly. Aku was never the only one who thought her a leech on the pirates' Dust supply, who saw her as a threat to the crew's very existence. And that voice across the deck last night, accusing—at least one person blamed her, as well, for the captain's and Nilam's deaths. But the pirates needed fighters, needed bodies. She could not simply throw around her accusations and expect people to get exiled, especially since she was the one who'd just arrived.

"Are you going back to sleep?" Baron asked a few minutes later, sitting upright in his new hammock as she handed him a mug of heavily sugared coffee. Several furs had been draped around his shoulders, but he was sickly pale, and swayed with every rise and fall of the ship. "I don't think—" And then he trailed off, his face gone slack as if he'd forgotten he was speaking.

Jordan clenched her fist. Slow dark rage pulsed through her; she would have killed Imni and Omni again, sliced them open slow and laughed as they screamed.

"Drink up," she said. "Your lips are turning purple."

Baron raised the mug, his hands unsteady. "But why?" he asked in Kebai, sipping carefully, and she knew he didn't mean the cup of gritty sludge she was forcing him to imbibe. "We haven't—*done* anything to them. They agreed to the fire bit, too. Aku was acting like—like he came up with it himself."

Billow of smoke, Nilam's heart torn open. The splash of sail-wrapped bodies sinking into the sea.

"Well, there's this," she said, raising her prosth. "There are the stories about the first captain, and half the ones that came after."

"Hm," Baron said, neutral. "And—is that something you want, too?"

Jordan gripped the edge of her hammock: a precarious proposition, with her prosth dead and her left shoulder aching, and the damned lurch of cloth every time she tried to swing herself in. But the pirates who wanted her out, however many there were, could not see her weak, and so she let Baron tug the fabric open, settled in cautiously.

She had come for Tink, and Tink alone; harbored no desire to lead a fractious group of mostly men, nor claim the fate that seemed to befall every captain on the Island. Yet, still sapped by withdrawal as she was, in so tight a space as her cabin, and two would-be murderers each at least half again her weight—there were limits to what she could fight.

And she could not stay awake forever.

She thought Dau liked her well enough, and Mateo—and even Jack Two, Aku's former first mate, who might have named himself the pirates' leader by now if not for the sheer density of myth-history-expectation wrapped around Jordan's residual limb. But she would sleep more soundly at night if the majority of the crew was on her side. They all knew how the story went: Anyone could cut off the lives of the other pirates, but captains—captains faced off against Peter. The crew itself did not touch them.

Baron was sipping the last of his coffee, his eyes huge in his face. Jordan thought of that brief, shadowed stillness before the attack—his cheekbones limned by firelight, the steady rise and fall of his chest.

A soundness of sleep that, knowing him, he would not find again for a long time.

"I promised," she said, still in Kebai, "that we would be all right."

His grin was wry. "I know your word means a lot to you, but—"

"Here, it does," she said fiercely. "To you, it does."

And then, because she could not stand the way he was looking at her, she added, "Eejit," flicked him lightly on the forehead, and lurched back out of the hammock for another lap around the hold.

PART FOUR

So much pretending
can bring a girl to her knees.
                    —Sally Wen Mao, "Anna May Wong Dreams
                                    of Wong Kar-Wai"

Chapter 27

Tier clambered through the damp undergrowth, his head the bruise-soft emptiness that always followed a hangover.

He'd lost control again, the night before. Returned from hunting treasure and repairing his ship to find the pirates smoke-smudged and grim as they wrapped corpses in sailcloth, no one to protest when he cracked open the whiskey barrel, and so he'd filled his cup again and again, let his sense of his body spin out from under him; swallowed with the urgency of not knowing when his next drink would come. A blurry memory of staggering through the hold, Baron's face squinting at him in the dimness, but the rest of the night was loose and slippery, and he'd lazed away the subsequent morning and afternoon in intermittent bouts of achy half-sleep.

Now—as the moon stared down again, chastising him for a whole day wasted—he felt raw and wobbly as an uncooked egg.

And his abdomen was still sore from Jordan's fist.

Starlight stitched the trees in faint silver thread. Through the blowing branches, he caught a rill of children's laughter, the thick smell of campfire smoke and fresh-cut wood.

A wisp of white fabric.

She tells Peter when to kill them.

Tier slowed, the throb between his temples lurching back toward nausea. Thought of Chay scrambling out of the creek, face alight with eagerness, her fingers daubing grey relief on his sun-blistered cheeks. He knew how a demon might put on a human face in the daylight, how smiles and good manners could be shrugged off as easily as a coat. But he could not believe she had set out to harm her Boys.

Jordan's smile, mocking. *Why would I lie?*

He found Chay dumping plastic buckets into a shallow trench, the sleeves of his jacket rolled up above her elbows. Strange grey spots rippled on her dress, and he thought they were moths until she stepped into a shaft of moonlight: scorch holes.

Tier breathed smoke again, and was afraid.

"Chay," he said softly.

She jerked her head up, scanning the darkness until she found him. Nearby, the Boys giggled and bashed what sounded like wooden planks; she held up a silent hand—*no farther*—and picked her way around the trench toward him, her brows drawn. Floating bright over the underbrush, her skirt hitched up by a delicately curved wrist, she could have been a girl out of a myth, she could have been a ghost.

"You shouldn't be here," she whispered as soon as she came close enough. "The Boys are right there, and it's almost their bedtime, they're low on Dust—"

"I know," Tier said, in a quick Erendite lilt. "I'm sorry. Something came up. But—what happened to you?"

"The pirates burned down our house yesterday. Everyone's fine." Her expression flickered in a way Tier couldn't place. Then she reached up and traced her thumb along the edge of his cheek, still an angry purple-red from its encounter with the tree, and his knees went weak. "What happened to *you?*"

"I—" Tier started, and wondered if she was ensorcelling him—her hand at the seams of his throat, his chest, and he would fall open, rib cage gushing secrets. He gathered himself hastily, or attempted to. "What d'you mean, the pirates burned your house? Have they ever done it before? Why now—"

"Hush," Chay said—his voice had begun to rise—and he clamped his mouth shut, face burning. Embarrassment bladed the insides of his knees: He didn't even need to be drunk to lose control. And soon, too soon, she would stop looking at him the way she was now. Her gaze would shift a little each time he stumbled, aversion building millimeter by millimeter, until she saw only the fumbling wretch at whom everyone else jeered.

But for tonight—

"We're all safe," she murmured, dropping her hand, and he grieved its absence. "We're all alive. That's enough."

Her eyes gleamed in the dark, orbs of polished onyx, and he thought: There had to be another explanation. He knew what it was to hate—to press the ice pack against an ankle, a rib cage, and imagine tearing apart the person who had tried to break him. But Chay had had a thousand chances to sic the Boys on him, and chosen not to.

Jordan's voice, grating. *Ask her.*

"I f-fell," he said, wincing at the twitch of the fricative. "The—floors of the coves are slippery."

"So the pirates haven't gotten to you yet?" Chay asked, not quite wry.

He thought of his vomit splashed chunky yellow-green across the whiskey barrel, a dozen pairs of staring eyes. "Not exactly."

She glanced over her shoulder. Far off, the thud of metal on wood, and childish voices arguing—the Boys still unaware of her absence.

"They're building a new house," she said, pulling her jacket tighter. "It's aboveground, this time. They have a whole crate of nails that washed up on shore this morning. So be careful where you step."

"I will," Tier promised.

Ask.

He hesitated. As he'd fitted new planks for his ship, scraped barnacles off ancient compasses, he had basked in the fantasy, however foolish, in which he invited her along. They would sail the islands together, ease their way back into civilization. She could leave behind the hurt she wouldn't talk about, whatever had caused her to clutch his jacket like it was the first gift she had ever been given; he would melt down his old armor, forge something new from the dregs.

But he needed to know that she was not who Jordan claimed she was.

He said, as neutrally as he could, "I saw your sister."

Silence, punctuated only by birdsong. They had wandered away from the clearing, and he could not read Chay's face.

She said, "She told you, then."

"Not the specifics." Not much at all. But the hatred in Jordan's expression had spoken as much as her words.

"It's not the sort of thing one can apologize for."

"The—" Tier swallowed. "The arm?"

"No, no. She was born with that." A patch of moonlight, and they skirted around it, the edges of her bare feet shining pale and lovely. "And I know it's no excuse, that I was ten years old. I've seen plenty of ten-year-olds do horrific things, Kuli is only eight—" She trailed off. "But I didn't *know*, back then. I'd never imagined Peter might—I didn't understand what would happen."

Tier waited, pine needles and mud tamped soundless beneath his heels. He did not remember being ten—or rather, he could, but only via extrapolation. His mother had taken him out of the private school by then in favor of home tutoring; his brothers would have been thirteen and fourteen and sixteen. There would have been riotous laughter—not his—and nights in his room without supper, and the private nurse only called when he had broken a bone.

The publicity team, with their powders and brushes and NDAs, would have taken care of the rest.

"She was a Twin," said Chay. "Or at least, pretending to be. They weren't—aren't—related."

"Ah," said Tier.

"They don't even look alike." Her mouth twisted in disgust. "But by the time I came to the Island, they were always together, flying off with their swords and their Dust. And I was just the Ama, washing their dishes—" A wet gulp, and when she spoke again, her voice was thick. "She barely looked at me. It was like—I wasn't even there."

Adrenaline prickled Tier's palms, sealed his throat shut. He may not have remembered being ten, but the belts and fists and locked doors echoed across time. Scattered its meaning until all he held in his hands was a fragmented mosaic of pain.

"I'm sorry," he said—to her, and to the child he'd been, curled up and whimpering in the corner of his too-large room. "Chay—"

She had paused at the base of a wizened pine, arms stiff at her sides. The collar of her jacket trembled with her shoulders. Tier felt another pang: He had stood that way so many times, facing the mahogany monstrosity of his father's desk.

"When she got her period—" Chay's voice faltered, and he reached out on impulse—found her hand in the dark, cold as buried bone. She squeezed gratefully. "And oh, gods, I knew what *that* meant, at least, my ama had told me before I'd left—"

She stopped again, at the ragged edge of an exhale. "I—I told Peter," she whispered. "I told him Jordan was a girl. And he went after her, he—I didn't think they—like she was one of the feral *boars* they chase through the forest—"

She broke without a sound. Her shoulders heaved, and then she was kneeling before the old pine like an altar, hunched into her own lap, her face crumpled in a silent howl. Above their heads, the trees murmured, the wind thick with coming storm; goose bumps rose on the back of Tier's neck, as if the dark itself craned toward them.

He folded his legs and sat beside her, her hand still fragile in his.

So this was the pain she had been tending, he thought, tracing his thumb in slow circles across her knuckles. This was the grain of sand hidden in her body, except sometimes when sharpness chafed and chafed, it produced no pearl—only a continuous flaying, an ugliness people recoiled from every time you opened your mouth.

Hush, he might have said, but her breath was barely a hiss out of her throat; she seemed as accustomed to silence as he was. *It's all right*, but of course it wasn't, of course some things could not be undone.

He said, instead, "When I was five—"

The *f* caught, jerked back on itself, and his lungs felt as if they had been shot through with crumpled tin. *No.* He couldn't do this. It wasn't worth it.

It was too late to stop.

"When you were five," Chay echoed, barely breathing.

"I b-b-b—I b-began—" Shit. Fuck. One sentence and he was already unraveling. He flattened a hand against his leg, his face hot. *Slowly. Slowly.* "Well." He gestured at his mouth, helpless. "This."

She gave him a look: stubborn, almost defiant. "What about it?"

Something rushed through him, so fierce he felt himself go limp. "My father and brothers hated me for it," he said, twisting his tongue into some approximation of a Glennan brogue before it could catch up to the fact that he was still talking. It worked, sometimes, when he wasn't shatteringly nervous. *No son of mine is going to go around speaking like a fucking refugee.* "They tried to b-b-b—to—" Pause, breath, reset. "To beat it out of me."

A twig pressed into his ankle. He turned it between his fingers, willing away the heat that had taken up residence behind his eyelids. When it subsided at last, he added, "As you can see, they f-f-f—they—it d-d-didn't—" His breath sputtered out, a whisper, and he was so, so small.

"Tier," she said.

"Yes?"

In the dark, she was little more than a shine of eyes, the fabric of her dress tented between bony knees. And then she leaned forward, and her mouth pressed into his, soft and deep and sweet, and Tier was a thing peeled apart, an open wound.

How easily she had broken him, he thought as her hands tangled in his hair, as something between a groan and a sob crawled out of his throat. He had spent two decades building walls that would hold up under siege, and she had laid waste to them in days.

"They're gone now," she whispered, and in the curl of her fingers against his scalp, the press of her other hand in the soft place between his shoulders, he felt something like safe, something like held. "They're Outside. You don't have to carry them with you."

And you? he wanted to ask. *What about your hurts, what about your ghosts?* But the words had slipped out of him, scattered to the night wind, and all he could do was pull her closer.

Here was the Island at night: velvet swaths of pine, the hulking shadow of the central mountain, creek gleaming silver under a fat gibbous moon. Tier draped his arm lightly over Chay's shoulders as she pointed out the stone pillars sheltering the Boys' lagoon from open horizon; the Pales' territory to the west ("Peter allies with them, sometimes, though we're never sure if they're about to eat us"); and, barely a smudge from the high cliffs on which they sat, Marooner's Rock, the jutting black boulder that divided the Boys' territory from the Pales'. The Boys were tucked into bed now—bedtime stories told, Pretend medicine (spiced syrup dissolved in water) spooned into the Twins' mouths to ward off the fake cough they'd developed—and a tightness had gone out of Chay's posture, as if she had laid down a heavy burden.

"I read about this place," Tier said quietly. The night air so still he dared not disturb it, stars glimmering in the vast dome of sky. "Long before I ever thought of coming here. Watched all the m-movies, p-p-played all the games."

"Why this story in particular?" she asked, leaning her head against his shoulder.

Heat flooded his hands, his face. That she would allow him to keep talking and not insist he loop back again, articulate *correctly*—his limbs felt off-kilter, as if he might lean too far forward and pitch straight off the cliff's edge.

"B-b-because—" He bit his tongue until he tasted iron. This was how it always happened: He would fuck up once, and muscle memory

would flood back like a burst dam, and he would break and keep breaking until Da belted him raw.

But there was just her hand resting on his knee, its lightness almost
sharp against his skin. Only her eyes intent on his face, as if he had just
spoken the first sentence of a new story. He blew out his cheeks, began
again. " 'Cause it was sort of—in this world, you know? Like there was
a chance P-P—*he*—might come to my window.

"And I'd always wanted to fly away," he added, his face warming
further. "To f—to find—I don't know. Something else."

"Have you found it?" she asked, her hand sliding up his thigh, and
then she was kissing him again, honey sweetness and ocean salt, and he
was a moan sealed into skin, he was dry brush sparked alight.

Another night, in the cave where he had been collecting his treasure:
crates of jewels huddled like conspirators in one corner, the bow of his
ship-in-progress a panther curve in the dark. There was a strangeness
to the way he was holding his mouth—*Didn't realize your face could
do that*, Jordan had called after him as he'd climbed out of the pirate
ship smiling—after which he had told her to fuck off, become painfully conscious of his expression, and hurried away before she could
interrogate him further. But Chay's hand smoothed his cheek, and he
tried to compose himself into something that wasn't all-out alarming.

"Did you do all this yourself?" she asked, breathless.

Tier shrugged, pride bubbling beneath his sternum as she swept her
lantern from side to side. He had built a system of levers and supports
to expose the ship's half-rotted hull; borrowed an axe from the pirates'
armory to cut fresh pine into planks; dredged up the more deeply buried gemstones and artifacts with an ancient fishing net he'd attached
to a long pole. The process was horrendously slow, but since his arrival,
he'd had nothing but time.

"It's not m-much," he said, and flushed. "There are a lot more ruins
in—in open waters and such."

"But you're rebuilding a ship from scratch." Chay's arms around his waist, her face tilted up open and beseeching. "On your own. When it takes the pirates ten men to just clean the bottom of theirs."

"I suppose," he said grudgingly, but when she touched the side of his face, brought him down to meet her lips, he realized his smile had returned.

And another: him and Chay walking along the beach, the ocean a galaxy awash with silver.

"Oh," she cried, "here's one," and she ran ahead to an indistinct mass the waves had pushed on shore.

Tier followed, words pricking his tongue like thorns—he'd sworn off alc for the night, and the world was sharp enough to hurt. Every edge a blade, except for hers.

"What's that?"

"Flour," she said proudly, tugging back the corner of the shape, and a laugh fell out of him—the label was Rittan, and though servants had always taken care of the groceries in his father's household, he found an odd comfort in the familiar shapes of the letters.

"And what's it for?"

"Cooking."

Strange—he'd thought they were always short on food; thought that was the reason her legs poked out from under her dress like twigs. "You use this to m-m-m—to cook for the Boys?"

"Yeah. Want to help me carry it up?"

"Of course," he said, nestling it in the crook of his arm like an infant, and they made their way back through the woods, a lightness to Chay's step as she parted the brush before him. And though his ship was not yet ready—though what had bloomed between them was still so new and tender it hurt his chest—as he took her hand, her fingers were as warm as he had ever felt them, and he thought: He would hold her this way forever, if he could.

Chapter 28

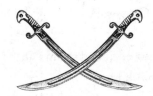

B aron."

Hands around his throat, squeezing.

"Baron."

Knife slash across his upthrown arms, distant shouts in a language he could not identify.

"Baron. Wake up."

He thrashed out of sleep like a fly in a spider's web, dreams swathed thick and sticky around his limbs.

"Don't," he wheezed, flailing in the dark. "I don't—no please—Jordan?"

And then his eyes shot open, and he could feel his body again.

His lungs squeezed. His heart drummed frantically, as if someone had been chasing him through the forest. The world was a lantern flicker, edges smudged like smoke, and he sucked in dizzy bursts of air, desperately trying not to make too much noise.

"I'm here," Jordan said, low. In the week that had passed since the attack, the two of them had moved back into her cabin—the walls muffled his voice at least a little, and none of the pirates were cruel enough to turn him out into the forest for the sake of their own REM. "Do you want Dust?"

"No, no, it's fine." Baron passed a hand over his face. His skull felt hollowed out, staticky, as if he hadn't slept at all; he did not want to think about Dust, or whatever battles they might soon be fighting, or the tension that had blanketed the ship in the daytime, the pirates watching and wary amid the vacuum of authority Aku had left behind. At least the Boys had lain low in the past week, presumably to work on their new house; Baron was grateful to not have been faced with them, too. "I—thanks for waking me. Sorry."

"Don't worry about it."

Beyond the door, someone muttered in their sleep; Mateo's footsteps creaked steadily around the hold, keeping watch.

The cot shifted, and Jordan's prosth came to rest heavily on Baron's chest, a real weight nudging out the tightness he could not shake.

It helped, a little.

She said, "Do you want me to knock you out again?"

He pressed two fingers lightly against his right temple, where a bruise had bloomed like a lover's mark. After the third sleepless night, he had all but begged for it: a starburst behind his eyes, blissful darkness slid open like a door. But he'd flailed awake from that, too, half sobbing, and in the end he was so afraid to surface that way again that he'd chosen this hazy insomniac haze instead. "Not yet."

"Alc?"

"No."

"All right."

A longer silence, the press of her shoulder almost feverish through the rumpled fabric of his shirt. On hot still nights, Peter had brought them out to the caves, shoved them one at a time into knee-deep water as the other Boys pelted them with pebbles. Calling out: *Where am I now? And now? And now?*

Training, he'd called it, like they were real soldiers, boys convinced they could go to war with beer-bottle arrowheads and rusted swords and a Pretend semblance of night vision. *Training*, except that after the first time, when Baron had curled into the water, shuddering silently—the irony, that he would be the one to break their disguise, after all the weeks Jordan had spent refining her Dust-glamoured hand—Jordan took his place. He'd stayed on the sidelines every night after, scream trapped in his rib cage, a universe away from anything that would have truly hurt him.

Was that where it had begun? With her sacrifice, and his shame?

Jordan shifted her arm. "Don't take this the wrong way, but—I thought you came here to die."

Baron huffed a breath, startled. "That wasn't the express purpose. Just a—a potential outcome."

"Yet your body is fighting it." Her fingers trailed across his furrowed brows, the aching knot of his jaw. "It's fighting so hard."

"Don't," he choked, as she traced the sweaty curve of his neck. "Don't try to—to—"

"Convince you?"

"I just—I don't know *why*—" The words were thick in his throat, and he swallowed, began again. He would hurt her even more, he knew, but the dark seethed around him, drowning—and they had both known from the beginning that they would not save each other. "Why do people even bother living, besides feeling like they should, or they already are, or that it would be an aberration to change what the gods have written?"

A long silence. The echo of Jordan's daggers, thudding into flesh; the watery groans as she cut the men open, a vow inked in blood that they would never hurt Baron again.

Her voice emerged as if out of the shadows themselves—slow, almost careful.

"I'm not sure," she said. "Maybe because your life is the only thing you've got. Maybe even if it sucks shit and you don't know if it'll ever get better, it's the only thing you've ever held in your own hands." After a pause, she added, "And there's still Dust."

Soaring blue sky, wind blustering against his face, the golden swell of knowing everything would be all right. He could not hold it in his mind.

"Sure," he said, hollow.

Jordan rolled back onto her right side, injured arm tucked between her and the wall. Ten minutes passed, or half an hour, and then her breathing grew deep and even—she was asleep.

Baron crooked his legs away from the edge of the cot. A strangeness had formed beneath his sternum, as if his ribs had come apart and were attempting to piece themselves together. In the dusky blur of the lantern, he could not remember the distances from the bed to the ceiling, or from wall to wall; the whole cabin could have been made of paper, poised to tear at the next intruder's first shove.

Maybe your life is all you've got.

But that was the problem, wasn't it? For as long as he could remember, he'd been frantically treading water, trying to stay above bullies' fists and the Lost Boys' swords and the storms of adrenaline that left him gasping over his textbooks at three in the morning.

This *was* his life. He could not imagine—for himself, at least—any other way to exist in the world.

The ghost of her ankle against his, her arm heavy on his sternum.

Dangerous, he thought again.

But she did not have to be his reason—just another person beside him, solid and sure. Her shoulders a measure and a bridge, letting him know the walls were not as close as he thought they were.

You'll be all right, she'd said that first night—as she touched him, as he shattered. *We'll be all right. I swear it.*

He had believed her then. Found, to his surprise, that he did still.

Baron closed his eyes, and when he slept, he did not dream.

Chapter 29

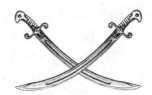

Jordan grunted as her dagger pinged off the side of the tree.

Her sleep had been thin and uneasy after Baron had woken her, underlaid by a bone-deep ache in her forearm and shoulder that lingered even after she'd applied her daily pinch of Dust. The air was cutglass cold, blue just creeping over the tin ribbons of ocean waves; in the crow's nest, the small figure that was Seida twirled a telescope between his fingers, supposedly looking out for Boys and Pales. Jordan could not shake the feeling he was watching her instead.

Her next knife embedded in the tree trunk, quivering.

"Hey."

Baron stood at the edge of the beach, two cracked plastic buckets swinging from one hand. He looked like shit. Dark shadows ringed his eyes, and his hair stuck up in the back; the early-morning light cast his face in pallid grey.

"Mateo wanted some of those brown mushrooms to cook with the boar," he said, holding out the buckets like an offering. The wind wisped up tendrils of sand, and he rubbed his eyes, his own morning Dust still kicking in. "I was wondering if you wanted to—"

Jordan wrenched the knife out of the tree, relishing the sear of her wrist, the clench of her fingers around the hilt. She'd once thought the Island temporary, for him: an on-off switch, there and back again. When he'd returned Outside at age thirteen, growing up had not been a defeat; he'd never needed to purge his internal organs while sitting on a stranger's toilet, or shore up his entire life against the biochemically staggering deficit of a substance he might never see again. His height, his voice, the stubble on his chin—in Burima, in most of the world, those were marks of honor, not shame.

But this place had torn him apart anyway. And if he chose to leave it again, there wasn't a single fucking thing she could do.

"Let's go," she said, jerking her head toward the forest, and he followed without a word.

Baron had volunteered to collect this particular ingredient, it seemed, for a reason. The mushrooms grew high enough that they did not have to kneel, but low enough that she wouldn't strain her shoulder reaching up. And there was a small catharsis in breaking the things off the bark of fallen trees—in the edges staring up at her, naked and beseeching. She dumped the caps in the bucket swinging from her prosth, scanned the forest for more.

At the base of an adjacent tree: a glint, metallic.

"What is that?" Baron asked, craning his head forward.

Jordan bent closer, hoping for a flask of Dust, perhaps a curved dagger. The patch of dirt was matted with pine needles, only a rounded rim visible between the tree root and surrounding humus. But as she reached, a second pulse beat hot beneath her bandaged skin; a strange longing snared her, like a thread pulled deep in her gut.

Then she realized what it was.

She had to be dreaming, she thought, as she scratched off the crust of mud. Dreaming—yet, as she brushed away filaments of moss and a jeweled beetle, the hook lay before her, stark and solid and darkly shining.

"Jordan." Baron's shadow lapped over her shoulder, and when she turned, his face was so full of concern, of *care*, that she flinched. "Don't touch that."

He had no right to look at her that way. Like they could belong to each other. Like he would stay until the end, if she let him.

"Fuck you," she said lightly, and shot off to dip it in the nearest branch of creek.

It fit like a charm.

There was a stiff leather harness, a complication of buckles and straps, but her teeth and left hand found their way around them as if she'd done this her whole life. The taste of tanned hide was familiar as an old storybook, its heft significant somehow, prophetic. Not the solid weight of her dead prosth, which she had stuffed in the bucket of mushrooms, but a scalpel slash, a karsa sharpness.

The weapon of a pirate captain.

Perhaps the Island was forcing her into a role, when it could come up with no others that suited her. Or perhaps every part she'd played before—Lost Boy, runaway, exile, fighter—had been in preparation for this one.

Beside her, Baron looked as if he had swallowed a frog.

"You know how the story ends, don't you?" he demanded, but Jordan could not keep the grin from spreading across her face.

She was done trying to be the hero. Done pretending. She was light as air.

"Yes," she said. "I do."

The pirates stared as Jordan made her way back toward the ship.

The hook did not glow in the pale late-morning light, did not whistle as it sliced the air. But she felt it anyway—the way their attention caught on its point, the way they shifted to make room for her as she passed. Nine years ago, her body had betrayed her in a manner she suspected no pirate captain had ever experienced; in that, and a dozen other ways, she did not quite have the *form* usually attributed to the figures in the stories. But this elegant curve of steel, this point at which she coalesced with history—it was impenetrable forest opening into sky; it was another weapon in her arsenal, both literal and figurative. She would make of it what she could.

And despite Baron's palpable distress behind her, or perhaps because of it, she felt the first upswell of pride.

"It suits you," Jack Two said as they ascended the deck, and Jordan's grin broadened.

Baron appeared at her shoulder again after they had dropped the mushrooms off with Mateo in the galley. She had gone back to throwing knives, which now involved calibrating her right side so she didn't accidentally stab herself in the thigh. His boots crunched the sand as she pried her last blade out of the tree trunk.

"Jordan."

"Yes?"

Baron's hands were shoved in his pockets, and he looked even more exhausted than when he had first approached her with the empty mushroom buckets. Yet she found herself staring at the curve of his eyelashes, the soft line of his mouth. Wanting for him so much that she could not give.

And, too—a grey dread, lurking as if beneath dark waters. Because she could not feel this way, could not *need* him. Or else, when he walked out of her life for good, it would destroy her.

"You know Peter will come for you specifically now, don't you?" he asked, his eyes flicking to her right arm. "Hunt you down, for wearing—that?"

Jordan straightened, the hilt of the knife heavy and cool in her hand. During her last stint on the Island, she had watched pirate captain after pirate captain die in battle; they'd lasted anywhere from three days to a couple years. Not all of them wore the hook—but a number of them *had*, and none of those men survived, either.

Yet she had never quite thought of herself as a man. There were surgeries for that—even affordable ones, if you caught the bus to Lamteng—but she'd never particularly longed for a beard or a dick, even if she despised the idea of being seen as a woman without them.

"Peter won't see it," she said. "We'll go after Tink tonight."

"Have you even scouted the new place?"

"No time." Another flare of irritation—at the dwindling pouches of Dust in Dau's pockets; at the way, every time she closed her eyes, she saw Gao Leng's trembling fists and slow, clumsy fall. It was not just Baron who was perpetually nearsighted. "The security here isn't exactly high-end. And we know when the Boys go to bed. Good enough."

"What if he catches you? What if you fail?"

She raised the hook—a bone-deep judder of air, as if its tip could cut through the very fabric of reality.

"I won't."

Baron's hands twitched. "Aku and Nilam thought the same thing. And you're already injured. If you wake up the wolf, or Chay, or one of the Boys—"

"Then what do you suggest?"

"If you need both Dust *and* karsa—" He swallowed, and the lump at his throat bobbed. "The pirates still have a bit of Dust. We could leave, while we're still alive. Take an extra pouch or two and find out the chemical composition, get someone to synth it for you. So you can have both."

"I tried that." A long syringe into her right arm when she was fourteen, a few grey-gold grains sucked out of the implant she'd installed there. The tech's eyes narrowed as they told her the results: calcium phosphate, trace minerals. Wondering why a scruffy teenager would have a sac of pulverized bone folded inside her skin. "All they found was ash."

"There has to be another solution."

"Maybe there isn't."

"Maybe," he snapped, "you don't understand enough science to make an accurate assessment."

There was a deadly pause. Baron looked mortified.

"You don't have to remind me," Jordan said coldly, "that my schooling ended nine years before yours."

"I wasn't talking about school."

"Weren't you?"

"I just meant we could still find a way that doesn't involve Tink, if there's no—"

"You're repeating yourself."

"That isn't what I—" His mouth opened, closed, a slow flush rising in his cheeks. "Saints. I'm sorry, all right?"

"Go," Jordan said. Her heart rampaged in her chest—this was it, this was it, but at least she had dismissed him on her own terms, at least he had not been the one to strip her off like a festering bandage. "Ask Dau for a pouch. It's a lower overall cost for us anyway. Go live your life. Find a better story to believe in."

He blinked. Swayed a bit, the bruise at his temple stark against the pall of his skin, and for a moment she thought he had gone to a place she couldn't follow.

Then he said, quietly, "What are we becoming?"

The question threw her. "What do you mean?"

Baron studied his shoes. "All this fighting," he said. "I just—what are we making ourselves into?"

He had always divided the world too easily, she thought. Right and wrong. Hero and villain.

"We," she snapped, "are staying alive."

He turned and walked back toward the ship, shaking his head.

Blood pounded in Jordan's ears; the straps of the hook's harness chafed her arm. They had both been coming apart anyway, since they'd left this place the first time. No matter that he'd let her kiss him, touch him in places he had never allowed anyone else—this was just the latest crack in a fissure that snaked all the way back to the beginning. Yet as the urge to hurl a dagger at his back slowly receded, a bitter relief flooded into its place. This new chasm between them felt like the hook: inevitable, once it happened. As if this was the distance at which they had always been meant to stand.

She weighed the blade in her palm. A dullness through her left arm—her grip not quite steady, not quite enough. But as she raised her hand, the world seemed to unfold around her, and for a moment she could feel every plank of the ship at her back, every pebble tumbling in the waves. The tree before her, poised to split open.

She threw, and the knife thudded dead center.

Chapter 30

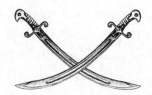

Baron slept alone in his cabin that night.

He'd gone through the rest of the day in a daze, barely registering the words said to him or the names of the pirates whose wounds
he cleaned and rebandaged. The crew regarded him with heightened
curiosity—he had been with Jordan, after all, when she'd discovered
the hook—but he staved off their questions with a tight smile, a quick
I'm sure she'd love to tell you.

Jordan had apparently flown off on the mission she'd planned that
morning. The bed seemed narrower without her in it; there was only a
suggestion of flame from the covered lantern, Dau's footsteps around
the hold as they kept first watch.

As Baron lay on his cot, the night his only witness, his fear spiraled
into the fathomless deep.

There was absolutely no reason he should have been surprised by
what she'd chosen. He was sleeping inside a pirate ship; had raised
sword and shield against the Lost Boys, seen Jack Two's wooden leg.
Most of the pirates were adults, according to Outside law, even if *he*

saw them as children who'd only lived long enough to wear out their innocence.

So why had the arc of Jordan's hook felt like a lens sliding into place?

And why had he lashed out, like there was no intermediary between his brain and his mouth?

Maybe you don't understand enough.

One sentence. One sentence, and he'd destroyed the single thing he had whittled down his hopes to. He may have washed up on the Island on the verge of several deaths—no college degree, no job, no one who would miss him besides his parents (and perhaps they wouldn't, either, when they found out what he had done). But at least he'd thought himself good. At least he had kept this one facet of his life pristine.

The way she'd looked at him. That utter disgust. As if he had become her enemy.

Then he was crumpling into himself beneath the sheets, gasping into the musty pillow. No invisible band vised his chest this time, no curve of spine released into thick dark—this was a gut punch, this was an ending.

He had lived his life terrified of becoming the villain, the moral of the story. That fear had loomed large over his high school and college days, while his classmates snuck off to drink on weekends or stayed up until five giggling and weeping over Hanwa historical dramas: that he would be the dreamer without the breakthrough, the butt of the joke, the one left behind. As other people's lives whirled past, brimming with color and substance, the desperation had smothered him until it fused with his skin. *You're hardly living,* his father had snapped during one of their late-night phone calls, when Baron made the mistake of confessing his lack of social life. *You barely know how to be human.*

But Baron had always, at least, been decent. Always, at least, been kind.

Tears leaked from his eyes, his body knotted in thin hazy exhaustion. He'd never expected *them* to last, not together, not as an entity;

had known Jordan too well for that, Island aside. Yet the first time she'd kissed him, a vision had taken root in the back of his mind—of a small flat in the San Jukong suburbs, when all this was over. Of walks in the park, and weekends spent hiking the Yeolong Mountains, and a little dog, maybe, cheerful and undemanding—

He hadn't expected he would be the one to blow it apart.

A quiet knock on the door.

Baron whipped upright, squinting to make sure he'd fastened the latch—as if he could even tell, from this far away. "Yes?"

The ship creaked and swayed with the wind, the lungs of some vast living organism. Against the swarming dark, he imagined another assassin, glinting eyes and black-gloved hands—or else Peter, grinning pearly white, the hold behind him a valley of severed heads. The voice that came through, however, was Jordan's. Baron would have laughed with relief if not for the fist still clenched beneath his ribs.

"Might do some recon tonight after all." Her feet shifted on the floorboards—*deliberately*, he thought, though he could not say why. "If you want to come."

As if this were some school sports club, some lunchtime lecture on the campus green. Baron wiped his nose with the back of his wrist, noting distantly that, in all his years on the Island, he had not once come across a piece of tissue paper.

"Have fun," he said, proud when his voice did not crack.

"We won't wait around."

A stone lumped in his throat. "Understood."

Jordan stayed a few seconds longer, a shadow against the shadow beneath the door. When it became clear Baron had nothing to add, her footsteps receded, and he lay back down and did not close his eyes.

The first time he had seen Jordan after the Island, those nine years ago—after her period, and the wolf, and her ten-year-old sister's knife-blade smile—a toothpaste-green hospital gown had been draped over her shoulders, her unglamoured right arm stitched up and furiously swollen below the plasticky sleeve. She glared at him, taking in his crisp button-down, his wire-rimmed spectacles, and he'd felt the sudden urge to run out and change back into furs.

"Hello," he said, and winced. His voice had changed all the way; it had occasionally cracked on the Island, but he'd let down his guard here, after a few days of hearing his father speak. Had forgotten about the Boys' giggling, the quick twist of Jordan's mouth on the edge of disdain.

"Where's your Dust?" she asked.

His hand lifted automatically to his neck—a lighter line of skin all around, coalescing in a patch on his collarbone where his pouch of Dust had once hung. He'd dumped its contents the moment his feet touched Burimay ground.

I'm moving on, he wanted to say, the words flickering on the tip of his tongue. *I want to grow up and work at an office and never think about the Island again.*

Come with me.

Instead he said, simply, "It's gone."

"You got rid of it." An accusation.

He shrugged, fiddling with the buttons of his shirt cuffs. Beyond the plastic curtain that bordered her cot, moans rose and fell like ocean waves, carried on air acrid with rubbing alcohol and sweat.

"I hope we can still be friends," he added, only half joking.

She glared. "You're giving up."

"That's kind of how it works, though, isn't it?" It came out more defensive than he'd intended. "We have our fun, we grow up, we leave. And it's not like we had that much to give up *on*, now that—"

"*We.*" A harsh laugh escaped her, and she doubled over with a sound halfway between a cough and a retch. Baron thrust out the basin lying by her cot, and she vomited something clear and slimy.

For the first time since his return, he was truly afraid.

The Lost Boys had each played sick perhaps once a season, when they wanted a little extra attention: begged for hot chocolate as Wen and then Chay dabbed their foreheads with warm rags; snuggled into the giant bed as their Ama spooned Pretend medicine between their coy pink lips. But they had always sprung up "better" the next morning, tired of their little fantasies of dependence. Had always rejected any weakness that would last.

Jordan didn't want his pity. One sympathetic look, one too-polite inquiry about her infection or the antibiotics, and he would lose what little of her esteem he'd managed to retain; would become just another uptight grown-up, trying to quiet her for his own comfort.

But they were no longer the Twins, either.

He thought, traitorously: He didn't know what to *say*.

"*We* don't have anything to give up on," Jordan continued, wiping her mouth with the back of her fist. "But *I'm* going back. And I'll make that bastard suffer."

Her own neck was bare as well—he assumed the nurses had thrown her pouch away when they'd brought her in. But there had to be other ways to return to the Island; he did not doubt she would find one.

He set the basin back on the floor. "If that's what you want."

She looked at him sharply. "What do *you* want, Baron?"

"I—I don't know," he said, his face warming. "To be happy, I guess."

Jordan laughed again, and the bitterness in her face was a hundred years old. "Good luck."

A brittle silence fell. Baron didn't want to leave—it seemed impolite, considering she was the one covered in stitches—but the space between them was a foreign country, a canyon over which he could no longer fly.

"What about you?" he ventured.

Her eyebrows arched. "What about me?"

"Don't you—" The words clogged his throat, but he swallowed, pushed on. "Don't you want to grow up? At least a little?"

"I'd rather be buried alive in a steaming pile of shit."

Baron nodded, resigned. A clear droplet—Saliva? Vomit?—beaded his wrist, and he made a show of scrubbing his hands beneath the nearby faucet so he didn't have to meet her eyes. A whisper of the Island ghosted across the back of his neck, then—sunlight slanting through birch trees, the chatter of the clear creek. The brush of her hands as she took his Dust pouch, so quick it might have been a dream.

The last time they'd touched. Perhaps, he thought, drying his hands with the stiff, uncannily flat paper towels, it was the last time they ever would.

"All clean now?" Jordan said, mocking.

The anger surged up faster than he could think.

"Stay with me," he said, lifting his chin. He would not *fear* her— would not cower before what they might become, without the Island to bind them. "Ask your parents if you can come over sometime. 265 Riau Street 10E, Arandak Township."

The same apartment from which they had flown to the Island. The same bedroom window. Her eyes narrowed, and for a moment he thought he'd lost her. Then she said, "*Your* parents will be delighted."

"They won't mind," he countered, reckless, and for a moment they were the Twins again—daring each other to walk across a morass of Everbird shit, or poking each other in the ribs beneath the covers until Wen scolded them for giggling. He pushed his glasses up his nose, cleared his throat. "They're, ah, concerned about me not having friends."

"Do you?" she asked, curious.

Baron shrugged, still halfway defiant. "What do you think?"

"Fine. I'll come," Jordan said, sticking out her hand for him to shake, and he didn't even wash his own again until he'd backed out of the room.

Chapter 31

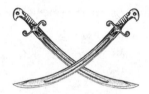

Tier wiped a sweating palm against his trousers as he led Chay
down the forest path.

They were headed back toward the coves—the ship he'd been repairing now almost seaworthy; the crates of jewels and coins and historical
artifacts stacked neatly against the walls, sorted into the cut he owed
the pirates and *his* pile, ready for loading. He'd come up with a short
speech for when they arrived, practiced it again and again as he rinsed
mud off ancient statues and ceramic figurines. But nerves writhed in
his stomach, a nest of snakes. Her hand crooked in his, starlight dancing through her hair—if he fucked this up, all of this, all of *her*, would
disappear in a breath.

"Tier?" Chay said, and he almost leapt into the air. "Are you all
right?"

Heat flushed his face. "I'm f-f-f-f—" he started, and then swore and
fisted his hand against his leg in frustration. "I'm—okay."

"Are you sure?" She was glowing, the reflected moon of a reflecting moon. Their fingers were intertwined, her heartbeat through her

skin alternating with his in erratic nonsynchrony, and he thought: He would miss the lilt of her voice, her eyes like constellations. He would miss everything about her. "If something's wrong—"

"No. No." Tier bit the inside of his cheek, grounded himself in the tang of iron. He'd only had one shot of whiskey tonight—enough to dull the forest's edges, but not enough to lubricate his speaking apparatus; he wanted to remember this, if it went well. But he hadn't felt this nervous since leaving Ritt. "I just have a—surprise for you, at the coves."

And then the mouth of the cavern opened before them, and Tier lit the lantern he'd stowed behind a stone.

The finished ship loomed out of the dark, solid and elegant and whole.

Chay's jaw dropped, awe breaking across her face as if she had never seen such a vessel, and affection surged through him for the childish wonder she was not afraid to show—that after all this time, the world, for her, could still be new.

Her small hand in his had gone slack. Still holding it gently, he knelt, electricity crackling through his lungs as he twisted his mouth into the shapes he'd practiced.

"Every day I worked on this ship, I thought of you," he said, and only stuck briefly on the first *d*. His diction was a mess—every word a different accent, all the sounds rolling and colliding in his mouth until they blurred into a frantic jumble beneath the pounding of his heart. "And I know you've stayed with the B—with the Boys—for a long time. But if you'd—if you'd like to come with me on a new adventure—and you d-d-don't have to say anything, now, you can just think about it— I'd like to—I w-wanted to ask—" And then something spasmed in his tongue and he couldn't force out another word.

A metallic click—Chay placing her lantern on the cold stone floor— and then she touched his forehead, ran her fingers through his hair. Seeing him, anointing him, the only crown he would ever wear.

What a joke, sneered his father, his brothers. *You have no idea how to do this.*

He had never been so certain of anything in his life.

"Yes," Chay breathed, and he was falling, he was free. "Tier, yes. All the ways yes."

The faintest twinge of released air, and then a thud, quiet as a pulse. Chay jerked back, eyes wide, and said softly, "Oh."

Tier looked down to see an arrow sticking out of his chest.

Chapter 32

As a child, Chay had watched every animated Rittan princess movie ever made.

Two years after Jordan and Baron disappeared, her ama had installed a small television in their kitchen, and on evenings when both her parents were working, Chay had spooned reheated congee from her plastic bowl and watched, round-eyed, as Cinda's foot slid perfectly into the proffered slipper; as Auri danced her way to Matthias's heart; as Nieve sighed awake to the kiss of true love.

Chay had wanted those lives so badly. As she kicked her feet under her desk at school, she'd dreamed of songbirds trilling at the window, of a king and queen pining for their long-lost daughter. Of a golden-haired boy on a white stallion, come to sweep her away. The princes had felt so close, then—reach through the screen and they would smile, delighted, pull you headlong into your own luminous ever after.

Rittan princes, Chay thought as Tier's chest hitched—more shock, at first, than fear—were never supposed to die.

Rittan princes—as his mouth opened, the huff of his breath still bruise-tender on hers—were never killed by people who loved them.

"Tier."

He slumped into her arms, his blood seeping hot between her fingers.

"Tier."

The kiss of true love, indeed. She'd given him the kiss of death.

"Please." She twisted herself between him and the patch of forest from which the arrow had come—thick shadows beyond the first row of trees, a phantom curl of laughter—and then she was fumbling with her canister of Dust ointment and stuffing its contents into his chest by the fistful, mechanical, automatic. He could not be taken this easily. Could not have been shot from afar like some common pirate. If she only worked fast enough—her fingers scraped the bottom of the container. "Tier. Please. Talk to me."

His mouth moved, but made no sound. His heart already slowing, and she could feel it in the surge-stutter-stop at his wrist, the shallowing of his breath, the sudden heaviness of his torso in her arms. Like he could break her with the full weight of him, though he never had before.

And when the smell of urine came, sharp against the thick dark, she pressed him to her chest, a final gift of warmth from some vengeful, twisted god, and cried and cried and cried.

Chapter 33

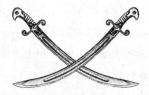

Tier had never trusted words.

They had always come to him unpredictable, sporadic, a loaded dice throw of shame and fear and doubtful neural connection. As a pilot, he'd practiced his announcements every evening, repeated each syllable in the mirror until no one noticed the wobbles in his diction but himself; in his work with the syndicate, his various foreign inflections had gone unnoticed by associates for whom every non-Burimay accent was a foreign one. But he was still, always, an undercover agent braced for a slipup, a high-wire walker who'd only stepped out into empty sky because he hadn't thought too hard about the height. Words, for him, were wounds, and walls, and scars.

As the blood leaked out of his chest, he realized he was down to his last few.

He could feel his pulse ebbing, his breath short and loud in his ears. Funny, he'd taken a bullet before, on a hunting trip, with less fear. But that had not struck him just below the heart. Had not protruded out of his back and rendered him a scream of pure, wordless pain.

Citrus pricked the back of his tongue.

Say it again.

"Tier," said Chay. Her eyes glistened, and he gripped her hand, felt her pulse racing through her palm. "Tier, please."

"Chay," he whispered, holding her name so carefully in his mouth, like the stem of a wildflower or a shard of glass, and in the clench of his fingers he wanted to give her everything: his still-beating heart and the rock-salt sky and a million secret futures they could have flown through like falling rain. He couldn't breathe. "I—"

And it might have become *I love you* or *I'm sorry* or *I wish we'd had more time*, but the stars split open above him and he was lost to the spaces in between.

Chapter 34

"Ama."

She was a stone sunk in a black glass pond. She was the silence after the explosion, ash rained down on stubbled foundations.

"Ama?"

His weight crushed her chest. His blood soaking her dress.

"Amaaaaa. Come on."

A tug on her pinkie finger. White-blond hair, grubby cheeks. *Jack*, she thought, dazed, taking in the rusted sword in his other hand, its dull edge gleaming. The sword he'd drawn—for what? She blinked, her eyes already swollen. Had the pirates attacked, too?

Slowly, like shadows detaching from their sources, the rest of the Boys drifted into the open: Kuli with his knives, Slightly gripping his staff, Tudo's and the Twins' blades like the tails of faint stars. Ael, whom she'd left behind every time she ran off to see Tier, loped her way with the ghost of a growl.

"Did you see that?" Peter crowed, brandishing his crossbow. "Straight to the heart!"

Chay's throat closed.

You, she thought numbly, though she could not speak the words for what he had done—naming it would make it real, would transfigure the already-fading warmth in her arms into something other, something inhuman. She knew the rule: *No grown-ups allowed.* Yet she had still walked with Tier within hearing distance of the Boys, had kissed him barely a stone's throw away from the new aboveground house. Had thought them invisible, the charmed exception.

Chay twisted away from Tier's body and retched, sour and empty. When she raised her head again, the Boys were staring, half revolted, half fascinated.

"Why're you holding him, Ama?" Kuli asked, tugging her braid.

"Why are you crying?"

"Did he try to thimble you?"

"Are you sure he's dead?"

"Of course he's dead," Peter cut in, touching a dagger to Tier's collarbone, and a scream rose in Chay's throat as she slapped his hand away.

"Leave him alone."

Peter blinked, slow, and for a moment she thought he had seen through her, that he understood. Then he kicked off Tier's back—a bubble of rage filled Chay's lungs—and into the air, Tink casting his face in heroic gold. "Come on, Boys, let's see if there are any more!"

"Are you okay, Ama?" asked Tudo, bending toward her as the other Boys darted after Peter. But the head of his axe still rested in his palm, and a moan tore out of her mouth, the blade too sharp, too *here*. If there had been more grown-ups—Peter always killed first, or he got cranky—any of the Boys might have struck the fatal blow.

"How?" she croaked. Her insides were raw, as if she had been screaming for days. The smell of Tier's blood a finger jammed down her throat. "How could you do this?"

Tudo blinked his long-lashed eyes. "We always do this, Ama," he said, as if he had suddenly decided to play at being Father, and she the unwitting child. "It's the Island. No grown-ups allowed."

"Then what about me?" she shouted, and the Boys still in earshot flinched, blades bristling. She was being reckless, but what did it matter? "I'm a grown-up, too! I'm nineteen years old! Why don't you shoot *me* right now?"

"You're nineteen?" one of the Twins muttered, turning back.

"You're an Ama," Tudo said, with simple authority. "It's different."

High on the mountain, a wolf howled, mournful and empty, and an echoing cry rose in Chay's own chest. She *knew* these boys—the way they giggled at the shapes of clouds and made fart noises with their armpits, clung to her in the dark as they thrashed against nightmares.

She knew them, and she had loved them, and they were utter strangers.

"I'm going to clean him up," she said.

"No need for that." Peter had returned, flanked by the rest of his crew, their search for additional victims apparently unsuccessful. Chay silently thanked the gods. "We're low on Dust anyway, after the pirates—"

"No," Chay snapped. "He will not be Dust."

Silence, thick as a wolf's growl. Amas were supposed to give everything to their children—wear down their bodies in the daily trudge of cooking and cleaning, numb their hearts to every sneer and thoughtless tease. Would the Boys allow Chay to do something that did not serve them? Or would they decide her time on the Island had run out, and that their swords were meant for her after all?

Tier's head lay heavy against her shoulders. She clutched it, fighting the sob that cracked her ribs—and stilled.

A pulse, beating faintly at his throat.

A phantom, perhaps, or wishful thinking, but she shifted her grip anyway, pulled him closer. She could not breathe, could not speak. Hope swelled in her chest, a bright obliteration.

Please, she thought, and squeezed her eyes shut. *Please.*

It was still there.

Sluggish and faint, but the *one-two* against her palm was unmistakable. The ebb and flow of his breath, near imperceptible in the dark.

He was alive.

He was still alive.

Tier in her arms, not dead but unconscious, and she was a creature split open, she was sunlight streaming through the dusk-sweet pines.

The Boys were still staring, though, and so Chay furrowed her brow, contorted her mouth in silent agony. She had to act as though they had succeeded in killing him—as if she was still begging them not to desecrate his body instead of for his very life.

But the Boys had never looked too closely at their Ama. She prayed to whatever gods were listening that they would not begin now.

"Please," she whispered. It was not often that she begged, but thinking back, Peter loved it when she did. "Please, Peter. Let me bury this man in peace."

"If you really want a corpse that badly," Peter said, and smirked. "Why, do you want to thimble it?"

"Maybe we'll catch a Pale instead." Kuli giggled. The sound grated Chay's ears.

"Go to bed, Boys," she said, suddenly weary.

"You'll still tuck us in?" Tudo asked.

"In a minute. Change and brush your teeth first."

"But I don't want to—"

"*Go*," she said, and perhaps there was a new steel that rang through her voice, because they stopped arguing. "I'll come back soon," she added—a lie, whether or not they allowed her to live—"and make you a nice breakfast. Pancakes and sausage and eggs. How would you like that?"

"Uh, okay." Peter shrugged and then shot back toward the forest, the Boys darting after him like a shoal of fish. Leaving her be.

The moment the last of them vanished into the trees, Chay pressed her face into Tier's shoulder and laughed.

From a distance, she hoped it sounded like weeping.

Nine years ago—to the extent that time could be seen as anything more than a rippling sheet of silk, a pale strand on endless loop—a girl had left the Island.

She was bleeding, and in more than one place—her single body a war of life and death, hope and hate; of the belief, stark-shining, that one day she would return to end this story.

When she vanished beyond the boundary with a blink, a teardrop-shaped darkness, the Island saw, and vowed to remember.

And then it began to die.

There was no sudden flattening, no tectonic ooze of slag. Only a slow rot, thread by thread, its boundaries going limp like the daisy chains woven by its younger guests. Planes crashed against the barrier instead of passing through, their twisted metal corpses sinking into ocean mud. Ships lost their way in clear blazes of afternoon, radios gone silent. The children heaped Dust on their heads, bathed in it, and still so much leaked from the fabric of the Island that they barely rose off the ground.

More, they pleaded from cliffs and coves and hollow trees.

More, they cried, hurling rocks into choked springs and sputtering waterfalls.

More, they demanded, as if they had conquered, as if they *owned*, as if they were not the battered bastard children the Island had saved from drowning.

The Island rumbled with discontent.

Perhaps it was the girl's fault. Perhaps her departure had broken something vital in the core of the land, spilled evidence of the laughing boy's corruption into open air where it had no place.

Or perhaps it was the children themselves. Across the seas, the Island heard the moans of sister Lands smothered by concrete and glass and toxic smog, cries carried through fault lines and the weeping of glaciers. Rumors of children who were told there was no Island, or worse, not *told* at all, the stories shut off in favor of class rankings and multiple-choice tests and a single image of skyscraper conquest so vivid that the shores of their daydreams grew dull as old photographs.

Perhaps the girl was only the symptom of a greater infection.

But in the end, it didn't matter what the sickness was.

The Island weakened with every aircraft that crumpled against its edges, its springs and streams growing more sluggish with every stale sunset. Deep in the night, when shadows unhinged their jaws and the land shifted in between, it felt itself sinking slowly back into the ocean, cold breezes slipping over its head like a blanket of falling stars.

So it sucked the wind between its teeth and cried, *Come*.

The words were a clarion call: hurled from the high places, flickered in the dance of dying fires, kissed by moths onto sweat-damp foreheads. A ragged shout across the thin, tumid river between sleeping and waking.

Surely someone would listen. Surely someone would believe.

Yet when the winds died away, only one child knelt motionless in the cave at the Island's heart: another girl, younger sister to the first, dark braid spilling down her moon-white dress.

Choose me, she said, and the Island scented beneath her skin the slow ripening of not-death, of sheer bloody potential, pink curdles of tissue that would burgeon into something raw and swollen and tender. Urgency radiated off her like falling leaves—the soft sad precipice in the air before winter descended, before every wooded hiding place was stripped to the bone.

Her time was almost over. Her time had almost come.

Choose me, she insisted, *I will serve you better than Peter ever could*, and the Island spoke again: a moue of salt-rimmed lips, a murmur from the heart of the forest.

And what do you ask in return?

Her smile was sweet and luminous and sad.

I want to stay, she said. *And to remember.*

To remember. To stay. A shudder in the deeps, vast columns of stone and sea shifting and grinding in the fathomless black. In the eons since the Island's conception—over millennia of drowned bodies and withered empires—only one child had ever stayed, and paid a price. He could not become a man, with those clever hands and hungry eyes, because he might try to build something that lasted. And the Island refused to become like its dying siblings, surveyed and drilled and pinned down with ink, sliced with so many names that it no longer remembered its own.

The Island would not facilitate its own execution.

That is the one thing I cannot give, it rumbled, and the girl pleaded and wept and bashed her fists on the ground until they bruised.

If you cannot give me what I want, she cried, *I will take it myself.*

The Island whispered, light as an uncurling vine: *You may try.*

So I will.

The girl pushed to her feet—an irrepressible pulse of cells, budding fate—and left the Island's heart to echoing silence.

PART FIVE

Don't laugh. Just tell me the story / again, / of the sparrows
who flew from falling Rome, / their blazed wings. / How
ruin nested inside each thimbled throat / & made it sing
                    —Ocean Vuong, "Seventh Circle of Earth"

Chapter 35

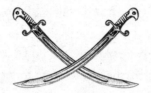

Chay had not considered, as she dragged Tier toward the Island's central mountain, just how heavy he would be.

She grunted as she adjusted her grip at his armpits, the lantern at her elbow clanking like manacles against her hip. Her face was raw from crying; her head pounded, dizzy with want for the sweet breads and scallion buns she had baked that afternoon and not eaten. But Peter's restraint would not last long—tonight or tomorrow or the day after, he would return, impatient to have his way with Tier's bones. To claim his newest kill like a trophy.

A touch at her elbow, wet and cold, and she startled: Ael, ears flicked back, teeth bared in a low whine.

"I'm sorry," she said. Since the incident with Jordan nine years ago, the wolf had clung more closely to her side—as if he, too, understood what she had done, and tasted her grief on his lolling pink tongue—and she had left him behind: not trusting him with Tier, or to defy the roles they were all expected to play. Now, he closed his mouth gently around Tier's ankle, and she stiffened.

"I don't think—"

But she was so tired, and her mind kept slipping toward soft pale rises of dough, the crackle of caramelized onions—a deep betrayal, this watering of her mouth—and so she staggered along, light-headed, as Ael dragged Tier farther along the forest path.

Come with me.

His voice in the dark, an offering. The waver of his lower lip against hers, barely perceptible, and her fierce rush of pride at the question it posed; at the uncertainty he had revealed, just to her.

Chay.

When she was nine years old, she had flown to the Island to look for Jordan. When she was ten, she had resolved to stay, whatever the cost, if only to prove she could. But in the fine fabric of Tier's jacket, which she could not bear to take off even if it stank of blood—in the way he had looked at her, like she *was* someone—even in the fish he had speared and presented to her on a tray, that golden afternoon, as if he could be the Ama for a day and she could simply eat—she had seen something like a future, something like a world, where she was not alone in bearing the burden of living.

She would have gone with him beyond the place where sea met sky. She would have abandoned the Boys and Peter and more, if it meant she herself would never be left behind again.

But as the crown of Tier's head slipped beneath the shadow of a massive pine, she thought: Perhaps she was too late.

The forest had shifted as she walked—thickets of trees nudging her this way or that, the ocean's whisper damped to silence. In the dark, slim shards of moonlight trickling through the branches, she could not quite tell where she was.

Ael stopped, snout pointed toward a gap in the underbrush, and she raised her lantern to a narrow cave, low to the ground. A place she had found, and entered, only once before.

"Oh," she breathed, "*oh*," and stumbled after her wolf into the forest's heart.

*   *   *

Tier's face was sallow in the stone-closed dimness, the stain on his shirt a monstrous flower. But when she held her hand beneath his nostrils, a slow warmth misted on her skin—his breath, his life, anchoring her to her own.

Chay settled on the stone floor, cold radiating through the thin fabric of her dress. "Tier," she whispered, and the sound fractured against the cave walls, a hundred wispy phantoms. "It's all right. You're safe now. You can wake up."

"Amaaaa!"

She tensed—the Boys somewhere above, all cheerful shouts and high-pitched giggles. "Amaaaa, where are you?" But their calls soon faded—"We never needed a mother anyway," Peter declared, his voice a knife sailed between hushing pines, "off to sleep, everyone"—and then quiet blanketed the forest again, moss-thick and watchful and very, very old.

The cold hardened in Chay's bones, until she was not sure where her body ended and night began.

Chay.

She squinted into the cave's depths, wary. The darkness beyond her lantern had thickened, grown eyes and teeth, and she had met no one else on her last sojourn to this place—only a few patches of blue-white mushrooms, softening the walls with their strange, sunless glow—but nine winters had passed since then. Who knew what others might have washed up on the Island aside from Tier, and hidden here instead of joining the pirates or Pales?

Who knew what they might have become, after all those years crouching in the dark?

"Yes?" she said, and her question ricocheted back at her, a mockery.

You should go back inside.

A faint warmth, cupping her face. Beside her, Ael's ears pricked, yellow eyes fixed on something she could not see.

"Tier?" she gasped, her voice breaking. "Tier?"

Nothing.

Chay pressed her hands to his stiffened shoulders, the clammy flesh of his neck. A twitch had started up in her left eye, a snowy static in the space behind her forehead, and she wanted to press herself into his chest, curl beneath his arm and fall asleep; to be, again, warm.

Never mind that he still reeked of blood and urine. Never mind that ever since Peter's arrow, the Boys' cheers, his eyes had not opened once.

"Tier, please." She'd cut off the bits of arrow shaft protruding from his chest, terrified she had left splinters inside to fester; scraped clean her entire canister of Dust ointment, the whole month's worth, and stuffed it into the gaping hole.

It had to be enough. It couldn't not be.

Go. A warmth brushed her forehead, too tender to belong to the Island. *Or Peter might forget who you are.*

In another time, Chay might have laughed. In another time, she might have shaken out her knees, unclenched her teeth, stumbled back toward the Boys' rickety tower of a house and their grating, heartless innocence. She could have another chance at pretending, another chance to play at being mother. After all, the Boys had not yet run her through.

Chay drew the jacket tight around her shoulders.

"No more," she said quietly. "Tier, wait for me, please—"

A breath of smoke, unfurled for a moment against the wind. A ghost trace of his thumb along the line of her cheek, copper lashes arced against pearl-bright skin. And then the lantern dimmed to embers, and she knew, despite the slow pulse at his throat, that she was alone.

Chapter 36

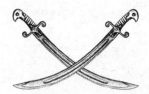

Jordan paced the deck, the hook whistling with every swing of her right arm.

The sickening lurch in her gut had been quelled temporarily with an extra half pouch of Dust—Dau reaching into their coat, when she'd asked, with a look of warning. Then a dinner of crocodile meat and the collected mushrooms, roasted over a spit on the beach, and for the first time since Jordan had washed up on the Island, she had felt herself uncoil a bit, buoyed by the fullness of her stomach, the flicker of a fire not stoked to destroy. Yet an ache lingered between her shoulder blades, a weariness that dogged her steps. Her body a constant precarity, the kind of wound that did not heal with time.

We could leave.

Baron's hunched shoulders as he trudged back to the ship, his cabin door latched shut. If she was honest, it didn't sound entirely awful to spend her final days somewhere with running water, glamouring thousand-mir bills with her last reserves of Dust. To know Baron would not be stranded here, or shot down over open water when she was dead.

Aku and Nilam had gone down trying to take Peter: two on one, their approach camouflaged by smoke to boot. With her sword arm shaky and getting worse—she gave her wrist an impatient flick, and almost passed out again as something spasmed the wrong way—she was in no position to launch her own strike, or ask the other pirates to fight for her.

But neither could she live with having surrendered. Not when she was in this deep. She had crossed an ocean to find this place again; she could not give up with Tink a mere kilometer away.

There are high-security vaults less than a kilometer thick, she heard Baron say. *Distance isn't the same as*—

"Shut up," she muttered aloud, and Koro, who was keeping watch at the stern, glanced up. "Not you," she added, and the archer—who, for whatever reason, kept his polished wooden bow slung across his back at all hours, including mealtimes—looked as if he thought her a little mad.

"Maybe you," Jordan amended, and paced in the other direction. If she squinted, she could make out a patch of greater darkness in the forest canopy, an ash-rimmed mouth where the hollow trees used to stand.

There has to be another solution.

You just don't understand—

Anger flared through her again, at once hot and freezing cold. She may never have taken a formal chemistry course, but she had fought enough people to know when she was outmatched. In the hospital, when she was stitched up and screaming through the sedation, the doctors had decided she was some sort of addict. Her drug tests had all come back clean, but there was nothing she could have done to change their minds.

Though punching one of them in the face probably hadn't helped.

She stopped in the middle of the deck. A firefly flicker, in the heart of the woods—a few hundred meters from Peter's new outpost, according to Mateo, who had spent the day scouting.

Perhaps the Boys had decided to celebrate out in the open.

Unless it was the Pales camped on the far shore, getting restless or seeking alliance. Or Tier, slinking back to the ship in the dark to avoid her, though she doubted he was stupid enough to proclaim his presence in the forest at night if he'd managed to survive this long.

Or someone else altogether, just washed up on shore.

"Think it's the Boys?" she asked Koro, who was gazing out across the black as well. He turned smoothly, though she had sensed the edge of a flinch at the sound of her voice.

She was not Aku. Didn't want to be. But she needed to move—needed to convince herself she was still fighting, because the alternative would swallow her whole.

"Possibly." Koro's dark eyes flicked toward her hook, then away. "You want to do recon."

"Yes." She thought of Baron, turning and turning in his cabin below; a dapple of sunlight, the press of his bony shoulder, when they were ten and leopard-crawling toward a valley of Pales. "Want to come?"

Koro raised a brow—surprise, at last. "Shall I wake Mateo and Ellis for second watch, then?"

"Go ahead," she said, and it was only when he had vanished down the hatch that she realized he'd been asking her permission.

The forest, at this time of night, was a silent tunnel: dark whip of branches, jeweled eyes reproaching, a grey gauze of smoke pulled in with every breath. She flew with Koro—and what a rush, to be burning Dust so extravagantly—along the ridge of a ravine, keeping downwind of where previous scouts had marked Peter's new house to be. The spark of amber she'd seen from the ship darted like Tink between the trees.

The archer kept to himself. He had remained stone-faced during Aku's and Nilam's burial, and she wondered if he harbored any of his own ambitions to become captain, or kill her on someone else's behalf. But in the week or so since Aku had passed, Koro had shown no inclination toward taking charge—or any human interaction, really. All she'd gathered from watching him was that when he shot, he did not miss, and that he rarely spoke more than a couple sentences in a row.

She told herself she would get used to it.

They came to the old clearing first—a haze of smoke and drifting ash, stubbed branches jabbing the sky like skeletal fingers. Jordan drew to a stop, massaged the round of her hook against her sore left arm.

"Saints above," Koro said softly.

It was an alien landscape, a devastation. She had lived here, too, for five years—spent hundreds of mornings sliding down her and Baron's hollow tree; worn the shape of her body into its unforgiving throat and the giant bed and her chair-stump at the dinner table. After she left, that first time, this ring of seven elms had morphed into as much symbol as memory—of everything that had gone wrong, every starry-eyed story of childhood innocence she was no longer fit to claim.

But before that, it had been shelter from the wolves and the rain. Before that, it had been home.

A rustle—Koro had unslung his bow and quiver and laid them on the ground, head bowed.

Jordan unsheathed her sword and followed suit, though unbuckling the scabbard felt too complicated and the hook remained firmly strapped to her right arm. For a moment, she considered guilt—this had been her idea, after all, a destruction left in her wake. But she only saw Baron's sanctimonious frown, the lines he had chosen to draw between them.

What are we becoming?

The trees would grow back, as they always had. In the meantime, the cleared canopy would give smaller saplings a chance at sunlight, the songbirds and foxes and small black snakes a few more places to warm themselves.

The Island clung to life, fire or no. All she could do was fight for her own.

"The pirates would have burned it down sometime," Koro said, as if he had, in silence, traced the bent of her thoughts. "I—and most of the crew—we just hope something comes of it."

Jordan sheathed her sword, turned again to the glint of distant flame.

"Yeah," she said, and the heat through her forearm simmered a warning. "So do I."

Chapter 37

Jordan thought she had learned all the caves on the Island.

Peter and the Boys had been obsessed with them: endless mazes in the near dark, stalactite spikes perfect for breaking off and throwing, narrow tunnels that unfolded into grottoes full of treasure. She had spent five years, herself, plunging headfirst into that shifting landscape of stone and shadow. But as she and Koro tracked the light—weaving and bobbing between trees whose branches tangled, perhaps deliberately, to block their path—it stopped, seemed to slip into the ground, and Jordan peered into the dark maw of a cavern she had never seen before.

Little more than a hole, it appeared at first. A small crack at the base of the mountain. But the pale mushrooms glowing along its edges increased in size and number as she ducked inside, and then she caught the cast of a lantern—the kind the Boys carried to piss after nightfall—slanting amber across the damp, moss-coated walls.

Chay huddled beside it, wrapped in dark furs. And, pacing around her—the wolf.

Jordan took a silent step back, her breath catching in her throat. Ael had gone grizzled and grey, in the years since they had last faced each other at close quarters, but his shoulders still bunched with lean muscle, his yellow eyes gleaming. And those teeth—it had not just been syndicate brawn she had thought of, when she'd asked Baron to tweak her prosths Outside. She had wanted machinehood, wanted to be empty. To strip away her soft insides until there was nothing left to cower.

Koro settled soundless beside her, firelight dripping gold across the tip of his bow. Murmured, "Isn't that your friend?"

"What?"

He pointed his chin, and Jordan looked. Looked again.

Holy shit.

She pressed the hook into her thigh, suddenly dizzy despite the Dust that still buoyed her. The dark shape she'd assumed to be another shadow resolved into a face, a curl of auburn hair. Red drenched his shirt; a tang she'd taken for cave damp sharpened into sweat and blood and piss.

And Chay—her arms draped not with strangely proportioned furs, as Jordan had initially thought, but a black pilot's jacket, so large on her that the sleeves pooled around her hands—Chay was moaning his name, over and over.

Something septic and raw twisted in Jordan's chest. She had stopped counting her kills around her second winter on the Island, the beheaded Pales and vivisected pirates; karsa addicts, afterward, far enough gone to attack a syndicate messenger in her own territory. A parade of bodies that had meant her harm, and that she had disposed of.

But only now the weight of a life. Only now, as she looked down at the corpse of a man she had taunted and fought with, who had flown across the sea at her command and borne the consequences, did the word *death* turn and ripen into fullness.

"*Tier.*"

Half-lit by flame, Chay's mud-smeared face was a thing turned monstrous, her mouth a gape of bloodied earth. Jordan thought of that last bright morning—the serene triumph in her sister's ten-year-old face as she'd strode across the beach, the Boys' riotous laughter—and the old convulsion twisted beneath her skin, the constant Dust hunger. Nine years after the fact, her crew had burned down the Lost Boys' house underground with a few strikes of flint against kerosene. It felt as if some rule of engagement had been broken; Sir Franklin himself might have gasped at their cruelty. But the pirates and Peter still stood at an impasse, one that had held for the last who-knew-how-many years.

Perhaps, she thought, they needed someone on the inside.

And if her sister was truly mourning for Tier—if the Boys still saw her as their Ama, which was likely, given that she hadn't been filleted and dumped at the bottom of the sea for making off with his bones—

Jordan motioned at the wolf, and Koro nocked an arrow quick as a breath.

"Keep it on him," she whispered. Her heart beat high in her throat, a roar in her ears like the Underground, and *gods* this was a bad idea, but there was no other way she could keep moving—not without being hunted down again, or else admitting defeat. "I'm going in."

It was indeed Ael who saw her first; who bared his teeth, remembering. The scars across her chest and upper arms needled pain, as if her skin had suddenly come unseamed. But Jordan did not draw her sword. Only raised her hands, the hook softly mouthing the air— damn. Nothing she could do about that now. She hoped it was the gesture that counted.

"Chay," she said. "I just want to talk."

Her sister stilled. Her eyes focused gradually, but there was a hollowness to them, as if she was not all there. It was a look Jordan had seen on dying hospital patients and their families, a pain so immense it swallowed you whole.

And she looked so *small*, kneeling there in the dirt. Like someone could tip her over and she would shatter like porcelain.

"You," Chay said, but there was no heat behind it. Her Rittan was crisp as Tier's—as Tier's had been.

"Me," Jordan said simply. Ael stalked forward, hackles raised, and she rolled to the balls of her feet, adrenaline lancing her lungs. Plenty of Dust glimmered in her veins—she would take off the second the bastard tried to start something—but still. "I don't want to hurt you. If the wolf moves any closer, though, it gets shot."

A twist of that perfect mouth. "The Boys will hear me if I—"

"I can't imagine you're particularly pleased with them right now."

Chay's face crumpled, as Jordan had known it would. There were many ways to die on the Island, but Peter had always been the quickest. "No," she whispered, cupping Tier's face. Then, barely audible, "He won't wake up. He might not—I don't know if—"

So he was still alive. Barely. A small loosening between Jordan's shoulders. "You were seeing him."

Chay nodded once, miserable. "He came with you, didn't he?"

"Yes."

"Why?" Her voice was plaintive, and for a moment she could have been ten again, eyes burning with a resentment that would never run out. "Why did you have to come back?"

"Why did you stay?" Jordan countered.

Chay ran a hand through Ael's fur, and the wolf sat back on his haunches, though his baleful yellow eyes still fixed on Jordan, unblinking. "It was the one thing I could do better than you."

Jordan stared. "That's super not how this works."

"Isn't it?" Chay lifted her chin. "I have everything I want here. The Boys built a little house just for me. Every night I tell them the most wonderful stories, and tuck them into bed. And"—a phantom sneer—"I never have to grow up."

"Did you do it better, then?"

A tear slipped down Chay's mud-smeared cheek, and Jordan sighed.

She'd never been good at comfort—never wanted to be, before. Even if it wouldn't have come off as *motherly*, she'd never seen the point in stopping or grieving—there was only the next step and the next and the one after, hours bleeding into tomorrows that marched too long into the dark. Acknowledging misery with platitudes and talk of *feel-ings* only made things hurt more.

As a tool of persuasion, however, it would have proven useful. She suddenly wished Baron was here instead of her.

Though Baron would be furious when he found out what she wanted to do.

"All right," she said. "Let me rephrase. When someone loves you, they don't shoot the one person you enjoy being around and forget about it the next day."

Chay's nostrils flared. "Peter doesn't *love*—"

"Oh, I know," Jordan said, hooking down the collar of her shirt, and her sister flinched at the puckered braid of scars. "But do you really think you're better off here, doing chores until you shrivel up and turn grey? Or until you fall and break one of those fragile bones? Fine, you've lasted a few years longer than most people. So what? You want someone to clap for you?"

"He's just a child," Chay said weakly.

"If Peter used to be a child," Jordan snapped, "he isn't anymore. There's always a cost to not growing up."

The lantern guttered, spat smoke; wind whispered through their hair. At last Chay folded her hands, weary. "What do you want?"

Jordan grinned. Perhaps there was some sibling resemblance beyond their faces after all.

"I came here for Dust." She risked a step closer; Ael twitched his tail but did not lunge. "For Tink. There are—people—Outside, former Lost Boys, who get sick when they don't have enough of it."

"You," Chay said.

Jordan swallowed. "Well, yes. But others as well." In theory, as Baron might have hedged, they had to exist, even if she hadn't met them yet.

"And you pirates are outmatched."

"Not necessarily." She could not bring herself to say otherwise, in front of her sister. And it wasn't as if she was fully responsible—the pirates had been fighting the Boys long before she'd washed back up on shore, and still failed to gather enough Dust to fly for more than a couple battles. Yet the fact remained: She was the one who had sought out Chay, presumably for help. "You still have access to the Boys, if you want it," Jordan added. "You're not dead yet, which means they'll still let you inside the house, cook their food, listen in on their conversations. You'll know what they're planning, where they're going, where they might rendezvous with the Pales or ambush them.

"So my question is: Could you go back?"

The words hung in the air, dust motes unlit by sun. Jordan could practically feel Baron glaring through the trees. *This is your idea of tact?* "Just for a few days."

Chay's fingers curled around a rumple of sleeve. "But he—he might wake up."

"And how long do you think that will take?" Her sister flinched, but Jordan waved her hook at Tier's motionless form, the massive crimson stain. "You think he'll last like that for weeks, months? He'll need some way to get nutrients, extra care if there are complications. If you help us, we'll get him off the Island as soon as we have the Dust for it."

"And if—if he doesn't come back at all—"

"Even then," Jordan said quietly. "This isn't just for him, or me, or the pirates. No, this is for the tomorrows. This is for all the other poor bastards who can't help growing up, the ones who can't rip it out of their DNA. This is for the kids who shouldn't be punished for existing in fucking *linear time*."

Chay blinked. Jordan realized she was breathing fast and shallow, as if she had just fought an Underground match. It was the most she'd spoken in a while, the most she'd ever said to anyone about why she had returned.

Granted, it wasn't entirely true. She was playing to her sister's altruistic side—clearly, someone who was this broken up over a Rittan man who'd washed up only a few days ago had more of a heart than she did. But as she watched Chay drink in her words—strange, still, to see the echo of her eyes and mouth on another, molded not out of Dust and will but ordinary chromosomes—she realized it wasn't a complete lie, either.

Someday, another kid with the "wrong" kind of body would wash up on the Island, dreaming of an adventure beyond darning socks and waving the Boys goodbye. Someday, they would learn to build their castles high—if not with glamour, then their own shields and blades and words; to forge a thousand kingdoms' worth of reasons they were more than the *thing* between their legs already conspiring to betray them.

Someday, that child's pretending would cost them more than they knew.

"The Pales are guarding the house," Chay said, hands twisting in her lap.

"How many?"

"Four or five, right now." She pointed her chin toward the Lost Boys' wooden tower. A glint of axe-head, perhaps, against the hard black of the forest, and Jordan's hand dropped to her hilt, but no Boys roared down to meet them. "Peter likes it when there are two by the front door and two in the back. It makes him feel like a king."

"And how is the house laid out? Where does Tink sleep?"

A flicker in Chay's eyes, unreadable. "You'll treat her better than Peter does?"

Jordan inclined her head. As a Lost Boy, she had always thought of Tink as imperturbable: Peter's aura, his bright un-shadow, when she wasn't lining her nest with fern fronds or tugging the Ama's braids. But perhaps Jordan hadn't known to pay attention, before—that the fairy had in fact suffered as much as any of them; had spent entire human lifetimes being stripped like a mine. "Sure. We'll build her a fucking palace."

Some of the tension lifted from Chay's shoulders. "All right. Well. She has an alcove by Peter's hammock. Toward the back, like in the old house. If you consider the door facing this clearing the front—"

As her thin fingers sketched shapes in the air, the cave walls seemed to press in close, listening; pine branches clacked, a slow cold percussion.

Jordan rolled back onto her heels, marveled at this small victory—as if her sister had been waiting to tell. As if all Chay had ever wanted was for someone to listen.

"Does that help?" she asked when she'd finished, hands dropping back to Ael's ruff. Her cheeks were flushed, and there was a poorly concealed eagerness in her expression. "How are we supposed to contact each other?"

"Sure," Jordan said. Something like pride flared through her rib cage—Chay would make a decent pirate yet. "As for contact—listen close."

She tipped her head back, garbled an Everbird call. For several long minutes, nothing. Then a glossy black male flapped out of the trees and settled on her shoulder, bobbing his head. Jordan grinned.

Nine years, and she still remembered.

"Hello there," she said, stroking his wings.

Chay's eyes widened. "How'd you do that?"

Jordan shrugged, and the bird nipped her ear affectionately. "Comes with the hook."

In truth, the first time she and Baron had arrived on the Island, they'd spent an inordinate amount of time by the Everbird coves. The creek widened there, and since the other Boys avoided it for the smell, it became their go-to spot for putting on their glamours. She had practiced her calls until the birds came at her command, until they recognized the sounds of her and Baron's names.

"They like seeds and shiny things," she said. "Give them little bribes and they'll carry your messages to me."

Chay held a tentative finger out to the bird. When he ignored it, she drew back, her hands rumpling the dark sleeves of Tier's jacket. Whispered, with her gaze fixed on the ground, "Why would you trust me?"

Behind her stood the wolf, with his tearing fangs. The Boys snored lightly in their rickety tower; Peter whimpered as he dreamed his terrible dreams. The sounds were engraved beneath Jordan's skin; still jerked her awake, some nights, clawing at air.

"I haven't forgiven you." She turned back toward the cave mouth where Koro awaited, bow still drawn. "But now you know what it is to bleed."

On her way out—a pale shape in the dirt, small enough to fit inside a spoon.

Jordan bent closer. A field mouse lay on its back, a half-bitten mushroom glowing faintly in its tiny paws. When she nudged it with her hook, its whiskers quivered, the black beads of its eyes staring up at her in supplication—but it did not run, did not move.

"Fascinating," she murmured: some kind of toxin, paralyzing the creature while keeping it warm and trembling and alive. And even as she felt Koro's gaze boring into her back again, a radiating conviction that something was truly wrong with her, she scooped up the tiny body and slipped it into her pocket.

Chapter 38

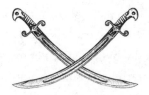

On the front stoop of the Boys' new house, Chay closed her eyes. For half a breath, she built the hollow trees back up in her mind: a warm silence filtering up from earth-twined roots; the Boys' sleeping faces sweet beneath the low flicker of fire; the fresh sailcloth curtains she had tacked over the trees' openings, pale and fluttering like ghosts. But screams drifted out on the cold air now, voices raised in argument. A couple Boys—Tudo and Jack, perhaps—wailed in great heaving sobs.

Murderers, Chay thought, but the word tasted of ash rather than accusation.

She gripped Ael's shoulder, suddenly nauseous. Despite Jordan's motives—and were they any more selfish than Peter's? Were they so wrong?—she had been right about one thing. Chay was still alive. She could still return to the right side of the story, pick up the pieces of herself that had shattered as Tier's heart-blood spilled into her arms. She could still put the Boys to bed, a smile pasted to her face like a mask, and act as if the last few hours had been no more than a passing nightmare.

Back in Burima, heady with stories of plucky princesses and sunset endings, she might have drummed up her courage, played this like just another game of Pretend. But now—she wasn't brave enough to face it. Wasn't clever or strong or good enough at pretending, couldn't even turn up the corners of her mouth without wires of pain coiling up her cheeks.

She couldn't do this.

She had no other choice.

Tier might not wake. She knew this as much from the weeping sisters and daughters and girlfriends she'd seen in her parents' late-night television dramas as from the broken stone inside her own rib cage; had even wondered—as she'd watched him lying there, his face cold and remote as a distant star—if she was drawing from the characters' fear and grief instead of the other way around.

But if she could not imagine a way forward, at least she could take one step with the Boys.

And she knew how *this* story went.

Auri, smiling for her prince even though she could not sing. Isabella, gliding between high bookshelves as a monster salivated below. Serana, weeping as she begged a trickster imp to spin straw into gold.

A strange calm washed over Chay. She had watched so many women manage the expectations of men. Now it was her turn.

"Boys," she shouted, slamming the door open, and they quieted immediately, as if they had been waiting for a grown-up to take charge. The living room was a mess of loose branches and rusted knives, the flask she used for Pretend medicine unstoppered and leaking onto the floor. Peter, Kuli, and the Twins were frozen mid-grapple above the stove; Slightly whipped his staff in sharp figure eights as Jack and Tudo sobbed in opposite corners. Chay bit her tongue—if she didn't, she was afraid she would burst out laughing and never stop. "Why aren't you in bed?"

"Our Dust bottle's empty," Tudo babbled, scrubbing his eyes behind tear-smudged glasses. "Do you have your ointment?"

"No," Chay said. Saw again the gaping hole in Tier's chest, red and ragged and wrong. "I'm—out."

"There's barely any Dust in that ointment anyway, eejit," Kuli snapped, and half the Boys' faces crumpled.

"We'll never fly again," one of the Twins wailed.

"Never ever ever," cried the second.

"I didn't say that." Peter ducked out of Kuli's headlock, Tink clinging like a faded golden limpet to his skeleton-leaf collar. "I just said you'd have to fight for it awhile."

"But I don't *want* to fight without Dust," Tudo shouted, which set off Jack again as well.

"No fun at all, I want to go *home*—"

"And Kuli was trying to steal Tink," piped one of the Twins.

"Was not!"

"I saw it, too," Slightly chimed in, and the room erupted yet again.

Chay swayed against Ael's warm weight, the space between her temples fracturing to glass.

If someone really loves you—

No. She swallowed, clenched her fists. The Boys' howling faces haunted by fire. *No. No.*

There's always a cost to not growing up.

And she thought at Jordan, in reply: *You should have killed me on sight.*

"*Boys*," she screamed, her voice cracking open, and the silence that followed rang in her ears like a bell.

Chay closed her eyes. Sealed on her mask.

She would be brave. She would be strong. She would pretend until it broke her, or keep pretending because she was already broken, and she of all people knew it didn't matter which.

"Go to sleep," she said, lower. The Boys fidgeted, Kuli giggling nervously. This was not the Ama they knew. Not the Ama who scrubbed their dishes and dirty clothes without complaint, who kissed them good night and woke them with scrambled eggs and congee the next morning. She desperately needed to lie down. "Save it for tomorrow."

When the Boys had all washed up at last—when Chay had scrubbed the dirt and blood from her hands and face, though she brought the stinking mass of Tier's jacket with her under the covers of the giant bed—sleep slipped over her, and she dreamed of Outside: her feet planted at the center of a stage, lights bright enough to stop a heart, her stomach torn open and spilling blood.

The Boys were eating breakfast when Chay heard the knock on the door.

A double thud, official sounding, and she lurched toward it first, blinking past the dull throb of her eyes, the stiffness in her knees. She'd been dragged awake before dawn to Kuli screaming out of a nightmare, Slightly and the Twins laying into him and each other as Peter floated, whistling and remorseless, above their heads. Between quieting them with a story—and what stories could she even think of, now, that ended happily?—and mixing a batch of pancake batter in a bowl big enough to fit Jack inside, her head felt at once fog-dull and spiked with nails.

Behind her, amid the sleepy clink of forks, came the soft *oof* of breath: Peter slapping Tink on the back until she was dull and grey, the other Boys watching hungrily. But there was nothing for it—the golden grains that flaked off Tink's skin did not spring from an endless well.

"Ama," Kuli started, "it's not *fair*," and then Chay swung open the door and found herself face-to-face with a Pale.

A shock, this close up. Vertical lines of dried blood were crusted across his mouth; his arms were corded with muscle, his barrel chest level with her face. Peter switched between allying with the Pales and fighting them as mortal enemies on a near-monthly basis, the former because they both enjoyed battling the pirates, the latter because it kept things interesting. This particular Pale was one Peter had recently selected to guard the new house—though, as his ice-blue eyes flicked down to hers, Chay rather wished Peter had chosen someone less *tall*.

"How can I help you?" she asked, her voice a husk.

"We fight pirates today." The Rittan syllables tumbled guttural and strange against the Pale's crooked teeth. A thin stream of saliva drooped from the corner of his mouth, and when he licked it back, Chay stiffened: The tip of his tongue had been sliced off, leaving a blocky, dark pink remainder. "We kill them."

"Woo-hoo, let's go!" Peter darted around them, Tink perched faint and grey on his shoulder. His eyes gleamed with battle hunger. "Come on, Boys, hup-ho."

At the table—newly built as well, from the door of an abandoned ship and some tree stumps—the Boys stared.

"Without Dust?" Slightly asked, tossing his staff from hand to hand.

"*I* have Dust," Peter countered, as if this helped at all. "You scared?"

"No, but—"

"Peter," Chay said quietly, but it was enough. A hungry grin was curling the Pale's too-dark lips, like a crocodile that had smelled blood. Beside her, Ael growled, the fur on his ruff spiking. "You—we—are no use to the Pales without Dust."

Peter shrugged, stubborn. "You Boys stay put, then, if you're wimps. I'll be back in—"

"No," Chay said, desperately wishing he spoke anything other than Rittan so she could keep the Pale from understanding. "The Boys will be—vulnerable."

Peter's eyes darted to the Pale, and then back to Chay, and she willed whatever calculations were clicking through his head to come out in her—and the Boys'—favor. And she was, in a way, still trying to save the others. They were only children, after all, Peter's playmates until they morphed into enemies and he cast them aside. The unfairness of it churned inside her, for everything they had lost and were still losing—and shame, for not having the courage to stop it. She swallowed it down. *This is for the tomorrows.*

"Actually," she said, injecting brightness into her voice, "how would you all like to visit the Cave of Spheres today?"

As the Boys burst into cheers—the Cave of Spheres brimmed with mermaids and strange rock formations, ever-shifting labyrinths of jewels and wonders they could explore for days on end even without Dust—the Pale shrugged.

"You fight beside us next time," he said, "if you are still interest to be allies," and then he turned and vanished with surprising swiftness back into the woods.

Chapter 39

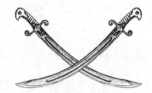

Perhaps these?"

Baron cringed as Mateo proffered another pair of glasses from the mud-caked basket on the ground between them. The cook had caught him on the verge of sprinkling Dust into his eyes that morning, and taken it upon himself to reduce the crew's overall usage by digging up his old cache of visual-assistance flotsam for Baron to try. The problem for Baron was twofold—first, because this meant Mateo had to *guard* him, clanking swords and all, and second, because without Dust or a strong enough prescription, Baron could barely see what he was picking out of the pile.

Adrenaline laced his fingers as he took Mateo's offering, avoiding a sunbeam that would have glinted off the metal for kilometers around. He peered close—not too much mud, that he could tell, and none of the tiny grey beetles he'd brushed off the first pair. But it was as if the entire world turned to fog when he couldn't see, as if he could not trust his eyes even at close quarters.

He slipped the specs on. The blur sharpened into blur with vague edges.

"Anything stronger?" Baron asked, even as fear twisted his lungs—that he would not find anything, that the pirates would decide a partial solution without Dust was better than a full solution with it, that Jordan would knife someone to get him his proper Dust ration—but no.

She would not fight on his behalf, not anymore. And he had no right to ask her to.

A twig snapped. He startled backward, but it was only Mateo rooting through the basket again.

"Hm. Maybe this?" A shape held out. Baron took it. "I almost didn't keep it, it's way beyond what I would ever—"

The forest slid into soft focus: dapples of sunlight, tree trunks emerging from the morass of shadow, though more in his left eye than his right. Baron breathed in, shaky.

"Good enough," he said. A shovel leaned against a nearby tree—the one, he assumed, with which Mateo had dug out his treasure trove. And here was Mateo, too, sun-browned and lean and watchful. Baron's ears heated. "I can help you bury the basket again—"

"No need," the pirate said, grabbing the shovel with an easy sweep of his arms. Dirt tumbled back on top of the hole, which he'd dug with a fluidity that made Baron think of Jordan. As if everyone had been born with a confidence in their bodies but him.

"Do they fit?" Mateo asked.

"They—what?"

The pirate winked, and Baron's heart lurched awkwardly beneath his ribs. "If not, I can bend the arms a bit. I've done it for a couple of the others—"

"No, thank you," Baron said, too loud. He pushed the spectacles up the bridge of his nose—they had already begun to slide—and wondered if this was how Jordan had felt every time he'd offered to fix her prosth. The old pang shot through him—for his rotten tongue, for the raw place inside him from which she had finally torn free. "But thanks for offering."

*   *   *

Jordan was deep in conference with Dau and Jack Two when he clambered back on deck, dizzy with his newfound semi-sight (and the beginnings of a headache—something off about the lenses, he couldn't tell what, and it made him want to scream). The map of the Island on the planks had been expanded yet again, and with her head bent toward the two pirates, the hook tracing invisible lines from cliff to cove to ravine, she could have been the first captain out of Sir Franklin's story, she could have been the commander of armies.

Baron walked as quickly as he could toward the hatch, shame jangling beneath his skin.

He'd heard her return late last night, as moonlight shifted through the grubby cabin portal, the tide murmuring across damp sand—a click of latch, a faint whiff of ash. In the morning, as he felt his way through the smear of faces and pressing bodies, there had been a brush of leather and buckled fastener at his elbow, cold and then gone.

And now—

He could apologize again. Get on his knees and beg in front of the entire crew. But her mind was not easily changed; if she felt like she'd been forced into forgiveness, whatever she offered would be for the sole benefit of those listening.

And a part of him still cried out: They had been the Twins. They did not bare their fractures so others could thrust their knives in.

"Ahoy!"

Baron turned. An Everbird had landed on the deck rail behind him, a whirl of black feathers and beady eyes. Jordan tugged at something on its leg, fumbled it open with the hook and her bandaged hand.

A scroll, he realized as she scanned it. Someone was sending her messages.

Jordan looked up at the crew, which had fallen silent. "The Pales are marching on the ship," she said, her voice carrying across the deck. "At noon. With torches."

"Ah, shit," someone said.

"We still have time," a freckled pirate named Sander pointed out, clambering down from the crow's nest. "If we can keep them from crossing the Ridge—"

The Ridge ran down the western flank of the mountain, walling off the Pales' side of the Island from the pirates'.

"They won't approach from there," Jordan said. "They've allied with the Boys again. A few of them have been guarding their new house."

"Could we booby-trap the pass, then, for next time?"

"Depends on how many they've left to guard their camp—"

"How sure are we that they'll all come down with the Boys?"

"It's not like they've ever let the Boys into *their* camp—"

"Who told you?" Dau asked, raising their voice. "Do you believe them?"

Jordan exchanged a look with them and Koro, and Baron felt an irrational pang of jealousy. Of course she would have wanted backup, when she went on recon. Of course someone else had stepped up while he was sulking in his cabin—someone who could truly defend her, who was not just another softness she had to shield in battle.

"I have a source inside the house," she said, and though the near-apexed sun had carved away their shadows—though, in the distance, Baron swore he could hear the tromp of a dozen feet, the thunk of halberd and pickaxe against beaten ground—a grin spread across her face. "And yes, I do."

In the subsequent whirl of activity—pirates scrambling for blades and body armor, Koro and Dau and Jack Two fleshing out Jordan's plan to head the Pales off in the depths of the forest—Baron found Jordan braced against a washroom basin, her head dipped below the curve of her collarbone.

"Your bandages are dirty," he said.

She exhaled, slow. Her knuckles clenched white along the basin's edge; in the sallow light of the deck prism, beaming down a faint refraction of sun from above deck, her face was tinged grey. "I don't have time to change them."

"They'll get infec—"

She raised the hook in the air, and he cut off abruptly. A small flame flickered beneath his skin, but he tamped it down—fat lot of good his anger had done him yesterday.

"So," he ventured instead. "Who is this spy?"

"Chay." Still she did not look at him.

"Why would she want to—"

"Peter shot Tier in the heart. He's in a coma now. Chay's taking care of him."

"What?"

Jordan pushed herself into some semblance of an upright position, arm trembling with the effort. A grin that was more of a grimace. "My sister had—feelings—for him."

"For Tier," Baron repeated. He thought of the Rittan stumbling out of the San Jukong bar, the curl of red-brown hair falling over his forehead. The peculiar lightness that had flooded Baron's own veins despite the miasma of alcohol, the simmering undercurrent of rage. "I thought he was fixing up a ship, looking for treasure—"

Jordan snorted. "Of a different kind, apparently." She lurched toward the faucet—ignoring Baron's hand thrown out to steady her, as if he didn't know better. As she splashed cold water on her face: "Peter caught the two of them wandering around and shot him in the chest. Which, apparently, was Chay's very first hint that Peter was not on her side. So I talked to her."

"Ah." He could not imagine how that conversation had gone—could not, if he was honest, imagine a scenario in which Chay walked out alive.

But then, perhaps it was more of a punishment for her to stay that way.

A hollow banging in the distance, the clank and shuffle of a dozen people arguing themselves into formation. He had the sudden sense none of this was real—that he would snap awake to crystalline daylight as he hurried across the campus green, the world sharp again through glasses he'd only dreamed he had dropped into the sea. Not an arrow stuck between Tier's ribs, or the hot gush of blood through clutching fingers.

Not Tier lodged in some swirling nothingness deeper than sleep, and all the damage on Jordan's head.

"You couldn't have told me earlier?" he said. The words wrong even as they left his mouth—accusatory, *not important*—but it was as if his tongue had broken its restraints and could not find its old shape.

Jordan raised a brow. "You were asleep."

"I wasn't."

"Well, I thought you were. Did you want me to check on you?"

Baron stuffed his fists in his pockets. Here she was again—the person who shoved into his lab at unholy hours, armored in bruises whose origins he dared not question. Who still held herself at a distance, as if there was any pretending left to do after fourteen years of blistering glamour and crossing the ocean twice and dragging corpses together through smothering smoke.

And here *he* was. A walking storm that could not help but blow itself apart.

The air congealed between them, dank and heavy with all the words they had not said. Then Jordan shoved past him and back into her cabin; reemerged, a couple minutes later, with a darker hem of body armor peeking above the collar of her shirt, sword swinging from her hip.

As she pulled the door shut behind her, Baron caught a snatch of color in the corner of her room: bird feathers and pine needles and—Saints above, was that a *rat*? Fear hummed through his blood, low and electric.

"Jordan," he said.

She barely paused. "You don't have to come."

"You shouldn't be going," he countered. Running his mouth again, and it didn't help that he hadn't slept well for the last—*many*—days, or that dizziness overwhelmed him every time he turned his head. "If one of the other pirates tries to kill you—if you run out of Dust again—"

"Don't *should* me, arsehole," she snapped, and the air huffed out of Baron's lungs like he'd been punched.

It shouldn't have hurt. She hadn't said anything remotely new; the name-calling was as much a part of their routine as their fake doctor joke, or the way he ribbed her for stealing his food. His throat tightened anyway.

"Baron," she said.

He fixed his gaze on the rafter above her shoulder, his face hot with shame. "Just go."

"Stay on the ship, all right?" In the torch-lit dimness, her eyes were near black, almost pitying. "Find some crates and block off the door. I can take care of myself. And we won't let the Pales get all the way down here."

Baron swallowed. That he would still be playing the victim, grown-up as he was; still making excuses for his weakness, when he was barely even wounded.

"All right?" Jordan prompted, an edge in her voice.

"All right," he echoed, hollow as a reed. "I can—help patch the crew up afterward." And then she was gone, and the pirates were clattering up the stairs, calling out to one another about weapons and tactics and to just know the others were there, and he shut himself back in his room and pushed the cot against the door.

He sat in the far corner, head in his hands, for a long, long time.

In the silence of noon, he dreamed of Tier.

Here an ivory crescent of rib cage slit down the middle, a stark line of clavicle bared to open air. Here the blood pooling in mud, the thick smell of flux, every slick detail Baron would never see.

Stop, he found himself crying, into thickets of pine devoid of sound. If only he could find someone to help carry the body, someone to hear. *Stop, or this place will break you apart and rewrite you in its image, and you'll never be able to leave.*

Chapter 40

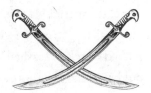

C hay shivered violently as she splashed through the shallows.
The day was brutally cold, her entire body clenched against
the wind that sifted through her dress. The fifteen minutes it had taken
her to scrub Tier's jacket in the creek that morning had felt like wading through razor blades, and afterward, with the sky overcast and no
sunlit rocks on which to lay her wet laundry, she had hunched with
the damp jacket by the fire, teeth chattering, and felt the minutes slip
through her fingers.

Perhaps she had found her own adventure in the bits of information
she snuck to Jordan, the rescue she was planning for Tink. Perhaps her
life had a purpose, now, besides watching the Boys dash off to battle,
or defying the Island with the mere fact of her habitation. But routines
were routines, and pride was pride. If she started eating like a Boy—if
she allowed her body to betray her, relinquished the one thing she had
ever accomplished—how would she live with herself, after?

And—she could not bear to think this, often—she would have
refused the fish that Tier had offered her for nothing.

"She's mine."

"No, I saw her first!"

"Amaaaa, Kuli's taking my—"

"Let go, both of you, you're hurting her," Chay said sternly, and Peter and Kuli pouted as they let the mermaid slip out between their knives.

Chay had brought the Boys, as promised, to the Cave of Spheres: a vast cavern scattered with pearls the size of human heads, algae-crusted bubbles suspended in midair that remained intact no matter how hard you hit them. And, of course, the mermaids, with their bared teeth and taunting laughter. But she had forgotten the chill that hollowed her bones every time Peter yanked a lock of seashell-adorned hair, or sliced a mermaid's tail so he could giggle at the spurt of blood. Forgotten the pit that formed in her stomach, knowing he must have behaved this way in every battle he'd fought, every trip on which he mysteriously disappeared for days—though she had only ever seen him flitting home afterward, his small hands still white as milk.

If he used to be a child, he isn't anymore.

"Give it back." Tudo, this time, chasing what appeared to be a severed chunk of his own ear. Slightly and the Twins scampered among the cave's small stone outcroppings, tossing it between them as Peter, high above, shrieked with glee. "Please," Tudo wailed, "give it *back.*"

One of the Twins smirked, flashing the bloody curve of cartilage in his cupped palm. "Come get it."

"Or keep begging, we don't care," said the other, and by some sleight of hand, some silent transfer from his brother, threw the half-ear across the water to Peter.

"Amaaaaaa," Tudo howled, wiping snot from his face, and Chay straightened, the old ache pounding through her skull.

"Boys. Stop it."

"You rat," Peter tossed over his shoulder, and then he swept away, Tink a tepid golden halo at his sleeve. "Come on, let's play something else."

Chay said, to his back, "Peter."

He turned—smiling coyly, all blue eyes and rosy cheeks. Even now, knowing what he was, her heart lifted at the sight. "Yes, Ama?"

The voice no woman had ever been able to resist. She kept her face like stone. "Give me Tudo's ear."

Peter sighed and uncurled his hand reluctantly. She plucked out its contents with two fingers. "And all you Boys, come give him Dust to reattach it."

Silence, brittle as glass.

One by one, the Boys gathered around her—an electric current running through them, something between dread and a fearful sort of rage. Healing wounds did not require nearly as much Dust as did flight, but they all knew, by now, that it would use up the meager pinches Peter had sprinkled in their leather pouches that morning.

For all their Pretending, they could not truly remember what it was to live without Dust. It was like running out of oxygen.

"But we won't have any left to fight the pirates with," Jack said in a small voice.

"The pirates aren't here today," Chay said firmly. Tudo's blood was drying in the cracks between her fingers, and she saw, suddenly, Tier's chest heaving in the dark, eyes glinting and wild, his life coursing inexorable through her hands—*stop*. "You Boys' health comes first."

"He doesn't even need that part of his ear," Kuli snipped.

"He does."

"Does not."

"Does t—" Chay ground the heel of her free hand into her thigh, exasperated. The Boys would never restore their Dust supply if they kept using it at this rate. Years ago, the previous Slightly had hurled a bottle of it down a cliff in an inexplicable rage, and Peter had put the other Boys to sleep for a week; when they'd woken again, a new wine bottle glowed from Tink's alcove, and Peter had informed them that that Slightly had returned Outside. Now, though, the Pales knew they were defenseless, and Chay was not eager to see another Lost Boy run off the Island.

"We should take bones from one of the Pales," Kuli was saying. "Tell them it was the pirates."

Slightly snorted. "You're so loud, they'd catch you walking out our front door."

"Am not." Kuli jutted his chin. "I snuck out of the Rankling Tinkerland and killed all seven kings without a sound."

"That was a story the Twins made up when they found a bunch of coins in the mermaid lagoon," Slightly snapped. "It wasn't *real.*"

The other Boys' eyes widened in unison. Slightly's voice had cracked on *real*, given way to something deep and rough and foreign, and in its wake the cave itself shivered, stilled. Slightly had always pitched his voice low—all the Boys did, from some inescapable instinct that lower meant better—but it had never before broken in earnest.

Kuli giggled nervously.

"Slightly," Peter drawled, and the tension screwed tighter, fissured across the dripping stone walls. "C'mere. I want to show you something."

A flicker through Slightly's face, his knuckles whitening around his staff. Then he stepped slowly toward Peter, head bowed.

"Without the staff," Peter said carelessly.

Slightly's jaw went rigid. "What?"

Peter arched a brow. The stick clattered to the ground, and the two boys flew out the mouth of the cave, a sheath of sunlight imprinting on Chay's vision in their absence.

As Kuli laughed into the ensuing silence, mocking the bray of Slightly's new voice, goose bumps prickled the back of her neck.

She could flee now. Beg for refuge on the pirate ship, curl into some dusty corner of the hold as her sister's armored knights slayed her monsters and whisked her safe into the dusk. Jordan would be disappointed, but Chay sensed she had been incidental to her sister's plan—insider information or no, the pirates were always going to fight until the bitter end.

Tier, she thought, would have sailed away with her already.

"Where are they going?" she demanded, rounding on Kuli, whose mouth clamped shut. The other Boys regarded her, as blandly incurious as baby rats.

"Out," the Twins said in unison.

"They'll be back." Jack laid a small hand on her elbow, and she jerked away—another wrong move, but she couldn't stand by and watch an arrow pierce another heart, a crimson gash draw tight across the soft of another jugular.

"Where did they go?"

The Boys shrugged, not caring, and Chay ran.

An hour later, she found Peter drifting above the Island's highest waterfall, alone.

"Where is he?" she demanded, ragged with exhaustion, but his cheeks only dimpled into that milk-tooth smile, perfect and untouchable and wrong.

"Where is who?"

"Peter." Her throat was a slash of sandpaper; her legs ached from the climb. "Please. Where's Slightly?"

"I don't know," he said, and before she could scold or tease or cajole him into something as messy and absolute as truth, he slipped back through the trees, whistling loudly.

Above her head, the afternoon sun seared the world white.

This place, Chay thought, her teeth gritted. The waterfall below her was a skein of silk, the Island shifting beneath it the restless mantle of some alien planet.

Peter's words weighed in her bones.

Her original troop of Boys had left her one by one. Some, like Baron, had asked and been granted permission in daylight; others had vanished overnight, and she'd believed Peter when he said they could not bear to say goodbye. She had assumed Jordan to be the single aberration, and for good reason.

But now—

Now—

How many others had Peter taken, in this long lightless span of years? How many other children had he renamed and then discarded?

Far off, a cloud of Everbirds flapped from a hillside, a swarm of velour. The Boys would expect her back soon, if they hadn't already cut each other to pieces. But when Chay closed her eyes, she could feel herself dissolving into the sky, motes of dust blowing off her like snow.

Her heart—how had Peter left it? An ash-dusted hollow, an exit wound, an open grave. Chay had never lashed out with her fear, her pain—had instead tucked it deep inside herself, allowed it to fester and grow thorns. But standing on the promontory, a curtain of water thundering onto waiting stone, she thought: If she could at least keep someone else from suffering. Ruin one life in exchange for those of future lovers, fathers, daughters.

Pay the cost of their growing up.

When she moved again, her joints creaked, a body wakened after an eon frozen in ice. Soon, she would return to Tier, at the heart of the Island—tend to him, and find a way for him to wake. But she could not stop seeing Slightly's hand uncurl from his staff, the almost obscene bounce as wood met stone. Could not stop hearing the squawk of his voice on *real*. And all the Boys before him, who had left without a farewell—she could not remember which of them she had watched fly safely over the horizon.

She bowed her head toward the sun, and murmured what paltry prayers she could remember, before slipping back into the cool shadows of the trees.

Chapter 41

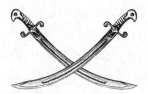

The thickest part of the woods: afternoon sun splintered through close-knit branches, shadows cool and still, Jordan's feet barely touching ground as she and the pirates crept toward the place Chay had marked on her map. Dau had buoyed them all with just enough Dust to lighten their footsteps, and Jordan's skin was shot through with gold, the throb of withdrawal faded slightly from the pit of her diaphragm.

A small bitterness at the corner of her mouth—that from now on, she would only ever feel this well in the face of impending death.

Koro at her side again, hard-jawed and unquestioning. She did not think about who might have stood in his place.

(The way Baron's hand had hovered at her elbow. The furrow between his eyebrows, the way he kept blinking and squinting as if the glasses she'd asked Mateo to find him still weren't strong enough. The flinch between her scapulae every time their eyes met; the bare want, in his, for her to trust him with her weakness.)

(But just because she'd broken in front of him before did not mean she had to again.)

At the head of their party, Jack Two raised his fist. *Halt.*

Jordan scanned the opposite slope, hand curled around the hilt of her sword. Dau, Jack Two, Mateo, Koro, and Seida were interspersed among the few remaining men on the crew she hadn't quite gotten to know— all of them tensed and wary, faces smeared with camouflaging mud.

Beneath the shimmer of noon light, the birds had gone silent, as if a hawk was gliding overhead. The forest a confusion of branches and brush, moss gentling the air a luminescent green—

There. A faint twitch, mud against mud.

The Pales emerged suddenly, as if they had sprung whole from the latticework of trees—chests crusted with silt, dried blood smeared across lips and hatchets. About two dozen, though it might not have been their whole camp; the last time Jordan had scouted their side of the Island, nine years ago, she'd counted more than thirty. She picked out flame-red Erendite hair, an aquiline Glennan nose, the olive-tinted skin of a Dal. Brought together to play a role, as the pirates had been, by some impulse old as humanity.

Jack Two waited for them to reach the bottom of the slope before bringing his fist down.

A twang of loosed string, a thud. The two leading men collapsed, arrows quivering in their throats.

The rest of the Pales' heads whipped up, and they charged.

Jordan had gone over the Island map again with Jack Two and Dau—marked out choke points for possible ambush, dense unclaimed swaths of forest where they might station themselves for raids. But then she'd spent precious minutes bent over the washroom sink, heaving up her breakfast, and who knew which version of the battle plan the crew had been told in her absence.

Whatever it was, the pirates' line scattered against the Pales almost immediately. Too many of them, everywhere, and though the pirates' slight boost of Dust softened the drag of gravity, the Pales wielded thick crossbows and heavy hatchets, throwing knives that whipped through the slick verdant air with a hum that burrowed beneath Jordan's skin.

"Back," Jack Two was shouting, "get back," but as their crew retreated up the hill, the Pales followed, a jumble of shields and bodies, steel edges and howling mouths. A dough-faced man bore down on Jordan with a blade-tipped staff and she heaved her sword up, her arm juddering with the impact; blocked again and again as he slammed into her at full strength.

Then a high keen of steel from her other side—Seida, a cut from his forehead pouring blood into his cold grey eyes, sword singing down toward her.

Too fast for her to dodge, her blade locked as it was against the Pale's staff. Too much force for her to block, as her hook was a needle in comparison. But as blood thundered in her ears, that strange sense of *unfolding* returned—the forest opening itself to her, every clump of grass and stone and glowing-green leaf vein composing itself into something she could read. And when Seida's sword arced toward her heart, she *knew* its beveled edge, the whistle of air parting around its facets. Felt its infinitesimal waver *away* as if she'd nudged it away with her own hand.

Seida's eyes went wide, and then her hook tore out his throat.

"Anyone else?" she called as he crumpled, gargling imprecations, and slung her sword toward the Pale as he charged her again.

In the end, she'd brought no clever strategies. No tactical maneuvers designed to earn the pirates' respect, or cement her place at the head of the crew. Her blade lashed out without control, her hook a flail, tracing red across wrists and cheeks and the insides of arms, and choking was an impossibility now—this was the desperation of her time ticking down, this was blind fury at her own withdrawal, this was every bloody seam she would have opened on the boy who took and took and did not even remember why.

"Charge," she heard herself scream, her voice already jagged from vomiting. "Now, now, now—" And *there*, the pirates shattering the enemy front, and the Pales who were still alive gripped their axes and ran.

Thunder fading to silence, and she roared after them, a warning:

She would paint the mountains with their blood; the rivers would flow crimson with their defeat. Her voice echoed through the hills, ricocheted off a hundred trees, and when she turned back, half the pirates' eyes were fixed on the gore-crusted curve of her hook, the corpses at her feet.

Five of them. If she was going to start keeping track. Red poured from mouths and chests, entrails spilling. Her ears rang.

Somewhere above her head, a bird warbled, testing the air.

"Saints above," Dau murmured. "Saints above, did we *win*?" And in the faces of her crew, Jordan saw something like fear.

Chapter 42

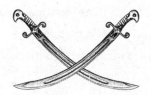

The pirates returned to the ship drenched in blood.

Baron's fingers tightened around the fuller of his two hand sanitizer bottles as he watched them mount the gangplank. The Lost Boys, fearing even the smallest cuts, had always retreated quickly and often, and so the wounds that Wen and then Chay patched up were the kind of scrapes one got from riding a bicycle down a San Jukong sidewalk, or playing ka ball at recess. But now—half of Ellis's nose had been sheared off, the lumpy brown severance cupped in one hand as he covered the remainder with the other; Jack Two was doubled over, palm pressed to bloodied shoulder. It was the kind of fighting that belonged more in the hospital than the movies.

Yet even as Dau lined them up by the severity of their injuries, an air of cheerfulness pervaded much of the crew. They had triumphed—a fact that became loudly apparent as they rehashed the skirmish to each other, clapped the backs and shoulders of those who could take it. Against slim odds and a scattershot strategy, brute force and Jordan's sword arm had saved them. And Jordan, in their midst—complimenting Dau for a quick bit of footwork, Koro's aim with his arrows as he ran. Her chin lifting as they acknowledged her in turn, as if she was an emperor simply accepting her due.

"Take your half over there," Dau said to Baron, shoving a makeshift first aid kit and several pouches of Dust into his chest. "And stitch them up as much as possible. We don't have enough Dust to dump it all into one person."

Baron nodded, his head pounding and hollow, and led his first patient, a pirate clutching his own intestines, toward the pallet he had conscripted as a temporary operating table.

"Do you need help lying down?" he asked, low, and the man nodded.

"Thanks."

The crew quieted as Baron and Dau began their work—out of respect for those being treated, perhaps, or a morbid fascination with the stretch-pull of black thread through human skin. At the press of their gazes, Baron braced himself against the old terror—for electricity to bolt through his lungs, for his hands to shake so hard he dropped his needle onto the planks. Yet as he stitched the flaps of stomach, the pirate chewing furiously on anesthetic herbs from Dau's stock—as he edged Dust into the hole in Jack Two's shoulder, and felt the man's breath ease—a remarkable calm filtered through him, as if a lens had snapped in place, shifted the deck into focus. For a caught breath, he saw himself in an operating room, scalpel flashing between his fingers, armored in a white coat instead of a sweat-sticky button-down.

Then the vision dissolved, and only blood remained.

"Hey."

Jordan stood at the end of his queue—her face spattered with dried gore, though she had not claimed any significant injuries when Dau surveyed the crew. The rest of the pirates had dispersed to toast their victory on the beach, more than a few of them nodding or even grinning at her as they went; aside from Ellis, leaning on the rail of the crow's nest for evening watch, the two of them were alone on deck.

Baron pushed up his glasses with his wrist—his hands were drenched with bodily fluids, and smelled like it. "You're alive."

"Yeah." Her mouth twisted, brief. "You're still here."

"Yeah." A basin sat between his and Dau's stations; he rinsed his hands in the rancid-looking water before pumping a fresh blob of hand sanitizer into his palm. His whole body was hazy with fatigue. "I am."

"Seida's dead."

Baron blinked. "What?"

"He tried to kill me."

A rush in his ears, phantom gurgle of a severed throat. "But he's a—in the middle of a battle—are you sure it wasn't just—"

Her face shuttered. "Are you fucking joking?"

Saints. Too late, he realized he'd done the same thing the doctors had, nine years ago, in calling her a drug addict. A weight pressed on his lungs—his rotten mouth, again. "I'm sorry, all right? I haven't slept in about a week, and—I don't know what else you want me to say—"

She fired up instantly. "What else *I* want you to say? You chose to come here, Baron. If you stopped playing the victim for one second—"

"Me," Baron said slowly, "playing the victim? What about you? Running out of your parents' house, living on the streets—"

"You think I wanted that?" she snapped, stepping toward him. "I was thirteen."

"You didn't want parents at all." His voice shook, and he was acutely aware of Ellis watching them from above, the handful of pirates listening from beneath the ship. But some instinct had roused in him, beyond the heat of his face or the alc-coated gore-slime on his hands, because Saints take him, he was right. The realization unfurled as he spoke. "You never wanted any part of that life, did you? You could have gone to some—some other hospital, one of those state-run rehab centers—"

"You think I knew what *rehab* was at that age? After five years on the Island? We were eight when we came here. What the fuck would I have—"

"But when you found out," Baron countered. "When you were fourteen, fifteen, sixteen—"

"Why do you care?"

"Because you're still running around this place *destroying yourself*," he blurted, his voice cracking. "The battle plans, the constant fighting, cleaning up afterward—you love it here, don't you? This is the only place you feel like your anger means anything."

A terrible silence. On the beach below, laughter and the cracking open of a fresh whiskey barrel, Mateo crouched in the sand as he stoked sparks from kindling. Baron clenched his fists, fixed his burning eyes on the darkened sky. He'd never made it through an argument of substance without shattering like glass. What made him think he could get through to her—and now, of all times?

"Well." A mask had come down over Jordan's face—one he knew by heart, from all the years she'd snapped it on in front of the Lost Boys. She swept her hook toward the water, a steel arc of reflected dusk. "If you're done here, you know what to do."

Raucous shouts below them, cheers as something thumped the waves. Baron shuddered a breath. A hitch in his lungs, a tightening vise at his temples—another storm was coming, and he couldn't do a thing about it.

"No," he said thickly. "Not this again. It's—we were going to leave this place together. That was the whole point, wasn't it?"

"So what does it matter how I make that happen?" she demanded, the hook dropping back to her side. "You think I'm fucking around with Pales and swords for the laughs? I have a plan. I'll get us out. If you'd just stop trying to—"

But the thunder was surging through him again, fracturing her words to static, and he staggered toward the hatch, one hand raised.

"Please," he said, hoarse. His limbs were sacks of stones; he could not pull in enough air. "I need a—a minute."

Something in his voice, or perhaps it was all he'd needed to say. When he climbed back down through the hatch, she did not follow.

He locked the door of his cabin, crawled back onto his cot. The storm blasted him apart in silence.

In the weeks that followed, the new respect with which the other pirates regarded her settled into fact, like sediment falling to ocean floor—a hush as she passed them around the bonfire, faces turning toward her with questions about ship maintenance or the day's plans or the deadliest way to throw a knife. Jack Two may have cut a more intimidating figure, and Dau may have established themself as quartermaster and Dust steward, but Jordan had proven herself as their loose cannon, their ace—at least, when she was functional.

Volatile, Baron overheard someone mutter one afternoon, *can barely hold a sword if she's not high*, but she *won* for them, the Pales fled before her blade, and in return Dau gave her a greater portion of the Dust they scavenged from the high branches near the Lost Boys' house. On the nights the pirates roasted their fish on the open shore, she smeared charcoal across her cheeks like war paint; blazed across the sand, glowing gold, her feet barely touching the ground.

And though Baron ventured out, in the days after their argument— though he sat with the pirates, and picked at his food, and wanted too much—she did not look at him once.

Chapter 43

J ordan fought.

Across white sand beaches and boulder-strewn cliffs, beneath waking dawns and bloody-fingered sunsets. The Everbirds called to her in a rush of dark wings and she followed, sword hot from its sharpening on cliff stone, right arm chafing against the hook's leather harness. And perhaps she did take more pleasure in it than was strictly necessary—perhaps sprinting across forest paths and leaping ravines made her feel more alive than any syndicate op she'd ever done—but she was still running out of time; the shadow of withdrawal still hovered beneath the surface of her skin. And so every Pale hand cut off was one that could no longer be raised against her; every bridge and clearing secured was one more channel through which the pirates could trawl for Dust.

The Boys themselves appeared infrequently—it seemed her little arson trick had dealt quite a blow to their Dust supply, or else the forests were shifting to keep them apart. But in the meantime, she led the crew out against the Pales, left slashed throats and spilled blood in her wake.

Baron bandaged them up afterward, his mouth a thin edge of disapproval.

She suspected he had begun to train, in her absence—she caught the pommel of the rapier in his cabin slick with sweat, scuff marks from his shoes across the cleared expanse of the hold. He wouldn't demonstrate, of course, not in front of her, but something like a grin sparked inside her at the thought. If he had picked up a sword, maybe he was ready to drop the bullshit. And if he was ready to drop the bullshit, maybe he would stop insisting on cloistering himself on the ship—

Jordan pushed down the thought. She was not here to relive her childhood, or coddle him for the sake of nostalgia. Once the pirates snagged Tink, they would all sail away, leaving the Boys and the Pales to their own petty campaigns, and Baron would finally feel like he had permission to do whatever the fuck he wanted.

But when she clambered down to the hold after a Pale battle one afternoon, ahead of the rest of the crew, and found him jabbing at a twist of hammocks, she couldn't resist.

"Your wrist should line up with the edge of the blade."

Baron startled, his sword clattering to the floor. He bent to retrieve it, fingers repeatedly missing the hilt; when he finally rose again, weapon in hand, his face had flushed pink. "I don't see why everyone here is such a prick about proper form."

"Because *everyone* looked it up on the internet once and has crowned themself the supreme authority." She drew her own sword—still streaked with Pale guts, but in the dimness of the hold it looked clean enough. "Fight me."

His eyes went wide behind his glasses. "What?"

"Come on." The Pale battle should have worn her out, but her veins still sang adrenaline, her limbs warm enough to not be sore. "First touch, winner gets half the loser's dinner."

"You'd kick my arse."

"Then at least no one else will."

"They still will, trust me," he said. By then, the other pirates were clomping down into the hold, shooting him and Jordan curious looks; Dau smirked as if they'd won a bet. "Maybe we should take this outside," he added. "More room."

And less of an audience, Jordan thought, but hey, if he wanted to impose conditions, at least he was agreeing to the initial proposal.

She sheathed her blade, and her grin was as wide as Dau's. "Name the place."

They squared off in a clearing that was both out of eavesdropping distance from the ship and decently removed from both Lost Boy and Pale territory. The sky a flat grey, the trees around them glowing as if lit from within. Baron's hands shook as he drew; his gaze darted from the rusted pommel to Jordan's bare forearm, the puckered line Peter had left. It still hurt to clench her fingers too tight, but she'd stripped off the last of the bandages a few days before.

"How's the arm?" he asked.

She rolled her shoulders. Her sword flashed silver against the dull clouds. "It'll get there."

"The Dust is helping?"

She nodded. The pirates had only built up such a reserve of Dust in the first place because they'd scavenged for years; only lately—because of her, everyone thought but no one said—had the supply in Dau's cavernous pockets begun to visibly wane. They had to capture Tink soon, if Jordan was going to be anything more than a drain on resources.

"Oh. And." Baron swallowed, jerked his chin toward her right side. "Swords only, yeah?"

Jordan saluted with the hook. "Wouldn't dream of anything else."

She lunged, light on her feet, and his hand shot up, their blades colliding with a crack that made him wince. Loose jabs toward his shoulder, knee, other arm, and he yelped and backed into a tree, his rapier held out awkwardly in front of him.

"Bend your legs a bit more," she called, pointing the hook toward her knee, "it gives you more flexibility." He mimicked her, grimacing. "And keep your guard up—" Another flurry of steel, mostly hers, and then her blade was poised above the soft of his throat, his head tipped back against the tree.

He made a face. "You've been waiting to do that."

"Of course not." She nicked the underside of his chin, and his mouth went into a funny little spasm. "Sparring is about learning, not posturing."

"And learning is about—deliberate practice, not being challenged to duels by obnoxious pirates who don't know when to stop fighting."

Jordan stowed her sword. "You should be glad I'm letting you off with one match."

"And you should be glad I haven't had my coffee."

"I'm sure it would have helped immensely."

He peeled himself off the tree, nudging his blade several times through empty air before it found the scabbard. And then he straightened, and stilled, spots of color rising high on his cheeks.

She hadn't looked at him, not *like that*, since that night in her cabin, the dark quiet hours before Imni and Omni had tried to kill them. Now: the strange cut of Mateo's glasses across his face, as if he'd applied Dust so subtly she could not read the seams of the change. The hands she'd watched dart across a computer keyboard on a thousand different nights, made incongruous around the hilt of a much older weapon.

Whatever this was, it did not feel like memory.

"Um," Baron said, articulately.

Jordan grinned. Wind gusted down from the cliffs, lifted the hair off her forehead, and she breathed it in, ocean salt and sharp green pine. As if the forest was, for the hour, theirs and theirs alone. "Yeah?"

"Question for you."

"Mm-hmm."

He blinked, hard. The longer she stared, the more he flushed, a hitch in his breath like he'd forgotten what to do with it. But it was not panic—that, he would have tried to hide. "What will you do, once you have Tink?"

She stepped closer, her hook hovering above the stilted rise of his chest, his eyes blown wide and blank and dizzying. Over the past few weeks, they had kept their distance. Even though he had stayed—even though she'd decided to forgive him because of it—there were Pales to fight, and the way the pirates' eyes at once pinned her hook and skittered away. There was the way she still canted off-balance when his gaze pricked hers across the crowded hold, the residual give of her knees.

But she had missed *this*—the raw hunger filling her mouth, the heat rising off his skin. Control like a marble on her tongue, shooting her sharp and high as karsa.

What will you do?

And she said, smiling, "Everything."

"No, I'm serious." He leaned back, an expression on his face that made her want to laugh. "When you're not in withdrawal anymore. You could glamour as much cash as you can imagine, make yourself into anything, anyone—"

He choked to a halt: She had cupped his chin in her hand. A drop of blood from the cut she'd made seeped into the lines of her palm.

"Maybe," she whispered, "let's not think so much about after."

And he shot back, almost mocking, "Who says you're thinking?"

"Nice try," she said. "I am, actually."

And then she kissed him.

It was the first time she had done it in the relative absence of pain, and the difference was startling—as if light had shot through her veins, as if she were quicksilver inside her own skin, bright and lethal and bursting at the seams. Baron made an extremely undignified sound, and she laughed into his mouth, tugged at his collar.

"Please don't." His hand around the hook's leather harness, careful as if it were a baby bird. "This is the only clean shirt I have left."

"Go without." Her head spun. A low drumbeat in the bowl of her pelvis, but it was one she had asked for, a song she had called in from the far reaches of the sea. Sparks at the tips of her fingers as she fumbled

THESE DEATHLESS SHORES   285

with the harness, shucked the sweaty thing off, touched the soft skin at his throat and his chest and the crook of his waist—

He said her name like an anthem, he said it like a call to war.

"See," she said later, as they curled together against the clearing's largest tree, "*that's* how you should spar," and he groaned and buried his face into her shoulder.

Chapter 44

Baron polished his glasses with the hem of his shirt, studiously avoiding the vague shape that lay beside him.

He had, in fact, spent as much time as he could stand with the rapier, given that his vision splintered and his chest went tight every time he even caught sight of a blade. It was the one fear he could imagine overcoming, as Jordan and the pirates battled the Pales on distant shores: the sword's geometry a graceful swoop against the dull planks of the hold, his formless terror distilled to that single cutting edge.

And perhaps, in some dusty corner of his mind, he'd *wanted* Jordan to catch him—to look at him again like they could be something other than strangers. They both spoke a handful of languages, but there was only one in which she would truly accept an apology.

Now, her thumb traced the rim of his ear, and he could have laughed. He'd been played like a symphony, held and kissed and touched until his rawest nerves seared clean and pure as a violin melody. Even thinking about it sent the insides of his knees ringing like steel chimes.

His first time, traversing this strange country—letting himself go, letting her hold him this way.

He could not help but wonder if it was also goodbye.

"Baron."

"Yeah?" He edged his glasses back on with his ring and pinkie fingers. Her face still slightly out of focus, close as it was, but he could make out a curve of mouth, her eyelids at half-mast.

"If we could glamour money—" She rolled onto her side, facing him. "And launder it properly. Saints above. The entire syndicate could eat shit. And we'd have an infinite supply of A-grade karsa."

"And then?"

"What do you mean?"

"I mean—" He paused. Words still difficult, his sense of his body split open and scattered to the breeze. "What would you do, after that?"

"Whatever's needed, I guess. Ten hells, don't ask me these kinds of questions." She shifted on her right arm—the hook still doffed, for now—and considered him. He was not sure if she was satisfied with what she saw. "You?"

Baron shrugged, suddenly embarrassed. It was the kind of cheesy thing asked on Meiri talk shows: *If you had ten million mir, how would you spend it? What would you do if money was no obstacle?* The kind of thing that was impossible to move out of the imaginary, at least for him, at least with his family. "I'd—I think I'd try and finish school."

She made a disbelieving sound.

"More slowly," he amended. The computer lab flashed across the backs of his eyelids, and the old lightning flared through his lungs. "And maybe, ah, a different course. But I've been—stitching up you pirates after battles, a bit—"

"You put Ellis's nose back on."

"With Dust, but—I suppose." He took her hand—a shiver of something like recognition, the tiny miracle of it, that he could reach across the chasm and return with the warmth of her calloused fingers. "I could do something like that. And it would be a—a reason to wake up in the morning."

She was still looking at him intently. "If that's what you want," she said, and he was surprised to hear no trace of scorn. "What?"

"I thought you were—" He motioned vaguely at the ocean, at what lay beyond. "Not in favor of—of office jobs."

"Everyone has to find some way to keep going, right?" Her thumb traced his brow, the line of his cheek. "Some reason to stay."

And then his throat closed and his eyes were spilling over and her arms wrapped around him, holding him the way he had never dared ask because he'd never believed it was something she would give. She was holding him and he was sobbing into her shoulder, the storm he had tried so hard to seal inside his skin howling out undignified, an obliteration, and still—and still—she did not let go.

"Sorry," he said thickly, when he could speak again. The inside of his chest felt as wrung out as old sailcloth. "Sorry, I—sorry."

Her fingers tangled in his hair. " 'S gotta come out somehow."

"Didn't—mean for you to—"

"I've *been* here, Baron," she said, almost patient. "Remember?"

"Oh." He swallowed, which hurt. "Right."

They lay there for a while, side by side, as he—far too loudly—attempted to regain control of his breathing. He flexed his fingers, clenched his toes. Focused on the press of her arm, and the dull ache of his lower back. Beneath the haze of their recent—exploits, his skin still felt glass-fragile, rattling. As if, with a push, he might fall apart.

"When you said you weren't afraid to die." Jordan's voice was a murmur beneath the wind, and he breathed, breathed, felt her palm pressed flat against the bruise that was his sternum. "When you said we'd lived by different physics, here."

"Yeah?" It came out a croak.

"I think, for everyone who leaves the Island, everyone who's allowed to come in the first place, that's kind of what it *means*, isn't it?"

He blotted his eyes with the cuff of his sleeve. Above them, fluffy clouds drifted past; pine branches clacked in the light wind. "I—I'm not sure I understand."

"The way we mixed Dust and death to get here. The way we'd rather be cut off cleanly at the end of the story than live out adulthood like some seventy-year depressing-as-fuck epilogue. It's almost like that's *from* the Island. Like that's the point of Peter."

"Oh," Baron said. "You—think about that stuff?"

She flicked his nose, but not hard. "Arse." And then, her head shooting up: "Someone's coming."

He blinked away the residual heat behind his eyes, drew a shaky breath. There—a crunch of leaves, getting louder. Unlikely that it was the Boys, if Chay's reports were to be believed, and the Pales always traveled in groups, their footsteps a susurrus snaking through the underbrush. Whoever—or whatever—was moving through the forest now walked alone.

Then Dau stepped out of the trees, hands stuffed in their coat pockets. "Oi. Thought I heard voices."

Baron flushed all the way up to his forehead, though the quartermaster gave no sign of how long, exactly, they had been listening. Beside him, Jordan had risen to her feet, sword in hand, hook donned again with astounding speed. He wondered how much she had practiced, alone in her cabin. If she had known on what occasion she would choose to take it off.

"What is it?" she asked.

Dau jerked their head toward the depths of the forest. "There's something I think you'll want to see."

The bodies were barely recognizable as flesh.

They lay on their backs, oozing blood and pus, bloated skin speckled with iridescent flies. A shard of green glass was jammed beneath the chin of the thinner one, and ridges of bare larynx showed through, pinkish fluid leaking from the seam where flesh met glass. But it was the open wounds at which Baron could not stop staring: the chewed-up gashes along thigh and forearm, spines and fingers bent liquid and wrong.

All the corpses' bones had been removed.

"Dust," said Dau quietly, when neither he nor Jordan spoke. "That's what they become, when they don't make it over to us."

"Saints above," Baron choked. There was a strange blistering behind his eyes, as if his corneas were unraveling. He had seen this before—the wet slice of steel between trees, the scream cut off in crimson; should not, at this point, have been surprised. But the stench crawled down his nostrils and he was reeling anyway, his head floating high above the canopy.

A fly was tangled in the tentative line of fuzz on the thinner body's upper lip, rubbing its tiny greedy hands.

Baron turned and vomited into the brush.

"You remember him?" Jordan gripping his elbow, an anchor. Baron wiped his mouth, noted distantly that his knees had gone unsteady.

"Slightly," he said, realizing. The round-cheeked boy who had washed up the day they had left, insisting his name was Henry. Maybe five years old at the time. Fourteen, now, his departure already late.

"Yeah," said Dau. "Those always get the most gruesome deaths. For pretending to know more about the Outside than Peter does."

"And the other one?" Jordan frowned down at the second body—gawky-limbed with early adolescence, dark hair crusted with blood. "A Pale. Huh."

"So much for their alliance," Dau said tartly. "If we bring this to their chief—"

"There's nothing to prove *we* didn't do it, though."

"The Boys are the only ones who extract Dust ingredients this way."

"It might not matter, if they take us in bad faith."

Baron sagged against the nearest tree—*letting the adults talk it out,* said a snide voice in his head. Two of Dau's fingers had been cut short, the remainders knotted with scar tissue, and he wondered if Peter had severed them as punishment, or Dust-tithe, or to fit them into their hollow tree. The latter had happened to the first Slightly Baron had grown up with, nine years ago—Wen stitching the loose flaps of skin as the Boy howled and the others turned away. A few days later, he had vanished.

"—return them to the Boys tonight," Jordan was saying. "Drop them off at the old clearing, and see what the Pales think of their alliance then. Baron?"

Baron jerked back—a beetle had skittered through a tiny gap between the glass and the underside of Slightly's chin. He felt tainted to the core, as if the stench had soaked into his lungs and would marinate in his bones forever after.

"Yeah," he said, clearing his throat.

"Let's go."

Then the arrows thudded into the tree behind him, and a mob of Pales and Lost Boys stormed the clearing with a roar of utter outrage.

He could not run, at first.

His feet churned too slow against the mud as if in dreaming; his arms windmilled, teetering him off-balance. Then Jordan yanked him down by the elbow and a dagger scythed through the space where his head had just been and they stumbled back through the woods, branch-whip and ankle-scratching brush and brief cleared patches of dirt. The ship unfurled like a shadow on the sand, the pirates emerging with swords and shields and hidden body armor.

"How could you *do* that?" Peter cried as he swooped toward them, his eyes glinting malevolently, and the Boys jeered. "He was just a kid—and what about that Pale?"

"Oh, stuff it." Jordan knocked an arrow away with her sword, and Baron stumbled again, his pulse a sick thud in his throat. "Was it your idea to put the bodies side by side?"

Peter shrugged, coy. Then the Pales surged forward too, all

blood-painted teeth and righteous fury, and the pirates raced across the beach to meet them and the world broke open, a confusion of screams and steel and crashing bodies. Baron's head spun as he allowed Jordan to maneuver him toward the edge of the melee. He'd neglected to put on a protective vest—had assumed, when Jordan said first touch on their fake duel, that she meant it. And now he was as good as naked.

"Run back to the hold," Jordan shouted in Kebai. Her sword was a starburst of light, a bright constant clang. "I'll cover you."

"What?" He dimly noted that he was wheezing again—his lungs only filling halfway, his limbs gone rigid and numb.

"Back to the hold." Another crash of steel, and Jordan wrenched her sword away from a Pale hakapik, kicked its wielder in the chest. "Go on."

Baron hesitated. His sword hand was shaking even harder than it had been a couple hours ago; his continued presence would hinder the pirates more than help.

Yet—the memory of her mouth brushing his throat, her thumb trailing the jut of his hip bone. Her arms around his shoulders, a promise to stand between him and the world if he wished.

We'll be all right, she'd said. *I swear it. If you stay.*

And for once, he *wanted*, a bright flash of desire through the storm-churned dark. To give her what he could; to show her he would try.

"No," he managed, raising his blade. "No, I'm here." And she gave him a look he could only describe as *blazing*.

Chapter 45

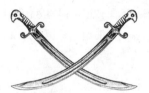

Truth was, Jordan didn't need him.

Truth was, she could have fought more easily without an extra body to defend. The pirates' line around the ship—downright fragile, against the seething mass of Boys and Pales—needed as much of her attention as she could give; it would have been more efficient to shove Baron deep into the forest, to fight only for herself and Dust.

But the solid warmth of him, as the Pales and Boys mobbed her in a scream of damson mouths; the bump of elbow and shoulder blade as he angled to cover her right side; the way he ducked as she deflected an arrow from his head. For so many years, they'd lost their rhythm—his thoughts leaping off cliffs she couldn't see the bottom of, hers locked in tainted circles she'd refused to pull him into. But now—now his ragged gasps quieted to something steady and familiar, and he jabbed at a Pale with a faint echo of his former surety, and it dizzied her, split her open, a high in her veins like no drug she'd ever tasted.

In the beginning, they had been the Twins. Their swords had flashed side by side, thrust into pirates and Pales—grown-ups—from whom they had looked away, pretending death was an adventure on which they could choose not to embark. They knew more of death, now—the way it stole your dignity before it stole your breath; the way it loomed over those you'd convinced yourself you were no longer holding on to. The way you might offer up your own life, hoping it would take you first.

But Saints, he was fighting. He was *fighting*.

Despite the corpses piling up on the sand—despite the Pales now heaving torches over the deck rail, and the fire that had bloomed across the planks—Jordan threw back her head and laughed.

Chapter 46

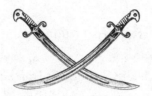

In the weeks since that first, terrible clash, Baron had not expected close combat to have grown familiar.

He and Jordan were both far removed from the bodies they'd had at thirteen—a strangeness to the nudge of their heels, the lengthened reach of their arms. Jordan moved with the kind of brawling grace he had witnessed a few times as he walked the poorer parts of San Jukong's First Circle; *he* could not stop thinking about his wrist lining up with the stupid blade, its cold and terrifying sharpness. Yet in the first clang against Pale steel, the force of it reverberating up his arm, the beach seemed to quiver, sand washed in silk and shadow, and he fell into a stance he knew as if from dreaming.

Jordan laughed, and it was the cruelest and most beautiful sound he had ever heard.

Do you remember?

The Pales circled, the Boys bearing down from above, and as the rest of the crew grunted and heaved their swords—as a scream lit the air, and Jack Two crashed to the ground—Jordan struck faster than Baron could see: throat, gut, unguarded temple, her hook slashing scarlet ribbons through a snarl of arms and swords and teeth. *Mad dog*, he'd heard the pirates call her, but the Pales and Lost Boys skittered away from Baron, too, as if she was making up for his shortcomings, and he wondered, foolishly, if the pirates had been mistaken; if she had simply been clearing the way for him all this time.

He thought: She had found the place she belonged.

He thought: In all the years he'd been looking, he had never truly seen her until now.

He knew: If he had ever loved anything in this life besides the promise of an ending, it was this.

The pain struck without warning. An iron-hot sear against the side of his head, and he cried out, fell to his knees. Then blood pooling in his hands—a curtain of it, a river—and he was falling, falling, his mouth a copper tang—

A sudden absence, beside him: Jordan had dashed into the forest after his attacker.

"Wait!"

A flash of lighter brown between branches. Baron heaved back to his feet and staggered past grown-ups and Boys still locked in battle, one hand pressed to the gushing warmth beside his ear. His vision had gone blurry again despite his glasses, his skull a molten throb, and he crashed into trees at random, scrambled back up in a tangle of knees and elbows and twigs.

"Jordan!"

Into the forest's green devouring maw—pebbles crunching beneath his feet, rain spattering his face through the canopy. Too slowly, another clearing opened before him: pines gouged with the scars of old claws, the stand of white birches stark against cloudy sky. The same place, he realized, that she had run to on the day of her final punishment.

The Pale was backed against a tree, trembling.

He was little older than a Boy himself—his forehead dotted with acne, tufty white-blond hair just beginning to darken.

"Please," he said as Jordan stepped forward, the Rittan words garbled with fear. His raised hands were empty of weapons. "Please, I did not see—I did not know he was—"

Jordan took another step. Fury radiated off every line of her body, her hook and sword already slick with blood.

"Please, please," the Pale babbled, raising his hands higher. "No weapon, mercy—"

A twisted smile. "Mercy," Jordan repeated, her voice unrecognizable. She bent down, lay her blade in the dirt. Straightened.

The Pale heaved a breath. "Thank you."

Then she lunged, fist swinging, the hook gouging skin and muscle and eye. The Pale was half a head taller, but she was Dust and steel and living flame, and he shrieked as she smashed his ribs, as the hook lodged in the softness of his lower lip and split his cheek in two.

Through it all: *Please... mercy...*

"Jordan," Baron coughed out. The left side of his face was on fire; he could not get enough air. No real code of honor existed on the Island, no behavioral constraints besides the Amas' rules and the limits of the Lost Boys' destructive energy, but this came closest—one did not cut down an unarmed man unless you had disarmed him yourself.

A wet sob from the Pale, his rib cage peeled open bloody, and Baron's vision spun dark. "Jordan. I'm right here."

Her eyes flicked to his. An unseeing to them, as if the Pale was not there, something inexorable in the set of her jaw. As rain stung Baron's forehead, coming faster, he thought: She had become someone he did not know.

She turned away.

An arching scream, then another. Her back bent with the grim doggedness of someone shoveling shit, or snow. Baron stumbled forward, hollow, the last traces of Dust-lightness drained out of his bones as he'd bled. His hand still clenched the hilt of his rapier—knuckles white, though he could not feel them. Another memory—her palm cupping his temple, velvet night and a smile like a dagger.

Maybe don't think so much.

Water down his face, too hot to be rain.

What are we becoming?

She would not forgive him for this.

He dragged his blade out of its scabbard and plunged it home.

A final, choking gurgle. The Pale's spine convulsed, and his head fell back as if weary.

Jordan rounded on him, breathing hard. "What in Taram was that for?"

Baron swayed, woozy with blood loss, electricity through his lungs like the roots of trees. The Pale's body fizzed before his eyes, as if the rain were already washing it away.

"Jordan," he said, and then he was breaking again, his face crumpled, ugly. "Don't do this. Don't become this. He didn't deserve—"

A murmur in the trees: Dau, Mateo, and a few other pirates had descended on the glade, their gazes darting from the Pale's gouged-out eyes to the curve of Jordan's hook, from the hilt protruding from the Pale's chest to the paint-red of Baron's hands.

To Jordan's own sword, laid out deliberately on the churned, muddy ground.

A heartbeat of silence, her eyes hooded and remote. And then she laughed. A strap of the hook's harness had come loose, and a welt was swelling her right cheek, but she was a fever brightness—her mouth twisted into a cold line that, through the blur of Baron's glasses, reminded him almost of Peter.

"No one *deserves*," she said, and wrenched Baron's sword out of the corpse with a faint sucking sound. A quick nod to the gathered crew, and he wondered at how easily she was able to play this role—not just because of her arm, but this hard core of her, this terrible armor. "But they bleed anyway. Are you going to wrap that cut or not?"

PART SIX

Someone has to leave first. This is a very old story. There is no other version of this story.
   —Richard Siken, "The Worm King's Lullaby"

Chapter 47

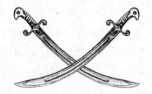

Tier was still breathing.

Chay knelt at his side, his jacket pulled tightly around her. Despite the afternoon sun warming the trees outside, cold permeated the cave; the blue-white mushrooms that bloomed from the walls seemed to leach heat from the air, leaving only an impression of dampness and spreading spores.

By daylight, the place had been stunningly easy to find. After the Boys hared off to battle, too quickly for Chay to send an Everbird to Jordan, she had slipped away from her chores—the trees almost seeming to part for her, the ground sloping down beneath her feet. The way a thought, often meditated upon, strengthens in the thinking.

"Hello, Tier."

In the lantern-dusk, he was pale and still, his face ragged with stubble. She stripped the old sailcloth she had placed beneath the lower half of his body, which stank of urine and excrement—averting her eyes, out of habit, from his naked legs. The second night, she had peeled off his pants, washed them, and waited all night for them to dry, but she'd since given up on maintaining his dignity; he wasn't conscious to appreciate it.

Shame twisted her stomach, already hollow from the banana bread she had not allowed herself to eat for breakfast. Her fault, for traipsing with him around the Island under the full eye of the moon. Her fault, for refusing to see what Peter would do.

"I have more Dust for you."

His wound had almost healed over, a raised pink circle where the ragged hole had once been—though, as bits of shaft were still potentially lodged inside, she wasn't sure this was entirely a good thing. Peeling his shirt from his chest, she dumped her leather pouch—its contents slipped from the Boys' near-empty wine bottle while the Boys (and Tink) played in the lagoon—into the divot of flesh between his ribs; watched the golden grains fade slowly, as if dissolving in water.

"I miss you," she whispered. A prayer, a promise. With the last vow she'd made in this place, nine years ago, bruises had colored her fists for weeks after; something in her skull had wound tight when she halved her food intake, as if her body sensed her determination and was itself afraid. But that day, she had asked the Island for the one thing it would not give. Tier's life should have been a trifle to it in comparison. *"Please."*

No flickering eyelids, no hitch of breath. Only the ocean's whisper, salt scent ghosted through mint-clean pine. As if the Island itself was conspiring against her.

Despair slid open inside her like a void. Dust was meant to heal— with it, she had patched up a thousand sword cuts, reattached ears and noses to their original heads; even, once, sealed a slashed-open throat that should have been fatal. But as she pushed to her feet again, legs stiff from the hard stone floor, she thought: There were some things even Dust could not put back together.

Then she was sitting with her back to a bowl of fried noodles, breathing shallow out of her mouth.

The house stood near silent—only the fire crackling in the corner, Ael snoring lightly at her feet. The Boys were still out fighting, and so she had busied herself cooking dinner, eyes skimming away from the place Slightly used to sit, the bile in her throat helpfully clogging the vortex of sheer need her stomach had become.

But now she was finished, and the Boys hadn't returned. And as the noodles—garnished with garlic and onion and tender slices of pork—steamed in the middle of the table, she could not stop her mouth from watering.

Ael roused, perhaps sensing the spike of her tension, and she scratched behind his ears, shifted as the bulk of his head came to rest against her knee. Tink had accompanied Peter, as always—a small pang in Chay's chest, as the fairy looked even more peaked than usual, but at least her absence gave Chay another chance to sneak Dust from the Boys' supply. And, too, the Pales were decreasing in number; lately Peter had been bragging that the Boys did not need their help, that the Pales were superfluous against a threat the Boys were meant to face alone. So as Chay scrubbed the dishes, and aired out the blankets, and climbed the branch-woven walls to dust the high corners of the new house, she had begun to tell herself: *Just a little longer.* A few more days, and then she could break.

Her stomach rumbled, and she pinched her nostrils shut. All her tomatoes gone, and she'd used the rest of the spinach for the noodles.

Chay.

Her heart squeezed. *Impossible.* She had just seen his body lying in the cave, unmoving as she rucked up his shirt and changed the sheets he had soiled. She was being self-indulgent. She was going mad. If this was a game of Pretend, she had not chosen to play.

She imagined the savory give of rice noodles between her teeth, and hated herself with every cell of her body.

Chay.

Exhale. A dull ache between her temples, the bone-deep tiredness that enveloped her every time she sat down. "Yes?"

A gust of wind pushed between her shoulder blades, oddly warm. *You don't have to punish yourself.*

"I'm not—" she began, but the rest of the words died on her tongue, tasting of ash.

One day you'll leave this place, and it won't matter. A brief lockup on the last *m*, and she thought she heard, quiet as a wingbeat, *Godsdammit.*

A bubble welled beneath her sternum, and she pressed her palm to it, the echo of a wound. She wanted to laugh, she wanted to cry.

I promise, he added. *There's something for you on the other side.*

She could not bear to taste his name in her mouth. Could only weep, knuckles crammed between her teeth, his jacket covering the cold patches on her back where the fabric of her dress had worn thin. It wasn't *fair.* The only person she'd ever wanted, in a way that didn't involve chores or struggling into her dress or proving the Island wrong. The only person who had ever shown her anything like kindness. As if the Island had found the one thing she couldn't bear, and pierced her with it like a knife.

Across the room, the fire flickered, casting the branches beyond the windows in deep blue shadow. Ael's tongue lapped warm against her cheeks, tasting salt.

It's not your fault.

"Please don't," she managed. Her hands were coated with spit and snot, and she smeared them against her skirt, sniffling. She could not lose control. The Boys might walk in at any moment and see her babbling at air, and then they would know what she was: a traitor in the face of their heartlessness, a doll shattered to pieces.

Can I ask a favor of you, then? Softer. Chay wrapped her arms around Ael's neck, buried her face in his fur. She was so cold.

"Mm-hmm."

Can I ask you to eat, just a little?

The resolution congealed inside her as if it had always been there, crouched at the back of her mind—that one day someone might love her enough to break the curse she had cast over herself. That one day, they might give her permission.

Even the idea of standing made her woozy. She pulled the massive bowl of noodles toward her and dug in with both hands.

She couldn't stop.

The bottomless hurt she had denied for nine long years. The empty vacuum of her stomach, oil and grease and flour shoveled into her mouth with tear-salted fingers. She couldn't stop, and the sheer energy stored in each bite pounded through her body, high and potent as Dust but a hundred times more terrifying.

Her hands scraped the bottom of the bowl. A miasma of soy sauce had lodged between her molars. She would have to cook something else for the Boys—could do it now, while they weren't watching, make double the usual portion, or maybe she'd choke that down too—

All right.

A cooler touch at her wrist, steadying. Her cheeks were flushed; a giddy fever burned beneath her skin.

Chay. The wind cupped her jaw, and she imagined sea-blue eyes, the soft part of his lips. *You'll be all right.*

She shoved back from the table as if burned. Her face smelled of grease and onions, and already she could feel the bolus of oil and flour bloating her stomach, huge and wrong, the bulk of her hips and thighs as she pushed to her feet. She had failed. All these years keeping herself pure, and she had allowed a whisper of wind to break her. And now she would bleed, and the Island would have its way, and she would be shooed back Outside with her second and final pouch of Dust to become grown-up and ordinary.

Her sister's voice: *Did you do it better, then?*

Chay had not, of course—and she'd committed to that belief the moment she agreed to help Jordan. But who was she, in the quiet of an empty house, if she wasn't fighting to stay?

A tendril of her hair, moving against the wind.

She was too high to weep. Instead she lay on the Boys' giant bed and folded her hands over her swollen stomach and watched the empty bowl gape at her, an accusation.

Chapter 48

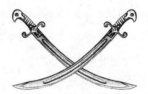

The sea was as dark as the inside of Tier's body.

He was floating again, time but a conjugation, his sense of his own limbs dissolved among the waves. Flashes of *elsewhere* hushed through him: wrought iron gates and the sharp vegetal smell of roses, lantern light tremor and a girl with eyes like wounds. But when his attention flagged, the images flickered away like pennies dropped down a well, became vague thin dreams of other lives.

Tier.

A tug of current, beneath the surface, and he drifted closer—though space folded in strange ways, here, and he could only gauge his progress by the slow fading-in of his vision, a golden bloom of firelight and the prick of a wolf's ears. And then he was *there*, in the close twig-woven walls, drifting among mismatched pots and pans—the Lost Boys' new house, he suddenly realized. His name not spoken but longed for, and he pressed his lips gently against the shell of Chay's ear, spoke as loud as he was able. Felt the warmth of the noodle bowl against her cold palms, the sluggish flow of blood through her veins.

Chay, he said, and did not stumble. *You'll be all right.*

He attempted to wrap his arms around her, only succeeded in ruffling a few strands of her hair. Yet she shuddered as if she had felt him; as if his fingers—if they could be called that, invisible and nebulously felt as they were—had caressed her skin in earnest.

You're so brave, he murmured against the crook of her neck. *I'm so proud of you.* And he wanted to kiss the tears from her face, and pull her to his chest; wanted to sweep her from these blood-soaked shores and hold her hand at sunset and waltz with her through his family's manse, their laughter echoing through those ancient halls in holy desecration.

But the current was pulling him away again, an inky rush as insistent as the moon, and it was all he could do to hold on until Chay finished eating before it tugged him back on starless waves.

Chapter 49

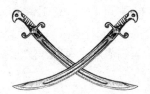

This was the forest after rain: glistening branches, thick green smell of moss, pine needles catching Jordan's hair like tiny fingers as she, Dau, and Koro plunged its depths in search of Jack Two. A bird, somewhere, mewling like a cat; the rush of clear swollen creeks; the high careless laugh of a boy, or perhaps the wind. As she swerved around an overhanging bird nest, the familiarity of it struck her again like a fist to the gut. Home. Hers. She had never belonged here, but it was damn well more than she'd ever fit in Outside.

That Pale didn't deserve—

Jordan wiped the blood from her mouth and spat. Baron was a prick. Baron was right. She didn't care. At the startled O of the Pale's mouth—and how dare he cringe, how dare he beg—fury had blazed through her, blinding white, split her open from collarbone to ankle.

And Baron's sword, plunged into the man's heaving chest—he'd had no fucking right. That Pale had been *hers*.

"They might have already thrown him into the sea," Dau said at her shoulder. Jack Two had not emerged from the forest after the Boys and

Pales had retreated, nor as the pirates stitched their two other fallen, Ellis and Sander, in their own sailcloth shrouds and lowered them into the deeps. Jordan had pushed against Dau coming to retrieve the other pirate's corpse, but they had insisted; she suspected that, to some extent, they felt responsible for his death.

"Where did you last see him?" she asked, batting aside fronds of Everbird-collected mermaid hair and spider silk that dangled from the branches. "Who was he fighting?"

"Kuli got a knife in his gut, I think." Dau's face was pale, and shadows stood out like bruises under their eyes. "And then dropped him from the cliff to break his neck. I swear, if they've used his bones for Dust—"

"Where are the Boys now?" asked Koro.

Dau peered up through the dusk-dimmed canopy. "Eating supper, probably—oh, look."

Jordan followed the line of their finger: vultures, straight-winged, circling dark against the grey sky. On the ground below, raccoons and opossums stood shoulder to shoulder with a hyena, all tearing into a bludgeoned mass of pink.

Jordan descended with Dau and Koro at top speed. Branches slapped her on the way down, trees that had been saplings when she was a Twin now rigid as soldiers. Dau drew their sword long before they were in range.

"Git," they snarled, swinging wildly, and the animals bristled, chunks of viscera still dripping from their mouths. "All of you, *git.*"

Koro nocked an arrow, his face contorted in disgust, but Jordan raised her hand. "They're going."

Sure enough, the hyena was loping away, one last rind of meat clamped in its jaws, the raccoons close at its heels. Dau heaved a breath and unfolded a square of old sailcloth from their immense coat.

"Saints," they said quietly.

Jack Two's bones had been cut out with a messy, vicious efficiency. Wet sockets gaped where joints had been; his hands and foot were bloody smears soaking into the ground. And his face—a mass of dried red, caved in on itself. Only loose flaps of skin and scraggled bits of beard to suggest its former shape.

A patina of flies scaled him like armor.

"You two take the feet and middle," Jordan said, when neither Dau nor Koro moved toward the corpse. "I've got the head."

They lifted the body in tandem, its sliced-open flesh mucking and oozing. The forest around them glowed gemstone-green—light seeping dense and grainy from thick clouds, the soft chirrup of songbirds pressed too close, suffocating.

No one deserves.

The puckered scar across Jordan's left forearm throbbed as if she'd slammed it against the ground.

"We can't bury him like this." Dau tugged the cloth over Jack Two's mauled face, their own a mask of grief. "Not the usual way. The others shouldn't have to see—"

"No. Let them." Koro's nostrils flared. "Let them see what the Boys do to our dead."

"Like they need to be reminded. You want to put him on display."

"Every single pirate who dies is put on display. You're being emotional."

"*Fuck* you."

"I'm just stating a fact."

"The rest of the crew should know what happened," Jordan said as Dau's hand went to their hilt. "But Jack Two has suffered enough. Let him meet the sea in peace."

Koro opened his mouth, and then snapped it shut; inclined his head toward Jordan. Dau's eyes flicked to her as well, but in silent thanks, and an ache hollowed Jordan's chest in the wound Baron had left only a few hours ago.

He had never looked at her with this kind of regard. Friendship, yes, and desire, but not this.

It was not an altogether unpleasant sensation.

"Come on," she said, bunching the sailcloth in her left hand and piercing it with her hook. It was an awkward angle, and the leather harness would chafe like ten hells once they started flying, but with Koro's inscrutable silence and Dau's gaze a weighted thing on her face, there could be no takebacks, no traces of weakness. "Let's get back before the Boys hear us arguing."

When she finally descended into the ship's hold that night, the door to Baron's cabin stood open.

After retrieving Jack Two, she'd gathered a few pirates to deal with the Pales' corpses, patch the hull, and roast the wild boar Koro had shot down in the tangled inner reaches of the forest. Baron didn't so much as show his face, even for food, and by the time the sun sank below the horizon, she was half convinced he had wandered off into the caves, or taken that extra pouch of Dust and fled back to Burima. All the better for him.

But as she walked down the dim hallway, the pirates' voices behind her fading into the rustle of waves and salt-eaten planks, her eyes caught the gap between door and frame.

Despite herself, she nudged it wider.

He was asleep, the torchlight from the corridor dancing across his forehead and eyelashes and the neat stitches along the side of his face. For a moment, she simply stood and watched—the slow rise of his chest, the fist clenched beneath his chin. He looked caught in between. Or perhaps her Island memories were swarming and colliding with the past few years: that last gift of Dust slipped into her hands breath-quick, the soft morning brightness, his eyes full of promises despite the blood between her legs.

A hint of that boy still ghosted his cheeks, the curve of his mouth. But she also caught a strand of silver in his hair, the beginnings of frown lines at the corners of his eyes. He'd have wrinkles before he hit forty.

She didn't want to think about Baron at forty. About the aura of gravity that would settle over him, the knife-edge of fear that time would dull to apathy or sharpen until he split at the seams.

Or perhaps he would meet someone else. Someone who could charm his parents over a table of dim sum, who rode the train to an office in the morning and returned at the same time every night. Who could coax a laugh out of him when his jaw set and his eyes went glassy and he fell into that airless place she couldn't follow.

Someone with whom he could grow old.

Beneath the collar of her shirt, her lacerated skin burned.

You fool, she thought, swallowing the apology that wormed up her throat. He wanted her to be the kind of hero they'd cheered for in the old Hanwa adventure serials, the kind who upheld the virtues of the gods as they bashed in the heads of demons and bandits. Even now, he'd believed enough in her fundamental goodness to stay.

But her virtue or lack thereof had never mattered—not to Peter or the Island or her parents, probably not even to the gods. Only that she had bled, and caused others to bleed in turn. Only that her heart was still beating, and she wasn't sorry for trying to keep it that way.

The weight of his hurt lay dormant between them, a meter and a half of creaking planks and flickered shadow. The moment he woke, it would thicken again, smother them both.

When she had raged at that Pale, back in the clearing, she'd meant every drop of blood she shed. She just hadn't imagined it would push Baron away.

After all, she'd already been doing *that* all this time.

A faint breeze riffled the hairs at the back of her neck. How many nights had they lain side by side on this Island, the squeak and groan of the Boys' giant mattress lulling them to sleep? How many times had their eyes flicked open simultaneously in the dark as Peter wept, babbling his senseless dreams?

How stupid would she have to be, to abandon her longest-standing ally?

Please.

Please. She saw the Pale's face before she tore it apart, terrified and shining in the rain. *I did not know he was...*

Baron was—what? Too grown-up to be her Twin, too queasy around swords to be a true pirate. But the Pales abided by certain rules on the Island as well, no matter how enthusiastically they consumed one another's remains. And one of them was this: The pirate captain was off-limits during a fight. Peter's alone.

And his first mate was to be killed by the Boys.

Saints dammit.

Jordan stepped forward and poked Baron in the shoulder.

"Hey," she said quietly. "You awake?"

He breathed in, a soft snuffling snore, but did not open his eyes.

Chapter 50

Morning—a quickening warmth in the air, the irritated squawk of an Everbird, rosy skies shot through with gold beyond the cabin's grubby window. Baron's back clenched as he rolled over on his cot—bruises everywhere, he felt like he'd been pummeled by a cricket paddle—and for a slow, weightless minute he just lay there, empty, before it returned to him: the stitches knotted beside his left ear, the thrust of his sword into heaving flesh.

And Jordan—seething, furious, flecked with blood.

Dread seeped through him. The last time he'd attempted to confront her had felt like peeling off his skin; the thought of doing it again made him want to hide beneath his covers and never reemerge. Yet he could see, more starkly than ever, their future hardening before them, paved with her tight-lipped fury and his inadequate apologies—the gradual distance, the increasing coldness, until one day they passed through the same corridor and barely recognized each other at all.

Jordan was the reason he was still here. And she'd said it first: If he didn't like what she was doing, he could leave.

He couldn't imagine going anywhere else.

When he had washed and changed, he limped up the stairs to the ship's deck, his head throbbing with every step—not enough Dust, still, to bind the gaping red beneath his skin. Under the open sky, a fragile quiet—shushing waves, the creaking wingbeats of herons overhead, salt breeze soft against his face.

Jordan stood alone at the stern of the ship, her silhouette traced in gold.

Her back was to him, but he knew that stance—arms folded, feet spread, shoulders thrown back like she could fight another platoon of Pales and Peter's crew besides. As Twins, they'd mirrored each other constantly, adjusted their postures and facial expressions so the Lost Boys would see them as identical; carved themselves into the shape of the roles they had chosen.

He wondered how much she was still acting.

A plank groaned beneath his feet, and he ducked back through the hatch before she could turn.

The rest of the crew roused themselves soon after. Dau appeared on deck with a large rolled-bark map and the scraps of Chay's messages; Koro dipped his head in an awkward combination of formality and camaraderie; Mateo even attempted to crack a joke. Baron sat heavily on a crate on the cargo ramp, out of view, and tipped his head back against the wall.

Jordan had found her place here. No one called her captain yet, but he read it in the tilt of the pirates' shoulders, the way they turned to her first when they spoke of the upcoming battle. In the presence of the hook—or perhaps just *her*, finally given the Dust she needed—they bent in her direction like plants toward sun.

And he couldn't help the pang that went through him—that whenever he lined himself up beside her, shoulder to shoulder, palm to palm, she would always shine brighter.

Outside the Island, he had *won* in every conventional sense: gone further in school, molded himself to better fit the shape of respectability. Here, it was she who had learned the rules.

Baron scooted his crate higher, peered above the hatch again. The pirates, bulky with blades and protective gear, had formed a circle, shifting in the gaps where their dead had once stood. Their voices pulled thin across the cool air; sunlight sparked off Jordan's hook every time she moved. Baron thought of the one live play he'd seen in college, the actors' faces animated by something more potent than real life. There had been a certain devastation to the tableau, something magnetic—the way the stage lights anointed them, made them worthy of being seen.

Nausea twisted Baron's gut. He was fed up with trying to perform; with the broken promise that, if he did it well enough, he might be truly known. Now he just wanted to lie back down.

Sometimes your life is all you've got.

"And you'll patch us up when we get back?"

Titters through the crew, and Baron realized Jordan was looking straight at him—the first time, he thought with some rancor, since they'd fought yesterday. He cleared his throat, acutely aware that his eyes and forehead now peeped above the deck.

"No."

Koro rolled his eyes; Dau's mouth twitched. For once in his life, however, Baron jutted his chin and stood (sat) his ground.

He would have said yes. Would probably cave anyway, when the pirates limped back with gashed shoulders and spilling innards. But the fact that she'd brought it up, *commanded* it, hardened the stubbornness that had brought him to this ill-advised protest in the first place.

He had denied her in front of the crew just to show her that he could.

Their circle parted for Jordan as she walked over—her steps slow, measured. A predator's walk. When she was out of the others' earshot, she said quietly, "Does this mean you're leaving, then?"

Baron flushed. Remembered her hand trailing down his chest, her lips soft against the curve of his ear. "No, no, I just—"

"You just *what*, Baron?"

"I'm not going to help you anymore." A rushing in his ears—like

spring wind, like spread wings. *You don't understand enough.* The coldness of her eyes, stripping him to the bone. "Not if you're just going to—"

"Then at least stay inside the ship."

That tone, still. "I can handle myself."

"I'll ask Mateo if he wants to keep watch for you—"

"Who do you think you are?" Baron demanded, lurching to his
feet, and despite the white heat that seared his vision and the indignity
of standing half a meter below her, a dull anger pumped through the
bruise that was his body. "You put on that hook and you're suddenly
entitled to everyone's obedience—"

"You think I wouldn't have done all this anyway?" she snapped in
Kebai, unbuckling the leather harness with a few flicks of her left hand,
and he winced: The skin beneath was roiling with blisters, and stank of
sweat and salt and a rancid sort of musk. "You think this isn't as much
of a tool as my sword? I *know* what they see when they look at me.
Don't blame me for using it."

"That's—that's not what I meant," Baron sputtered. Behind her,
the pirates were staring—she'd never doffed the hook, not in front
of them—and a wild laugh bubbled in his chest. *Surprise!* "It's just—
I'm—I'm not your *subordinate*—"

"Stay inside," she repeated, tugging the hook back on. "We'll talk
about this later."

Dau came up behind her, their mouth half-open in protest, but Jordan said, "Let him," and they both returned to the circle, leaving Baron
feeling like a petulant child.

He spent the day defiantly outdoors, scraping long-dead barnacles
and seaweed off the hull, waterproofing the planks with a bucket of
pine resin and an ancient paintbrush. Despite the calm blue bowl of
the sky—despite the birds and creek burbling their hearts out among
the forest's thick verdancy—outrage spiked through his skin. That
she would command him like some cabin boy. That she would take
the hurt between them and air it out before the crew as if he was just
another misbehaving member.

The echo of hospital fluorescents—of her eyes, burning into his back as he scrubbed his hands of her—and he felt a pang. He had shut her out first; had kept doing so, in a way, with every midterm cram session, every weekend he'd retreated to his parents' apartment because he couldn't fall asleep in his dorm. But how long would he have to atone? How long would he have to pour himself into a wound so large it would swallow them both whole?

He saw the towheaded Pale's face mid-battle, unseamed by steel. The bottle-glass green shoved into Slightly's/Henry's throat, and the bloated remains of the corpse beside him. The thin diagonal cuts across both their torsos, slashed vicious as—

The bucket of pine resin tumbled from Baron's nerveless fingers.

"Saints." He flattened his hand against an unpainted plank, the wood rough and warm beneath his palms. The ground tilting beneath his feet, his vision bladed by too-sharp sunlight. "No. No no no no *no*—"

The gouges through skin, not quite matching up with bone. The bloody curve of hook against red-flecked mouth. The look on Jordan's face when she'd borne down on Baron, vicious and incandescent and not quite there.

She'd cut them open, hadn't she? The two bodies Dau had found. Even if she hadn't killed them directly—a still-growing teenager and a Boy she'd *known*—

A dull pain branched through Baron's chest, and he gulped a breath, screwed his eyes shut against the spinning sky. At age eight, he'd watched Jordan hack off a Pale's right ear and several fingers; at ten, she'd stabbed the pirates' second mate through the stomach and laughed as she twisted the sword deeper. The Island had demanded that she harden, and she'd risen magnificently to the occasion.

But didn't she always have a reason? Or—the Pales' mutilated faces swam in his vision, and Slightly/Henry running his chubby five-year-old hands along the root walls of the house underground—had Baron been too naive to see that she had lost it long ago?

The waves licked his feet, foaming before they slid back across silk-smooth sand, and he shuddered, pressed his forehead to the hull. He couldn't know for sure that Jordan was at fault. The Boy and the Pale could have turned on each other, or run into a bear, or been killed separately by their respective factions and dragged together by hyenas; some might call it disgusting that Baron had jumped to his conclusion first. But he knew this Island, too, knew the rules by which Boys and Pales and pirates cut each other open, and he had to be sure.

He peeled himself off the ship; winced as pain pulsed through his skull, the wound beside his left ear a crimson heat. More than a day had passed since Dau had led them to that small gap in the undergrowth, and the bodies would be half-rotted; perhaps the Island's animals had cleaned them up the rest of the way. But if there was anything left—if there was still a chance he could prove himself wrong—

His lungs at half capacity, adrenaline splintering glass shards beneath his skin, Baron limped toward the forest as if it might hold anything resembling an answer.

Chapter 51

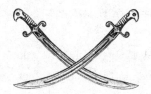

Night had fallen again by the time the pirates returned.

They emerged from the forest one by one—shadows unfurled between trees, eyes reflecting lantern flame like monsters out of a storybook. No blood on their hands or clothes that Baron could see, but he sensed some secret triumph in their faces, some knowing from which he had been shut out.

He straightened beneath the ship's hull, pulse singing, and breathed out through his mouth. Slightly's and the dark-haired Pale's bodies lay on the sand beside him, leaking slowly. He'd dragged them across the beach with his hands wrapped in wet leaves; gagged at the squelch of torn-open intestine, the soft give of boneless wrists.

He was overreacting, he thought as flies swirled a cloud around his ears. He was overwrought. They would take one look at him and laugh.

But could they not understand what they had done?

Jordan appeared last—her face like stone, hook slashed silver against the dark sand. She did not look at him as she approached, though she had to have seen him. Cold blew through his jacket; he had torn it for the first time yesterday, fighting the Pales. Evidently the material was not as unbreakable as the tag had claimed.

A large black spider crawled out of Slightly's mouth, and Baron clamped down on a scream.

"You might better help your cause," Jordan said, coming to a stop before him, "if you didn't make a spectacle of yourself next time."

Her eyes did not even flicker toward the corpses, and Baron felt at once the absurdity of it and a sort of sick thrill. She'd mentioned a next time—maybe he'd get another chance, despite all this. Maybe they could still start over.

"What part of this *isn't* spectacle?" he asked, desperately trying for his old ease, though he could not remember how they'd managed to make conversation yesterday, or three weeks ago. He stuffed his hands in his pockets. "Do you like playing this part of the story?"

Her eyes narrowed. "What do you want, Baron?"

He motioned to the bodies at his feet, their eyes wide open and staring. A dark sweep of Everbirds had gathered on the edge of the forest, cawing raucously. "All this fighting. All this death. And—" He gestured at the thin lacerations across the cut-out ribs. "What is this supposed to be?"

Her face was a mask. "I didn't kill them, if that's what you're thinking."

"But you used their bones for Dust."

She only shrugged. "We become what we need to be in order to survive."

The quiet grated between them, grimy with the residue of daylight violence. Baron could have sworn he heard the Island move—the rumble of rearranging hillsides, grinding stone, carcasses sloshing as they drifted out to sea. The Everbirds plunged into the woods, shrieking triumph, and he looked away.

"What did you think it would look like," Jordan said, low, "for us to make Dust?"

Baron threw his hands skyward. "I thought we'd use *funeral urns*," he said, exasperated. "People who'd already been buried. People whose bodies we could respect, at least a little. And then we'd fly back on Tier's plane, and you could get what you needed from Outside—"

Jordan snorted. "So, what, you thought the ingredients changed, after the crash?"

"No, but you could have found some way to get them without— without becoming a—"

"A what, Baron?" she said sharply, but he could only bite his tongue, a lump in his throat he could not swallow.

"I—never mind."

Jordan closed the distance between them in a single step, her eyes blazing.

"Don't you dare," she spat. "Don't you *dare* call me the only villain, or monster, or whatever the fuck you were going to say, because you couldn't think through what it would mean to get Dust on the Island. Don't you dare act all righteous and disgusted now because you've seen the mess up close."

"I'm not saying I—"

"You chose to come here, Baron." She said his name like a curse, forced between her teeth. "You were part of the crew. That makes you as guilty as the rest of us."

"I didn't know you cared about guilt."

She laughed, short and bitter. "But you do."

Baron didn't realize he had backed away until his head bumped the hull.

"I chose to come, yes," he said. His heart beat double-time; a rankness coated his tongue from breathing the dead boys' fumes. "And I'll spend the rest of my life regretting what I did here. But at least I'm trying not to repeat my mistakes."

Her eyes flashed. "As am I."

"There's a line, Jordan," he countered. "We *knew* that Slightly. You attacked that Pale after he'd surrendered. It doesn't matter how much you've been hurt, there are things you just don't do—"

"What have *you* not done, then?" she snapped, and in the rising glow of the stars she was all bared teeth and barbed-wire edges. "What are you innocent of, O Greatest of Lost Men?"

Baron squirmed despite himself. "Don't call me that."

"Did you hold Peter back when he vanished our Slightly?"

"I didn't know—"

"Or when they threw rocks at me thinking I was you?"

"You offered to take my place—"

"Or cut off the head of that first mate and sliced him open from mouth to di—"

"Jordan."

The hook was hovering centimeters from his face, her breath coming hard and fast. A wild wheeling nothingness in her eyes, as if she were looking into a mirror and seeing only the sky behind.

He realized she was shaking. They both were.

She lowered her arm slowly. The air had broken between them like a fever, something gone cold and missing and sad, and he wanted to weep, he wanted to buckle the leather strap that dangled loose at her elbow, he wanted to shake her by the shoulders until she turned back into the Jordan he knew.

"It's all right, Baron." Her voice was disconcertingly even. "You can grow up now. None of this is real. Take a fistful of Dust, and tomorrow you'll wake up back in your dorm room pretending this was all just a story you told yourself as a kid."

Baron blinked, found his eyes wet. From the deck of the ship, he could sense the other pirates' breathless silence, the sharp admixture of wariness and curiosity as their new captain meted out her first round of discipline. *Discipline*—even the word made him nauseous. He wondered if they were already mocking him—if he would spend the rest of his days aboard this wretched ship turning and turning to whispers behind his back.

But he hadn't come for them.

"I loved you," he said, and the past tense lodged in his throat like a broken tooth. "I loved you because you didn't care what people thought, because you weren't afraid, because you never stopped fighting. But using Slightly and that—that *kid* for Dust? You're just as bad as Peter."

She only stared, impassive. Baron hunched his shoulders, heart roaring in his ears. At his back, an owl hooted; a curl of breeze, warm wood and night sky, and he thought of Tier wandering the dark of the hold all those weeks ago—asking, out of nowhere, if there was a limit to his affections.

You know how the story ends.

Finally, Jordan leaned toward him, lips crooked in a half smile. "Want to know something?"

He breathed out, slow. "What?"

An eerie emptiness to her face, a glint of canines, and a strange heat passed through his bones. They had been each other's mirrors, until they weren't. Had laughed away the burn until their own mouths split them open.

"You say you loved me," she said, and he could not read her at all. "But me? I was always pretending."

Pulse-skip, darkness. For a moment he was the wheeling stars, he was the murmuring trees, he was the frigid, empty air.

"I'm sorry," he mumbled at last, and stared down at his shoes. It seemed like the right thing to say.

"Don't be." Jordan's voice dripped acid. "After all, it's not your fault."

A firing squad of pirates' eyes lay heavy on him as he trudged toward the woods. His face burned. He'd come to the Island expecting steel and blood and ashes, but not this. Not exile from the exiles. Not a canyon between himself and Jordan so wide that the only way to cross it was to fall.

The wind angled toward him, smoke from some distant fire catching in his lungs until he coughed. As Jordan reclaimed her place at the helm of the ship, Baron slipped into the dark, eyes blurring. Perhaps the Lost Boys would shoot him like a fish in a barrel, slice out his bones and crush them for fuel.

Perhaps there was only one reason he had cared, before.

Perhaps that reason was gone.

Dangerous, he knew, to live for someone else. But it had been too late fourteen years ago.

He thought, then, of stormy afternoons on the Island: cliffs echoing thunder, pines swaying wild as omens. The two of them shooting into the clouds, heads thrown back, laughing and unbreakable, and all the world could not have convinced them of what lay ahead. He hadn't known he was happy—or if he had, it was in the distant way he was aware of breathing air, that his lungs were cycling oxygen into his arteries to nourish the rest of his body.

Only now, as he stumbled over a root or a stone in the dark—as his palms scraped dirt, and blood scored them like a warning—did he wish he had stayed oblivious.

Chapter 52

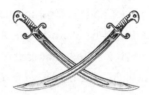

Jordan watched from the deck as Baron vanished into the trees.

She couldn't claim he *wasn't* the person she had known. For fourteen years he'd been her voice of caution—slow to injure, quick to hesitate. Just yesterday she had held him as he broke open, stroked his hair as he pieced himself back together; they had fought the Pales back-to-back. She'd expected him to at least understand.

Just as bad as Peter.

The wind blew through her, fanned her anger like flame. He would not last long, crashing through the forest alone and unarmed in the middle of the night; who knew but that Chay's wolf already had its nose to the ground. Yet the last time she'd fought on his behalf, he had turned around and called her an aberration.

Let him play at surviving on his own. Let him map her on the wrong side of his arbitrary boundary, shut her out for dissolving his image of her innocence.

And if a wild, keening grief still rose within her at the thought of a Boy thrusting a sword into his heart—if a scarlet rage clawed her insides when she imagined his body broken and flayed beneath the trees—well, she had been bracing for this her entire life.

No one ever stays.

As the stars brightened against bruised swaths of sky, Jordan leaned against the deck rail and stared into the forest.

He was right about her, of course. She was missing more than a moral compass, more than a sense of what was and wasn't appropriate. There was an absence wired into her frame—a chasm between knowledge and empathy, between correct behavior and true compassion—whose sides would never meet. Perhaps the Island had torn it out of her, or perhaps it had never existed to begin with, but all that mattered in the end was the lack.

And if it made her broken, if it made her wrong—if it made her as bad as he said—well, hadn't some ancient Hanwa scholar once claimed adaption was the price of victory?

"Need someone to keep an eye on him?"

She turned. Dau stood at the hatch, silvered in starlight, and something immense and complicated stirred at the base of Jordan's sternum: what they might have seen in each other, had they met Outside. If she would have felt this strange tug of recognition, as if toward a mirror tipped at a different angle.

Her fingers clenched around the rail. *Focus.* The Pales were dwindling in number—one last push, and the rest of Peter's defenses would fall, and Tink would be theirs for the taking.

If Baron didn't want a cut of the Dust, all the more for the rest of them.

"No," she said, and ignored the pang in her chest as Dau's eyes went wide. "I'll take first watch with Koro, and Mateo and Rien can take second as usual. We'll need everyone at full capacity for tomorrow."

Dau's face was unreadable. "As you wish," they said, and dipped their head in something like a bow before vanishing back into the hold.

Nine years ago—the stitches across Jordan's arms and shoulders newly snipped away, the alc-and-linoleum stink of the hospital still acrid in her nostrils—she'd shown up on Baron's doorstep at two in the morning.

265 Riau Street 10E: the address recited over and over in her head, spelled forward and backward, worn smooth until it fit the creases of her palm. Through her hospital stay; as she crossed the glossy marble tile of her parents' new apartment; as she read their faces, pale and set because the daughter who had returned was not the one they had wanted; through blood-drenched dreams and reaching for a sword no longer there.

Now, it was her last resort.

After her parents tore into her for the karsa they'd found under her pillow—though that was just the last straw, really, after she'd skipped weeks of school and started fights on the street and disappeared for an entire afternoon with the seedy syndicate lowlife Obalang, who frequented the nearest corner store—after her mother's tearful wails of *where did we go wrong* and her father roaring *demon* and *animal* and *get the fuck out of my house*—Jordan ran out the door, clutching only a wad of cash. Baron's was a temporary solution; she would owe him for every night, and besides, she could already feel her brain softening to mush from all the hours she'd slept under the concrete roof of her parents' flat. But she had no idea where to find a sword here, and she couldn't return to the Island if someone knifed her in some First Circle alley.

It was just a place to sleep, she repeated to herself as she knocked on the door. Until she could find another.

Inside, the shift of couch cushions, bare feet padding across tile. She waited, swaying slightly from the drug still sharp in her veins.

The door swung open. Baron's new glasses glinted beneath the hallway lights.

"Jordan?" he said, taking in the hair plastered to her forehead with sweat, the plastic baggie of mir bills bulging awkwardly from her pajama pocket. "What on earth—?"

"Karsa," she said, widening her eyes to show him the jitter, and he shrank back into the dark. "They wouldn't give me any other painkillers for the Dust withdrawal, they wouldn't believe that it hurt, I had to—"

"Come in," he said, cracking the door wider. "But be quiet about it. I don't want to wake my parents, and they won't like this."

"No?"

"You know how they talk," he said hastily as she toed off her sandals, slipped them behind a large potted plant. "But we won't get caught if you leave after—hang on. Stay where you are, okay?"

He vanished behind a wall, leaving her to survey the familiar granite countertops, the round-leafed plants atop glass shelves with their protective plastic stickers still unpeeled. When he reemerged, his hands were draped with antiseptic wipes.

"My mother has a sixth sense for dirt on the floors," he explained, grimacing. "If you wouldn't mind—"

Jordan took one sheet and ran it dubiously over the soles of her bare feet.

"Thanks." He looked slightly constipated. "Sorry."

She stuffed the dirty wipe into her pocket just to see him flinch.

Baron's room, to her relief, still felt relatively unlived-in. A new set of school uniforms hung from matching plastic hangers, and a few manga posters had been tacked to the walls in place of the old elementary school drawings and honors certificates, but the air of the place was still too sterile, too forced, to be his. She almost giggled as she shuffled under the crisp white sheets, breathed in the clean-laundry smell—on the Island, between the salt and the mud, very little pure white survived—and then Baron joined her, and they were two sightless ghosts facing each other across a rumpled sea.

"Is this all right?" he asked, tugging off the blankets, and the grin faded from her face.

A week in the hospital had refreshed her on the rules of Outside: Soiled things went in trash chutes, shoes on feet in public places. But the sight of Baron moving through this apartment in a soft red T-shirt and plaid boxers—as if he belonged, as if this was *easy*—had knotted something in her gut.

She was alive. She was safe, for the time being.

But she was so, so angry.

"It's fine," she said. And then, "Thank you."

The window spilled blue across his face. "You're welcome."

They lay down, silence crystallizing between them. Baron placed his glasses carefully on the bedside table; a few minutes later, he began to snore.

A crack fissured across Jordan's sternum. In the coming years, she would learn to hide it with her face and her fists, hard words and harder silences. Most people assumed, after all, that there was nothing wrong with you, and lying was only a matter of not contradicting them—of performing decency consistently enough that no one saw the damage beneath.

Lying on Baron's bed that night, awake and alone, she could only prod it with her fingers and try not to breathe.

He may have been sleeping beside her, but she already missed him.

She shot awake the next morning to a shout that made her ears ring.

"Teoh Jinfei! Who is *that*?"

"Wh—Ba—you're not supposed to come into my room—"

"You. Girl. Get out!"

The warm comforter was ripped off Jordan's body, baring her legs and the red tangle of scars across her chest and arms. Baron's father— who else would it have been—slapped her across the face.

"What the f—"

"Out," he bellowed, and she stumbled off the bed, eyes streaming, landed flat on her arse on the floor. Sun blared in through the window, washed the room white. She'd slept harder than she had expected.

The man turned on Baron. "Do you want to shame our whole family? You are *thirteen years old*—"

"It's not like that—"

"Shut up. Shut up and get ready for school. And why are *you* still here?"

Ironic, Jordan thought as she ducked toward the door. Peter had taught them to sneak past grown-ups, to outwit them in swordplay, to ambush them behind boulders and trees and creeks running with blood. But he'd never lived in a world where the grown-ups could truly win.

Over her shoulder, she met Baron's gaze.

"I'm sorry," he said.

But the fear in his eyes was stark as the hour before sunrise, and as Jordan walked out of his room, out of the apartment, tongues of smog pressing themselves against the narrow hallway window, she knew that fear was truer than any semblance of hospitality.

Stay with me.

Jordan had won, in the end. Caught Baron in his lie, scraped the varnish off his grown-up hypocrisy. But it was the hollowest victory of her life.

Her whole face hurt.

Stay.

The front door clicked shut behind her—it couldn't have been past eight in the morning, after all, and Mr. Teoh would not want to wake the neighbors. For another minute or so, Jordan stood on the landing, sucking machine-chilled air through her nostrils, the clean smell of Baron's blankets still wafting off her skin.

Then she took the stairs down. The stairwell door slammed like a gunshot behind her and she whipped around turn upon dizzying turn, exit signs flashing at every landing. The air was a windowless column of heat, despite the cool residue of night; as her sandals hammered out the intervals of her descent, sweat pooled under her arms, her thin new armor of air-conditioned cold molting into something musk-sharp and animal.

By the time she hit bottom and strode back out into the waking city, the scent of Baron's sheets had washed away like rain.

Chapter 53

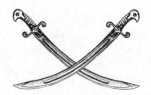

Voices. Out in the shifting dark, on the edge of Baron's hearing, moonlight faint and delicate as gauze. He'd fumbled through the woods for what felt like hours—fisted his hands without seeing them, shuffled his feet along ground more inference than reality. The torn-paper edges of his breath reaching, curling, gone.

You can grow up now.

He hadn't needed permission. Had only ever wanted her to come with him—the one thing she could never give.

I was always pretending.

There was a time, sitting at the edge of a creek, that she had used him as a mirror.

But hadn't they met in a place that was a fiction? Hadn't they built their story out of Dust and the other Boys' unwillingness to see?

Hadn't it only collapsed because he'd sought the truth?

Your choice, she murmured in his ear, and he could almost taste her, cut-flower stillness and obsidian eyes.

Perhaps she'd been putting up another front. Perhaps she'd only struck back at him in the heat of altercation.

Or perhaps he just couldn't stand to tell himself otherwise.

One thing was certain, though: She would not come for him, when the Boys discovered him here.

The ground gave out under his feet, and he tumbled into a pit.

Voices, closer. Branches stabbing his cheeks, his palms, a faint blear of light overhead. His glasses still dangled from one ear, and relief flooded his stomach as he shoved them back onto his face, though against the close earthen walls it made little difference. He couldn't tell how far down he'd fallen; his hands met mud on either side, small crawly things crunching beneath his fingers. When he stepped forward, the toe of his boot caught on something solid, and he hoisted himself up, grasping, scrabbling, before sliding back down in a rain of dirt.

"Did you hear that?"

Baron froze, heart in his mouth. A Lost Boy, though not Peter, not yet. And no footsteps—they would approach from the air. He curled into the shadows, panic jittering through his palms, and willed the night to hide whatever twigs and grass he'd broken on his way down.

Jordan would have told him to swallow his fear. To pretend until the disguise crumbled between his fingers, and then fight with every damn thing he had.

Jordan was not here.

A high giggle, and Baron's throat clenched like a fist.

"—pirate stupid enough to—" the Boy said cheerily.

"—isn't bedtime yet." Another voice, higher, and Baron pressed his knuckles to his teeth. He had left his rapier on the ship—a final, foolish act of protest—but even if he hadn't, any fight would be two or five or seven against one, and he couldn't even hold the thing correctly.

Not to mention the Boys seemed to think Dust was more potent when the bones were cut out still steaming.

"Ama won't—"

"Don't you think she's been acting weird lately?"

A snort. "Well, she *is* a girl."

The night birds had stilled, the air gone heady and monsoon-thick. Baron exhaled, shaky. Terror wired his windpipe shut; adrenaline arced down the insides of his knees.

And yet—a still-lake quiet, at the core of him. A taste in his mouth like relief.

He had wanted this for so long—a quick death, a new beginning. A reason to offer up his life, brief and devastatingly beautiful, at the altar of some insatiable god. No one spoke ill of a martyr; no one would laugh at him again, or call him a coward or a villain or a tragedy. He would be perfect forever, remembered for the million lives he could have lived instead of the disappointment of the one he had.

Two shadows loomed over the mouth of the pit, blotting out the stars.

"Why, hello there," one of them said, and Baron closed his eyes.

He had never thought of his body as fragile.

As Jordan's Twin, he had been untouchable, almost brave, a defiance of light and momentum and gravity. In high school and college, hunched over unintelligible textbooks and lines of code, his body had morphed into a clockwork ticking on against his will, so traitorously vital that winding down seemed a laughable impossibility. Even when lightning jagged his skin—even when an invisible weight crushed his sternum, and he grew dizzy from lack of oxygen—it had always felt like his choice, somehow, a physical reaction his mind had conjured to justify all the ways he fell short. But his symptoms were never severe enough to send him to the hospital, never given a name, and that meant he was fine—he just needed to try harder, to stop being lazy.

As the first blow detonated pain behind his eyes, he realized he had been utterly, disastrously wrong.

"A grown-up," one of the Boys exclaimed from above, and another kick knocked Baron onto his back. His ears rang; his lungs had gone flat, and he could not remember how to fill them. "D'you think he's a pirate or a Pale?"

"Dunno, carve him open and see."

Fire down the line of his sternum, and he cried out, spine arching against the dirt.

"Get his arms first," another Boy suggested, clinical. "Keep him from hitting you—"

"*No.*" Baron's voice cracked against the starless dark, but hands pinned his wrists and ankles, a weight settling on his stomach, and then a knife-sear down his shins and the arches of his feet and he bucked again, screamed.

So this was death, he thought, as a Boy boxed his ears—as his abdomen was sliced open crosswise, and something hot and vital spilled out. Not the television actors with their painted-on sweat and breathy last words; not the faceless grown-ups crumpled at his feet like toys, the way he'd thought of them as a Twin. Death was ugly, it was undignified, it was being *gone* where gone meant forever.

Fingers of panic crawled up his throat. He did not want to leave yet. Not into the permanence of this dark, not when he had left Jordan with so much unsaid. Not when his heart was still thundering in his chest and the night smelled of stone and moss and starlight and he wanted to go back, he wanted to apologize, he *wanted*—

A blade pierced the meat of his right palm, and he burst into tears.

Chapter 54

Chay knelt before the dirt hole that was the Boys' latrine, hands
pressed to her stomach, and wished she had the courage to
vomit.

Some of the older girls had spoken of it, in her hazy memories of
school—their voices carrying while in line for assembly, or as they dis-
dained the snack stands in the courtyard. *Easy*, they'd said, bone-thin
and heavyset alike, *I do it every day*, and here she was, seven—eight?—
years older than they had been, unable to push her finger past the first
curve of her tongue.

The bulge of noodles pulsed in her abdomen like a second heartbeat; the folds of her dress clung too close, revealing. She imagined the
broken-down sugars ferried to the soft pink tissue between her hips,
destruction blossoming inside her without an ounce of the Island's
help.

One day you'll leave this place.

A roasted fish atop a salt-scoured plank. Her grease-slick fingers
scraping its fatty residue against a pine cone. His steady gaze flooding

her with light, as if he was trying to guess at all the ways she had made herself small, and imagine her free instead.

What she wouldn't have given to live that hour again, without the cold clenched between her shoulders. What price she wouldn't have paid to have been fundamentally *all right*—to feel his arms around her waist without hunger running constant through her veins.

Her eyes were dry now, red-rimmed. She was still too high from gorging herself to weep.

"—one caught in the pit—"

Peter's voice, sharp in the cool night air, and Chay stiffened. The Boys set booby traps all over their territory for pirates and Pales alike, but an animal occasionally sprang one of the snares, and the Boys would skin and gut it and bring it to her for dinner. Her mouth watered betrayal—to fry the slabs of fresh pork over the spitting fire, fat sizzling, a thick savory crust of herbs blooming on her tongue. To consider her own cooking *food* again, and not just the tomatoes she piled on the dish rack. To reinflate her aching stomach, even as she despised the greasy smell of her own face. Even the stink of the latrine pit could not tamp down the pounding of her midsection.

"—you sure?" Kuli, his voice veering close.

"—said he was just sitting there." One of the Twins. "—doesn't even have a sword—"

"Trust *Tudo* to find him."

Chay frowned. Boars were not expected to wield swords. And if the trap contained, instead, a person—

Hot blood gushing through her hands. Tier's mouth a trembling wound in the dark.

She pushed to her feet, acid curdling in her throat. *Enough death.* Enough men speared like beasts, and Boys vanished in the shadows between trees. Enough shame at the cracking of a voice, and stretched-out gawking limbs, and—

A step forward, a gust of breeze, and the white fabric of her dress wrapped tight around her hips.

Revulsion reared through her like a wolf with bared teeth. She wanted to hide, she wanted to run. But there was nowhere she could go to escape her own body.

An echo on the wind, tinged with cave damp: *Chay.*

Chay shivered and pulled Tier's jacket tighter around her shoulders. Pretending had been difficult even with her discipline intact—smiling as her heart was torn from her chest, as her sister's voice taunted her through lantern smoke; as everything she'd lived for, these past ten years, crumbled to ash in her hands. But it hurt twice as much with her appetite unstitched, the seams of her self-control ripped open to reveal the ravening hunger beneath. When she might be communing with ghosts, or losing her mind.

Yet Tier had believed in tomorrows, up until his had been stolen from him.

A twig snapped up ahead. Chay levered herself forward, a spreading grey numbness where her heart had been, and followed the sound of breaking.

The Boys were already beating him when she arrived.

An air of revelry hung about them, as if they were fairies dancing in a ring—wide wild mouths, eyes blacked by night, Tink's coin-gold aura shifting across fists and feet and daggers.

And at their center—

Chay steadied herself against Ael's side, her stomach gone hot and sick.

The man lying in the dirt was too injured to scream.

Even in the token light of the eyelash moon, she could tell he'd been broken—his arms mottled ink-wet against the faint glow of skin, his torso a pulped mass. Something *wrong* about the arrangement of his limbs, as if the Boys had snapped a few of his bones in preparation for their removal.

Ael juddered a growl, though to whom it was directed she could not tell.

"Boys," she said, her voice pulled thin and tremulous against the thump of fists and blades. A vicious glee curved their mouths, a spark kindled behind their eyes, and nothing in the world could douse the conflagration.

Nothing except, perhaps, an Ama.

Chay fisted the sleeves of Tier's jacket. The face of the Boys' newest victim was ravaged beyond recognition; she could not have said whether he'd just washed up on shore, or once called her by the same name as those now dancing violence around his body. Perhaps there was no one to miss him. Perhaps he was a pirate driven to despair, as others had been over the years, and had come tonight seeking release.

But she didn't know for certain. She didn't know anything at all.

Chay hitched up her skirts and stepped into the ring of knives.

Chapter 55

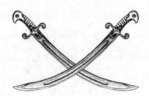

Full capacity for tomorrow, Jordan thought as she paced the deck, had been an utter lie.

The hour or so in which she'd kept first watch had proven uneventful. Koro was about as compelling a conversationalist as a rock, and the sliver of moon morphed the beach into a second shifting sea, drowning everything in darkness. She hadn't been able to hold still—kept fidgeting with the hook's harness and the flakes of leather peeling from the hilt of her sword, pushing away the vision of Baron's back sliding away beneath the trees.

His eyes, as the tip of the hook hovered over his left cheek, needle-fine—as if he was still surprised at what she would do.

I loved you, he'd said, and she had hated him for speaking in the past tense what neither of them had ever dared say in the present.

No one ever stays.

She wanted to break something. Tear off her own skin, douse the whole damn Island in kerosene and burn it to the ground. He was going to get himself killed—maybe that was even what he wanted—and it was not her obligation or her duty to chase after him, or beg him to return.

But if she didn't fish his arse out of whatever he'd inevitably stumbled into, she was going to regret it by morning.

Or perhaps—the thought sluiced through her like cold water—he was already dead.

She took her leave of Koro, who nodded begrudgingly; stepped over the Pale's and Slightly's decimated corpses, on which a handful of gulls had descended; and followed Baron into the heart of the forest.

He was not difficult to track. Snapped twigs and churned pine needles drifted in his wake, and the air around her hushed like held breath, like the taut second before the falcon swooped down. Thirty or so meters in, a round hole opened in the ground, muddy debris giving way like punched-in teeth to empty darkness, and Jordan curled her hand around her sword, the hook poised midair, and listened: bullfrog croak, a mourning dove's coo, the soft damp smell of rotting leaves.

The faintest moan, as if from the earth itself.

Forward at a run, her head barely attached to her body. The tree trunks splintered to fragments, her Dust-lightened footsteps a soundless scream. Phantom wolves lunged at the edges of her vision; the shadows of Boys sprang from the canopy like the jaws of a trap.

He was crumpled in the dirt like a broken toy.

She knelt—the forest's hidden eyes crowding her, accusing. A faint sheen of starlight caught the edge of split skin.

"Baron."

He did not answer. She felt nothing, then, but a numb cold. Later it would crash down on her, what they'd done to each other, but now there was only his body split open and spilled into the earth—only the miasma of red blood-smell, her hand and hook alike outstretched and helpless.

"You there?"

She prodded his arm—soft, clammy. Slightly's bottle-shard throat seared green across her memory, and the Pale that she and her crew had deboned to stretch Chay's Dust, but her heart did not race, her gorge did not rise. She couldn't reconcile those Boys, those men, with this. Could not lay them side by side.

This was just Baron. Could only ever be just Baron.

"Hey."

She fumbled for wrist, shoulder, throat. Searching for a pulse, though her own beat so loud that whatever she heard might have been an echo. Still, a strange absence of panic. She tugged open her emergency pouch of Dust with her hook and poured it over him, tipped another pinch into her own mouth. Gold sparkled on her tongue, heady and heartless.

"This is probably going to hurt."

His head lolled too far to the side as she dragged him by the elbow, both of them drifting upward as she willed his Dust to defy gravity. Branches snagged his shirt, jammed in open wounds; he shuddered, half waking, and she swore fervently under her breath. But slowly, surely, they cleared the dense inner forest, his arm heavy over her shoulders. The curve of her hook—their only defense, now—felt thin and almost fragile above the sweat-damp harness.

She tried not to think of the last time she had carried someone this way.

They sailed back to base in silence. The shadows were somehow thicker than when she'd first ventured out, every breath out of Baron's lungs wet and labored. She did not look at him again until they touched down on deck—when he slid too easily out of her arms, head thumping the planks with a hollowness that made her wince.

"Get Dust," she snapped at Koro, who was drifting over. Her voice a thing detached from her mouth. "And bandages."

He hurried off without a word.

Then she was alone again with Baron, the slow seep of his blood into wind-weathered wood, and fury flared through her so bright she couldn't breathe.

The Boys had *played* with him—deep slashes across his face weeping crimson, his hands and rib cage split down to the bone. Cuts meant to make him scream for as long as possible before he passed out, or bled dry. And she could all but taste their glee, hear the giggles as they broke him slowly. Some insatiable desire, or perhaps just curiosity, to pry open the thing they would soon become; to feel some illusion of power over it because their hands could make it hurt.

But they had not killed him.

A thump of dark wings: an Everbird alighting on the rail. No scroll tied to his legs—just a reproachful caw, and a bent spoon dropped pointedly to the deck.

Chay.

Jordan reached for the spoon, studied the fitful rise and fall of Baron's chest. Her sister, saving her Twin—ushering the Boys toward bedtime or some other distraction.

She thought of Tier, and the bloodied smear on his white shirt. His jacket swamping Chay's small body, some secret tenderness she still did not understand.

Baron moaned, his cut-open hands twitching, and the spoon dug into Jordan's palm hard enough to bruise.

Koro returned with a pouch of Dust and several strips of torn sail-cloth, trailed by Mateo, who blanched when he saw. And then a quick glance at her—she didn't miss it—as if he was wondering why she had allowed this to happen at all.

Baron's voice: *The only place you feel like your anger means anything.*

"Gods," Mateo choked, peering closer. "He's still alive?"

"For now." Jordan pushed to her feet. Her legs had gone loose and unsteady, and a high whine needled her ears like she'd been punched.

Perhaps there *was* a line, she thought. Perhaps she had crossed irrevocably beyond the boundary of Baron's moral kingdom, and upon waking, he would hurl himself straight back onto the Boys' waiting swords.

But who was he to have drawn that line in the first place? Why should she hold back when they had all lost so much?

And were the pirates not, now, the ones keeping him alive?

"Bandages," she repeated when Mateo remained frozen. "I'd appreciate if you could take the arms, and Koro, his face—" And the three of them stripped off what remained of Baron's shirt and set to work.

Chapter 56

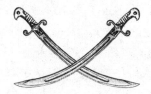

Baron could finally see.

He swooped through sky as blue as eternity, the Island below a knife-sharp labyrinth of cliff and pointed pine, the white-capped wavelets that nudged its shore so clear his eyes felt peeled open. His body lay somewhere on the pirate ship behind him, unwaking: muscle and tendon and nerve patched up with Dust, an anchor for whatever—Spirit? Essence? Consciousness?—was allowing his perception to fly free.

And it did feel, at last, something like freedom. Up here, no fist clenched in his chest; no fear thudded relentless through his veins. When he breathed in deep, brine and wind and blooming sunlight, it felt something like a first time.

A cool draft nudged him—his not-body—downward, and he spotted a blowing white shape on Peter's side of the shore.

Chay was surrounded by Boys: six of them scrambling up a cliff and clanging their swords, a restless many-headed creature that mostly ignored her. Her hair braided with brutal precision, her expression serene. But a sourness lingered in the turn of her mouth—or perhaps

Baron could taste it, somehow, in air wicking around her—that spoke of the night before, and what it had cost her.

"Ama!" Jack dipped down from the cliffs, a crab cupped gently in his palms. His hair sparkled with drops of seawater, his cheeks rosy from exertion. "Ama, look what I found!"

She took the crab in her hands, and despite the pain her face had just held, her smile was luminous. "Beautiful," she murmured, stroking its shell. "It's beautiful, Jack."

Baron remembered the pale flare of her dress, a starlit blur against the punishing dark. The ring of her voice, commanding, as his consciousness curled in a small dusty corner somewhere outside his body.

The way the Boys had obeyed her—had, for whatever reason, stayed themselves from killing their Ama—and in the process left him alive, if barely.

They still terrified him. Their faces reared up sharp in his vision as he swooped among them, and he balked at piercing heartless eyes, the cruel curve of a mouth. But as the Twins raced barefoot across the sand, arms raised in identical Vs of victory, he thought: They were still so young. He and Jordan had killed far more than they.

He *needed* to believe there was something of them worth saving.

He woke to pain.

Everywhere, a slow constant throb—his face a mass of heat, lines of fire down his arms and legs. A deep wrongness in his rib cage, as if he would drown the moment he breathed too deep.

He attempted to curl his fingers, and almost blacked out.

"Don't move your hands." A shadow on his left, silhouetted against amber torchlight. Jordan. "Or just don't move at all."

A low animal moan that he struggled to recognize as his own voice. He attempted to open his mouth, choked as his jaw popped like a gunshot.

"Try not to talk either." She stepped out of his periphery and reappeared with his glasses, their lenses so spiderwebbed he was prob-ably better off without. "Here." Maneuvering them carefully onto his nose: "Dau just took out the stitches in your face—*don't* touch it—and you've got four broken ribs and fucked-up hands and more stitches all over your—fuck this." A crack, and he suspected her cabin, or wherever he was, had gained another opening. "*Fuck*"—another crack—"this."

He un-gummed his lips gingerly, felt an unfamiliar strain across his cheeks. "How long—'ve I been out?"

"A week."

"Oh." He shifted on the cot, gritted back tears as his ribs *moved* beneath his skin. Nodding at the wreck of his body: "And still—?"

"Yeah," she said, and something hardened behind her face. "We couldn't get enough Dust."

He ventured an inhale, thin, careful. Small waves lapped against the hull; the lanterns pooled shadows in the splintered hole Jordan's fist had just made, and on the small unmoving circle of woodland creatures—a field mouse, a squirrel, a couple small birds—in the corner. So he hadn't been hallucinating that day, when he'd glimpsed them through the crack in her door. "What are—those for? They're—*dead?*"

"Peter," she said, but did not elaborate. "And they will be, soon."

She'd begun to pace in front of a salt-crusted milk crate, fist still clenched at her side. Her face was drawn—dark rings beneath her eyes, the lines of her mouth pressed deeper, weary—and he wondered what time of day it was; if she'd sat here with him through all seven.

"I swear on Taram," she said suddenly, pivoting back toward him, "I'm going to destroy them."

"They spared me," he mumbled, and the look she gave him was haunted and terrible. "They—didn't have to, but Chay—" His hands pulsed heat, and he rested his head back on the pillow with a pitiful half breath.

"You're incredible, you know." More shuffling, and then she reap-peared beside him with several strips of yellowish gauze, a pair of steel scissors hanging from her ring and pinkie fingers. He remembered, somewhat belatedly, that she hated scissors—they were always sharpened the wrong way. "They just handed you the beating of your life."

"And?"

She peeled a disconcerting length of bandage off his chin—he braced for it to tear, but her fingers were uncharacteristically gentle, knuckles barely pinked from their encounter with the wall. "Maybe you *are* just better than the rest of us. Unless you're purposely being an arse so I'll mess up your medical care."

He drew himself up with what scraps of dignity he could muster. "You're—terrible—fake doctor."

She tugged away the last of the gauze. It was dark with old blood. "Why's that?"

"Fake doctors don't—*argue* with patients—while they're—convalescing."

"I'd hardly call this an argument—"

Then she caught the upward crook of his mouth, and Saints, it hurt to smile, it hurt to move, but the look on her face—as if she wanted to murder him, as if she wanted to laugh. As if she was almost on the verge of tears.

PART SEVEN

Is that child still alive in the belly of the beast? Or is there nothing left but rage and teeth?

—Neon Yang, "A Stick of Clay, in the Hands
of God, Is Infinite Potential"

Chapter 57

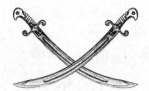

Chay stood beneath the stand of birch trees where Jordan had arranged to meet her, shifting uneasily on her feet.

She felt strange out here in the wind, cold and exposed. Her dress had tightened further around her chest and shoulders, and she could feel the flesh gathering at her hips the way her mother's had. There had been another—incident. Her bottomless stomach demanding more and more, in the long silent hours the Boys left her to when they flitted away from the crooked wooden house. The echo, beneath her eyelids, of broken bodies in the dark—

A glint of steel, and Jordan stepped into the small clearing, her hook sharp in the light of the half-moon. "Chay."

She smoothed her dress, resisted the urge to pinch the bulge at her waist. "Yes?"

"You saved him." Jordan's eyes were liquid pools of shadow. Chay could not see the resemblance between them. "Thank you."

"I—who?"

Her sister raised a brow. "Baron," she said flatly. A pause. "My Twin."

"Your—" Chay blinked. "That was him. In the pit."

"Yes."

Chay rocked back on her heels. She had not devoted much thought to Jordan's fellow Lost Boy, in the nine years since she'd bid him good-bye; had barely even envied him his place with her sister. It was always the living flame of Jordan's attention she had longed for—the only sur-prise was that Jordan had turned it on him instead. As if he'd had so much more to offer.

"Oh," she said.

Jordan jerked her head, unsmiling, as if it was something she'd wanted to get over with. "I have one last proposal for you."

Chay garbled out a laugh. "Something else?"

"This one's easier. Start acting like you want to go home. And con-vince the Boys to go with you. Can you do that?"

Chay nodded slowly. A couple weeks earlier, she might have doubted—to both the Boys and the pirates, every plan was the final plan, every battle the last strike. But with the Pales so reduced in number, and the Boys' Dust supply still low—thanks, in part, to her own smuggling of it to Jordan—an inkling of change shifted beneath her skin. The turning point of a story skulking beneath the surface, like a knife slid out of its sheath.

Peter was going to die, she thought, numb. Alone in the little wooden house, because he would sulk when the Boys decided to leave him, and he would stay. He always stayed. She and her sister both knew how that part of the story went, though he always forgot.

And then—

If he used to be a child, he isn't anymore.

"The Boys," she said, rubbing her thumb over the hem of Tier's jacket. She had dropped a dash of garlic on it, and the reek clung to the fabric no matter how hard she scrubbed. "Will they be safe?"

"If they don't try to interfere." Jordan smiled, humorless, and in that moment Chay saw her as the Boys might—a malevolence in the dark, a furious accumulation of scars. Jordan drew a glint of glass from her pocket. "Know what this is?"

Chay leaned closer. The vial of clear liquid was small as a thimble. Perfectly innocuous, but something deep inside her shuddered at the sight.

"What?" she asked anyway, on reflex.

"You know those little glow-in-the-dark mushrooms growing in that cave where you keep Tier?"

Chay stiffened. She had come to see that dank cavern at the heart of the Island as hers; the idea of Jordan sneaking there in her absence, harvesting the flora for her own ends and gawking at Tier's half-naked body, felt like a violation.

"Turns out when you juice them, they have some rather interesting effects." Jordan slipped the vial back in her pocket. "Put at least three drops in that Pretend medicine you always give Peter when he wants attention. It's tasteless and odorless. And it works quickly."

Chay emphatically did not want to know how her sister had found that out. "What time do you want the Boys away?"

A flicker of surprise crossed Jordan's face—and then she grinned, unexpected. "How's tomorrow night?"

Chapter 58

Baron woke to silence.

It was not complete—the ocean still murmured its slow lullaby, and he caught the low groan of wind that sometimes blew off the cliffs—but no pirates' snores reverberated through the walls; no ropes creaked as hammocks strained against ceiling hooks. Perhaps the crew had been gone for a while—it could have been afternoon, or evening. The flat grey sky was not forthcoming.

He pushed upright cautiously, felt around for his glasses on the windowsill. Pain still shot through him when he moved too fast, wound tight through his joints and the soft of his abdomen, but when he touched a foot to the floor, the resulting pang did not unravel him, and he eased himself upright, breathed, breathed.

Something nudged him toward the upper deck. The promise of fresh air, perhaps—the cabin had gone stale with the smell of his own sickness—or else a sort of morbid curiosity about how far he could actually walk. He made it halfway across the room before his legs gave out, and then he sat on the floor for a while, dazed, gingerly holding his ribs and trying not to gasp. In time, however, he hobbled up the cargo ramp. Tasted wind thick with the promise of rain.

The pirates stood in a circle, bristling with weapons.

None of the usual laughter and teasing, no last-minute instructions called out by Jordan or Dau. Only a tension strung between them, high and humming—a razor edge Baron could not, at first, understand.

Then Rien, opposite the hatch, caught sight of him, and a current rippled through the assembly: shock on Mateo's face, a twist to Koro's mouth. At the head of the circle, Jordan raised her chin, almost appraising.

The realization punched the air out of Baron's lungs.

Whatever she was planning, it was because of him.

Heat flooded his cheeks, and he shuffled back belowdecks, leaning heavily against the wall for balance. In the earthy closeness of that pit, before the pain had started, he had longed to be a martyr; had wanted his absence to mean something more than his presence could ever have. But all he felt now was detachment—that the pirates were only finishing what they had started. Fighting on top of fighting.

And, too, the disconcerting sensation of being stared at, the too-long beat of hesitation. The Island lacked mirrors—there was the creek on windless days, a handful of small pools near the Boys' territory that filled with crabs and silver fish at low tide. But as Baron ran his fingers across his cheeks—ridges of skin uncoiled like a map, seams of chapped canvas stitched not quite flat—the old lightning branched through his solar plexus anyway.

He could use Dust, of course, at least until the pirates ran out. But glamour would have been a waste, and his face hurt enough as it was.

And there could be something of Jordan, of the way she wore her own scars. The way she refused to apologize, in a world that would have preferred her to hide.

Or perhaps, he thought, he'd just been hit too hard on the head.

"You all know why you're here." Her voice rang out above him and he startled, elbows ramming the crate behind him with a thump that lanced pain through his forearms. Boots creaked across the deck—she must have been pacing—and he envisioned the black fire of her eyes, the hook a proud slash against luminous grey sky.

"You're here because you're angry," she said. "You're here because you're tired. You're here because Peter tried to erase the fact that you existed, but you survived, and for weeks or months or years you hid in the shadows while he hoarded Dust and murdered kids who trusted him. You're here because you've been locked out of your own story, and you want to take it back."

Ocean crash, blustering breeze, gulls screaming like vengeful ghosts. Baron closed his eyes and tried to see the Jordan with whom he'd flown out his San Jukong apartment window, the one who had pulled his bedsheets over her head and giggled something about ghosts. The wide-eyed person he'd kissed, uncertain for a precious fraction of a second.

He knew how the adage went—if he could not love her as she was now, then he must not love her at all. But for the space between two breaths, he allowed himself to miss what never could have been.

"The Lost Boys will be leaving tonight without Peter," Jordan continued, her footsteps steady against the cadence of her voice. "Our—spy will make sure of that. There are seven of us for six of the Boys. We'll hide in the trees around their clearing. When they fly out—and it'll be mostly one or two at a time, they'll all want to make their grand exit—we capture them quietly, knock them unconscious, and keep them out of the way. And in case anything goes wrong"—a pause, weighted, as wind gusted cool against Baron's face—"we'll each be carrying an equal portion of all the Dust we have left."

An explosion of voices—the pirates eager for their last strike, their one chance, *why now*—clipped back into silence, and Baron imagined that Jordan had raised her hook; that she stood at the bow, glowing beneath cloudlight, the spit of the engraving in Sir Franklin's book.

"Because we can," she said, to the loudest question curling like smoke through the air. "Because we've been fighting for too long, and too many pirates have died. This poison"—and Baron assumed she was showing them some sort of plant or tincture; thought of the animals lying in her cabin, the eerie stillness of their small bodies—"is going into Peter's Pretend medicine. Which will leave the way clear to take Tink."

Another spate of muttering, and Baron caught the word *Dust* from several different voices.

"And if they fight back, or all come out at once?" Koro asked.

"If they get in the way, do whatever your heart desires," Jordan replied. "But it won't be said"—another silence, pointed this time—"that I didn't try."

"All right."

"For Jack Two," Dau shouted, and other voices added *Aku* and *Nilam* and *Ellis* and *Sander*, and then they were chanting, a declaration, a prophecy, their boots and shields thumping the planks like a heartbeat.

As Baron pushed carefully to his feet, both hands braced against the wall, dread crept through him, cold and dark and viscous. Back when death was mostly theoretical, he had opened his arms to it passively—invited it to take him, if it wanted, though he was too much a coward to make the first move. It had been his shield against disappointment: If he could have been dead, then anything he accomplished, however paltry, might be framed as a triumph against formidable odds. Now, though, having brushed the edge of oblivion—his hands scrabbled helpless against unyielding earth, the snap of his elbow as a foot slammed down—

A stone formed in his stomach. He did not want to lose her.

She was marching the pirates back into that dark fold, and it was all his fault.

Eventually the chanting gave way to a barrage of last-minute logistics. Jordan talked the pirates through their positioning around Peter's house; Dau distributed the rest of the Dust reserve, and despite their warnings—*don't get cut, or you'll fall out of the sky*—murmurs rose up of barely suppressed glee. No one on the crew, save Dau themself, had held so much Dust in their leather pouches since they were young teens. Baron tucked himself into a corner, sucked in air tinged with lantern smoke. The tightness of his chest pushed down against his still-tender ribs, pressed him flat until he was nothing but shadow.

You know how this ends.

They were all dying anyway.

You know how this ends.

All he'd ever wanted was to not be the villain of his own story.

You know how this ends.

For half a breath, he had a vision of Jordan's hook sinking back into wet earth, jeweled Dust swirling bright in its wake. Enough to fly them home, to make them whole, to pry them free of all their bloody yesterdays.

But who was she, without her fury? And who was he, without his Twin?

The sea rustled, laughing. The gulls held their breath.

Baron turned and limped back toward his cabin.

Chapter 59

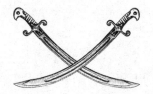

By the time Jordan made her way back to the hold, Baron was tucking his meager belongings—his Dust pouch, a couple ragged pairs of underwear, a handful of cured meat—into the mouth of his still-ludicrous climbing pack. His back was to her; beyond, the round window had dimmed slightly, clouds bleeding from flat grey toward crushed velvet dusk.

"So," she said, and a faint vindication shot through her when he stiffened—he had not heard her coming.

"So," he echoed, turning slowly. "This is it, huh?"

The single lantern on the wall threw deep shadows across the new planes of his face. Jordan had not spoken to him since the morning he had regained consciousness; had only poured Dust into those ragged red wounds and watched his skin knit, hour by hour, into some semblance of its old form. Now that he was fully upright, however, she could not help but think that, though neither of them had died, they had still paid a price.

The air between them was sour and thick as wool.

P. H. Low

"You're really—killing the Boys, too?" he asked.

"If necessary. They've killed a good number of ours."

He winced a little when she said *ours*. Perhaps that was the problem, she thought—he'd never truly taken ownership, of this or anything else. "They're—just children. *We* were just children."

"Exactly," Jordan snapped. "And look at what we did."

At his silence, she stepped forward. "I didn't know Aku well," she said, low. "Or Nilam, or Jack Two. But I'm not going to stand in the way of the others if they want their revenge."

His mouth contorted. "And they do."

"Of course."

Their old familiar rhythm, for just a moment, and something like sadness blazed through her, high and pure: at the thousand ways the Island had brought them together and then torn them apart; at the invisible hourglass above their heads, every grain plummeting toward an ending. As pirates' footsteps thumped the ceiling, the shadows poured over Baron, rendered him fragile and whip-thin and new, and she wanted to hold him, to crush him, to pour herself into the warmth of his skin until she was obliterated, or they both were.

"And then?" he asked, an unexpected gentleness in his voice. "Or did you never plan for After at all?"

She hid her surprise. "There might not be an After. Even if we fight with everything we have."

"You were always the one who *wanted*, of the two of us." A lock of hair had fallen across Baron's forehead, and he nudged it away, grimacing as his hand spasmed in protest. "You were the one always—searching, for more than the Outside could give you. So—if you had to pretend. If you got everything you could ever dream of."

Jordan wrapped her fingers around the hook, her skin chafing worse than ever under the leather straps. She'd never been one for speculation, for building castles where there was only swamp. The Island had been her only Pretend for almost a decade, and even it was barely imaginary.

"I don't know," she admitted. "Fly around the world. Make Obalang eat shit."

"And then?" Baron swallowed, painfully. "When you get old?"

She stared at him: his pupils huge in the dark, scars trailing furious red from brow to cheek to chin.

A silent understanding prickled beneath her skin.

The thing he had seen in her all along. The thing she had been loath to admit, even to herself. That she *did* like it here; that she had returned not just for Dust, but to take back the only life she had ever truly believed in.

That she would choose dying on the Island with a sword in hand over the shame of having left it behind.

He said, a soft accusation, "You're looking for an excuse."

"At least I," she said coldly, "have a cause."

Quiet again, words crackling under the surface. Jordan dragged her hook along the doorframe, mostly to watch him cringe.

"You're leaving?" she asked, and jerked her chin at his pack, the pouch of Dust inside.

Baron leaned against the cot, his hand still twitching. "I'll—wait until you get back."

"If I don't—"

"Don't—*say* that." Two unsteady steps and he was in front of her, a couple centimeters taller but she could blow him over with a breath. He smelled; they both did, something musky and slightly metallic that their daily dives into the ocean couldn't quite rinse away. But the clarion call of him—night sky and thunderstorms, his hands and mouth opening into her like flowers—sang again through her body, and she wanted it almost as fiercely as she'd ever wanted to fly. "Just don't," he said. "Please."

A dozen replies rose on her tongue. *Don't tell me what to do. Don't wait for me—it's not like you did before.* Yet in the heat of his closeness, as her thumb traced the part of his lips, she could not bring herself to hurt him. Not when it might be the last time.

She forced herself to step back.

"The only way we'll get an ending to this story," she said, keeping her voice light, "is if we write it ourselves."

The corners of his mouth curled up, his eyes quiet and sad. "As long as it isn't your end, too."

Chapter 60

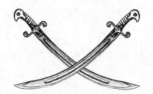

*A*t least I have a cause.

As the creak of feet ceased on the deck above—as the ship fell silent and lonely as an abandoned temple—Baron lay on his cot, dry-eyed and still, and watched the ceiling swirl above his head.

There might not be an After.

We'd rather be cut off cleanly at the end of the story.

He heard, again, the crack of sword hilt against his kneecap, his screams as the Boys slit the arches of his feet; felt the wet leak of intestine and the smack of his useless hands as they clutched at gushing warmth. He thought his mind had blotted out most of that night, but now it surged through him again: mirror shards of sensation, pain refracted endlessly in the midnight cavern that was his body.

If Jordan was placing the pirates' entire Dust reserve on the line for such a cause—if dying for this, for *him*, was the one thing she had ever truly wanted—

The hurt of it stole his breath.

She'll come back, he thought, but they were only words, crested like smoke against the wall that had crumbled suddenly inside him. And then he was spinning, his throat tight, pain lacing his ribs as he struggled for air. *She'll come back*, but he could only hear the faint whistle through his nostrils, the hiccuped edge of his own pushed-down sob.

Jordan—

Her bag digging into his knee at the computer lab. A blanket draped over him as he'd dozed on the plane. Her arms around his shoulders as they lay on the forest floor, holding him close as he broke apart.

Forget the way his leaving might shatter her like glass. If she was gone, what would be left of *him*?

And what had he been fighting for, if not the very life she was holding in so little regard?

Baron lowered himself gingerly from the cot, one leg and then the other, and then his knee spasmed and he was clutching the bedpost, the wood scraping his raw palms.

Jordan wanted to burn the pirates' Dust all at once, capturing the Lost Boys as they left for Outside; wanted the poison slipped down Peter's throat, and Peter bowed flightless at her feet. But visions of disaster were flooding through Baron, too late to warn her or the crew: If even one of the Boys cried out and alerted the others, the pirates would be locked into another pointless battle, their Dust supply—and the secret they'd made of it—ravaged for nothing. And years had passed since the pirates had fought in the air; it was not in their bodies to flinch at the barest swipe of a blade, to back away when their vision hazed red with revenge. They would fall to earth at the first nick of a rapier; would be twisted with the Boys into the same tortured Möbius strip as before—

Jordan's plan was a headlong rush toward death, the fireworks-bang of an ending she'd always wanted. But another idea tumbled from the darker corners of Baron's mind—the flutter of a white dress, a girl's high piercing cry. He could go to Chay instead. Ask her to keep the Boys inside tonight, to continue depleting their Dust until they were truly tied to gravity; to stay her hand from Peter's drink until they knew for sure that the pirates would win. Then he could talk to Jordan again, with the time he had bought, until she could envision a future—tether *her* to the ground, too, until she was no longer bent on going up in some bright burst of self-immolation and telling herself it was for him.

In the end, she would see, and she would live. And that would make all the difference.

His ribs still felt fragile, more bruise than bone; his left knee clicked disturbingly as he walked. But as he unlatched the cabin door, something like belief solidified inside him: He had spent nine years figuring out how to want his life. And there was only one person to whom he would have ever given it.

The planks groaned as he made his unsteady way down the hall, wood pores opening to release old sunlight and the vegetal smell of kelp and brine. The pirates would be deep in the forest by now, but they would travel mostly by foot, lest they squander their precious Dust. If Baron flew, he could reach the Boys' house in half the time.

Dau had handed him a leather pouch, too—a slow solemn nod as they'd shouldered into his cabin, as if they expected, even more than Jordan did, that he would flee while he could. He daubed it on his wrists and knees and spiderweb-cracked glasses, and then, blinking away the remaining grit, flew out into the waning light.

The pirates were nowhere to be seen.

Baron hovered at the edge of the Lost Boys' clearing, his breath a cloud curled beneath the thick shadows of trees. The thunder beneath his skin had quieted while he was flying—something about the wind against the flayed heat of his face, the infinite line of ocean as it smudged into sky. But as he touched back down on the ground—as the canopy closed over his head, and a high-pitched giggle rose from the Boys' house—it surged again, blood roaring in his ears. His skin a palimpsest of agony and old knives.

He squinted into the forest, forced himself to inhale on five. No people, as far as he could tell—only thin membranes of shadow, shifting and sliding. A couple hundred meters away, the forest thinned against the Island's northern cliffs, a precipitous plunge onto waves and sharp rocks. Perhaps he'd arrived before the pirates, and still had time to call an Everbird or toss a pebble at Chay's window; perhaps Jordan's scheme had already sprung into motion, and the crew was trussing up Boys one by one like ducks for New Year's roast.

Or perhaps their bodies were already cooling beneath the trees.

Then a gleeful whoop from the Boys' house, almost a war cry, and memory crashed through him again in a wave.

The wet thud of his head against hard-packed dirt. Hands peeling back the flaps of his opened stomach, reaching *inside*. Baron clamped a hand over his mouth, nausea lurching up his throat. *Breathe.* He had to get Chay's attention, and only hers. If the Boys heard him, they would leave their house too early, and if they left too early, they would see Jordan and the pirates before the ambush—

The crimson gape of his own open flesh. The ominous shift of his shirt against the wet of his torso. And the dark, the all-encompassing dark, dragging him down into nothing—

Not yet.

Breathe. Breathe.

He'd hoped, over the years, that the excess adrenaline would wear him down. That the equivalent of calluses might form across his neurons; that he would so habituate himself to fear that one day he'd stride into a life-or-death fight with a movie star's wink and daring smile. People loved a man with scars, after all.

But all he had now were wounds, torn open and bleeding. All he had were festering sores.

Breathe.

His heart pulsed an eedro bass. Copper on his tongue, sharp and bright. A stone against his chest, his throat in splinters, sharp metal grate of lungs *in out*

you're fine

in

stop

in

please

He'd triggered some kind of system shutdown, a full-blown panic attack instead of mere anxiety, something that uni and almost drowning in the ocean and being beaten nearly to death by a gang of flying children had failed to induce. He was a rag doll tossed into a hurricane, he was a nonsense of sensation, he was a heart bashed over and over against the hull of a sinking ship. Every storm before this had been a trial run—only now the thunderclap, the cataclysm.

Baron was finally going to die.

And if Jordan and the pirates had not yet arrived, he would take them down with him.

He staggered sidelong against the nearest tree, shattered, drowning—and at last an involuntary sound tore out of his throat, and Peter's house went silent.

Chapter 61

A nd the men and the lady went out into the world," Chay said, piling more dumplings onto Tudo's plate, "and lived happily ever after. All because of a mother's love."

The Boys made approving sounds. They were shoveling down dinner, their chatter the burble of a clear spring, and despite the narrow weight of the glass vial in her pocket, the sick twist of her stomach, Chay ached with the purity of the tableau: the fire glowing soft and familiar at their backs, everything that was soon to happen bundled into dim, distant abstraction. Within these walls lay light and warmth—she could still choose to go on washing the dishes, burrow oblivious into the giant bed; dump the poison in the grass and tell Jordan that Peter had refused his medicine. Tink could continue as she had been, knowing no other life but her perch on Peter's shoulder. And if—when—Tier woke, Chay would wave him away from shore apologetically. Tell him that she belonged on the Island, that he should find his place Outside without her.

And if he did not wake—if he passed in silence, in the dark span of hours she could not tend to him—

She wanted to lie down. She wanted to scream. She wanted to shove the rest of the dumplings in her mouth, despising herself more with every bite.

"Say," said one of the Twins, as Chay had been both hoping and dreading, "I wonder if our mother's waiting for us, too."

"She must be," said his brother. "Last I remember, a lovely lady."

"And mine." Tudo fiddled with his fork. "At least, I hope she is."

Chay smiled indulgently. "I'm sure she would remember as lovely a child as you."

"Blech. Mothers are toads." Peter scowled, stabbing a pork rib with his knife. "A long time ago, I thought mine would always keep the window open for me, so I stayed away for *ages*. But when I flew back, my window was barred. She'd forgotten about me. And another little boy was sleeping in my bed."

"Oh, Peter," Chay murmured, reaching out to touch his hand, even as her heart raced. Ever since last night's meeting with Jordan, she could not stop imagining those bright blue eyes gone glassy and still, the fast flicker of expressions across his elfin face stiffening into a death mask. This story wasn't quite hers anymore—she had taken it from the Sir Franklin movie she had watched over and over as a child, and from Jordan's assurances that it went this way in every iteration; the Boys' own selfishness and forgetfulness would do the rest. Yet she did not have to fake the tremble that slipped into her voice. "What if *my* mother thinks I'm already dead?" Pause, breath. Head up: resolution. "What if she's forgotten me, too? Peter, I think—I want to go back Outside."

"But who will be *our* mother?" Jack asked immediately, and the Boys burst into a chorus of indignation.

"—no one to cook—"

"No more stories—"

"We could chain her to a Never Tree—"

"Make her stay—"

"No," Peter said sharply, "you will not harm any girl who wants to leave the Island," and they quieted, though their eyes still burned with pique.

Chay straightened and brushed off her dress, tamping down the impulse to check her pocket.

"You could come, if you'd like," she said—looking down at them through her eyelashes, the picture of injured dignity. The Boys gaped, spoons stilled in midair. "I'm sure my parents would love to adopt you."

"Really?" Tudo asked, pushing up his glasses shyly.

"There will be more stories," she promised. "Whole buildings full of them. And toy shops, and movie theaters, and motorcycles—"

"Oh, can we?" Jack bounced out of his chair, and the Boys turned imploring eyes on Peter, whose face had gone dark. "Pleeease?"

It was the sheer newness of the thing that appealed, Chay mused, the shining possibility of a life that wasn't theirs. Once upon a time, she had believed in it herself—that you could shuck off your past like an old skin. That it would never come crawling back.

"Pretty pretty please, Peter," said Kuli, clasping his hands, "can we go?"

"Of course," said Peter. "Tink will see you off." And there was no bitterness in his voice; there was nothing at all.

Then a sound outside the hollow tree, halfway between a gasp and a sob, and Chay nearly jolted into the fire.

Use the door chime, she thought incongruously, as the Boys stilled. Static roared in her ears. Peter took his medicine right before bed, whenever he picked some small fight with the Boys and wanted to be fussed over by his Ama, but dinner had just begun; the light of the overcast sky still filtered in through the windows and the cracks in the walls. Why would the pirates come for her now? And why would they announce themselves? Or perhaps it was one of the remaining Pales, come to renew their allegiance after the pirates' atrocities?

"Who's there?" Peter called, and the curtains fluttered in a sudden gust of cold air. The Boys craned their necks, listening. "Hello?"

When no one responded, Peter motioned to the Boys. "Get ready," he said, hefting his sword. The grin on his face was bright and feral and triumphant—all the Boys' thoughts of Outside had flown out the windows, and he knew it. "We're going out."

Chapter 62

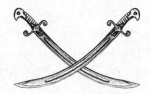

The Boys' new house, Jordan thought as she knelt in the cold dirt, looked strangely at peace.

It was built entirely from twigs and small branches, a lopsided three-story thing that seemed to regard gravity as a guideline rather than a hard-and-fast rule. From the open windows, she caught the flicker of a massive fire—enclosed by Dust, probably—but only a couple Boys' voices piped through the cool evening air, chirping and indistinct.

The pirates fanned out around the house, visible only because she knew where to look. Dau crouched behind a tree several meters to her right; Koro checked his arrows on her left; Rien and Jack One and the others tucked themselves into the shadows beyond, faces smeared with mud. Her crew, now, their oath etched in blood and Dust and the inexorable shine of the hook she had chosen. Poised to bundle the Boys away the moment they flew beyond view of the crooked house.

Jordan could not remember the last time she had felt at home. It sure as Taram hadn't been on downtown San Jukong's smog-thick streets or Baron's rolling green campus, or even the Island, those nine long years ago. Yet as she met each of the pirates' eyes, edgeshine of a blade in the falling dusk, she wondered if they would be the ones she would die fighting beside, and it was almost the same.

Baron's absence tugged at her—a hush of air at her shoulder, the missing half of a heartbeat.

He'd promised to stay this time. To wait until she returned. But he had not fully forgiven her—not that she deserved it—and his injuries had, thus far, kept him from venturing off-ship. What kind of fool was she, after all the walls she had flung up between them, for thinking he would not leave as soon as he was able?

A rush of memory: the shadows in the pit congealing into blood-mottled skin, his cautious clever hands bent and broken. The high keen of grief as she knelt, mud seeping into her pants, and touched the red mask of his face.

No more.

The forest was a labyrinth in the cloud-pressed half-light, the subterranean shift of earth transforming it into a place she did not know. She was past anger now; past the explosive fury, the simmering desire for vengeance. The only thing left inside her was certainty, cold and sharp as ice.

The Boys' goodbyes floated through the trees—more distinct now, their voices pealing like birdsong. Jordan felt a shot of admiration for Chay. She'd never accounted for her sister—had set out for the Island ready to fight for her own life until the place stripped her down to Dust. But Chay had, even while tending to Tier on the side, been a better spy than Jordan could ever have hoped for.

"Say goodbye to Father," she heard the Ama admonish, an utterly convincing waver in her voice, and at Peter's silence—the bastard was probably throwing a silent tantrum—the pirates exchanged a tight, wordless nod.

Another memory—Baron cast in shadow by the cabin torch, the accusation in his eyes thick enough to swallow—and Jordan's grip tightened around her sword.

Even if the Boys made it off the Island, even if they flew home to soft beds and stove-cooked food and mothers who firmly locked their bedroom windows, it would be to a world that would applaud when their voices cracked instead of setting out to kill them; that would take their newly hatched cynicism and call it sophistication, the dregs of their violence and call it ambition. The Boys would grow into men, and saunter through life expecting it to bend to their will, and though they might forget the Island, it would always be rooted in their blood.

And so Jordan did not dread the pirates' vengeance. Did not feel anything at all.

In the distance, one Everbird cawed, then another.

She froze. A weight tugged at the edge of her awareness—a subtle shift in the air, the ripple of a pebble dropped in water. Smoke curled from the new house's copper-pipe chimney, dissolved soft as moth wings; the trees leered at her, sharp branches bristling.

Something was wrong. Something was very wrong.

A flash in her periphery—a bird, or perhaps a dress, white as moonlight shot between branches.

"*Charge!*" Peter shouted, his voice coming from everywhere at once, and the Lost Boys exploded out of the forest behind her, screaming war.

The pirates were winning.

The pirates were *winning*.

This was not how the stories went. The Boys, having ambushed the pirates' ambush, were supposed to rush forward and press their advantage; only as they raised their blades to strike the killing blow should their opponent surge to full strength and beat them back for a while. So ran the grain of narrative, the arc carved into the heart of the Island— villains did not simply take the fight from the start. Yet as the Boys closed in, their outer circle squeezing the pirates in toward the house, time slowed and sharpened its edges, and the pirates rose off the ground with their last glorious burst of Dust, and at the Lost Boys' widened eyes—*Impossible, where did they get it? Flying is for kids!*—a grin broke across Jordan's face, fierce and giddy.

A Lost Boy's blade whipped a startled hairsbreadth from her elbow, and she dodged and spun—whirling forest, snap of fading sky. Euphoria jangled gold through her veins. Her sword clanged off a brass-knuckle hilt, and it sounded like laughter. Level with the Boys, now, the pirates had the longer reach and comparable wrist play; the Boys darted at them like mosquitoes but never struck deep.

Then a scream cracked the air, and Jordan whirled around, a shout escaping her before she even registered what she was seeing.

"No!"

A huff of breath like shadow, tearing.

He wasn't supposed to be here. Had promised her the easiest fucking thing in the world—to do nothing, to wait, to stay—and here he was, backed against the Boys' front door, his face crumpled in pain.

And one of the Twins was holding a knife to his throat.

"He was the one who warned us, you know." Peter—who was not, as she'd hoped, lying immobile on the Boys' dining room table—hopped down from the roof of the house, from which Dau still dangled by one arm, groaning and clutching their bloodied sword hand to their chest. Tink thrummed gold around his face; his blue eyes shone flat as a fish's. He flipped and caught his own dagger—a solid thud as the handle met his palm—and Baron jolted back, whimpering. "He got here ahead of you and told us everything."

"I'm sorry," Baron said in Kebai. His face was wet with tears, the words blurred by the rigidity of his still-healing jaw. "I wanted to tell Chay to—to wait a bit, and keep depriving the Boys of Dust so they'd be weaker when you finally met them and—I was afraid you'd *die* but I—I panicked and they found me and threatened to—" And then the Twin's blade pressed in and he clamped his mouth shut, his throat still working furiously.

The other Boys and pirates faded into the canopy dark, and for a moment Jordan just stared. Memorized the slope of his nose, the two gentle creases between his brows. The clench of his hands, still ragged and red with scars.

This was the face she had once made hers into.

This was a boy who had lost a war.

No one stays, she thought, and the sweet sharp crush of pine needles washed over her, his eyes clarion clear.

I loved you.

You know how this ends.

She had always told herself he would leave. That when he hit his breaking point—and he would, inevitably, as everyone else did when she no longer served their purposes—he would retreat back into the world that made sense: one where disintegrating beneath the anxiety of final exams meant more than swordplay and vengeance; where he might be confined in a cubicle for the rest of his waking days but could at least afford a hospital bed to die on.

She had never expected that, at the worst possible moment, he would choose her instead.

"So, Captain," Peter said, sweeping into a grand bow, and when he smiled, it was with every one of those infamous baby teeth: curiously flat, like two neat lines of gravestones. "Are you ready to die?"

And she had dreamed of this fight—had spent her early years in the Underground fantasizing about meeting Peter again, unbound by gravity—but now she simply wanted it to end.

She leveled her sword, and against its keen silver edge, she felt nothing at all.

Chapter 63

Jordan circled Peter above the forest canopy, her eyes locked on his heart because faces lied and hands were a distraction.

Her vision had narrowed to the edge of his sword, the curve of her own hook, Dust a steady hum in her veins. Below them, the surviving Lost Boys and pirates were gathered in a ring, just as they had in the original story, and she felt a grim twist of amusement—that this was just the Underground but shittier; that the Island had deemed her worthy of this role unto its end.

Baron, still half-crumpled in front of the Boys' house, was letting out small breathy gasps, the occasional strangled sob. It was a tactic she'd seen Peter use against former pirate captains: Comrades in pain distracted even the most hardened sailors; only Peter could remain truly unbothered. But there was a particular viciousness in the watching Boys, too, that thread of poison smoke she'd sensed while peeling Baron off the ground last week. Because they despised the length of his limbs, the lump at his throat. Because they knew, deep in their marrow, that they themselves were destined to belong Outside as much as he.

Just remember. Her own words, once, as her feet scuffed the sand of the Underground arena. *I took it easy on you.*

Stupid, the swagger she'd put on. She'd gone soft in San Jukong— too used to retreating to her air-conditioned apartment after she fractured a rib, too certain she would wake the next morning regardless of whether she won or lost. Victory hadn't *mattered*, at least by the measure of the Island, and each triumph under those conditions had built a false carapace around the real loss, the one that echoed red and brittle inside her.

And brittle things were easily broken.

"Peter," she said, and tasted his name in her mouth like a dare. "Do you remember who I am?"

He scoffed. "What kind of stupid question is that?"

And they fell to it.

For a full minute there was nothing but the dance of strike and counterstrike, bright slash of sword and hook, her own hard breathing and cloud-silk swaths of sky. On a good day, they would have been evenly matched—Jordan's wrist play had not atrophied as much as her predecessor's—but her limbs felt strangely out of cadence, her skin stretched wrong across the frame of her bones. The arch of Peter's spine became Baron's body, slumping to the ground; the mouths of shadow that danced between arm and sword were wet as split skin.

Fire whipped across her wrist and she jerked back, a shout dropping out of her like a reflex.

"Gotcha," said Peter, as Jordan began to sink.

She had forgotten the feeling of it. The loosing of a clenched fist, a puppet-string tug at her ankles; the Island enacting its final judgment, or just petty vengeance. As a nauseating warmth bloomed through her sleeve—as a murmur rippled through the pirates and Boys, and their circle spread out among the trees to make room for her and Peter at its center—her feet flattened against the mud, and she heaved her sword up just as a shattering impact reverberated up her elbow.

Then Baron began to beg.

"Please," he choked, his voice carrying through the trees. "No no don't *please*—"

She thought, without rancor, that she should have left him to die.

Peter struck again from above, and their blades skidded sideways, met hilt to hilt.

He grinned, delighted. "He's pretty when he cries, isn't he?"

She lashed upward with the hook and he flitted away, giggling.

Another scream, but she didn't dare look. Baron weeping as if his voice was being ripped out of his throat—as if the Twin's knife was slicing him open, limb by limb, bone by bone—and she was going to flay the Boys alive, cut Peter's heart out of his chest, let the Everbirds masticate them all organ by organ.

He would have grown old, she thought as Peter drove her toward the Island's northern edge. Beyond the trees lay wind-sharpened cliffs and cold frothing waves, a long view of the central mountain so swathed in mist it was more ghost than stone. She thought of Baron curled in a dripping-dark cave, the shamed relief on his face when she'd stepped into that icy pool in his place. *Godsdammit, he would have figured out how to live.*

A whip of steel, Peter ducking low, and Jordan's right leg lit up in white fire. She staggered through the brush, twigs and thorns snatching at her face and arms, and then tripped and landed flat on her back on a ledge over the ocean, her thigh a shattered mass of agony.

Don't look, she thought, and looked.

Peter had sliced her open like an envelope.

Dark yawned through the center of her vision; distantly, she felt her limbs slacken, her head loll to the side, the old blood-fear reared up like a dragon out of the deeps. But before she could pass out, Peter's sword—the kiss she had spent nine years running from, the touch that had haunted her waking days—came to rest against her neck, cold and deadly and light as butterfly feet.

"I didn't think it would be *this* easy," Peter said, and in that one sentence, she was stripped of armor. "But I guess you're a girl, so. Drop your weapons."

The piercing wrongness of the gap in her flesh. Her hand somewhere outside herself, still fisted around the hilt of her sword.

Peter's blade bit her skin. "I said drop 'em."

Moving hurt. The drag of sharp steel through mud, the maneuvering of elbow and forearm when her lower half was a crimson scream. But it was easy enough, in the end, to let go.

Her broadsword flashed over the cliff into raging surf. Somewhere below, an Everbird squawked, unsettled.

"The hook, too."

She eyed the thin fluted bones of his wrists. If she struck out and disarmed him, grabbed his hilt—but her reflexes were shot; she felt as though she were moving through tar.

From the clearing, Baron made a sound that was barely human.

She was dead. She was in love. She was in pain. Three sides of the same story, and in no version of it did she survive this fight.

The hook thunked to the ground in a waft of sweat and blister pus. Peter wrinkled his nose. "Wow," he said, kicking it over the ledge. "I didn't actually think it came off."

Jordan glared and spat in his face. In response, the sword prodded her chin.

"Any last words?" Peter singsonged. "Or are you going to jump?"

In nearly every version of the story, the captain jumped—into the ocean or the crocodile's jaws, onto his own blade. Better to break yourself, to choose your own end, than be crushed by this child-who-was-not, this little boy you should have bested so easily.

The trees pulsed grey, the air bleached with fault lines. This was what she got for falling in love, she thought—and she could finally touch that word, now that it had been drained of all meaning. Even when all her and Baron's promises had crumbled to ash, even with the thousand layers of armor they'd donned to defend themselves from each other, the possibility of his absence—his nonexistence—stripped her bare, left her shaking.

And she had promised him an ending. Could imagine him, still—clean and less emaciated, his scars healed over—sitting on a marble-tiled porch in San Jukong, rich off glamoured mir; flying off at midnight to sit on Gann's highest peaks; soaring over farm and valley and sea until the air grew clean and the stars burned bright and for a few stolen moments he could breathe in deep.

It didn't matter if *she* lived. It was almost easier to imagine herself gone—and quickly, without the humiliation of weeks- or months-long karsa withdrawal. But with Dust, Baron could have survived. Could have learned to be free.

She pushed slowly to kneeling on her good leg. One of the Twins was leading him out through the pirates' half of the watching circle, shoving him toward the cliff beside her; Baron stumbled with exhaustion, his face screwed into a gargoyle's bawl.

But he was not *cut*, besides a nick at his throat where the knife was poised.

The Twin's dark eyes glinted, mocking—that even an echo of that bloody night had been enough to undo her.

"I'm sorry," she said in Kebai, and by the flare of his nostrils, she knew he had understood. "You deserved better than what I gave you."

Then she turned back toward the drop.

"No," she heard behind her, as if through gritted teeth, "Jordan, *no*—" but she was hauling herself toward the edge—fist clenched against the obliteration that was her leg, Peter's sword sliding cold across her nape. All the Dust had leached out of her, left her a shell of meat and pounding bone, and when she leaned out into the night air, it was with something like relief.

At least it was over. At least she had fought.

At least she knew how badly she'd lost.

Her toes curled inside her boots.

"She's going to do it," one of the Lost Boys stage-whispered.

"About time."

"That's not very nice. She could have been our mother, too."

"Shut up, Tudo."

"Yeah, why don't you jump with her then, if you love her so much."

"Jordan—"

The gap yawned beneath her, whole and welcoming. A flock of Ever-birds spiraled toward the knotted clouds. Sticky heat oozed through her pants, dizzied her in its wrongness.

No shame in breathing hard, not anymore.

And then.

Then.

This was the stuff of which stories were made—myths and shifts and corners turned, beats like the ones her heart would soon run out of—and Jordan had imagined her death a thousand times but she'd never thought it would unfold like this.

A tug at the edge of her perception, like the twitch of a finger she did not have. Then memory poured into her, bright and surging: the whip of Dust withdrawal through her veins, the beetles crawling out of Slightly's mouth, every night she'd stepped out of the training cave and seen Baron's face shuttered in the aftermath of fear. The cries of a thousand children who were dead, or might as well be—the ones who'd been shattered so thoroughly that their pieces never quite fit back together.

Someone had to pay. And as new rage blossomed in her lungs, a waking wind shuddered through the forest and she *became*—every branch and beating heart grown as sharp in her awareness as her own limbs, every creature and stone and slow-breathing fern entwined in a symphony of pure sensation. The obliterating fury she'd felt while tearing that Pale apart, or hauling Baron out of that open grave, steeped in a sudden *knowing* that thrummed hot through her veins.

She thought she'd understood what it meant to grow up—that you could not win against time or death; that you could not attempt to kill Peter *and* escape with your life. In the past few weeks, when withdrawal lanced her gut, she had wondered if the Island was simply toying with her, shrugging her around its vast stone shoulders before the final proof of her insignificance rang down like a hammer blow.

But across a vast span of sky—before the pirates and Boys, still watching from their strange temporary truce circle with an air of something like ceremony—she willed the dagger out of Kuli's sheath as if she were holding it in her hand. Sliced it upward, and true.

A gasp, just behind her, tiny and intimate and wrong, and Jordan looked back one last time.

The dagger was sticking out of Peter's chest.

Holy shit.

Even dying, he was a picture.

He drifted side to side like a feather, his face blanched and flawless as a Rittan doll's. A whimper escaped him as he touched the tiny metal triangle between his ribs; blood pooled in the creases of his palms and—finally—stained them. A child, and not. A murderer, and more. The hilt of the dagger wobbled between the wings of his scapulae, stark and irreversible.

She had stabbed him in the back.

She had not touched him. Had not known, even a few moments ago, what she would do. But she had felt something like it on that morning she'd thrown knives into a tree, her hand shaky from its still-knitting wound; on that sun-drenched afternoon fighting Pales in deep forest, Seida's sword scything toward her chest and then suddenly, improbably swerving away. And now—she had *believed* enough to drive Kuli's knife between Peter's ribs with the sheer force of her want, and he could only thumb the tip of the blade, his grip suddenly feeble, his expression one of utmost betrayal.

"You cheated," he cried, and Jordan knew that—knew she'd washed up on a tainted shore of too much anger and too little honor. But she hadn't trained and fought and dosed herself with karsa for nine years just to hold back when a new weapon presented itself. She wasn't here to show good form.

She'd come to win.

A cry went up, and the pirates and Lost Boys crashed back toward each other in a wave, the strange spell that had kept them apart during the duel shattered among the steel clangs and screams. Evenly matched, now, without Peter. Without her.

Jordan swayed and fell back on her arse. A flicker of shadow—as if a hand were covering her eyes, her cut-open leg a mindless serrated pulse—and the cliff yawed at her back, the black rocks below sharp as iron gateposts.

She was losing too much blood. She did not have to look down to know this. But the golden glow that was Tink rested on Peter's forehead only a couple meters away, and Baron was struggling to his feet beside her (the Twin holding him at knifepoint had sailed gleefully into battle), and so she attempted to lever herself back onto her feet, her bad leg juddering like a motorcycle engine.

Her elbow bent at an awkward angle, and she crashed sideways into the mud.

Fuck, she thought dimly. Darkness a blanket folding over her, the hot metallic smell of her sliced-open thigh coating her tongue. All this fighting and bleeding and dying, and in the end she would succumb with Tink a mere meter away.

Then a white dress flared in her periphery, and the fairy vanished into Chay's pale, steady hands, and Jordan heard the sound of weeping.

Chapter 64

Peter was dead.

    Chay knelt, sobbing, his body cradled in her arms. She had watched him dart and dance around Jordan as they fought above the ledge—delicate curves of wrist and knee, edges of shoulder blades like birds' wings; had watched Kuli's dagger fly as if thrown by the wind, and pierce its bull's-eye like paper. And the Boys would expect her to cry, now. No one mourned more than a mother for her son. So she crushed her fists around the sleeves of Tier's jacket; remembered the weight of another body, so great it would smother her. Allowed grief and fear to wrack her from the inside out.

In her other hand, Tink fluttered, warm and bursting with gold.

This was not exactly what Jordan had asked for. Chay was meant to usher the Boys out of the house, slip the poison into the glass flask of Pretend medicine, then hurry off to retrieve Tier and let the pirates do the real fighting. But Jordan had collapsed in the mud; the rest of the crew seemed otherwise occupied, as Peter's prohibition on fighting in front of her seemed to have dissolved with his last breath. Chay was the only one whom the Boys would not turn on for grabbing Tink; the only one whom the pirates wouldn't appear suspicious for not attacking.

But side by side with her real and acted grief, an unfamiliar feeling rose in her chest, hot and sharp as burnt tin.

She thought of Tier, drowning in his own blood. She thought of Slightly, fidgeting without his staff as he followed Peter out the Cave of Spheres' sun-bright mouth.

She thought, *No more.* And though her nose was swollen and pink, though she had cried so hard her eyes felt like bruises, that scorched-metal feeling flooded her mouth, tingled her fingertips. Vindication.

No more.

Tomorrow we start anew.

And when the pirates began to stumble back into the trees, retreating—Had they *all* been cut? Were they running out of Dust?—and the Boys swooped down in a vicious flock of swords, she called out, thick-throated but dizzy with her own sense of accomplishment, "Boys! Remember the story about the fairy who drank poison?"

Shadow flicker, ringing steel. Fear yawned a chasm inside her—if she could not distract the Boys, if there were no pirates left, no one would save her; she would be left behind yet again.

"And died?" Kuli asked eventually, bobbing back in her direction.

"Yes. But she returned to life." Chay tipped her head up and met the gazes of each Boy, who had drifted close as if for a bedtime story. *Listen to me, one last time.* "When children all around the world clapped for her, their belief pulled her back from the dark in-between-lands. What if we do the same for Peter, now?"

Leaves rustled. The Boys' gazes pressed into the mask that was her face. But they looked at her tears and saw a mother; they looked at her arms around Peter's shoulders and saw someone who did not lie.

Slowly, slowly, the Boys began to clap. The pirates looked to her, alarmed and grateful, and slipped quietly back into the forest.

Chay blew out a shaky breath, shivered as adrenaline leached out of her system. Even if the pirates did not capture the Boys tonight, she had at least allowed them to get away; with Peter dead, and Tink's wings brushing her palm, they would find some way to sneak her—and Tier—to safety.

Because she knew, in the end, the clapping would fail.

Chay had adapted her tale from the Sir Franklin story, though she'd clad the fairy in her version a bit more modestly. There had been a mustachioed pirate captain slipping cyanide into Peter's nighttime eggnog, Tink darting in at the last moment to choke down the teaspoonful of death meant for him. But Sir Franklin had been wrong about as many things as he'd been right. And even if there was a mote of truth in this particular anecdote—even if there were rules to Dust, and the Island, that Chay did not fully understand—Peter had called on every child in the world to revive Tink in that story. Surely five or six, now, would not break the finality of death—and Peter's death, no less. The Boy who was never supposed to die.

"Boys," she cried, "do you truly believe?"

They clapped harder.

"More," she shouted, waving her arms. "Come on, come on!"

"Is it working?"

Chay whipped around. The barest crunch of boots: Jordan, limping slowly through a gap between trees, her torn-open leg bound up in some kind of tree bark. As the Boys booed and hissed, the slap of their palms rubbing thin in the clouded evening air, Jordan's eyes flicked to Chay's, and Chay mused at the strangeness of this last collaboration, this story folded in on itself. The way they had come to look each other in the face at last.

Jordan spread her arms mockingly. To the Boys: "How much longer are you going to try?"

"As long as it takes," Jack shouted, and as the others took up his cry, Jordan jerked her head toward a figure slumped beneath a bush.

Chay turned again and thought, *Oh, Saints.*

Baron lay spread-eagled on the ground, unconscious.

His skin was ashen, the knife slashes across his face and arms still a puffy, half-congealed mauve. Chay tucked Tink in the pocket of Tier's jacket and picked her way toward him, unsteady. Eight nights ago, as she had approached the Boys' mud pit—the dark viscous mess, more spillage than person; the arch of a foot split open and bone shining through.

Jordan had told her, with obvious reluctance, about the pirates' Dust supply, the way they scavenged the Boys' dregs from the lagoon and cave walls and high trees. But there was no way they could have saved enough in a week to fight this battle *and* take away Baron's pain.

He groaned when Chay moved his arm, eyelids fluttering, and her chest loosened—just the usual kind of unconscious, then. But Jordan probably wanted him well enough to fly off the Island on his own, and for that, Chay would have to apply the Dust ointment she kept in her pocket, and for *that*, all the Boys would need to conveniently look away—

She looked to Jordan again. A nod between them, like something out of a dream, and then Jordan took another step toward Peter's prone corpse, her leg quivering as if about to buckle.

"It's too late." Her chin tilted up, that sardonic smile Chay used to despise. "He'll probably turn back into Dust soon. Though if you hang around, maybe you can see it happen."

"Shut up, you eejit!" Kuli called, and Chay could hear the sneer in his voice.

"Stupid pirate!"

"You don't know anything!"

"You're supposed to be dead!"

"Keep clapping, then," Jordan drawled. "See those vultures up there? All for him."

As she continued to taunt the Boys, Chay dropped a glob of ointment onto Baron's face, and he moaned again, his back arching.

"Shh. Shh." Nausea bubbled in her throat, and she clamped her teeth down. "It's just Dust."

He squinted at her, the edge of one eyelid crinkled by a scar slashed halfway down his cheek, and she thought: She could not remember him as a Twin. Could not see in his face the boy she used to know.

"Jordan?" he mumbled.

Chay nearly broke open again. She knew the way he held that name in his mouth—like it was the last word he was clinging to, when hurt had scattered all the others like sand.

"No." She fumbled more ointment out of the canister. Her fingers had gone stiff with cold, and her eyes burned. "No, not Jordan."

Then the clapping stopped.

A hush of wind, branches clicking like teeth. Velvet absence where her sister's voice had been, and Chay shivered, felt inexplicably as if someone had called her name.

Peter still lay near the cliff's edge, delicate as a flower crown. His chest did not rise; his eyes did not lampshade-slide open in slow, glorious revelation. A couple of the Boys clapped again, tentatively, but the others hissed and they stopped.

Below them, Jordan leaned casually against a tree.

Her eyes were hard, her chin jutted in defiance. It was the same face she made while fighting—feral and sharp-edged, dancing on the edge of control—but Chay caught the pallor of her cheeks, the catch in her breath. The way she resisted putting her weight on her wounded leg.

But Chay could not go to her, not without the Boys noticing. And, anyway, she'd run out of ointment again.

Above them, the clouds had darkened, a cupped hand easing them slow toward night. Inland, past the dark fringe of leaves, smoke from the Lost Boys' chimney curled skyward in a bitter exhale. The wind had died, and an unnatural stillness lay over the Island—as if the earth itself was waiting, alive.

Then, from the blood-matted mud, Peter gasped awake.

Chapter 65

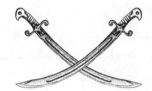

Baron was absolutely sure he'd seen Peter die.

He lay flat on his back, a dull ache radiating from every bone in his body, the forest canopy a black-toothed jaw snapped shut above his head. His grasp on time had slipped—one moment the Twin's knife cold at his jugular, his legs shaking as he was shoved through the forest; the next, Jordan limping toward the precipice, and a lightning tang on his tongue, and dark spilling across Peter's skeleton-leaf shirt like a prophecy. And as the Boys bellowed rage—as Chay called them to believe, and they clapped, and Jordan scoffed—Baron had even dared think: They'd done it. Mangled the script, shattered the ending.

Yet here was Peter's voice again, that unmistakable peal of laughter. And Baron had lived all his life terrified of failing school and life and the people who needed him, but tonight—allowing the storm to sweep him away, the one time it truly mattered that he hold on—was the worst thing he'd ever done.

Jordan may have dragged him back into a war, but he had lost her the final battle.

Chay's Dust ointment was working slowly through his body, the throb of his hands and face and rib cage fading breath by breath. He clenched his toes weakly, attempted to twitch limp fingers. His head still lolled back, leaden and elsewhere.

He had to apologize, he thought. His brain felt sluggish and viscous, but—if he could just make it to his feet. He would not save himself, nor any of them. But if the Boys, spurred by their evidently unkillable leader, were going to slaughter the pirates tonight, at least Jordan should know he hadn't meant to hurt her.

"Find them," Peter was shouting, "find them and kill them all!" And his crew crashed back through the trees with a howl of triumph, scouring the ground for grown-ups to finish off.

Baron propped himself up on one elbow and almost vomited.

There were too many joints in his body. Too many ligaments and tendons and nerves, all of them still bruised and screaming, and he had longed for this sometimes when the fear took him—proof etched in his skin of the wreckage of his mind—but this hurt, it *hurt*, and everything in him revolted against it.

Stand up.

His other elbow dug into the mud, as did the raw tender mass of his lower back. His jaw ached from clenching; pain shot through his ribs whether he breathed or held his breath.

Up.

As Jordan had once stood for him—pelted by pebbles in Peter's lightless cave, and tilting his chin up with her sword, and all the hours in between.

His heels churned the dirt. He attempted to tense his abdomen, and heard a squelch.

Up.

To his knees, then his feet, a tightness pulling between his temples as he tottered shoulder-first into a boulder. Dirt smudged his glasses; his pants clung to his legs, damp with sweat and mud. But he was still fighting, still here.

If he made it off this cursed place alive, he thought, he could live through anything.

One step, another. On his left, deep in the tangle of brush, he caught sight of Jordan wading forward on her knees; on his right, near the cliff's edge, Peter stomped his feet and shrieked for Tink.

Baron only had a moment to wonder at this before another rush of ozone howled through him—a force like magnetism or gravity, sucking him in—and the Boys began to scream.

Chapter 66

Peter was alive.

Jordan sat back against a tree trunk—hidden, for now, from the Boys, who had poured back into the forest to hunt down the few remaining pirates—and screwed her eyes shut. Peter, sitting up with the dagger still protruding from his chest. Peter, impish grin and drawn sword as the Lost Boys' triumphant howls rebounded off the cliffs. *Impossible*—even the Island had rules. Even belief had its limits. Dead boys stayed dead.

But then, Peter had never been all boy.

A rumble, deep in the earth, as if a giant had breathed in for the first time in millennia. Jordan thought of the fear that had lit the Boys' faces as the pirates kicked into the air; thought of Chay, the pale waft of her dress lit by Tink's heady glow.

But if Peter could not die—if the Boys could pull him back from that final threshold simply by believing—

"Tink," he shrieked, stomping on the ground, a funny little twitch of his knee Jordan realized was an attempt to fly. "Tink, c'mere, you little bitch."

She crawled away. Toward thicker tree cover, mud cold beneath her palm, legs canted awkwardly to keep from jostling the moss-and-vine bandage she'd knotted around her thigh. In the spaces between Peter's shouts, quiet rang through the air: a held breath, a watching. And though she had lost track of the Boys—though she'd seen the white flash of Chay's dress slipping into the woods toward Tier's cave—Jordan could sense her own death barreling toward her like a train, two hundred tons of steel and thunder. See the fragile husk of herself, snapped in half like a reed.

Her hand clamped down on a forearm.

Jack One, his face crumpled against the red spill of his intestines into the soil. *Dust*, she thought, with a twinge of guilt. And a weapon. She pried the sword out of his clenched fist, the glint of fresh blade like a prayer; fumbled for the leather pouch at his throat.

Empty.

"Hook."

Peter's voice, too close, and Jordan whipped around—that eerie echo through the woods again, as if he spoke from every stone and pore of bark. But a thud like a shovel and she spotted him still stark against the open sky, slamming his sword again and again into grass and dirt. Something rageful and broken behind his face, as if he was no longer quite there—or perhaps more fully himself. "Hook! You stole Tink. You took her, didn't you? Boys—*Boys! After her!*"

Yet no one swooped down on Jordan; no arrow speared her through. It would have been relatively easy, right then, for them to spot her groping a corpse in the ivy. But it seemed the Lost Boys, upon discovering Peter could not fly, had left him to thrash and wail like a tantruming toddler.

A grin cracked across Jordan's face. She hoped he remembered this. She hoped it was the one thing he would never forget.

Then a couple Boys drifted back toward Peter. Kuli's voice, low and almost ashamed: "Um. Peter—why can't you fly?"

Peter's mouth framed a perfect O. "*Because*," he spat. "I died for a while and they took Tink and—*Tink!*"

"I think Ama has Tink," one of the other Boys piped.

"And the pirates have *her*." Peter rammed the flat of his sword into a stone. "Where are they, I'm going to kill them all—"

But neither the surviving pirates nor Chay dared show themselves. Jordan squinted through waving plant matter, past thick oak trunks and hulking shapes of wind-roughed stone. No hint of Dau's long sweeping coat, or Koro's resin-varnished bow, or the glint of Mateo's spectacles.

"Cowards," Peter roared—alone, now, at the center of his tiny stage. "Come out and fight. Tonight you're going to die."

Die. Jordan crawled on slowly, slowly, soft white circles crowding her vision. More bodies, as she rounded a clump of bushes: Naowen, Rien, Koro. With each face, a new fissure cracked the pit of her chest. A wallowing numbness, at how easily they had fallen.

Peter *could* die—if there were no Boys clapping to resurrect him. If there was no one left to believe.

And if Peter could die, she would do whatever it took to kill him.

Jackpot, in the Dust pouch around Koro's neck. She tore it off and dumped half of it beneath the makeshift bandage at her knee (*don't look*). The other half went straight into her mouth, fizzing on the way down, the amber glow filling her with something quick and hard and irrevocable.

There would be no tomorrows, for her. No more growing up or linear decay. Only her rage, here and now; only the memory of what had been done in this place, burned dark as the void between stars.

Then the Dust hit, and the world splintered, and she knew every branch of every tree and ten thousand ink dashes of Everbird feather, salt-damp stone and spider silk and the Boys' hot pounding blood, and she opened her eyes into the seething screaming everything and *pulled*—

"Jordan."

Baron's voice sounded a thousand kilometers away. Closer, trembling vivid in her mind's eye: her hook hurtling back up the cliff, dragged by her will from the ocean deeps; her sword close behind, a straight skyward plunge. Above her head, the six Boys were being pulled—with only Dust, only her *want*—into a midair semicircle, a dozen of their own knives angled at their throats in perfect synchrony, and she could have stopped their hearts in their chests but she wanted them to see their deaths coming, to cower at the blaze-bright burst of her fury before she plunged them forever into oblivion—

"Hey."

She smelled the pirates' piss and shit and blood pooling in the mud. Could *feel* Baron's ravaged face and the underbrush scratching Chay's ankles and the memory of the wolf's claws tearing her own burning-bleeding body.

The knives in her control trembled, electric. She was a live wire. She was death itself.

"*Jordan,*" said Baron, and she opened her eyes.

He was standing. Swaying precariously, his glasses cracked, his wan face soaked with sweat. But he was upright—shit, he was *alive.*

Jordan swallowed. The Island thrummed in her ears—the baying of a mountain lion and the rapid-fire jar of a woodpecker's beak, mermaid giggles and scuttling crabs and the slow quiet stretch of fungi in the dark. And always, always, the relentless crash of sea. But her sword was singing in her hand again, her hook settled on her right arm, and she kept a firm hold on the new weapons she had seized, the blades the Boys had collected so they could play at war.

"You came back," she said. Her voice a rusted hinge.

"I'm sorry." Baron's breath hitched, and she felt it through the lines of knowing the Dust spiraled out before her—his racing heart, the pain still threaded through tendon and muscle and bone. In Kebai, he added, "I was so afraid of losing you. I thought if I flew ahead and—and asked Chay to keep taking the Boys' Dust, we'd have *time.* To—to talk about how to live. Learn how to say things to each other that weren't goodbye. But I got here, and had a"—he gulped, and his throat moved, and she felt that, too—"I lost control. And I'm sorry."

Jordan exhaled slow through her nostrils. In the failing light, he was all jagged shadow and shining black eyes, an agglomeration of joints still too raw to walk all the way toward her, and she thought: *This fucking Island.* The way it had forced them to latch on to each other to survive, cut them open to feed its promise of flight. The ways they'd tried to piece themselves back together, Outside, just for the cracks it had left within them to strain and tear apart.

She said, still in Kebai, "There is nothing to forgive."

He sketched a half step forward, wincing. "We got what we came for," he said quietly. A nod toward Peter and the semicircle of Boys before her, still trembling before the swords and daggers she held beneath their chins—then to the woods, where she sensed Chay stepping into the cool stone shadow of Tier's cave, Tink cupped in one careful hand. Jordan inclined her head: Yes, she'd seen. "We can leave. Will you let the Boys go?"

"What about the other pirates?"

"They're—coming, too." A breath, labored. "Remember?"

"No. What about the ones who were killed?"

Baron frowned. "The Boys are unarmed."

"Because I disarmed them." The forest shifted, surged through her again—burbling creek and hollowed-out caves, padding bobcat paws and silver flash of fish and—*Focus.* "None of them are innocent. None of them are just kids anymore."

"So you're—doing Peter's job for him."

"No. Even if I kill at the rate that he did, at least I'll have the decency to die at the end."

He flinched, and she wondered if there was still a leak inside him— if the spaces between his bones and organs were, even now, flooding with blood or other fluids. But she couldn't think about that. He would either follow her and the pirates and Tink or march off again, brimming with righteous fury, and neither she nor Chay would be able to save him in time.

"Look, Baron," she said, lower. "This is just how it goes."

"This is what—you've chosen," he countered. "Isn't that what you told me? That we made our decisions, and—and now there are consequences?"

"So I should have just rotted from karsa instead?"

"No. I'm saying—" A twinge through his torso, as he attempted another step forward, and he let out a tiny *oh*. "You don't have to do— either. Peter lets anyone leave any time they want. We don't have to— play these parts anymore. We don't have to stay."

A yelp from the clearing: Peter, going cross-eyed as Jordan nudged the dagger against his jugular. A thread of crimson leaked from that pearl-perfect skin, pooled thick between his collarbones—blood like any other boy's. His eyes squeezed shut, his breath rabbit-fast.

She felt a triumphant pang—it seemed he had a little fear in him after all.

The only place you feel like your anger means anything.

The wind shifted, thrumming low through the arc of her hook, and from the direction of the dead pirates' bodies she caught the bitter tang of urine.

"Let the Boys go," Baron said. "Please."

He was so fragile, she thought. A singular heartbeat against the entire Dust-illuminated mass of wood and wind-beaten cliff and hidden spring. Standing so carefully, as if with one cough he might come undone.

He stretched out a hand, slow, as one might to a wild animal.

"Do you remember—what you said to me, that one time?" he asked. "About—hanging on to life, because it's the only thing you've got?"

The solemn weight of the Island's mountain, night wind brushed across feathered fronds of pine. She thought of their faces reflected double in the river. Of clouds churning low and thick, the heady smell of a thunderstorm, snow glimmering in fairy-tale heaps between pale tree trunks. Of the ringing quiet before a fight, that infinitesimal prick of knowing as they planted themselves back-to-back, the world tightening to planes and hard lines and the millimeter split between life and death.

She cleared her throat. "What about it?"

"There were a lot of times I thought about—dying," Baron said, still in Kebai, his outstretched hand wavering. "The simplest solution,

really. And I don't *know* if there's more for me out there. At least, anything worth fighting for." A pause, and she felt rather than heard the
speeding of his pulse. "But—that day when we were sparring? After
that—after we, well. That was the first time I thought, maybe we could
stick around and see. Together."

Last gasp of sunlight over the mountain, the clouds parted by soaring gold, and it washed him in amber, made him translucent as old film.
She had felt many things about him, over the years—not the headiness
of exchanging glances with a new fighter in the Underground locker
room, or eyefucking a stranger at a bar before a night of karsa-sharp
pleasure, but something solid, something sure.

She could map every crack in his armor. Could conjure from memory, centimeter by centimeter, the warmth of his arm when it draped
her shoulders.

And she so, so wanted to believe him.

"Baron," she started, her voice not entirely steady. The Island should
burst into flames now; the ocean should crest into a hundred-meter
wave and swallow her whole. But the clearing was deathly quiet. The
Boys squirmed and sniveled in midair; Dau and Mateo emerged from
the woods and, meeting her eyes, tied up Peter's wrists and ankles.

Bound by both rope and gravity, his own dagger still resting light
across his throat, Peter looked smaller than Jordan had ever imagined
him.

"You know, we're not so different," she said, raising her voice. The
gash in her leg pulsed against its makeshift tourniquet as she made her
slow way toward him, acutely aware of Baron's eyes on her back. "We
both love the Island. We're both afraid of losing."

Peter sneered. "You're a grown-up. I'm nothing like you."

"But you've lived a long time, and you've been doing the same thing
for years and years. Is it really so different?"

"Yes," he snapped. "Because I'm having *fun*, and I don't have to do
boring grown-up stuff, and I'm not—" His eyes darted to Baron. "I
don't—"

Chay's tear-stained face, stark in the lantern light, as she knelt over Tier's inert body: *Peter doesn't love*—

"No," Jordan said, almost gently. "You don't."

And then she turned away.

Ironic that this, in the end, was what distinguished her from him. For all the Pales and pirates they'd killed, together and in opposition, for all the malicious laughter and stones thrown in dark caverns and overgrown Lost Boys they had hunted down skidding slopes, this was the reason—not Dust, not the promise of vengeance—that she was still living. She was no longer carefree and innocent and heartless; perhaps she had never been. But as she limped away from him—as Baron's fingers slipped through hers; as the knives at the Boys' throats dropped to five, and then three, and then one, a warning—she saw something like a future: her laughter echoing off the Yeolong Mountains, thousands of kilometers away; sea breezes blowing like pale flowers through her hair; Baron's hands, his hands, young and smooth and old and weathered, cupping her face, bringing her home.

Peter, with his whims and his killing, was trapped in suspended animation. There was a word he would never know, a world he would never learn.

And she wondered, for the first time, if the real shame was not in growing up, but in never being able to.

"Jordan," Baron said hoarsely.

"What?"

He was staring as if he'd never seen her before, mouth twisted into an expression she couldn't yet decipher. But she would learn. They had time enough, now, for that and everything else. "You're bleeding."

"So are you," she said, and for some reason this struck her as unutterably funny, and they laughed and laughed and kept laughing, even as the ground beneath them began to shake.

Chapter 67

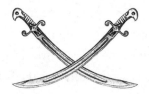

The earth was quaking.

Only a tremor at first, a burr of vibration in the bones, but as Baron's mouth opened—*Did you feel that?*—the ground beneath him *rose*, an incomprehensible tide of earth and tree and stone, and his knees buckled, his teeth rattling like makeh tiles, fingernails scrabbling useless across ground that was now pike whipping him hard toward darkening sky. Someone shouted his name. Too late—he had *become* the storm, a flail of limbs, the trees around him folding and bowing at uncanny angles—

As he tumbled through the air, a groan seemed to emanate from the land itself, some gargantuan door rumbling open in the deeps. Hills jostled like shoulders in a crowd. Yet the cry that went up from the Boys—which meant Jordan must have let them go, but where was *she*, her hand had slipped out of his at the first roll of ground at his feet—was: "The sky! Look at the sky!"

Baron looked up, and almost impaled himself on a branch.

Nosing across the line of the cliffs was a helicopter.

It was a sickle slashing through curtains of cloud, an eclipse in reverse. No logos blazed from its sides, no corporate colors striped its tail, but the hardware beneath the machine-gun whip of its propellers struck him as vaguely military, and its windows shone black as insect eyes.

"Shit," one of the Lost Boys shouted over the earthquake and engine scream. "Where's Peter?"

"Where's Tink?"

"Where's our *Dust*?"

"The barrier's breaking." Chay appeared suddenly at Baron's elbow, and he startled—Tier's jacket was draped over her shoulders, its inner breast pocket glowing a distinctive gold. Trailing behind her was Tier, or Tier's body, wrapped in some kind of sailcloth, eyes closed and sunken in his face. "Have you seen Jordan?"

"How did you—is he—" Baron started, and then the forest heaved again and Chay was dragging them both through the canopy, the hand not gripping Tier's makeshift harness vised iron around Baron's wrist.

"There!"

Flash of silver, bright edge of a cheek. Chay yanked Baron toward a thicket of close-grown saplings, and then they were face to face with Jordan, who immediately pointed the hook at her sister.

"You."

Chay's mouth tightened, but she held her head high. Confusion yawed through Baron—hadn't she just used up her entire Dust supply to patch his wounds?—but then he remembered the clapping, dim through the haze of pain. Her voice, corralling the Boys to raise Peter from the dead: *Do you believe, do you truly believe*—

"Your pirates had all gotten cut," Chay said, ducking as the saplings around them bent like bows. "And I thought you'd passed out. The Boys needed a distraction."

"Quite a distraction," Jordan snapped.

"I didn't know it would *work*. I thought it was just a story."

"Just a story? On the *Island*?"

Chay fished through her breast pocket and then thrust its contents toward her sister: a canvas bundle, chiming indignantly. A wall went down behind Jordan's expression, gave way to a weary sort of exultation.

"Ah," she said. "Hold on to that, will you? And stay below the tree line."

"Where are you going *now*?" Baron croaked.

He wasn't sure she'd heard—his throat was hoarse from the sheer amount of screaming he'd done, after seven days of silence—but her eyes flicked to him as if they stood alone in their cabin on the ship.

"To find Dau and Mateo," she said. "And whoever else is left."

Before he could even nod, she limped off in the direction of the Boys' house, dead leaves drifting like snow in her wake.

Chay cocked her head, and in that moment she looked remarkably like her sister.

"So," she began. Above them, the helicopter had slipped behind the mountain, though Baron was sure it would return. *My father's people,* Tier had said—what felt like years ago, as Jordan crushed him against his own cockpit—blasting their way in just as Tier was about to leave. Trees clashed crowns like crooked fingers; squirrels vaulted from branch to branch, above the chitter and patter of a thousand nocturnal creatures flushed from nest and knothole and burrow.

"So," Baron echoed. "Thank you."

Chay's eyes searched his, and he flushed when he realized she might still remember Kebai. Might have understood what he'd said to Jordan.

I thought about dying.

The simplest solution, really.

But she only said, "Those knives."

He did not have to ask which ones. "Yeah," he said, articulately, and her lips pursed—a shadow of fear.

"I've never felt anything like it, before." Tink jangled again, and the Ama's thumb trailed the bulge of the cloth, absently soothing. "Like she was using Dust on the whole Island."

Baron attempted to shrug, stopped as pain lanced between his shoulder blades. His mental film of the past few minutes was slowly respooling, edged in razor wire: the soft *oof* of impact as the dagger embedded in Peter's back, at a speed and angle none of the pirates could have thrown from; the Boys' weapons, sliding out of their own sheaths without hands to guide them. And the half breath before all that—a pop in his ears like the air had been sucked out of the world, a scream reverberating inside his bones. Jordan's rage poured out like stars or teeth or broken glass.

"Maybe she was," he said. "Maybe there are things we can do with Dust that we haven't even imagined yet."

"And what will you do with your portion?" Chay asked, but Jordan dropped back between them—airborne now, her wound at least sealed by skin, Dau and Mateo drifting like smoke-smeared shadows in her wake.

"We should head out."

"How close are they?" Baron asked. Chay studied him a moment longer—Knowing? Wanting?—before she lowered her gaze again.

"Still behind the mountain. But—" Jordan lifted Tink's sail bag from her sister's hands, tugged the knot tighter. "We need to be over the horizon before they realize the Lost Boys aren't the only ones here."

Dust itching over the rest of their cuts, and then they kicked off together, the earth groaning back into stillness beneath them. A weighted silence—blue and cool, the trees settling half-cocked atop newly formed hills—and as they wove between trunks like aerial ka ball players, Baron could almost breathe.

Most of the Pales were dead. So were Aku and Nilam and Jack Two and Koro and Slightly—a trail of corpses left behind for whoever sat in the helicopter, or else had paid to have it flown across this nowhere patch of ocean. Yet as Baron broke out onto the beach—as he looked back for the last time at the Island's hazy grey peaks, the light mist rising off the waterfalls, the clouds of pine pinned flat by the waning light—something that was not grief surged through him, wild and terrifying: It was over.

It was over, and they had broken the script, and the future sprawled ahead of them, wide and free as the sky.

Then the copter edged back over the Island's central peak, and small black canisters began to drop from its belly. *Bombs*, Baron thought, *or parachutes*, until slivers of sky flared open between catenary black threads and he understood.

"Nets," Jordan said beside him, eyes fixed on the falling payload. Tiny shapes thrashed and kicked above the trees, reeled upward like fish. A copper flash of hair—Peter, bundled by gravity into the bottom of the mesh.

As his head vanished through the aircraft's steel door, Baron imagined he could hear screams.

"I hope they grow up," he said, low. "I hope they don't feel the need to come back."

Jordan looked at him. "They might not have much to come back *to*."

Quiet for a while—only the sigh of waves, Dau hissing through their teeth as they attempted to un-peel the coat sleeve from their scabbed-over wrist. Cold wind cut Baron's face; far off, a low moan echoed across the water.

"Peter," he said, breaking the silence. "He *did* die, didn't he?"

"Yeah." Jordan turned. "Why?"

He tried to stretch his crooked fingers, grimaced as something cracked like bone. "I wonder if what happened to him weakened the barrier around the Island, somehow. When he came back to life."

"You mean it broke some kind of rule?"

"Maybe."

She twisted back toward the Island. The helicopter had shrunk to an inkblot against the grey-gold sky.

"Maybe Peter really *was* the Island, in a way," Mateo suggested from Jordan's other side. "Or at least linked to it. He was always talking about being its messenger—his death could have punched a hole in the—oh."

They had flown through a patch of air that might have been a vestige of the barrier or blowoff from some undersea geyser, only a buzz of heat to mark their passage. Baron stopped and trailed his fingers through it, searching for more—a ripple of light, an infrasonic whisper, any hint that the line between Before and After still walled off the waters. All he heard was the slow lap of gathering waves.

"Oh," Chay breathed, curling her fingers tighter around Tier's sail-cloth, and Baron looked up.

The Island had slipped beyond the horizon.

Jordan darted upward, and then back down—checking, Baron assumed, that she could still see the mountain peak over the line of the water. Then she was silent for a long time, as if before a monument, or a grave; when she turned back, her eyes shone with what might have been tears.

"What?" she snapped when Baron's gaze snagged on hers.

He shrugged—a lightness spreading through him, potent as Dust. "I told you," he said hoarsely. "I told you there would be an After."

"Shut up," she said, and then her forehead was pressed against his, her hand cupped against the back of his neck, and he was spiraling into the sky, he was a comet fallen back into orbit, he was here and he was here and he was home.

She had terrified him, once. He'd cowered before her the way he had the rest of the world: his disappointed parents and the classmates who breezed past him, stones thrown in the dark and arms that drew away before you could even think to fall.

And Peter. That dagger hilt thrust out of his chest, a pointing finger—Jordan had not needed to touch the blade in order to make it fly.

That she could have held such a possibility inside her head, and slammed it against the walls of the *real* until it bled through the cracks—it felt dangerous, even more than swords and ships and snarling wolves. Who knew if she was the only one who could do such a thing, or how else Dust might change them all, given time? Yet as her lips opened into his—that petal softness, that murmur of heat—he felt strangely steady, as if whatever malevolent power that was writing his script had finally given him a moment to play himself.

Another impossibility, he thought as the ocean sprawled before them, open and surging. The smallest of them, and the largest.

Chay cleared her throat and Baron pulled away, dizzy and shot through with adrenaline. "You're in company."

"I know," Jordan said, motioning with her hook. "Turn around."

"Goons," Chay muttered as Dau batted their eyelashes mockingly. Resigned, she added, "Do you want me to fairy-sit?"

Jordan handed her sister the folded sailcloth, and then she was holding Baron again, her cracked-open grin like a mirror, and together they flew out over the boundless sea.

Chapter 68

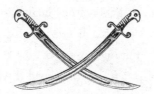

The man in the hospital room doorway looked nothing like Tier.

He had the same auburn curls, albeit threaded through with grey, the same sea-blue eyes and aquiline nose. But a cold disdain edged his mouth, and his height imposed rather than comforted. His suit and polished leather shoes seemed at once an impenetrable armor and a natural extension of his body.

When he walked past Chay, it was as if she did not exist at all.

"How long has he been in this state?" he demanded of the doctor trailing him, and they ducked their head, almost a bow.

"Six days in the hospital," they said, their gaze flicking to Chay. "But before that, a few weeks."

Chay willed her expression to remain politely neutral. Jordan, true to her word, had dropped Chay and Tier off at a gleaming steel-and-glass medical center in San Jukong's Second Circle ("Not Hanak," Jordan had muttered, "in case you have billing issues"), along with a rather intimidating stack of glamoured cash; Chay had spent the subsequent days rotating in and out of the ward and the hotel across the street, designating Tier's bedside a no-food zone to keep herself from buying out the hospital cafeteria.

Disgusting of her to be thus preoccupied, when plastic tubes trailed out of Tier's forearm and abdomen. The pinnacle of selfishness, when a dark screen kept time to his heartbeat and nurses entered every few hours to stretch his limbs. But she hadn't been able to stop. And as the man Chay assumed to be Tier's father grilled Dr. Yan on the cause of Tier's injury—*a casual shooting session among friends* the official story, on a tropical island in which neither healthcare nor transport were readily available—Chay's stomach twisted: Disgusting she may have been, but it was too late for anything else.

The red-haired man paced the room as if it were his. "How quickly can he be sent back to Ritt?"

"A few hours," the doctor said, polite but wary, and the man frowned. "Nothing faster?"

"Sir, medical jets are used only in extenuating circumstances. Our network of hospitals in Burima share a single—"

"Then I want him transported to it by helicopter."

"Sir, with all due respect—"

"I'll pay for it," the man snapped, turning on his heel. "I don't want my son lingering in this shithole backwater a minute longer than he has to. If he passes, it should be at home, surrounded by family. And even if he woke"—his voice broke, almost convincingly, Chay thought— "even if he does wake, after this long a time, the sheer amount of rehabilitation—"

Chay told herself the man's rudeness was understandable; that, as Tier's father, he hurt more for Tier than she could ever imagine. But Tier's voice, beneath the shushing pines—*they hated me*, he'd said, and given her no reason to disbelieve him.

She caught Dr. Yan's gaze, but they shook their head infinitesimally, and her eyes filled.

She was not family to Tier. Nothing to him that the Outside would care about. She had known this—prepared for it on the flight back, as Baron refreshed her on how hospitals worked; as Jordan explained exactly who Tier was and how they had found out. But she still felt as if her heart had been scooped out of her body.

In the most precise Rittan she could muster, she said, "Excuse me, sir."

Tier's father, on the verge of shouting again, paused—stayed, perhaps, by her accent. "And who are you?"

"A friend of his, Sir—"

"Ardmuth." He frowned, as if she was supposed to have known, and Chay's heart clenched. Tier had not told her his surname—had not warned her that even the doctor would flinch, as if the hearing was a wound.

"Sir Ardmuth," Chay said, her hands fisting around Tier's jacket sleeves, and the man's vivid blue eyes narrowed. "I spent a lot of time caring for him in the last few weeks, when he was still in the—the tropics. And I was wondering if I could say goodbye."

This last word drew a look of distaste, as if Chay were a turd Ardmuth had found on his expensive shoes. "I don't even know who you are."

"I'm a *friend*," Chay repeated, hating the desperate edge that had crept into her voice. "My name is Charlotte Makta, I'm from—the area—"

"She has stayed by your son's side all this time, sir," Dr. Yan added, something like steel in their tone.

Ardmuth's mouth snapped shut on the edge of a protest.

"All right," he said, though Chay suspected this was more to save face in front of the doctor than any specific goodwill toward her. "Fifteen minutes."

"*Fifteen?*" Chay cried, abandoning all pretense.

"Ten," he said brusquely, and she reeled back as if struck.

And then he and Dr. Yan were gone, leaving Chay to the harsh white lights, the incessant beeping of a dozen machines.

She threaded her arms through the steel rail around Tier's cot, and felt time streaming out of her fingers like water.

He was beautiful even in absence: red-gold curve of lashes, lips slightly parted, freckles dusted light across stark high cheekbones. She ran her fingers along the curve of his temple, the bridge of his nose, and felt despair well inside her, a current dragging her under.

She thought of him waking in that cold grey country. Thought of him padding barefoot through vast flagstone halls and echoing rooms, surrounded by people who had spent their best years punishing him for being alive.

Thought of the rows of buttered pastries in the hospital cafeteria, and the life she was supposed to make for herself in this noisy, stinking city, and him not being here for any of it.

"Please," she whispered—to him, to the powers above. To the Island, as if it could hear her from this far away. "Tier, *please* wake up."

She had seen him comatose for more days than she'd known him conscious. Every time she'd left that cave, it had felt like goodbye—always accompanied by a deluge of guilt, for being the reason Peter had shot him in the first place. But to imagine him the rest of the way gone—to imagine his slow breath stilling, the pulse emptied from the soft curve of his throat—

No.

From her pocket, Chay pulled out the pouch of Dust Jordan had left her with—the remnants of the Boys' wine bottle, filched from their house at the tail end of their last battle. Beneath the glaring fluorescents, the blipping monitors, it was difficult to believe it was anything more than oddly colored sand.

But Chay had lived half her life on the Island. Magic was carved into her now; for as long as she lived, it would never let her go.

She bent close. Her breath was mint-sharp—one of receptionists at the front desk had handed her a toothbrush and a small tube of toothpaste, when she'd claimed to be Tier's only family—and she thought of Rittan princesses, of locked towers, of kisses and long sleeps and true love. Over the past few days, restless and desperate to stop eating, she had queued up the newest Sir Franklin movies on the small television in Tier's room; passed her visiting hours leaning against his shoulder and pretending, perhaps pathetically, that they were watching together.

There could be no such fairy tales, Outside. There was a reason a barrier had divided the Island from the rest of the world. And, too— she wanted him too much. In life, as in the stories, girls who let their hunger consume them did not get what they desired.

She thought of the Boys' clapping, of Peter gasping upright. Of twelve daggers flashing through dusklight, held by no hand but the waking air.

Please.

With a furtive look at the door, she lifted Tier's hospital gown, Dusted the faint pink circle of his wound for the last time. And then she lowered her lips to his—carefully, as if bending to a pale puff of dandelion, his mouth slack but still warm, his tongue unmoving. Pressed in, searching, hungry for that spark that would bring him back to life.

Please.

Electronic patter synced to his heartbeat, counting down the time.

At last she sat back, the residual brush of his lips fading from her own. Watched the frozen half-moons of his eyelids; felt the faint pulse at his wrist where she had wrapped her hand.

Nothing.

And nothing.

And still.

"No," she whispered, "Tier, no," and then her tears splashed onto his cheeks, bloomed dark spots on his paste-green gown. She was being left behind yet again, and she did not know how to survive this cracked-open future, this nothingness gaping through her rib cage as vast as the sea. Could not hold together the wreckage of her heart, stripped of the Island and the Boys and him all at once.

"I'm so tired of pretending," she said, pressing her wet face into his collarbone, and Ardmuth would see the stains but what did it matter? "Tier. Tier. I don't want to be alone."

The shift came so quietly she almost didn't notice. A door sliding open in some far-off corner of her mind, an inexplicable *knowing* of his bones and muscles and the dark channels of his heart. And as remnants of Dust tingled on her palms, she knew—understood with the certainty of his jacket pulled tight around her torso—that this was what Jordan had wakened in that last battle with Peter, this was Dust and magic and everything living.

"Tier?" she repeated, hardly daring to breathe. Holding the wholeness of his body, every hair and freckle and tiny vein, and she did not know what parts of him needed to spark to life, could not directly traverse the labyrinth of his sleeping mind, but she imagined him sitting up, and the low ruffle of his laughter. Imagined the air itself, fritzed through with fluorescence as it was, bending toward her, listening. "Tier, *wake up.*"

And slowly, slowly, he opened his eyes.

Chapter 69

Three Months Later

The San Jukong University Medical School was the most fancy-arse building on campus.

Arching skyways and patterned glass, windows glowing against the wet-blanket dark that was ten p.m. A handful of people in white coats strode purposefully through the halls; they all seemed to be staring into the years to come, lit with some mysterious inner fire, and as Jordan tugged Baron toward the entrance, she thought: As an epilogue, as a way of continuing to live, perhaps this wasn't so bad.

It wasn't for her, but nevertheless.

Beside her, Baron's face was blanched with exhaustion, the hand that wasn't twined in hers curled awkwardly around a student ID card that no longer looked like him.

"Remember, you're just taking a tour," Jordan said, low, and he looked at her, eyes wide and blank behind his new wire-rimmed glasses.

"What?"

"Your alibi," she said, and when he pressed his card to the door lock, she pulled it open and bowed him in.

He was not there as a student, though his ID still let him into nearly every building on campus. After showing up at his parents' front door, several weeks missing and sporting several muggings' worth of bruised bones and barely healed stab wounds, he'd gone on leave for the semester; once out of the hospital, a month had passed before he could cross his living room without stopping to catch his breath, even longer until he could set foot on campus without breaking into a panic. There were still physical therapy exercises and a cane on the bad days, open-fingered compression gloves and mornings he sobbed himself awake. But Jordan had stuck around—paying for overindulgent hotel suites and secret non-Hanak-affiliated apartments with glamoured mir, hindered only somewhat by the way Dust could create the illusion of cash but not credit. Now, as they passed through the lab's brightly lit hallways, he leaned a little against her shoulder, and she let him.

She was still growing accustomed to the fact of *them*, Outside. That he had not let go; that he wanted her with him.

That she, too, had chosen to stay.

The lab was all fluorescent lights and stainless steel, the air sharp with the scent of rubbing alcohol and peeled skin. Baron's mouth contorted as she pulled away, tugging a rumpled white jacket from her pack.

"What?" she shot at him as she shook it out.

"I—this feels like sacrilege," he muttered, his face pinking, and she raised a brow.

"I bought this myself."

"Not the point. It's still—"

"Fake?" she teased, and he flushed even deeper.

Left sleeve first, her prosth catching the lapel securely between thumb and forefinger. Baron had patched the thing up as much as his hands would let him—even if, prick that he was, he'd refused to build a switchblade into the palm. (Though now she had the hook, too, for the days she needed a sharper edge.) As for the others: Chay and Tier had dropped by once, to pick up some sort of audio feedback system Baron had rigged to help Tier with his stammer; Dau and Mateo had slipped into the clamor of the city, rendezvousing with Jordan every weekend to pick up their share of Dust. Tink bumped happily around Jordan's and Baron's apartment, trailing Baron like a stray cat because he'd padded her new alcove with sequins and dryer lint. But Dust required two ingredients, and as such, additional risks had to be taken.

"Second thoughts?" Jordan asked, for the tenth time that evening. In the week or so that she and Baron had spent planning this, there had been moments—the glint of sunlight off a motorcycle rim, a sharp cut of his breath—in which the stink of Slightly's and the Pale's rotting blood reared up between them, so pungent and *there* that the air curdled in her lungs. And, too—if Baron was caught, she doubted he would be allowed into the medical course, or back into the university at all. But he'd conceded that medical school cadavers, or the ineffable spark that once burned within them, had at least volunteered to be used for science, and that this was as respectful a Dust-making scenario as they could achieve given the circumstances, and so he'd been the one to jam the transmissions of the relevant security cameras, scope out the lab's class schedules and traffic patterns.

"And third ones," he muttered, stationing himself at the door. "Just don't take too long."

"So we'll state for the record—"

"This was *entirely* your idea."

The bodies were shrouded in linen, laid out on rows of metal tables with conveniently wheeled legs. Jordan folded back a corner of fabric: crook of bare arm, leathery rib cage, skin peeled back above dull white bone. "How about this one? You can already see half the ribs."

Baron shook his head. "Another."

"Why?"

"It's someone's homework."

"*That's* where you draw the line?"

"It's like—four or five different people's homework."

"Oh, boo."

"I am categorically against stealing the fruits of other people's academic efforts." His mouth crooked, not quite a smile, and she saw the ghost of another lab, flat blue computer screen and his eyes glazed with fear.

"Fine." She seized an empty rolling table—the adjacent room, according to their recon, contained an entire host of embalmed bodies in steel drawers—and was rattling it across the linoleum when Baron cleared his throat in warning.

"People coming. Students, I think."

Voices—out in the hall, fast approaching—and Jordan shoved the table into the nearest gap between homework assignments. They had planned for this, devised false names and a script an actual (albeit rumpled) medical student might deliver while giving a personal late-night tour. But Baron was already stooping a little, the way he'd begun to do when he was tired—and who knew how long the students would stay, or what medicine-related conversation they would try to make?

She hadn't dragged Baron out of the house to godsdamned *socialize*.

A muffled sound came out of him as she crushed her lips to his, angling so neither of their faces were entirely visible from the slit of glass in the door. His mouth was as soft as she remembered, falling open at her touch, and as her tongue swept the arch of his lower lip—as she pressed in closer, sucking gently—he groaned deep in his throat; slumped against the frame, eyes hooded and hazy.

"*Oh.*" A nervous giggle, footsteps pausing outside the door. "Maybe we should come back."

Baron's head turned toward them, unsteady, and as the tap of shoes receded down the hall again, Jordan grinned in triumph.

"How's that for a first date?" she whispered, drawing away.

Baron's mouth remained half-open, his expression dazed. Their last real kiss had been over the ocean—before the endless barrage of hospital treatments; before the walks through San Jukong University campus in which he'd fought, every time, to breathe. "You never said—this wasn't supposed to be—" He struggled for a bit, and she thumbed the creases between his eyebrows, which seemed to make things even more difficult.

"What?" she said, teasing.

"Jordan." His dark eyes serious. The way he said her name, like it was a word he was just learning. "Now that we're Outside, I want to do this righ—"

He jerked away. She had touched a new swell on the upper curve of his lip, reddening slowly beneath the stark fluorescents.

"Better ice that quick," she said.

"Saints above, what did you do?"

"Don't worry, just tell your parents you tripped over the coffee table—"

"*What did you do?*"

"What did *I* do? I heard an *extremely* enthusiastic—"

He elbowed her arm away, and then they were grappling lightly against the wall, a flail of limbs. And she had thought, once, that no one ever stayed—that he was not bound to her by law or blood, that his choice to remain might be revoked as easily as slamming a door. But as she pulled him back to her, both of them breathless with laughter and the press of new bruises, she found herself thinking, just for a moment, that the future could not hurt her if she had this.

The Island watched its visitors slip over the horizon.

It did not grieve as they abandoned its charred cliffs and blood-steeped coves, teardrops of shadow curled above memory-thick sea. Did not cry out as they passed beyond its boundary, now blooming holes the way ink unfurls in clear pools at low tide. The Island itself had been birthed from destruction: crimson veins of volcanic slag, seeds burrowed deep in slippery seams, wolves tearing smaller creatures limb from limb and spattering the earth with their blood. Everything died in order to be reborn; that was the way of things, and the Island was no exception.

But it would not be held captive to the will of another.

The humans in the helicopter would leave—taking with them the boy who had never grown up, an absence of the laugh-bright creature pooled dark between his hands—and return as conquerors. They would smother the Island in concrete and glass and toxic fog, choke it with apartment complexes and bent-backed laborers and children starved of stories. Never mind that the very land they chained had once been a story in itself.

More, the men would shout as they lashed steel beams to proud peaks, pumped waste into springs and clear waterfalls.

More, they would beg as waters rose and storms raged, fueled by poisoned dreams and the nameless drowned.

More, they would command, because they had conquered, because they owned, because they had grown up with multiple-choice tests and windowless cubicles and a reality of steel skyscraper conquest so vivid the Island's shores were dull photographs in comparison.

The Island would fall, a mere symptom of greater infection. Deep in the winter of its discontent, when its shadows no longer opened their jaws at night and the land lay mapped and paralyzed under moonless skies, it would sink slowly back into oblivion, crude tungsten lights yawing over its peaks like blotted stars.

Yet it only watched as the fliers slipped beneath the line of the sea like shadowed moons, battered bastard children gone to seek a new shore. As the helicopter, too, turned away, its kerosene reek smeared across the Island's canopies like a planted flag, or a vow.

And then.

Then.

A heavy silence, a geological heartbeat in a lifetime of stone faces. It was the final pause after the telling of a story, the hush after the humans have gone to bed and the house lies still again save for the tide-rush of traffic outside sealed glass windows. The Island reveled in the silvery lightness of it, the spreading absence, a body burned to ground as its soul broke toward the clouds.

And then: the memory of a voice, carried along a cold breeze. A whisper of the boy who lived, and the girls who had left, a question light as the wings of moths.

What is your desire?

The Island's answer welled from dark springs and silken pines and the secret places where the land shifted in between, two words laden with the grief of a thousand fading suns.

To survive.

When no one replied in kind, the Island knew, as a stone knows its mother continent, that it was cold and alone.

Slowly, slowly—in the churn of basalt, dormant for millennia; in the shift of high mountain winds, waking and watchful; in its ash-dusted forest, the thick snap of owl beaks and the unhinging of wolven jaws and the wings of vultures sifting the air—it armed itself for war.

When the conquerors came again, in a month or ten years or a thousand, the Island would respond in kind.

Credits

Notes

- "Walk on" on pg. 26 with love and gratitude to Rachel Hartman's *Tess of the Road*.
- "Villains only pretending" on pg. 125 from Leanne Yong.
- "The continual *yes* of her heart to her body" on pg. 146 after Ocean Vuong's *On Earth We're Briefly Gorgeous*: "Perhaps to lay hands on your child is to prepare him for war. To say processing a heartbeat is never as simple as the heart's task of saying *yes yes yes* to the body" (13).
- "The forest floor a switchblade opened only in flame" on pg. 167 after K-Ming Chang's *Bestiary*: "Someday this story will open like a switchblade" (3–4).
- "He would know that stride from its barest gesture, a single flickered frame" on pg. 169 after Madeline Miller's *The Song of Achilles*: "I would know him blind, by the way his breaths came and his feet struck the earth" (134).
- "Here, it does...To you, it does" on pg. 185 after Euripides's *Orestes*, translated by Anne Carson, *An Oresteia*: "Not to me. Not if it's you" (218).
- "Words, for him, were wounds, and walls, and scars" on pg. 222 after Amal El-Mohtar and Max Gladstone's *This Is How You Lose the Time War*: "Words can wound—but they're bridges, too... Though maybe a bridge can also be a wound?" (95).

- "A million secret futures" on pg. 223 and "the million lives he could have lived" on pg. 337 from Tana French's *The Likeness*: "I hope in that half hour she lived all her million lives" (466).
- "The kind of wound that did not heal with time" on pg. 239 after Sleeping at Last's "Eight": "My healing needed more than time."
- "That's super not how this works" on pg. 246 after Yanyi's *The Year of Blue Water*: "I thought love was a trapdoor out of loneliness. Hint: it super isn't" (49).
- "But then, perhaps it was more of a punishment for her to stay that way" on pg. 262 after Madeline Miller's *The Song of Achilles*: "Perhaps it is the greater grief, after all, to be left on earth when another is gone" (84).
- "The forest... composing itself into something she could read" on pg. 273 after Amal El-Mohtar and Max Gladstone's *This Is How You Lose the Time War*: "I will try to compose myself—to order myself into something you can read" (171).
- "She would paint the mountains with their blood" on pg. 274 after Seth Dickinson's *The Traitor Baru Cormorant*: "I will paint you across history in the color of their blood" (396).
- "*What will you do?* And she said, smiling, 'Everything'" on pg. 284 after V. E. Schwab's Shades of Magic series.
- "He was not sure if she was satisfied with what she saw" on pg. 287 after Madeline Miller's *The Song of Achilles*: "You would not be displeased... With how you look now" (94).
- "Edgeshine of a blade in the falling dusk" on pg. 376 after Arkady Martine's *A Memory Called Empire*.
- "What it meant to grow up—that you could not win against time or death" on pg. 385 after Amal El-Mohtar and Max Gladstone's *This Is How You Lose the Time War*: "Love is what we have, against time and death, against all the powers ranged to crush us down" (165).
- "Still fighting, still here" on pg. 394 after Amal El-Mohtar and Max Gladstone's *This Is How You Lose the Time War*: "Keep fighting. We're all still here" (201).

Acknowledgments

The book you now hold in your hands is the work of a tremendously talented crew. I am so, so grateful to Brit Hvide and Angelica Chong for picking up *These Deathless Shores* and offering such insightful feedback (also, when "blorbo" was uttered during an edit call, I knew I had done something right in my life); to the rest of the Orbit team—Tim Holman, Elina Savalia, Alex Lencicki, Natassja Haught, Angela Man, Lisa Marie Pompilio, Stephanie Hess, Rachel Goldstein, Bryn A. McDonald, Rachel Hairston, Barbara Nelson, and Kelley Frodel—for their work, both visible and behind the scenes; to Desola Coker at Angry Robot for fighting for this story from the slush pile (please enjoy your firstborn), and the rest of the AR team—Eleanor Teasdale, Amy Portsmouth, Caroline Lampe, Gemma Creffield, Simon Spanton—for your enthusiasm and transparency in bringing this book to the UK; to authenticity readers Bella Lamos and Ennis Bashe, for nuancing my understanding of limb difference—all remaining errors are my own.

I have been blessed with not one but two covers beyond my wildest imagination. Thank you to the Balbusso twins for the US cover and Alice Claire Coleman for the UK one.

Thank you to Sara Megibow and Savannah Brooks, for your business acumen and patience through the entire process, and for the kindness you bring to this work; to the literary agents and other publishing professionals who have taken the time to educate me about the industry, especially Sam Morgan and Jim McCarthy for introducing me to adult SFF, and Claire Harris and Amy Bishop-Wycisk for taking a chance on me when I was a wee intern.

To Grace D. Li and Em X. Liu, best of mentors, for seeing my characters in ways I never had before and Sisyphus-ing this book back to life; to my Viable Paradise faculty and friends, for helping me level up and being the best writing community and definitely-not-a-cult I could ask for; to Valo Wing (gifted with prophecy), Clare Osongco, Mia Tsai, Shannon C. F. Rogers, Em Dietrich, Ai Jiang, Lily Lai, Craig Church, the rest of the Pitch Wars 2021 cohort, the Pitch Wars 2024 subcohort, There or Square, and everyone else with whom I have been braving the publishing wilds; to the Revenge Crew, for welcoming me to New York.

To my English and creative writing teachers over the years, especially Melissa Jensen and Kathy DeMarco Van Cleve, for encouraging me when I stood at a crossroads; to my friends in Philly, for loving me while I was still figuring out how to be a person; to my MFA classmates and professors for your friendship, wisdom, and inspiration.

To the many authors to whom I owe a creative debt, including V. E. Schwab, Madeline Miller, Amal El-Mohtar, Max Gladstone, Tana French, Alix E. Harrow, Fonda Lee, Alyssa Wong, Seanan McGuire, and Philip Pullman; to Halsey and Billie Eilish, whose music formed the brainstorming soundtrack for this book; to Leigh Bardugo, Sally Wen Mao, Ocean Vuong, Richard Siken, and Neon Yang for allowing me to place your words alongside my own. To every bookseller, librarian, reviewer, blogger, bookstagrammer, TikToker, and reader who has spread the word about *These Deathless Shores*.

To Leanne, Soonyoung, and Stephanie—you're the reason I can write friends; you're the reason I can write about love.

To G, through a glass darkly.

To my family, for keeping the window open.

To my past selves, for surviving in the ways you knew how.

And to you, for coming on this journey with me.

extras

orbit

meet the author

P. H. Low is a Locus- and Rhysling-nominated Malaysian American writer and poet with work published in *Strange Horizons*, *Fantasy Magazine*, *Tor.com*, and *Diabolical Plots*, among others. They have a bad habit of moving cities every few years but can be found online at ph-low.com.

Find out more about P. H. Low and other Orbit authors by registering for the free monthly newsletter at orbitbooks.net.

if you enjoyed
THESE DEATHLESS SHORES

look out for

THE SCARLET THRONE

False Goddess Trilogy:
Book One

by

Amy Leow

Binsa is a "living goddess," chosen by the gods to dispense both mercy and punishment from her place on the Scarlet Throne. But her reign hides a deadly secret. Rather than channeling the wisdom of an immortal deity, she harbors a demon.

But now her priests are growing suspicious. When a new girl, Medha, is selected to take over her position, Binsa and her demon strike a deal: To magnify his power and help her wrest control from the priests, she will sacrifice human lives. She'll do anything not to end up back on the streets, forgotten and alone. But how much of her humanity is she willing to trade in her quest for power? Deals with demons are rarely so simple.

1

THE FALSE DEVOTEE

A woman had been crushed by a goat that fell from the sky.

Her husband, Uruvin Vashmaralim, humble spice merchant, now kneels before me, haggard bags lining his eyes and tearstains slashing down his cheeks. He laments the loss of his wife and the suspicious circumstances hanging over her death. She was a pious woman, he claims, who always set the mangoes and wine before the family shrine and prayed to them three times a day. One day, however, a terrible illness befell her. She didn't place her offerings before the family shrine. She died the next week, not from illness, but from a goat falling on her while she was drawing water from the well.

Lies, a childlike voice hisses in my head.

The man bursts into sobs at the end of his tale. I observe him with my back straight and hands folded demurely on my lap. My lips are pressed into a thin line, but my brows are soft and relaxed. My brother has told me that this is my best regal pose, assuring everyone that the spirit of the goddess Rashmatun lives in me, with every muscle, every limb perfectly poised.

Even if Rashmatun never possessed me. Even if Rashmatun doesn't exist.

"My goddess!" the man wails. "Please, have mercy. I know not what my wife has done wrong, save for the one day she forgot to placate our ancestors' spirits. Her death has grieved me so. Rashmatun, what can I do to rectify the calamity that has fallen upon me?"

I stay silent, contemplating the situation. A goat dropped on an unsuspecting woman. It would have sounded ridiculous if not for Uruvin's solemnity as he delivered the tale. In fact, I am still in disbelief, even though I allow him to continue wailing.

extras

Meanwhile, Ilam, the demon inside me, trails slow, taunting circles in my mind, his presence as unnerving as a monster lying beneath still waters.

"Uruvin, how long has it been since your wife's demise?" I say, my reedy voice amplified with deeper, overlapping echoes. The acoustics of the concave niche carved into the wall behind my throne creates an incandescent quality to my tone. My brother did it himself, claiming that the sculpture of Anas, the ten-headed snake god, would protect the living goddess from any harm. What the temple dwellers do not know about is the hollow that lies beyond the niche, large enough for a grown man to squeeze into and eavesdrop on my daily audiences.

"Two weeks already, Your Grace," Uruvin replies. He wipes a tear away from the corner of his eye. "I miss her terribly."

Two weeks. Snivelling Sartas. They'd have cremated the body by now. "Pray, tell me," I resume smoothly, "was she a good woman?"

"Why, of course, Rashmatun! She was everything a man could ask for." He waves his arms in a vigorous manner, as if it could convince me of his sincerity. "A wonderful cook, a meticulous cleaner, a patient listener. Oh, my dear Dirka!"

He falls into another round of incoherent sobbing, forehead planted onto the fiery red carpet beneath him.

I narrow my eyes at Uruvin, studying him intently. The hems of his suruwal are suspiciously clean, neither a trace of ash nor dust on them. He probably never visited his wife's remains after the funeral. The Holy Mound is where we keep the ashes of our dead, open to the public and frequently flooded with visitors. If he were truly mourning her, he'd have spent plenty of time there.

Or perhaps he is so overwhelmed with grief that he cannot bear to step into the Mound.

Lies, lies, lies, Ilam chants with sadistic glee.

Where is the lie? I ask.

Open your eyes, girl. Open your eyes and see.

I draw a breath, and Ilam gets to work. He worms his way to the front of my mind, shoving me aside and suffocating my thoughts.

After nearly ten years of communing with a demon, you'd think I'd have become accustomed to the constant crawling up my spine.

But I endure it to have this power.

The demon burrows straight into Uruvin's mind; the man himself is unaware of the intrusion. A rush of resounding *truths* pours into me, and a brief flash of pain splits my skull before fading into a dull pulse. My senses sharpen, so sensitive that I can hear Uruvin's erratic heartbeat and catch the faint scent of perfume on his smooth, creaseless clothes. Ilam's magic amplifies the truths such details carry. Each of them pierces through my mind like a fire-tipped arrow streaking across a moonless night.

Throughout this, I maintain my tall, regal posture.

Then Ilam is done. He slowly retreats, and the world fades into its usual palette, the saturation of sounds and scents ebbing into the background. I inhale deeply. Using blood magic always leaves me with a discomfort that burrows deep into my bones. After all these years, I still cannot tell if it's an inherent side effect of blood magic, or if it's my own revulsion towards the practice.

Meanwhile, Uruvin is still choking up with melodramatic sobs.

I wait for him to swallow his tears. Now I see where the lie reveals itself. If not for Ilam, I would not have caught the subtle yet alluring fragrance of frangipani on him, commonly used as a perfume by Aritsyan women to usher good luck in love and life. I would not have seen the shrewd gleam in his eyes.

The part about the falling goat must be true—as absurd as it is—Ilam did not say it was a lie. A mystery to be dealt with later. But Uruvin is no honest, grieving husband.

He hopes to earn some sort of compensation for his unprecedented losses. Just like many of the insufferable fools who walk in here. Some devotees are genuine, but plenty are out to take a bite out of the goddess Rashmatun's bursting coffers.

Fortunately, I'm not as gullible as these people would like me to be.

"You live by the banks of the Nurleni, Uruvin?" I ask after the man wrests his sobs under control.

"Yes, my goddess. I'm sure that the chief priest would have told you all you needed to know." He sniffs loudly. Perhaps he's wondering why the great Rashmatun is asking such menial questions.

"Is it Harun who will relieve you of your plight?" I say, allowing an edge of irritation to creep into my tone. "No. It is I. So answer my questions without hesitation nor falsehood."

Uruvin's fingers drum against his thigh. "Yes, Your Grace. My humblest apologies, Rashmatun."

"Excellent." I tilt my head. "Is your business doing well, Uruvin?"

"Why, of course! The demand for spices is always there, no matter how poor the economy. And the river always brings good business." His fingers continue to *tap, tap, tap*.

Interesting. It hasn't been raining for the past few months; the waters of the river have receded so much that large boats can barely sail down without their bottoms scraping against rocks. Does the merchant think that I am ignorant to the workings of the world at large because I don't step foot outside temple grounds?

I stay silent for a while, tempering my anger.

"Do you think me a fool, my child?" I finally say, voice dangerously soft.

His eyes spark with alarm. "Your Grace?"

"I have given you a chance to speak the truth, and yet you have lied to me." I lean forward ever so slightly, careful to not let the weight of my headdress topple me forward. My shadow, cast by the braziers above my head and distorted by Anas's ten snake heads, stretches towards Uruvin. "You call yourself a follower of Rashmatun, yet you dare to let falsehoods fall from your tongue in my presence? Why must you use your wife, even in her death, to compensate for your failing business?"

Ilam cackles in delight. He loves it when I truly *become* a goddess, when none can defy me and all must bow to me.

Even I have to admit I enjoy the feeling.

The rhythm the merchant taps out grows even more erratic. "Your Grace. I assure you that I have been speaking nothing but the truth. My wife—"

"Is dead. That much is certain." I pitch my voice low; the echoes induce trembles in the man's limbs. "But for all her wifely qualities, you never did love her, did you?"

Uruvin's lips part dumbly. "I—I—Rashmatun, no," he stammers. "I loved her, with all my heart!"

"You are lying *again*." I slowly adjust my arm so that my elbow is propped atop the armrest encrusted with yellow sapphires, my temple resting against my fingers. "If you did love your wife so, why have you found yourself another lover already?"

His eyes widen in shock and guilt; his expression is stripped bare of pretense.

I cannot tell if the satisfaction welling in me is mine or Ilam's.

Uruvin sinks into a panicked bow. "Oh, Rashmatun!" he cries. "Your eyes see all. It was foolish of me to even think of deceiving you. Please, my goddess, I beg for your forgiveness! Please grant your servant mercy!"

I close my eyes, exasperated. Sweat trickles down my neck; the back of my jama is uncomfortably soaked. I am eager to peel off the four gold chains weighing down my neck, and my rump is sore from sitting the entire morning. I've given this idiot more than enough time to redeem himself.

"For your transgressions, you shall be prohibited from entering the temple for the next five years," I declare, opening my eyes languidly. "And you will pay a twenty percent increment of yearly taxes, since according to you, your business is bustling. My priests will ensure that the necessary paperwork is filled out."

His face takes on a sickly pallor. "My Rashmatun has been merciful," he murmurs.

"Get out," I say, tone quiet.

Uruvin ducks his head and rises to his feet. He scuttles backwards until he is out of the worship hall. Ilam's amused laughter continues ringing somewhere at the back of my mind.

With a tired sigh, I sink into my throne. "Harun." A portly man whose eyes resemble a bulging frog's steps into my direct line of sight. I've grown somewhat accustomed to the chief priest's permanent expression of gross surprise. "Anyone else?"

"No, my goddess," Harun replies. He adjusts the orange sash thrown over his left shoulder. "That was the last worshipper for today."

"The maximum number of devotees is twelve." I pinch the bridge of my nose. "That was the twentieth."

"The land is in a dire state now, Rashmatun. We did transport a sizeable portion of our grain stores to the armies' supply centers before the drought hit us." He stares at me with his frog eyes. "Your people are growing desperate. Many are flooding your temples, and more still wish to have an audience with you."

"I see."

Clever, clever goddess, Ilam laughs. *How your people love you so.*

I try not to bristle in reflex. No use getting furious at a demon you cannot control.

Harun clutches the length of prayer beads around his neck; his eyes slide towards the priests lining up behind him, their mouths shut in an eerie, complete silence. "My goddess, perhaps if you actually do something about the drought—"

"The Forebears bide their time, Harun," I say, waving a dismissive hand. "Is Hyrlvat thriving? Are the cornfields of Vintya lush and abundant? The gods are staying our hands for reasons that will be clear in a time to come."

Harun presses his lips into a thin line. I've been using that same vague reason for the past two months now. Even as most of our supplies are being given to the Aritsyan army, which has been battling the Dennarese Empire for decades, leaving precious little in our silos. Even as our crops wither and the prospects of a hungry winter grow exponentially with every passing day.

Do I have a choice? No. The only reason why the people of the city of Bakhtin have not rioted against me is because the rest of the country is suffering as well. Anyway, this is not the first time such a drought has occurred, and certainly not the first time Bakhtin's goddess abstained from bringing food to her people.

The chief priest still doesn't look convinced, though.

"Why do you not use your own magic to enchant the clouds, then?" I suggest scathingly. "If you're so worried about the drought?"

"My goddess, you know that our power has greatly weakened over the years. Besides, we can only cast enchantments—"

"When I'm around. Yes, I am well aware," I cut him off. *Excuses*, I think, but don't say out loud. The priests have no problem coaxing trees to bear fruit and casting needles to mend their elaborate garments when they think I'm out of sight. Minor spells, but ones that speak volumes about the temple's priorities. "Enough," I continue, vexation growing in me the longer this topic drags out. "I will only admit twelve devotees per day. At most. Am I clear?"

He dips his head in deference. "Yes, Your Grace."

"Good. And see to it that the necessary compensations and punishments are dispensed."

"Of course, Your Grace."

I dip my head. "Till tomorrow, Harun."

"Till tomorrow."

I stand up and step off the elevated dais. My bare foot touches the carpeted floor. Immediately my posture is not as straight, my head not held as high. I let my knees buckle, as if they were not accustomed to the weight of the ornaments I wear. Harun reaches forward to steady me, a fatherly smile on his face.

In a split second, I am no longer Rashmatun. I am Binsa, vessel of the Goddess of Wisdom, an ordinary girl whose life was touched by the extraordinary.

"What did she do today?" I ask Harun. My routine question after I've broken out of my "trance."

"Many things. Many great things." His routine answer.

"Will she bring rain soon?"

"She..." His grip on my shoulders tightens ever so slightly. He shakes his head and presses a hand against my back, guiding me out of the Paruvatar, the worship hall. "Come, child. You should rest."

I follow his lead without another word. We exit into a courtyard shadowed by long, straggling branches and lush emerald leaves. The rhododendron bushes planted all around the space are at full bloom, the vibrant red of the flowers resembling cloaks woven out of fresh blood. The sun overhead blazes bright, yet its full heat is lost on me with the mountain winds cocooning the temple, which lies high atop blustering cliffs. All enchantments by the hands of the priests; while the rest of the city withers, the sanctity of the temple must be maintained, which includes tending to its environment.

Harun claps his hands. Muscular palanquin bearers materialize before us. I step into the litter; the chief priest walks alongside.

The palanquin sways with a rhythmic lull as the bearers walk in perfect synchrony, marching through the various temples in Gha-natukh's complex at a languorous pace. They let me down before a two-tiered building, its red walls basking in the glow of the sun. I enter the Bakhal, the goddess's place of residence. A tall, imposing woman appears from behind one of the pillars, her generous girth clad in white. Jirtash claps her palms together and bows her head. Harun nods, leaving me to her care.

We wind our way through the sprawling maze of the pillars and shrines in the Bakhal's lowest floor, the scent of sandalwood drift-ing lazily through the air. We cut through another courtyard—a dry fountain in the middle, a luxury the priests didn't bother with—before arriving at my chambers. The furnishings hardly match the grandiosity of Rashmatun's power; while they are not falling into decay, they are as plain as a commoner's taste in fash-ion. The size of the room makes up for the lackluster decorations, though.

Any room is better than where I used to live, back when I was a child.

Jirtash tugs me towards a full-length mirror. I follow her like the obedient girl I'm supposed to be. She's the chief of the hand-maidens and the oldest, having attended to four other vessels of Rashmatun before me. She carefully lifts the headdress away and places it on a finely embroidered cushion; the absence of its weight is liberating.

Meanwhile, Ilam has curled into a comfortable ball at the back of my mind. The demon rarely emerges during my day-to-day activities, only coming to life when something catches his interest or offends him, or when he wants to taunt me. Typical of a demon, only giving attention to matters that involve them, and remaining apathetic towards everything else.

More handmaidens scuttle towards me, peeling away the layers of my uniform with reverent efficiency. The four gold chains, each with a different design, representing the four cardinal directions. The bhota and jama, both fiery red and embroidered with golden flowers, catch the brilliant rays of sunlight streaming in through tall, narrow windows. My earrings and bangles are removed. Jirtash wipes my forehead with a cloth soaked in coconut oil, removing the seven-pronged star painted onto it. She whispers a quick prayer, a plea for forgiveness, as she temporarily breaks Rashmatun's connection to her chosen vessel. With the star gone, she moves on to the rest of my face—the thick lines of kohl around my eyes, my bloodred lips.

Soon I am left naked, save for a pendant of yellow sapphire hung from a crude length of woven threads. Its uneven surface rests comfortingly against my chest, where my ribs protrude beneath my skin. My arms and legs are as thin as sticks, and my breasts are pitifully small. Not that it matters, since no one dares to comment much about my appearance.

The handmaidens unwind the thick coils of hair piled atop my head. It falls almost to my knees, thick and luxuriant, a soft sheen running down its trails. The only physical trait I am proud of.

Jirtash takes my hand and leads me towards the bathtub. I sink into its waters, contentedly allowing the handmaidens to lift my arms and legs and scrub them clean. A layer of grime gathers and floats on the water.

When I'm done, Jirtash towels me down and outfits me in a red kurta—I must always wear a hint of red somewhere—and a loose-fitting suruwal. I sit before the vanity table, and she braids my hair as her helpers tidy up the place.

"Oh child, what a woman wouldn't give to have hair as gorgeous as yours." Jirtash sighs in admiration.

Ice seems to gather at the nape of my neck. The ghost of a rough hand yanks the ends of my hair and sets it aflame.

extras

I play with a near-empty bottle of perfume on the table, pushing the memory away. Jirtash has combed my hair almost the past ten years. This is just another day, another routine. She has no ill intentions. She has nothing to do with my past, I remind myself.

A past that she can never learn about.

I hope she doesn't notice the slight tremor in my fingers as I run them over the perfume bottle. "Thank you," I murmur.

She doesn't say anything else. I know what is on her mind: If only the rest of me were as gorgeous as my hair. I am close to sixteen now. Other girls my age have developed bosoms and swelling hips already. Me? I might as well be a withering tree trunk.

It's unusual for a girl to not have menstruated already, she told me two weeks ago, and what is even more unusual is that I have not shown signs of puberty. She once suspected that I was malnourished, but quickly dismissed the notion when I pointed out that I ate three full meals a day.

I did not tell her that I always dispose of two of those meals.

She finishes braiding my hair and claps her hands over my shoulders. "All done," she says. "There now, don't you look pretty?"

I don't agree with the sentiment. My nose is too large for my pointed chin and thin lips, my cheeks are as hollow as an empty bowl of alms, and my eyes are too large, too fierce. But she is trying to be kind, so I muster a smile. "Thank you."

She nods, then releases me from her grip. A platter of food has been served, placed on a table by the window. I polish off the meal thoroughly; it's my only one every day. When no one is watching, I retrieve a vial from under my table and pour a drop of its contents into the clay cup of water, turning it into a murky solution. I drain the cup, trying not to wince at the foul taste. This is forbidden medicine that poisons my ovaries—another one of my methods to delay my bleeding for as long as possible. A small price to remain a goddess for a little while longer.

But my medicine is running dangerously low.

I haven't heard from my supplier in weeks. I grit my teeth, suppressing the anxiety rising up my throat.

445

When I'm done, I head towards the exit. I sense a hint of grim disapproval from Jirtash. "Off to your lessons, now?" she asks, more out of courtesy than genuine interest. She does not think that I should be paying so much attention to books and education. I should be more concerned about growing into a woman and finding a good husband, like the many girls who came before me. The latter won't be too hard, considering that everyone wants to receive some form of blessing from a former living goddess. Assuming that I choose to marry.

However, that means that I have to give up my status as the vessel of Rashmatun. The thought hollows out my stomach, as if someone carved my skin open and emptied my insides.

Who am I, if I am Rashmatun no longer? A scrawny girl with no inherent title or wealth to her name. A nothing, someone whose face will fade from the memories of all who have seen her.

I shake the notion out of my mind. I am still a living goddess, I remind myself. "Of course, Jirtash!" I chirp innocently. "Lessons won't wait!"

I traipse out of the room.

if you enjoyed
THESE DEATHLESS SHORES
look out for

FATHOMFOLK
Drowned World: Book One

by

Eliza Chan

*Welcome to Tiankawi—shining pearl of human
civilization and a safe haven for those fleeing
civil unrest. Or at least, that's how it first appears.
But in the semiflooded city, humans are, quite literally,
on top: peering down from shining towers and aerial
walkways on the fathomfolk—sirens, seawitches, kelpies,
and kappas—who live in the polluted waters below. And the
fathomfolk are tired of it.*

*When a water dragon and a half-siren join forces, the path to
equality is filled with violence, secrets, and political intrigue.
And they both must decide if the cost of change is worth
paying, or if Tiankawi should be left to drown.*

Chapter One

A late arrival elbowed past Mira, knocking her out of position. His jaw was tight, and he wrinkled his nose as he met her eye. "Keep in formation, saltie."

Mira fist-palm saluted sarcastically. She had heard it all before; got into fights with pettier human bureaucrats than him. The delegates continued at a snail's pace, ambling as if perusing market stalls on a Tiankawi festival day rather than inspecting a rooftop military parade in the baking midday sun. The wax coat of Mira's border guard uniform was akin to a simmering claypot. If she strained, she could hear the ocean below, but thirty floors up where they stood, the breeze didn't provide much reprieve. Sweat dripped from her forehead and she cricked her neck.

The captain of the kumiho – the city guard, led the politicians down the line. "And this is Mira, newly appointed as captain of the border guard." The older man was de facto Minister of Defence, but he stroked his silver moustache like an indulgent grandfather offering candied lotus seeds. Mira had seen the other side of him. She saluted the delegates, the Minister of Ceremonies and two junior officials.

"Ah, we've heard a lot about you," said the Minister of Ceremonies, a tall middle-aged woman. "Helping out the Minister of Fathomfolk. The siren."

Helping out was not how Mira would have phrased it. It was more of a partnership really. She pushed a smile into the corners of her mouth. "Half-siren actually. I'm glad to be here today."

"You should be," the man on the left said. "First fathomfolk in the military and now the first to reach captaincy. Integration at its finest." The words were well-meaning enough but she could hear the abacus beads clicking in his head. Not satisfied with putting her name out as a fathomfolk success story, now they wanted to paste billboards all over the city. Mira had refused. It was difficult enough to do her job without her face staring back from every sky-bridge, walkway and tram platform. "With all due respect, sir, I hope to inspire fathomfolk to join *all* branches." Her emphasis was deliberate. While she was a trailblazer, there were only four other folk in any aspect of government. All on the military side, all in her chinthe border guard rather than the more influential kumiho city guard. Titans forbid that folk get into the offices of agriculture or transport; the glamour and influence they could have . . .

The remaining official who had not spoken simply pinned Mira's captain badge on the front of her coat: the golden liondog name-sake of the chinthe. His hand shook, eyes decidedly not meeting hers. He was afraid. Afraid of the siren mutt without a leash. He did well not to flinch. Mira nodded and smiled, went through the motions of small talk the same way she got dressed in the morning: automatically, perfunctorily, with her mind sorting through end-less lists and jobs that needed to be done. If she kept pretending it didn't bother her, one day it might be true.

"Did you see the look on his face? Pale as a sail," a voice whis-pered behind her as the delegates moved on. One of her lieutenants.

"Bollocks, he'd probably forgotten where he was. Doddering fools refuse to retire until they have to be carried out." Lieutenant Tam's baritone carried above the other voices.

Mira allowed herself a half-smile. At least some people had her back.

Despite everything, it had been a good day. Two of her good friends had been promoted and a rusalka had just completed advanced training. The border guards were never invited to the kumiho celebrations in City Hall. The steamed dumplings and free-flowing wine would be missed, but the entitled city guard would not be. They flaunted their ceremonial swords like children's toys. The chinthe only got symbolic daggers, another slight to add to the heap. Mira ran her thumb down the worn hilt of hers.

This group had been with her for nearly as long as her chinthe dagger; patrolling the waters in the southern districts of the sprawling Tiankawi city state. The border guards' jurisdiction was supposedly only around resettlement and trade. But over the decades, the city guard had refused to have anything to do with the folk-concentrated south. The whole region would have fallen into the hands of gangs had it not been for the chinthe.

From the rooftop training ground, sea level was quite a drop. In her younger days, Mira had clambered across buildings, vaulted and scrabbled through various shortcuts. But the long way had its own charm. The city stretched out, monolithic pillars a canopy above the shanty towns below. At low tide the planks of the walkways oozed with muddy water, threatening to warp faster than they could be fixed. At high tide they were completely submerged, beholden to the mercies of the waters that surrounded Tiankawi. Not that this presented a problem for the folk.

Mira's usual after-work haunt was nothing more than a street stall near the port in Seong district. An elderly couple of stallholders seared skewers of spiced tiger prawns and whole fish over coals, bottles of moonshine floating in the water by their feet.

"To the new captain, Mira o' the chinthe, we are not worthy," Lieutenant Tam said with a mock bow.

"Oh piss off." Mira prodded him with the toe of her boot.

"Don't forget about us when you're a lofty council member," he added. Mira rolled her eyes, not wasting her breath on a retort.

"He has a point," said Mikayil, her other lieutenant, his thick eyebrows wiggling at her from an amiable brown face. He wiped his hands neatly on a square of cloth from his pocket.

"They want you for leadership," Lucia agreed. She was one of the newest ensigns, her uniform still pressed every morning and her face free from the worn river lines the others had. She held her sheathed dagger like they'd given her a nugget of gold. Mira remembered that elation. Wished she had a little of it left.

"They want a tick box in the Council; a head-bobbing, arse-kissing recruitment pamphlet. Well, what do you think?" Mira said, posing with her hand on her hip, a caricature of an enrolment notice. They laughed, clinking bottles and turning to talk of other things. Mira took a long swig of the local brew. She wished it was that easy to brush it off inside as well. The faces of the delegates today confirmed what she already knew. All they saw was a half-siren. No matter the uniform she wore, the exams she passed, the ideas she brought to the discussion; they always saw her as fathomfolk first. She'd never lived in an underwater haven – the semi-submerged city was her only home – and yet she'd always be an outsider.

She helped herself to another bottle, raising it until the stall-holder auntie nodded in acknowledgement. Heard the merry-making fall silent suddenly.

A group of folk made their way down the walkway. Walking four abreast, they took up all the space. Mira recognised some of them: the whiskers of the ikan keli catfish twins, the swagger of the broad-shouldered kelpie leader in front. Drawbacks: a group of dissident folk who had been openly sceptical of her appointment. They walked with confident purpose, stopping too close to the border guards' celebration for comfort. Mira felt the wariness of her colleagues, drinks being placed down on tables, hands inching towards baston sticks.

"Congratulations are in order, *Captain*," Lynnette, the Draw-back leader said. Sarcasm tugged on the edges of her words. As if she wasn't tall enough, her tousled mohawk added inches to her height, like the crest of a wave.

Mira stood slowly, closing the distance in their heights a little, trying to defuse the situation with a light-heartedness she did not truly feel. "My thanks, you're welcome to join." Eyes glanced over the makeshift seats; nothing more than upturned wooden crates. The table a couple of damp pallets, mildewed around the edges.

The younger catfish twin was staring at Ensign Lucia, baiting her to look away first. He bared his teeth with a sudden hiss, barbed fins fanning down otherwise human-looking forearms. The effect was startling. Disquieting. Lucia toppled off the wooden crate she was sitting on. Only the quick reactions of those beside her prevented her from falling entirely into the water. The folk cackled.

"We've somewhere to be," Lynnette said.

"Another time perhaps." Mira kept her voice steady. Neutral.

The kelpie flexed her generous biceps, the sand god amulet around her neck swinging. "Unlike some, we're busy making a difference for folk in the city."

Mira heard Tam curse quietly behind her, the tension thick. Despite the alcohol, she suddenly felt very sober. Of course, just because she'd been made captain didn't mean all folk approved her appointment. "Should you have any suggestions for change, I'd be glad to hear them."

"Try changing yourself," a whisper from the back of the new group snarked. Loud enough for all to hear. Not enough of an insult to warrant anything really. What was Mira – the first folk captain in the history of the city – going to do? Arrest the most vocal protest group on her first night? The Drawbacks knew it as well, Lynnette seemingly swaggering up to make this exact point.

"Good night, *Captain*. I'm sure our paths will cross again soon."

The Drawbacks did not wait for the response. They jumped, cannonball-diving and flipping from the walkway into the water on either side with whoops and jeers. Making splashes so big that the border guards were drenched completely.

Saltwater ran down Mira's face and coat as her colleagues swore and stood up around her. She sat back down, taking a sip of her now salty beer. She'd hoped to enjoy her promotion for at least one day, but there would be no such respite.

Mira had almost succeeded in putting the Drawbacks out of her mind by the time she caught the tram. It was mostly empty apart from a drunk sleeping in the corner and a fathomfolk couple talking in whispers by the doors. The carriage lurched forward on the raised rails as it headed towards the central Jingsha district. Here stood the proud buildings at the heart of the city, the steel-boned monuments to humanity's prowess. Built during the Great Bathyal War, when it became clear that fighting between humanity and fathomfolk would not change the rising water levels; before the decades of floods. Built to endure. The rest of the city was made up of scattered semi-submerged neighbourhoods sprawled around Jingsha. Mira herself came from one of those districts, a shanty town really. She'd never thought that one day she'd live in the centre.

When she opened the door to her apartment, it was snowing. A layer of white covered everything as if a flurry had passed through the room. It was like the stories her ama had told, tales set in winter palaces on top of mountains she'd never known. Flakes like tiny flowers drifted towards her and despite herself, she stuck out her tongue. The cold sliver melted and sharpened her senses. She could've stayed there all night, head tilted as if towards the sun, and let it fall on her face. The sound of familiar footsteps made her turn. Her partner Kai stood waiting for her to notice.

"You have no idea how much I love you right now," he said with a smile that spread from his mouth into his warm brown eyes. He soaked the scene in, clearly pleased with himself.

"What did you do, you mad fool?" she said, unable to stop herself from laughing.

He came towards her, hugging her tight and warm. "Congratulations!"

"What, what is all this?" she said again. Insisting this time. She extracted herself briefly, even though she just wanted to bury her nose in his shirt. He smelt of home. Of soup broth and lemongrass soap. Though he was impeccably dressed, his fingers were nonetheless stained with black ink. She took one of his hands, rubbing at the smudges as he talked.

"I have to be impartial, I know. And you didn't want it to be a big deal. But how can I not celebrate this? You made captain!" he said. Mira cupped the side of his jaw, the bristles on his chin tickling her palm. He could still make her heart sing after two years.

"So," he continued, turning to plant a gentle kiss on her hand, "we can celebrate your promotion here – at home – with all the fuss I want to lavish on you."

"Yes, but what is *this*?" She gestured around. Now that she had a moment to look, she realised he had covered the furniture with blankets, rendering the sofa and the dining table into soft white mounds. The snow falling around her was real though. It was all Kai. He demonstrated, flicking water into the air and using his waterweaving powers to freeze the droplets as they fell in perfectly defined snowflakes. It hardly looked like he was putting any effort into it, a level of skill that would make any other fathomfolk sweat with exertion. Delicate precision that only someone of his upbringing could achieve.

"You wanted to see snow; you've never been north. Honestly, I want to take you there. I *will* take you there! But for now, this will do."

Despite the cold, Mira felt her skin tingle where it touched his. Her head spun with his words. Kai was never one to do things by halves. Even after all this time together, he could still surprise her. She wondered if all folk born in the sea havens were like this, but she doubted it. He was pure sincerity and joy.

He presented her with a scroll in both hands, bowing ceremoniously. The lotus-leaf paper was protected by a glass tube. It had become a tradition of theirs to give each other mock documents: salacious newssheets, penalty notices for missed dinners, or strongly worded complaint letters about the quality of lingering glances. His eyes laughed merrily as she struggled with the wax, finally cutting it loose with her ceremonial blade. He'd made a certificate in flowing legalese, a document verifying that she was captain not just of the chinthe, but of all fathomfolk. And beneath it, images brought to life by a couple of deft brushstrokes. Mira leading a parade of dancing, laughing, singing folk along a riverway. His light touch had captured familiar faces, the idiosyncrasies of people they both knew.

"It's, it's . . . " she began.

extras

"I know," he quipped.

She pushed him lightly onto the sofa, the snow puffing up on impact and making them both laugh as she sat across his lap. A tremor ran through her, the whole room swaying. Kai's face was the one clear thing. "Look at me, I'm shaking," she said in a whisper.

"As much as I'd like to take credit, that's an actual earthquake." He put his hands on her hips and anchored her.

The overhead light was swinging but nothing else was out of place. Growing up on the water, Mira barely noticed the minor tremors, but in the imposing towers of Jingsha she felt them more acutely. They waited for it to pass. She piled the fluffy snow on Kai's topknot, dabbing it into his dark facial hair and on his nose. Giddiness bubbled up through her as he shook himself free, the snowflakes flicking onto her face and down the front of her top. And when he complained of cold, she kissed him better; butterfly kisses down his neck and shoulders. Her hands untied his robes to reach down across his smooth skin, her lips caressing the pearlescent smattering of scales on his collarbone, across his torso and down one arm. She loved that he wore his true colours even when in human form. A water dragon, the only one in the whole city state. The notion still took her by surprise now and then. The closest thing to fathomfolk nobility, and here he was, looking up at her with hungry eyes.

He ran his hands across the fabric of her chinthe green uniform, tracing the braiding, rubbing the brass buttons in a way that made Mira involuntarily exhale. "*I'm* supposed to be treating *you*, remember?" he murmured. The coat fell away and his hands ran down her back. Their lips met and she leaned in, pushing her hips, her chest, her mouth into him, pressing close so he could feel the ache that filled her entirely.

"So . . . how do you want to celebrate?" he asked.

Her response required no words.

Follow us:

/orbitbooksUS

/orbitbooks

/orbitbooks

Join our mailing list
to receive alerts on our
latest releases and deals.

orbitbooks.net

Enter our monthly
giveaway for the chance
to win some epic prizes.

orbitloot.com